bLinD a

gRaCE hArWOod

castaway pRess

PUBLISHED BY CASTAWAY PRESS

A CIP record for this book
is available from the British Library.

ISBN 978-0-9568050-0-3

Printed and bound in Great Britain.

Castaway Press
BM 2156
London
WC1N 3XX

www.castawaypress.co.uk

To Martin

1. Blank Generation

*(Written by Richard Hell. Appears on Sire/Warners: Blank
Generation, 1990. Performed by Richard Hell & The Voidoids)*

I bought The Blank because I could see him. I couldn't see
the details of course. I couldn't see the stumpy limbs, the oversized
hooves, the too large head. I wilfully ignored other factors. I
didn't, for instance, take any notice of the fact that his body was too
short to be an indicator of any real show jumping potential. I turned
my blind eyes to his pigeon toes and took no notice of the fact that
this horse was what the British Horse Society, or indeed anybody
else with eyes in their head which worked properly, would call
"ugly". I suppose that just as little girls are not considered to be
especially pretty unless they are equipped with golden curls and a
pair of blue eyes, horses are perceived as "ugly" and "poor
specimens" if they fail to please the eye. The human eye that is.
Horses, as far as I am aware, do not care very much about it.

I didn't care very much about it either; but then again, I am
as blind as a bat. Well, maybe not as blind as a bat. It's difficult to
quantify just exactly how blind a bat is. Perhaps, a bat does enjoy
better eyesight than me. Bats probably don't get Stargadt's Disease.
However, despite the fact that I am considered to be, to all intents
and purposes, blind, I do have some sight - although, I can only
really see anything in any detail on the sidelines of my vision.
Whenever I look at something directly, all I can see is a blur; and it
is an unfortunate fact that when you see something out of the corner
of your eye, instinctively you turn to look at it directly, at which
point, I lose sight of it altogether. It's a shame, but my greatest
moments of clarity come before I've even seen them. However, it
should be made plain, even though it's generally all a blur, I *can* see
some things. I can, after all, see large objects and bright colours. I
could, for example, see The Blank. Even slathered in mud and
sweat as he was – sweat had begun to foam up on his neck and
withers and he had begun to snort in fear from the very moment

1

which his then owner, Keith Denby, had appeared at the gate to his muddy puddle of a paddock – I could see a large white horse that would be impossible for me to lose in our field when I turned him out to grass.

A further reason I bought The Blank was because I felt sorry for him. I could tell how things had been for him whilst Keith Denby had been his owner. Keith Denby; small-time show jumper, amateur horse-breeder, erstwhile owner of the greatest horse who ever lived, *The Blank*, and Total Shit. I can imagine what Keith Denby would have had to say about The Blank upon the day he emerged from his pedigree mother. I can imagine Denby's response to the trembling, pale-eyed, pigeon-toed creature in the stable that night all too vividly. How he must have sworn and cursed his never-changing luck. How furious he would have been. All of those hours spent scrutinising breeding lines. Which dam would be the best mother, which stallion to pair her with in order to sire his next great show jumping hope. All of that time spent in what he pretentiously called his "study"; only to be rewarded with an albino foal. God's consolation prize. A throwback. A miscalculation. A mistake of Nature. A little bit like myself really; if I consider how Nature has betrayed me and genetics has destroyed my sight.

Still, Denby is nothing if not an optimist. You don't lose as many times as he does in the show jumping arena and still persist in your attempts, *without* being a blind optimist. Anybody else would have given up years ago; but not Denby. So, he gave The Blank a fancy name *"Le Blanc"* and set out, once more, to conquer the show jumping world. And, once more, he failed.

Le Blanc, I presume, was Denby's attempt at French sophistication. I suppose he didn't realise that he'd actually named his horse *"The White"* – which just doesn't make sense – in French, or indeed, in any other language. But then Denby is an idiot. I don't know why his not knowing this surprises me. And after all, he wasn't alone in his ignorance. Half the commentators in the Greater Manchester area mispronounced the horse's French name until he became known as just *The Blank* in time. It was a name which, as Denby would argue to anyone who would listen to him, suited the animal well because it would (in his own words) 'never win 'owt' and was 'a waste of good stable space' and 'not worth *nothing*' (another imbecilic grammatical error – but one, this time, which, to Denby's cost, would prove prophetically true. The Blank, the greatest horse who ever lived, is definitely *not* worth nothing). The Blank not only failed to win under Denby's direction in the show jumping arena; he *spectacularly* failed. By the time The Blank had a new name and his show jumping career was over (at least in Denby's mind), he had refused to jump or, alternatively, demolished, nearly every type of fence that horse and rider might ever reasonably encounter in the show jumping ring.

When I first saw The Blank, or the white shape of him anyway, through the habitual fog of my vision, he was *not* wasting good stable space in Denby's yard. In fact, Denby had not even bothered to stable him at all (and, make no mistake, Denby had good stables and plenty of them, where his prized show jumpers can stand up to their knees in clean bedding, freshly plumped up by some fresh-faced stable girl; who, coincidentally, had probably also just been freshly plumped up by Keith Denby – I know Denby and his methods of old). The Blank, however, undeserving, I suppose, in Denby's eyes, was standing up to his hocks in a filthy mire of a churned up paddock in a neglected corner of Denby's yard. All that remained of Denby's great show jumping hope was a tired, jaded, broken-down animal. It was clear to me, as it was to anyone else who was present that day, that if I didn't buy The Blank, then his next stop was the *Whiskas* factory.

It was raining slightly. A mizzling, fine rain of the type that soaks everything through within just a few minutes of standing out in it. Even I could see that The Blank had been standing out in it for more than just a few minutes. From the feel of his hot damp fur, the unwholesome scent emanating from his hooves which had clearly begun to rot in the mud, The Blank had been stood up to his hocks in the mire forgotten for something more like a month. Perhaps

3

longer. Then there was the shape of the animal. Oh, I'm not talking about the confirmation thing. What do such things matter to me? I'm talking about the way he was holding himself. The weary way he rested his back legs, one at a time, as if the effort of standing in the mud was becoming too much for him; the way in which he hung his head, his pink-tipped muzzle almost dipping in to the mud before him as if his next logical step was to immerse himself entirely in the sludge which surrounded him, and thus utterly extinguish what remained of his miserable existence. Even I could see the desolation in this picture. Nor was the sight entirely wasted on the freshly-plumped-up-stable girl who accompanied Denby and myself to this forgotten corner of his yard. I heard the sharp hiss of her shocked intake of breath. Clearly, there had been no plumping up of soft beds in cosy stables for this horse. Evidently, The Blank had remained forgotten for some time.

My attention was diverted from the picture of dejection which stood before me by overhearing a whispered aside from Denby to his luscious stable girl.

'She can't even see the state of the thing. You watch this. We'll be rid of it in no time. I might even bump up the price.'

Now, contrary to popular belief about the visually impaired, my senses have not compensated for my blindness by developing an extraordinary sense of hearing which enabled to me discern Denby's murmurings at this point. No. That was quite simply down to the fact that Denby's "whisper" was the equivalent of anybody else's shout. He never did have any subtlety. His undertone was just too loud for me (or indeed, anyone else for that matter) to miss. Perhaps he thought I was deaf as well.

Still, he was right about one thing. He would soon be rid of The Blank, because I'd already decided I wasn't going to leave without him.

I paid two-and-a-half grand for The Blank. It was probably more than you would expect to pay for a horse in the poor condition that The Blank was in. I'd have paid twice as much; particularly

4

when I ran my fingers over The Blank's rump and flank and felt the accumulated scar tissue, just a small reminder of the beatings he had received at the hands of Keith Denby. I told you he was a Total Shit.

I didn't know then that I'd got a bargain. And, Keith Denby, smug look upon his face as I handed over the money; (I didn't even need to see that one. I just knew it would be there - as I say, I knew Keith Denby of old) didn't know that he'd been ripped off. But I didn't know then that The Blank was the greatest horse that ever lived, and even if I had, I wouldn't have cared that I was ripping Denby off. I would have been glad. I heard what he said as I followed The Blank as he was led stumbling weakly, by another (equally luscious stable girl) to where Scotty waited for us with the horsebox.

'Look at them. Two freaks together. A match made in heaven.'

Bastard.

This is how I discovered that The Blank was the greatest horse that ever lived. I had owned The Blank for approximately a month. During that time I'd made sure that he knew what it was to stand up to his knees in clean bedding in his stable, just as he should have done from the very beginning. I'd dressed his poor heels, cracked and starting to rot from standing in the mud, with antiseptic wound powder and stuffed him with as many oats as he would eat in an attempt to get some condition on him again. Already the white of his coat seemed just that little more lustrous through the fog of my vision. When I went to the stable early on those dark, freezing mid-winter mornings, as I led him across the stable yard, often he would seem to my limited vision to glow with an almost luminousness, his white coat reflecting the hard frost which was at that time laid thick upon the ground. When I ran my fingers through his coat as I groomed him, less and less I felt the thick scar tissue which would never entirely disappear from the flesh of his rump. More and more I felt the soft luxuriance of a glossy coat. Best of all was that first morning around three weeks after that first encounter with The Blank, when as I stumbled to his stable in the early morning winter darkness, still stupid with sleep, I heard him whicker to me in affectionate greeting. Keith Denby had done much damage in his attempts to "train" The Blank, but he had not managed to utterly annihilate his faith in humanity.

At first I did not ride The Blank very much. Or, in fact, at all. I confess I was afraid to. The whole experiment of horse-ownership for the blind had just been a mad scheme at first. A dream which had been pursued too far. Something which for so many practical reasons, it would have been best if it had remained as fantasy alone. But it was nobody's fault but my own. Scotty had warned me about the insanity of my scheme.

'What do you think you are playing at?' he had demanded when I had first announced that he should get our ancient horsebox going again because I was going to start using my grandmother's stables and paddocks for their original purpose.

'What's it going to be?' he had demanded 'Are you gonna put a fluorescent yellow bridle on it and call it a guide horse for the fucking blind?' (At this point, I should explain that Scotty has the most incredibly filthy mouth. He uses swear words as adjectives, nouns, verbs and as substitutes for punctuation. However, because he loves me so much and because he has spent most of his life looking out for me; because he puts up with so much from me, I somehow manage not to notice).

'What will you do with the thing? Take it into Tesco and when they say "Sorry Madam, you can't bring that animal in here," you'll be able to tell them "but this is an official assistance animal, you have to let him in with me."'

Before I'd actually bought The Blank I was adamant that my defence for horse-ownership was sound. Once upon a time, before it had all started to go down the pan, I'd almost believed that I could have made it in Keith Denby's world. Once upon a time, those dreams had almost become real. And, okay, it had gone down the pan... My sight... The burgeoning career... Everything really...

6

But being blind didn't stop me dreaming about those horses or riding those horses or owning those horses again. In my dreams, I can still see. But now that this particular dream had become a reality, I had to admit that Scotty had a point. Oh, I could manage most aspects of horse-ownership by utilising what little vision I had, or by touch alone. I could, for example, as I had initially predicted when I first met The Blank, see him to catch him and bring him in from the field to his stable. Using my fingertips, I could find the spots where the mud had caked into his fur to brush it off with my hard dandy brush and thus keep him clean. Other chores, I could manage with Scotty's help, although that did not prevent him from complaining volubly and with much profanity about any assistance I required of him. But when it came to actually riding The Blank, I admit it, I was terrified. Scotty was right. How was I going to manage? I couldn't see traffic well enough to hack him out safely on the road and Scotty couldn't (well, wouldn't) come with me. In addition to this, I was not the person I had once been. I admit it. I was afraid. I had lost my nerve. Which brings me back to how I discovered that The Blank was the greatest horse that ever lived, because I couldn't just carry on stuffing him full of oats. He was already showing a penchant to gain weight, and fast. It would not be long before he was positively fat. He needed exercise. What was more, as the person solely responsible for his welfare, it was down to me to ensure he got it. I had broached the subject tentatively with Scotty, almost in the hope that he would offer to ride The Blank for me (*what was I thinking?*) Predictably, he had responded in no uncertain terms.

'Fuck off. Your horse. Your problem. You sort it out. I've fixed the horsebox for the millionth time. I've driven the thing and helped you out in its stable. Anything else, you can forget. I never signed up for this shit in the first place.'

I sometimes wonder what made Scotty stick around in those days at all.

So, it was my problem, and I had to sort it out. Therefore, it was with some trepidation that I carried The Blank's bridle and saddle from where it had lain discarded in my bedroom ever since the day Keith Denby's girl had handed it over to me and tacked The Blank up. The Blank himself didn't seem particularly surprised by this turn of events. He was quite patient whilst I fumbled with the unfamiliar straps and buckles. He didn't seem to mind my clumsiness with the saddle, even when I cast it too far over his back and it slid over his other side to land with a soft thud at his feet. He even seemed to be positively helping me as he poked his snowy nose through the noseband of his bridle to take the bit gently into his mouth. Still, even with The Blank's assistance that first attempt at tacking him up was a painful process; slow in the extreme, and punctuated by a variety of impatient expletives from Scotty, with every new error I committed; ('Oh, for fuck's sake.... Oh, Jesus Christ! Oh, *fucking hell!'*) which didn't really help, if I am honest about the matter.

Still, I managed it; or rather *we* managed it, since The Blank seemed to be doing his best for me. We also survived getting out of the stable and into the yard outside. I even had courage enough to let down the stirrups and swing myself up into the saddle; the first time I had sat upon a horse in a very, very long time. I have to say that, nerves aside, it did feel good to be back there again. Despite the fact that I couldn't see very much at all in the dull morning light (I was riding out early in an attempt to evade excessive traffic on the roads), I felt safe sitting on The Blank. Almost secure. And when I took that final leap of faith and nudged my heels into his sides and The Blank, as if sensing my trepidation, moved off at an even steady walk, I could feel the rhythm of his stride echoing familiarly through my body, just like the beats from a well-loved, never forgotten song. By the time I'd reached the end of the drive, with Scotty's eyes following our retreating figures all the while, I was starting to feel something of the old confidence creeping back. I even risked turning back to wave at Scotty as we halted at the end of the drive, before scanning left and right for moving objects in the blur. Nothing. I nudged The Blank on, turning left into the road. Not much of a road really, more of a lane. I should have been able

8

to detect anything coming towards us quite clearly and, that day, there was no movement in the lane ahead. We pushed on around the corner towards the end of the lane. This bit was trickier; a main road to cross into the mouth of another lane. All seemed quiet and we risked the crossing. More traffic on the second lane. Sweat began to prickle in the palms of my hands. The reins became greasy between my fingers. I could see The Blank's ears in blurred outline, flicking back and forth at the sounds of the traffic as it passed us - red blur, blue blur, metallic green blur - noise of something which I couldn't see... That one must have been a silver car. I never could make out cars of that colour very well. I urged The Blank into a trot. I just wanted to get off that road. Again that well-remembered beat. 1, 2... 1, 2... Up, down... Up, down, as I rose and sat with the rhythm of the pace. We reached the end of the lane and halted again. Look left. Nothing. Look right. Nothing. Silent Cheshire countryside all around. We risked the right turn. Another lane, fields surrounding this one on either side. I began to relax a little, my initial terror subsiding. I even started to enjoy myself, holding myself lighter and not quite so stiffly. I could feel The Blank respond in turn by loosening his stride, his steps becoming smoother and more fluid.

Right again at the end of a high wall which formed the boundary between a house and the lane. This was a useful landmark. I couldn't see the right turn too well. And then slow, slow, slow... My hand brushing the hedge on the right, riding on the wrong side of the road, desperately hoping we wouldn't meet any traffic, until, at last, after what seemed an age, the hedge disappeared and I felt the opening to the bridlepath which led back to the lane where our cottage stood. Now, at this point in time, I really began to relax and enjoy myself. No traffic to worry about on the bridlepath. It was just a mud track. Feeling more daring than I had done during any time in the past six years since my sight had begun to deteriorate leading to the perpetual fog I existed within, I urged The Blank on until he broke into a canter. I can't very easily describe how I felt at that moment. It was as if over a decade's worth of happiness had risen out of the gloom and begun to bubble up inside of me. I felt the familiar beat and rhythm of the canter... 1, 2, 3... 1, 2, 3... But it was like no canter I'd ever experienced before. I was relaxed, filled with light and happiness, a fluid being moving in precise symbiosis with The Blank... The Blank, whose every step was perfect, measured; smoothly beating his hooves against the ground. It was like flying. We were as one, invincible... Until the moment a large orange object (I'm guessing it was one of the neighbouring farmer's Highland cows) stuck its head curiously over the hedge and The Blank shied violently. I can't blame The Blank. The bloody thing made me jump too. No excuses. I was unprepared and lost my seat. I hung over the side of the saddle knowing I was going to fall, knowing that I didn't stand a chance of regaining my seat when I had lost the support of both of my stirrups and The Blank was still in full canter. I was going to fall. I was going to lose The Blank; at best until I'd limped back home all bruised-pride-and-bottom to find him standing with a gloating Scotty. At worst... I couldn't bear to think. What if he didn't know his way home again? What if he ran out of the bridlepath into the path of an oncoming car? All of these thoughts flitted momentarily through my mind, so certain was I that I was going to fall, when The Blank surprised me again by stopping dead, from canter to halt in one single fluent movement, allowing me to flop gracelessly back into his saddle. Thus, I didn't fall that day, or indeed, any other day from The Blank, with one notable exception. I never fell because The Blank wouldn't let me. Which is how I discovered that The Blank was the greatest horse that ever lived.

2. Outsider

(Written by Dee Dee Ramone. Appears on Sire/Rhino Records: Subterranean Jungle, 1983. Performed by The Ramones)

If The Blank's beginnings in the world were inauspicious, then my own inception was no more of a favourable event. Picture the scene: my grandmother's house; my mother, eight-and-a-half months' pregnant, comes lumbering down the stairs, steps over the stair-gate which my grandmother has only just had installed that very afternoon to prevent my two-year-old brother from clambering up the staircase to the treasures she stored in her bedroom above, when in the process of this, one leg straddled either side of the gate, my mother's waters break and an accelerated labour ensues. Twenty minutes later, I was born, forcing myself out into a world which was entirely unready for me to land in my grandmother's reproving arms. (It was she who had been reluctantly conscripted in to act as emergency midwife). Now, my grandmother never made any secret of the fact that she would happily wish me – well, both of us really – no point taking it personally: her wish applied equally to my brother and I – out of existence. My mother I am not so sure about. Did she ever really want me? It was always so difficult to tell with my mother. In the small time I knew her, she never spoke beyond a handful of words directly to me and never, to the best of my recollection or knowledge, looked directly at me (except once, but I'll come to that later). For the main part, however, she was always too busy, I assumed, studying the contents of her own mind and becoming increasingly flustered and harried by these to consider very much else.

My father I never knew beyond the faded photograph of a grinning, stocky, balding man which my grandmother kept on her dressing-table. He had, somewhat inconsiderately, stepped in front of the 11.32 a.m. to London St Pancras when he had been declared bankrupt just two weeks prior to my birth. Unfortunately for us, and somewhat uncharacteristically, the 11.32 was running to time that day and killed him instantly. The driver did not notice the shattered remains of what had once been a man (my father) that was spattered all over the front of his train until it pulled into Bristol Temple Meads, at which point my father – or what little was left of him anyway – was discovered, and the 11.32 stopped running to time that day. It would all have been rather inconvenient, I expect, to the passengers on that train. Except to my mother, who spent most of her days lost inside of her own head anyway, that inconvenience represented suddenly having to face the horrible reality of dealing with the angry creditors her husband had left behind; the loss of her home, the people who she might have called her friends who suddenly didn't want to meet her eye in the street anymore (back then bankruptcy was so much more shameful and less common than it is nowadays). More horrible still, having to face all of this with one hyperactive toddler clinging to her ankles and another baby expected imminently; and, perhaps most horrible of all, the only person she could turn to in this crisis was her mother-in-law.

My father's mother, my grandmother, was – and remains to my mind (although my brother and I learned to fear her more than most as we progressed through what was termed our childhoods) – a fearsome personage. It shows, I suppose, just how desperate my mother was, that it was to her whom my mother turned for help in what was the greatest test of her life thus far. But, then again, I don't suppose there was anybody else. And maybe... Just maybe, there was a sneaking thought lurking in the back of her addled mind, that this way, by moving herself and her children into the house of her mother-in-law – a cottage with an adjoining stable yard, stable blocks, paddocks, and even a clapped-out ancient horsebox employed by my father in his more prosperous days and still bearing the legend: "Jim Devlin's Show Jumpers" blazened in triumphant (if somewhat faded) blue and red across the tailgate – there might have been room for her to bring her beloved hunters with her too. Maybe she wouldn't lose it all to my father's creditors. Maybe, just maybe, this way she could retain some scraps of her old life. My poor deluded mother. It cannot have taken her

12

long to realise that those grounds only stood as they did because my grandmother's own father had pursued equestrian interests; a love that had resurfaced in her own son (my father) before the drink and the debts had destroyed him. After the demise of both of these protagonists, the grounds attached to my grandmother's cottage were only ever retained as a status symbol. Any equestrian interest or aptitude had definitely skipped a generation. My grandmother had no love of animals. Nor, indeed, did I see any evidence of love for anyone or anything for that matter. Once ensconced in my grandmother's dreary house, however, there was no going back, and, indeed, nowhere to go back to.

I'm not saying that my grandmother didn't actually help us when she took us in all those years ago. My mother was, if my grandmother was to be believed - and it seems highly likely that it was true, being as my mother remained in this state for the remainder of her days - a total mess after my father's suicide. And even if she hadn't been that way, she didn't have the first idea of how to provide for us anyway, having been accustomed to more than a modicum of luxury for most of her life. (Usually at this point during my grandmother's tirades concerning how she came to be stuck with us, my grandmother would always purse her lips with disapproval, leaving unsaid, but managing to effectively make known anyway, that it was my mother's love of opulence which had led to my father's – her son's – downfall in the first place. *Not true*; the true causes were collectively the pub, the betting shop and just simply living beyond his means. Keeping competition horses is never cheap, especially if you never win any of the competitions you jump in). After this point had been effectively made, my grandmother would adopt an air of saintly, if slightly injured virtue, and state that she had seen no alternative but to rescue us, because life in a dingy council flat with two whining brats (accusing look at me – I was always the whiney one) would have finished my mother off for good. Instead, as you have heard, my grandmother provided a home of sorts for us in her dreary, old-womanish cottage, and she finished my mother off instead.

It must have seemed strange to her, my mother, to be surrounded by all of those trappings of happier times, all of them falling into disrepair around her. Those dust-filled stables and the horsebox that would never again start in her lifetime must have seemed a strangely potent reminder of the wreckage of all that remained of her old life. There, in those dreadful decaying surroundings, my mother must have seen all of these vestiges of her happier days when her handsome husband had been known as bold, brave Jim Devlin who always jumped the fastest, cleanest rounds and she herself had been the envy of all the other show jumping WAGs with her classic English beauty, and wondered how she had been brought so low: surrounded entirely by fussy patterned wallpaper and dreadful Axminster carpets - one of which she had just ruined with a sudden gush of amniotic fluid. I could not blame her if she did not welcome my intrusion into her crumbling world and matters certainly did not improve for her afterwards. It was no wonder really that she lost her mind.

It was my grandmother who named me. Even from the very beginning my mother had minimal involvement with her new baby. Perhaps the process of losing her mind had already begun. Perhaps those blank spells which I would come to associate with my mother had already taken hold and set in. Perhaps she just gazed glassily at her newborn child, just as I would see her stare unrecognisingly at a curtain, an ornament or a vacant chair, for hours upon end, so many times throughout our short acquaintance. And, perhaps, witnessing this lack of response from my mother, my grandmother decided to take control, and named me, predictably, boringly, after herself. Or perhaps the very fact that it was her censuring arms which I landed in gave her (to her mind) the right to be given naming-power over me. What would I have been but a damp, scrawny creature, all flailing arms and legs, screaming blue murder, which had unwittingly launched itself into this scene of blood, tears, and

14

devastated Axminster carpets? Who was I to resist as she cursed me with her name? As I landed in my grandmother's reproving arms, legend has it that my brother toddled happily into this scene of unfolding tragedy to announce:

'Pretty lady up nose, Mummy. Up nose.'

It transpired that my brother, in those brief moments when my grandmother had not been watching him like a hawk around her china collection, had happened upon a tiny porcelain thimble with a miniature painting of a ballerina upon it. So transfixed by this object of extreme beauty had he been, my brother had felt an urgent and compelling desire to stuff it up his left nostril, where it had, unfortunately, lodged itself. Thus it was that both my mother and my brother were hospitalised within the same day. Only my mother was required to stay overnight, but she discharged herself immediately that dawn broke upon the next day, preferring to take her chances with puerperal fever and my grandmother, rather than spend another night with me screaming my lungs out, effectively ensuring that the rest of the maternity ward remained mutinously awake around us.

Once settled at my grandmother's house again, and once all the china had been relocated to a higher shelf, out of reach of little hands and noses, I suppose we all settled into some kind of routine. It was one in which, I am told, I was extremely and noisily vocal in making my feelings of dissatisfaction with the new situation I found myself in perfectly clear. In the meantime, however, my mother became increasingly withdrawn and silent and my grandmother's resentment of us and our noisy intrusion into her life amplified. It was a routine, in short, in which we all made each other miserable.

My poor mother. Everything of her life before the 11.32 a.m. to St Pancras was gone, and we, her children, my brother and I, were no consolation to her whatsoever. Just wretched brats; the only evidence that remained of her marriage to handsome, daring, reckless Jim Devlin. Already, I suppose, under my grandmother's "care", my brother would have begun the metamorphosis from boisterous toddler to strangely silent and fearful child. It was no wonder, really, that my mother did the one extraordinary thing I ever knew her to do, which was to calmly put on her shoes and coat one evening, pick up her handbag and walk down the lane to the blue bridge which spanned the river there and jump from it. I never really knew my mother at all.   She was always so insular and introverted, locked away in a prison of her own making, the cell of her own disintegrating mind.   And, of course, during those first years of my life - the principal years in which I must have spent the majority of my time in her company - of that time I have little or no recollection.   In fact, I don't have many memories from my early childhood at all.   I certainly do not recall being particularly miserable or conscious of the unhappiness of my state.   Nor, it is true to say, do I recall any appreciable happiness either, but then maybe this isn't so surprising in a child of early years.   No; I suppose I only came to a full realisation of the knowledge of the lamentability of my deplorable and pitiable existence when I came to see how others viewed me and the contempt with which I was held by them.   It was only then that I came to know the outsider I was.

When I was five years' old, as was to be expected, I started school.   I say I have few memories from my early childhood, but I can remember the feel of my new school uniform as I slid my scrawny arms into the sleeves, almost tangibly.   I can remember the peculiar "school" smell of institutions and old school dinners as if it was emanating from that faded material now (I have called the uniform "new"; in reality, it was an old one of my brother's).   I can recollect perfectly the pinch of my grandmother's bony fingers into the top of my arm – pressing on bruises which were already there from previous grasps by my grandmother's fingers - as she marched me into the shabby sitting room, forcing me into the very spot where my mother was, as usual, staring vacantly before her.

'There now, what do you think?'   My grandmother demanded.   'Uniform's a little too big for her, but I'm not buying new when this one will do just as well.   Anyway, she'll only grow out of it in a couple of weeks' time.' This last comment was passed in an accusing tone as if I had made a conscious decision to grow as much as possible, just to inconvenience my grandmother. My mother, forced to look at me by the very fact that I had been pushed into her line of vision, looked away quickly as if the sight of me pained her a little and continued her intense scrutiny of the swirling, nauseating roses in the carpet.

'Well?' My grandmother demanded. 'Is that it? I expect you'll be wanting to walk her down the lane to the school now, won't you?' With a final sharp jab in the back to convey me firmly in the direction of my mother, my grandmother left us.

For a moment, I solemnly regarded my mother as she studiously kept her gaze fixed on the dusty flowers before her. She made no movement whatsoever. With a sinking heart, I knew. I was going to have to walk to school alone. I walked across to the armchair where my mother was seated trying not to see me. I leaned across the chair and kissed her smooth, dry cheek. Still no movement. I turned and walked out of the room. I could already feel the fear grappling at my insides as I closed the front door behind me and headed for the lane.

The school, St James' Infant School, was only at the top of the lane on the main road, but I didn't want to have to walk there alone. At the top of the drive, I hesitated, torn between a desire to run back and seek comfort from an adult, and the sure and certain knowledge that the only adults available for this purpose were my grandmother, whom I knew enough to be afraid of, and my mother, whom I could just see in outline through the window, still staring vacantly at the pattern of the flowers in the carpet. I took a further hesitant step into the lane and watched with an even heavier heart as a smirking Sarah Braithwaite tripped past clutched solidly and securely by her mother's hand. Her school uniform fitted her perfectly. It was evidently shop bought, brand new. Her face had been freshly scrubbed, her blonde curly hair was secured neatly by two shiny jet black clips. She was to be in my class at school and would remain in all of my classes throughout my school career. My heart filled with a species of jealous hatred at the sight of her and her enviably present mother. (Even at this early stage, I possessed an extraordinary capacity for hatred). I looked down despondently at my own too-large school shirt and boys' blazer. The sleeves of the navy-blue jacket almost covered my hands. I could only just make out the tips of my grubby chewed-down nails poking out at the end of them. I decided there and then I was going to hate school. I didn't want to go. But then what choice did I have? The only other option was to return home to my mother and, worse, my grandmother. I took another reluctant step into the lane. I could feel tears prickling at the back of my eyes and an urgent desire to urinate. It was thus, dithering at the top of the drive, that Scotty found me.

'Are yer walkin' up to't school then?' He, of course, was also alone. I stared up at him with wide tear-filled frightened eyes. He took me by the hand and began to lead me down the lane. We walked to school together that day, and every day after that. It was from that moment on that Scotty became my best friend. My only friend, come to think of it. When I was with Scotty, if I wasn't quite strong, I was at least not quite so alone anymore and the girls in Sarah Braithwaite's clique didn't bother me so much. But Scotty was two years older than me and he wasn't in any of my classes. It was then that the taunts of those other girls affected me. It wasn't very much at first. It never is. Whisperings behind plump babyish hands, but I just knew somehow that those murmured spiteful comments and the muted laughter that inevitably followed them concerned me. I could feel a prickling awareness moving down my spine as I saw their baby blue eyes watching me. I felt awkward, gauche in their presence, and their sniggerings only exacerbated this. Later on, things stepped up a gear. My hair (cut by my grandmother with the aid of the kitchen scissors and a bowl) was wrong; my clothes (cast-offs of my brother's and worn until they were as thin as paper and much too small for me) were wrong. My home was a hovel, my mother a loony, my grandmother a witch (they may have had a point there). Suddenly, nobody wanted to sit with me in class.

Nobody dared incur the wrath of beautiful, blonde, blue-eyed Sarah Braithwaite and her equally exquisite friends. Even the other school losers didn't want to sit with me; Susie Crofter who was massively overweight, Leon Rimmer who was stick thin with malnutrition, the neglect of his parents painfully apparent from his unwashed face and body, which to be frank, smelled quite badly, and Pamela Casey, who never washed her hair. I suppose Leon Rimmer must have pitied and hated and avoided me for the same reasons that I did him; but there is a hierarchy even amongst losers, and, well, to be frank, I was just about as low as you could go.

I don't think even the teachers knew how to take me. From some of them, I thought I could detect a sneaking sympathy although they never went so far as to do anything so rash as to actually interfere in the bullying that was being enacted beneath their very noses. After all, Sarah Braithwaite's mother was a Parent-Governor at the school. Her closest friends, Jane Baker's and Rachel Williams' parents were wealthy landowners – part of the "Cheshire Set" - and could usually be relied upon to contribute generously to school funds. Also, whatever I thought of them (they were cows, all of them), there was no denying that all of those girls were so much more charming than me with their uniform blonde curls and laughing blue eyes. Even at the age of five they had learned how to widen those baby-blues innocently as they smiled girlishly up into our teachers' faces. Me, with my dirty blonde hair hacked off with the kitchen scissors and permanently sullen features just couldn't compete. As for the other teachers, teachers like Mrs Harris (P.E.) and Miss Sizer (Art), they were just Sarah Braithwaites with thirty years added onto their ages. They had no sympathy or understanding for me. Besides, they could see where Sarah and her pals were coming from. There *was* something subversive about me. And they were right to be concerned. I knew I was different to them. I didn't want to be the same. I had treasonous leanings even then.

3. In the Brownies/Nothing

("In the Brownies" Written by Billy Connolly, Polydor Records: 1975. Performed by Billy Connolly)/ ("Nothing" Written by A. Appears on Hi-Fi Serious, London: London Records, 2002. Performed by A)

When I was seven years' old my grandmother decided that this reckless desire for nonconformity needed to be curbed. She could see the way I was headed and she didn't like it one little bit. I should at least *try* to be the same as those other, much better, much prettier, much more charming girls than me, and I was forced to join the Brownies.

Now let me make this absolutely and utterly clear; *I did not want to join the Brownies.* My desire to join the Brownies was equalled only by my desire to attend school (i.e. non-existent). However, in both cases, I had no option in the matter. My grandmother had seen Sarah Braithwaite skipping blithely past the end of the drive on her way to school each morning and with my grandmother's characteristic determination, she had decided that I should be more like that happy, pretty little girl, instead of the morose, surly child I seemed destined to be. So, when she saw Sarah Braithwaite gambolling past, immaculate in her Brownie uniform, my fate was sealed. The very next day, my grandmother walked down the lane to the village to engage in emergency talks with Mrs Asquith, or "Brown Owl" as I was to know her during our (brief) acquaintance. The result of this crisis summit, unfortunately for me, was myself, standing in a brown uniform, complete with yellow neckerchief and woggle, and even smart new knee socks, so white they almost glowed in the evening light. The only advantage to this extension to my wardrobe was that every item of clothing I wore at that point in time was brand new and fitted me precisely. I had never experienced such luxury before. In an unaccustomed fit of generosity, my grandmother had purchased the entire outfit so that I would 'look as if I was one of those smart wee Brownies and fit in straightaway.' This uncharacteristic display of beneficence, in itself, was just a further illustration of the extent of my grandmother's determination to make me conform to Brownie life and set me one step further on the road to becoming the happy, carefree little girl (who was "such a credit to her" as she could imagine the other villagers saying) and that she had decided I should be.

I suppose there are two ways of seeing this. On the one hand, it was a good thing that the uniform had been bought to fit me; i.e. I, at least, did look very smart in it upon the one occasion on which I wore it. On the other hand, however, being as I only wore the uniform once, I suppose it was a bit of a waste. Anyway, if my grandmother thought that by my merely donning the uniform, I would be magically transformed into another Sarah Braithwaite, she was to be tragically disappointed. I felt uncomfortable in the uniform, and I looked it too. Sadly, the only transformation which had realistically been effected was that of a sullen-looking child in a grubby school uniform to a sullen-looking child in a (clean) Brownie uniform. I could see my grandmother was disappointed, but she was made of sterner stuff than merely to abandon her efforts just because the initial results had not met her original expectations. No doubt after a good session at the Brownies I would return home a different child; one full of the joys of Brownie-ing and childhood.

As for me, I knew I was in for trouble when she told me that she'd arranged for me to walk down the road to the Church Hall where the Brownies assembled upon a weekly basis, with Sarah Braithwaite and her mother. Of course, Sarah Braithwaite was impeccably behaved whilst her mother was present, but as soon as her horsey-looking mother was waving goodbye to us from the kissing gate which served as entrance to the grounds of the churchyard, she dug her fingernails into the soft flesh of my forearm and hissed viciously at me, 'Don't think you're hanging around with me, you *freak*.'

Sadly, Brown Owl had other ideas. Before the small crescent imprints of Sarah Braithwaite's tiny nails had even faded from my skin, Brown Owl was cheerily announcing that since Sarah and her mummy had brought me, Sarah should take care of me during my inaugural visit to the Brownies. This announcement itself was greeted by mutinous mutterings and sharp glances exchanged between Sarah Braithwaite and the other elves (the sub-group of the Brownies to which Sarah and her chums belonged); however, to Brown Owl herself, Sarah responded with an equally cheery 'Yes, Brown Owl!' That girl was pure poison, but it would have killed her if an adult had seen through the clean-cut charming little girl image she sported to the venom that coursed through her veins below. It would have been better for me that evening if she had, just once, let that façade slip and told Brown Owl directly that she, in fact, hated me and had no intention of taking care of me whatsoever. It might have been better for her too, come to think of it.

I hated Brownies. No surprise there. I knew I would do as soon as my grandmother had forced me into the uniform. I hated the stupid, seemingly pointless rituals of standing in a circle and pretending we were dancing around a fairy ring. I hated promising solemnly to do my duty to a God I wasn't sure I even believed in, a country I thought dull and uninspiring and a Queen who seemed remote and far-removed from my pitiful existence. And what was my duty anyway? The words of the Brownie promise seemed vague on this point. Besides, as Sarah Braithwaite mockingly pointed out, I got the words wrong anyway.

I got most things wrong that evening. After the recital of the Brownie oath and the insane dancing around the fairy ring, we did a craft activity.

'Right, girls,' Brown Owl chirruped cheerily (she was perpetually cheery; even later after the *incident*, she remained cheerful whilst simultaneously managing to convey to my grandmother her profound disappointment in me). 'We're going to be making a beautiful purse for you to take home to your mothers. We're going to make it from these sheets of brown felt, to match your Brownie uniforms, but you can decorate them *however you like*.' (This last was said with emphasis, as if the decoration of a rubbish cloth purse with a few sequins and different coloured

23

buttons was the greatest treat experienced thus far in our childhoods). Indeed, most of the elves around me beamed as if it *was* the greatest treat experienced thus far in their childhoods, which led me to silently question the nature of their home-lives; because even I could think of better things to be doing, and between my grandmother and my mother, I really didn't get many treats at home.

Brown Owl demonstrated how to fold the square of felt into three and stitch along the sides to form the basic structure of the purse. The first part of this process was achieved without too much trouble. Admittedly, my stitches were large and uneven; but then I was only seven years' old. It was when we came to decorate the purse that the problems began. Brown Owl had provided a plastic tub which looked as if it had once contained margarine filled with different coloured sequins, buttons and embroidery silks for us to decorate the purses we had made. By the time my stubby, clumsy little fingers had negotiated the task of attaching the sides of my purse together, Sarah Braithwaite and her cohorts had completed theirs and had already commandeered the plastic tub of gimcracks. When I moved to choose something for my own purse, Sarah Braithwaite blocked my path, arms crossed resolutely, little mouth set in a grim line of determination. She was like a miniature version of my grandmother.

'Oh no you don't! You don't need any of these things. Who are you making your purse for anyway? Your mum's a loony!'

'She's not! There's nothing wrong with my mum.' I'm afraid my tone lacked conviction here. Even at seven years' old I knew that my mother was different from the other girls'. Whilst theirs took them swimming, to play-dates and gossiped together at the gates to the school, mine simply sat motionless for hours upon end staring vacantly at an occasional table; or whatever else happened to be in her line of sight at the time. I knew it wasn't normal behaviour. Therefore, to add the necessary emphasis to my argument, I resorted to one of Scotty's favourite methods and gave Sarah a little shove. Just a little one you understand, but it was a *big* mistake. It was what Sarah Braithwaite had been waiting for. As soon as I touched her, she flung herself backwards (I certainly never pushed her that hard) scattering her unwary admirers. The sequins and buttons spattered across the floor.

'Girls! Girls!' Brown Owl with a well-practised eye, had immediately spotted the eruption. Cheery façade aside, she had years of experience of policing little girls. 'What on earth is going on here?'

'Emily won't decorate her purse, Brown Owl, because she says her mother's a loony and doesn't deserve a lovely new purse,' Sarah Braithwaite piped innocently, before I had even had the chance to think, never mind conjure up something plausible to explain the situation.

Brown Owl regarded me with suspicion. In indignation at "my" comments upon the state of my mother's mental health, Sarah Braithwaite's blue eyes had filled with empathetic tears for my poor mother. Even I had to admire the calibre of her acting. For a moment I was almost taken in myself. I almost believed I *had* said those things. Brown Owl surveyed my sulky little face. Obviously, she knew about my mother. Everybody in the village knew about my mother.

'Emily! What a dreadful thing to say. Your mummy's not feeling very well at the moment, but she'll soon be better and then I expect she'll love this little purse.' Brown Owl looked down doubtfully at the strip of grubby material I still clutched in my sticky little hands. The only decoration it currently sported were a few spots of blood streaked across it from my needle-pricked fingertips.

'No doubt that beautiful little gift will cheer your mother up no end,' Brown Owl concluded uncertainly.

It was my turn to look doubtful; and Brown Owl must have read my mind and silently agreed with me, because she quickly changed the subject.

'Anyway, girls, let's leave this now and do something new. We're going to go outside to the little wood where Tawny Owl has laid on a *lovely* activity for us to do.'

25

My heart sank. Whatever the activity was that had been laid on for us, I was certain it wasn't going to be lovely for me. Miserably, and with sore little fingers, I followed the rest of the Brownies outside.

Outside, adjacent to the church, there was a small copse of trees. It was only tiny, but big enough for there to be a couple of paths wending their way through them. I would never have said it was large enough to lose a group of children within those woods for any length of time. Still I was only seven years' old and that scrubby patch of woodland seemed a lot larger to me then, simply because I was a lot smaller then than I am now. At the centre of the woods there was a clearing where on summer evenings, such as that one, the Brownies and the older Girl Guides used to gather around a small, carefully controlled campfire to toast marshmallows and sing "Gingangoolly," etc. I suppose I imagined that this was to be the purpose of our visit on that particular evening. Certainly, the light was fading quickly that evening and it wasn't really fit for anything more. So it was a surprise when Brown Owl unveiled Tawny Owl's scheme for a grand adventure for us.

'What we're going to do, girls, is this: Tawny Owl has laid a path for us to follow through the woods. It's a trail made up of sticks and leaves and materials you would find *naturally* in the woods. We're going to use our Brownie *tracking* skills to follow Tawny Owl's route through the woods to the prize at the end. There is a reward for one of you from each of your individual groups if you follow the track successfully. The first from each of your groups to reach the end will win it. Now, hurry along, girls!' Brown Owl continued to jolly us along, ushering the separate groups of girls through the narrow entrance to the woods until only I remained with Sarah Braithwaite and the other elves. Again, just as there had been mutinous mutterings at Brown Owl's announcement that I would join the elves at the commencement of the evening, once more the other elves hesitated at the entrance to the woods.

'Well, come along girls, let's go and follow this trail,' Brown Owl urged. Still more hesitation. I could see that even Brown Owl's legendary patience was beginning to crack.

'Well? What's the matter *now*?' The emphasis upon the word "now" spoke volumes about lost tolerance for the private strategies of little girls.

'Please Brown Owl, we don't want to go into the woods on our own with Emily,' Jane Baker piped up, her eyes wide with mischievous innocence.

'Yes, Emily's mother's a loony. I bet Emily's a loony too. She might hack us up with an axe,' Rachel Williams added. Sarah Braithwaite herself kept her features carefully neutral, but I heard her snigger a little under her breath. Not enough for Brown Owl to hear, but enough for me to hate her and her horrible cronies even more.

'Now that's enough, girls! Brownies always make new friends welcome. Now come on, Emily, you lead the way and show these other elves how efficiently you can follow Tawny Owl's trail and win the prize. Off you go now, go on.' She gave me a little shove in the small of my back to convey me through the entrance to the woods. I got the feeling that Brown Owl was getting heartily sick of it all. I knew how she felt; but it was nice in the woods. Cool in the evening shade and not too bright. (Even at this early juncture in my life, a light which was too harsh would disturb my eyes.) Tawny Owl's trail was pitifully easy to follow. She had made arrows out of pebbles and sticks every few steps along the path. An idiot could have followed them and reached the prize within a few minutes. Behind me on the path, I could hear the chants of the other elves directed at my retreating back: 'You're a loony too! Loony too!' After a while, the words began to merge together and it sounded like they were singing "Loony tunes! Loony tunes!" It reminded me of the cartoons of Bugs Bunny *et al* which I used to watch with Scotty on Saturday mornings on my grandmother's old-fashioned television set. I hated those chanting girls; all of them. And then I had an idea.

27

I speeded up a little until the elves behind me were just tan and yellow blobs in the distance. As I followed Tawny Owl's trail, I hurriedly scrubbed out the childish arrows on the path with my feet as I went. As I had initially predicted, it only took a matter of minutes to reach the prize at the trail's conclusion (a bag of Maltesers which I split with Scotty later). I smirked to myself as I saw Sarah Braithwaite and her clique of friends in the distance. They were wandering off the marked path into the undergrowth, still chanting "loony tunes, loony tunes" to what they must have imagined to be the figure of me in front of them.

It was dark before Brown Owl called around to see my grandmother. I was supposed to be in bed, but I had heard her still-cheerful-if-now-slightly-disappointed tones echoing through my grandmothers' fusty cottage breaking the perpetual silence. I crept out of bed to the top of the stairs to listen in. The prize of the Maltesers still clung to the crevices of my teeth and I poked at them with my tongue, tasting their cloying sweetness as I eavesdropped on the conversation below.

'...Oh, I know it's only a small wood, but those girls wandered away from the marked path because the trail had been... Er... *Removed*... And I'm afraid when they realised they were lost they panicked a little and ran through some brambles. Little Sarah Braithwaite scratched her face rather badly and both Rachel and Jane were nearly hysterical when Tawny Owl and I found them. Their little arms were quite badly scratched as well.'

'And what has this to do with my granddaughter?' I heard my grandmother enquire in her sternest tones. I almost felt sorry for Brown Owl.

'Well,' Brown Owl continued delicately. 'Tawny Owl remembers quite clearly where the markers on the path were left, but after Emily had passed, they were no longer there, you see...' There was a short silence whilst Brown Owl let the implication of this statement sink in. 'And as a result the other girls became lost.' Another silence. I could imagine; almost see in my mind's eye my grandmother's lips tighten into a thin line at Brown Owl's words. 'I'm afraid the girls were a little mean to Emily at the beginning of the activity...'

'There's no need to make excuses for her behaviour,' my grandmother cut Brown Owl short.

'But I don't think that Emily would really enjoy the Brownies,' Brown Owl continued quickly. 'I think this... er... *incident* would make it difficult for her to integrate... The girls have rather taken against her.'

'I see.' My grandmother's response came out stiffly and I knew I was in for it as soon as Brown Owl left the house; but I couldn't bring myself to regret my actions of the evening. I felt an immense sense of satisfaction at the thought of Sarah Braithwaite's scratched face. As my grandmother brought the discomforting interview to a rather formal close, I hastily scampered back up the stairs to my bedroom, dived under the bedclothes and remained as motionless as I could as I heard my grandmother's footsteps lumbering up the stairs towards me. I hardly dared to breathe. I kept my eyes tightly closed as I heard the creak of the opening bedroom door.

But she knew. Somehow she just knew that I was awake that night. Or maybe she just didn't care whether I was awake or not. The first blow she directed at the side of my head made my ears ring for around two days.

'After all the things I've done for you... You stupid little cow. I'm ashamed of you. When I think of those pretty little girls you frightened. You're not worth one quarter of any one of them. You're *nothing*.'

I suppose I cried a little bit at what she had said. Or maybe just because of the pain of the beating I'd taken. Still, I never saw that Brownie uniform where it hung discarded at the back of my wardrobe for several years afterwards without a sense of achievement. I was different to those other girls and no uniform would ever make me the same.

4. Learn to Fly

(Written by Foo Fighters. Appears on Roswell Records Inc.: There is Nothing Left to Lose, 1999. Performed by Foo Fighters)

I describe myself as having "treasonous leanings" and "subversive" tendencies; and there is no doubt, that I did not "fit". But there were some ways in which I was just like so many other little girls. For I, like so many of those other little girls, was utterly, completely, absolutely, entirely, wholly, unreservedly, *obsessed* with horses. So there, at least, was one thing we had in common, those girls and I. Oh yes, I certainly lacked their charm, but we were all predictably pony-mad. There is no doubt that there are lots of little girls who dream about ponies. It is, apparently, a stage which all little girls progress through, before moving on, somewhere during their teenage years, to rock stars. The only exceptional thing about me was that I never moved onto the rock stars. Well, that is, at least, not until *much* later; (and even then I never left the horses behind.) I always was a late bloomer.

First, there was the horses. And foremost there was the horses. In fact, excluding Scotty of course, there was little else to occupy my mind except the horses. I suppose my father being who he had been; the once-oh-so-nearly great show jumper, only added credence, at least to my reasoning, to my dreams of one day making it big in the show jumping world. In my imagination, my grandmother's dilapidated stables were restored and populated once again with horses whose bay coats were polished like mahogany. Like Velvet (I had happened upon an ancient copy of *National Velvet* in my grandmother's attic and devoured it avidly) I dreamed of bits as other women dreamed of jewellery. My dreams, like her and her sisters', were the shape of horses; horses dark as treacle, palominos, pretty dappled greys with large eyes and manes of silver. In these fictions I rode a horse who pricked his intelligent ears as he cantered his approach to the last jump of the ring, who tucked neat little hooves up underneath him as he soared in a perfect arc to clear the round to the roar of an approving crowd. My grandmother's

31

cabinets were stuffed to overflowing with rosettes and trophies as opposed to the dusty, fussy little porcelain figurines which we were never allowed to touch. I was the toast of the village. Believe me, I never anticipated how things would ultimately turn out: how the dilapidated stables, even when occupied by The Blank, never really improved that much. How the roar of the crowd, when it came down to it, was not quite so approving. But then I really never anticipated being able to ride in the first place. My childish dreams of equestrian glory were just that, dreams; and set to remain that way. My grandmother would never have consented to the expense of either keeping a horse or paying out for riding lessons, and I had no money of my own. Despite my dreams, and in spite of my family history, I was enough of a realist to know that I was not Velvet. I was never going to be the child to whom wonderful things happened. My mother was not a larger-than-life, solid, comforting presence who had once known greatness of her own. My father was noticeable only by his absence. I had no Mi Taylor; no mentor other than Scotty who was already turning into the disillusioned and foul-mouthed person he would ultimately become. The colour of the childhood belonging to Velvet and her sisters was pink; the colour of the Dover cliffs washed in a sunset or the rosy glow of the dawning of a beautiful day; the pink wallpaper and coverlets of a girls' shared cosy bedroom. Mine was grey; the colour of Dover in the rain. In the desolate hours when I was not enduring school; not doing anything other than consciously avoiding my grandmother and trying not to think too much about the latest bruises or the pain in my empty stomach, I was leafing through an archaic child's riding handbook which must at one time have belonged to my father. I was memorising the correct way to hold the reins and how to manage the different paces of a horse, even though I had no pony of my own to test this theoretical knowledge out upon. Then, one day, quite by accident, my subversive streak reared up in me once again, and I found a way in which I could apply this knowledge in a more practical manner.

It must have been on one of those empty days when I was immersed in those ancient colour-plates of reins threaded through fingers when I heard it: the sharp, ringing beat of a horse's hooves pacing along the lane outside at a spanking trot. Immediately, I jumped up on my bed to peer through the narrow bedroom window. When the horse rounded the corner, I saw it was a classy looking dun Connemara pony, the horses' metal shoes almost chipping sparks from the timeworn pitted tarmac of our lane as his feet connected rapidly with it. The pony was trotting with his head tucked obediently down in the textbook fashion, mouthing the bit as if listening intently to each and every instruction Sarah Braithwaite conveyed to him through her reins (for, I realised, with a sudden and almost fateful knowledge, it was *she* who rode and presumably owned the pony). I would later discover that she was using a drawing rein attached to her pony's girth and threaded through his bit so that the pony pulled against his own strength and thus it was that his head was tucked in at the angle most desired by the Pony Club. If it had been any other pony, belonging to any other little girl, I would have left it at that; a single, brief, transitory flash of pleasure afforded to me by the sight of that smart little pony, illuminating an otherwise dull afternoon. But because it was her, a species of jealous hatred loomed up in me, and I couldn't bear for her to have him, when I could not. (Oh yes, I was no Velvet). And so it began.

I watched Sarah Braithwaite carefully with her pony for a long time before I made my first move. She was a lazy rider. The drawing rein, the Pelham bit coupled with the too-heavy hands which were much too harsh for her pony's sensitive mouth, the vicious looking crop which Sarah always carried in her dainty little hands; any measure, no matter how punitive, to force the animal to bend to her will. I suppose all of these were lessons she had learned from Keith Denby in whose livery stables she kept her little horse. Similarly, all of the duties and chores which a rider should perform in order to secure the welfare of their horse, all of the little tasks which contribute to the rapport between horse and rider, I saw her neglect. As I watched her, I saw her alternatively flatter or threaten her group of admirers into grooming and tacking up her little pony for her, and I observed as whilst she rode the pony, her cronies completed all of her stable chores for her, mucking out her pony's stable, sweeping the yard, cleaning out the water buckets, preparing its feed. It stands to reason that if you neglect the care of your animal, he will never care much for you. Indeed, I never saw any evidence of a bond exist between that horse and rider. I would watch as she turned out her horse into the field and whereas with the other riders, their horses would stop when their head-collars were removed to nuzzle affectionately at their owners' pockets and beg for treats; her horse simply turned its back upon her, shot her a final spiteful glance and ambled off to graze. I got the feeling that given the opportunity, and if he thought he might have got away with it, he would have aimed a sharp kick at Sarah Braithwaite as he turned to depart. (I knew how he felt there. I often felt like kicking her myself). Given all of the above facts, it was really quite easy to ingratiate myself into that little horse's affections. Starved of human kindness as he had been (and I knew how he felt there too; we had a lot of common ground between us, that horse and I); he was longing for me as much as I had longed for him on that first afternoon when I had glimpsed him through my narrow bedroom window.

Her horse was named Pepper. He had some fancy show name which she used to enter him under when they rode in the local shows; Pepperpot Mill, or some such thing. I always just called him Pepper. At first, I was careful. I only snuck into the field just to be with the horse; to feed him sugar lumps and carrots filched from either my grandmother's kitchen or the local allotments, or to stroke the hard muscle that ran along his neck, or to stand next to him and chat to him as he grazed. It didn't really take very long for Pepper to accept my presence. I flatter myself he even looked for me. Certainly he used to whinny a brief hello when I first entered the field and went to greet him; the same affectionate snicker that The

Blank calls to me when we greet each other in the mornings. Then, when I was certain that Pepper had come to accept my presence and, when I was equally confident that neither Sarah Braithwaite nor any of her cronies would be around, I risked mounting the horse. Nothing fancy. Just a little sit on his back. It felt weird at first, I have to say. With no insulating saddle between my thighs and the horse's back (out of necessity, I was riding bareback), I could really feel the distinctive lumps and bumps of the horse's spine along with the surprising warmth generated by his body which radiated through my jean clad legs. However, I soon became accustomed to the sensation and hazarded a little walk around the field. Nothing elaborate, just a tiny turn around the perimeter of the field. I learned to sit with the correct seat, and to feel and respond to the movements of the horse; to sway my hips with the rhythm of his pace and permit my wrists to become elastic to allow for the movement of the horse's head. I practised this movement as if I was holding reins, pretending I could feel the strips of leather as if they were woven between my third and fourth fingers and threaded through my hands to be secured by my thumbs on top, just as described in my father's antiquarian riding handbook.

I learned to steer using my calves, exerting a gentle pressure on Pepper's left side to ask him to veer to the right, and with my right leg to request a shift to the left. It was easy. I followed the limited guidance of the book, but mainly I followed my instincts, and just did whatever felt natural. If Sarah Braithwaite had ever given him a chance, she would have realised that Pepper was a horse with a kindly heart and a generous nature. If Pepper had belonged to a riding school, he would have been a schoolmaster and taught all the beginners to ride. As it was, I couldn't have "borrowed" a better horse.

I grew more daring. I attempted a trot. My father's handbook reported this as the bumpiest, most uncomfortable pace for the inexperienced rider. It was right. I spent a large amount of the time bouncing from Pepper's back into various weed-filled corners of the field, until I got the hang of it. There are two types of trot in English riding. The rising trot, which, according to my father's manual was easiest for both horse and rider (maybe if you had some stirrups – not so easy when you rely on the strength of your thighs alone to elevate your body weight) and the sitting trot. Of course, the only real difference between these two types of trot is the action of the rider during them; i.e. either alternately rising and sitting for the rising trot, or just sitting. Whichever action the rider chooses, the trot follows the same 1-2, 1-2 beat. I practised. I drilled myself in it, until by dint of repetition I could do it without falling off. 1, 2... 1, 2... Up, down... Up, down... Up, down for the rising trot. Sit, sit, sit, sit for the sitting. When that too had become habitual to me; when I could weave serpentine loops and figures of eight around the field, I moved on. The canter in my father's book was described as a "blessed relief" after all of that jolting around at the trot; and once again, my almanac proved correct. The canter is a pace in three-time, which is to say that each complete stride has three hoof beats followed by a moment of suspension. It has a rocking motion and is divinely smooth compared to the two-beat hoof pace of the trot. I didn't canter much. I didn't want to overwork Pepper. After all, he was also being ridden by Sarah Braithwaite. The canter became an occasional treat I permitted myself if Pepper didn't seem too tired, and I felt I had ridden especially well that day. Whilst I am on the subject of the paces of the horse, let me tell you about the gallop, the fastest of the horses' paces. Of course, I never experienced the gallop on Pepper. In the enclosed environment of the field, on a horse which was probably being overworked, it really wouldn't have been possible. Space is required for a gallop. Miles of rolling fields, as far as the eye can see to cover; stretches of empty sand. But I galloped much later, on other horses when I was with Keith Denby and, of course, on The Blank.

The gallop is a four-beat pace. Within the gallop there is a point in the pace when all four feet are suspended momentarily from the ground, so that it goes 1-2-3-4-pause-1-2-3-4-pause. It is probably as near to flying as man can ever come. It is perhaps from the gallop that the myth of Pegasus, the winged horse was born into the imagination of man. Just before a horse accelerates into a gallop, he will lower his head until it is level with his body and thus streamline himself to maximise his speed. In that moment, as he evens the contours of his body, he will drop away from you, leaving you hanging briefly in mid-air, and then will come the sudden rush of air and landscape sweeping past you as the horse streaks away with you clinging to his back. I advise you to try it. Put it on your list. Don't die without doing it at least once.

However, the gallop was not something I experienced for a very long time. In fact, when I think about my descriptions here, of these initial times when I first sat astride a horse and moved with him; something I would continue to do throughout my life, a connection between this animal and myself which existed before I was even born in the form of my father's and his grandfather's history, an alliance between us which has precipitated all of the most important events in my life, I realise I have made it all seem far too simplistic. I have conveyed it as if I merely walked into a field and *hey-presto!* I could ride. Clearly this is not an accurate portrayal of the events as they happened. When I got together with Keith Denby, total shit though he is and much as I dislike his methods, he probably knows more about riding horses than I ever will, he told me that those first few times he watched me riding Pepper, my riding was abysmal. My seat was all wrong, my legs flapped about in my efforts to cling onto a bareback pony. The position of my hands was completely out of line. Indeed, I could not have been further away from being the perfect little rider that I so longed to be. No, I was certainly no Velvet. Still, he told me, even then, he could see some natural potential in me that should be nurtured; that, in short, he could see that I was my father's daughter. He promised me that I too had what it took to make it. Words, just words. Words hastily said to flatter me so that he could get what he wanted from me. Words just as hastily retracted when things went bad between us. He soon changed his tune then.

And, yes, Keith Denby had seen me riding Pepper in his fields. A little girl riding a pony with no saddle or bridle; and not the little girl who was the rightful owner of the pony, the one whom he had just seen being driven away from the stable yard by her mother. Because no matter how careful I was, and I really wasn't that careful during the latter weeks of this period of my life, I was always going to be found out. I had got into the habit of riding Pepper and habit made me incautious and forgetful of the fact that I shouldn't have been riding him at all. I became more daring in the times I chose to visit Pepper. It was inevitable that someone, sooner or later, was going to discover what I had been up to.

However, Keith Denby finding out was one thing. He didn't particularly care what I was up to as long as I kept out of his way and didn't cause any trouble on his yard. I think, in a perverse sort of way, he even enjoyed the spectacle of me illegally riding that pony. No. It was when Sarah Braithwaite learned what I had been up to that the real trouble began. And, that too, was always inevitable.

It happened like this. It was late August. It might even have been the last week of the long summer holidays from school. Perhaps already that cold hand of dread had begun to claw at me, to nag and gnaw at me every time I recalled that in just a few days' time I would again have to don the hated school uniform and face Sarah Braithwaite and her gang of fawning imbeciles with whom she surrounded herself upon her own territory. Still I found it all too easy to dismiss the notion of school from my mind, and the certain knowledge that once I had returned to the dull routine of the classroom and the autumn evenings had begun to draw in, there would be less opportunity for riding Pepper. In those moments, all that existed were the long evenings of golden August sunshine for me to misspend as I saw fit. I was hiding in the usual place, waiting for Sarah Braithwaite to leave with her mother; i.e. I was crouched in a corner of the horses' field concealed partly by the water trough, but mainly by a clump of long grass and ragwort which grew in that particular corner. I could see Sarah Braithwaite standing at the

38

corner of the stable yard laughing with Jane Baker as that girl completed the sweeping of the yard. The sound of the hard bristles sweeping across the pitted concrete surface of the yard echoed in the still early evening air, so that I could discern each individual brushstroke quite easily; as I could the sound of their laughter. Once I even thought I heard my own name mentioned, followed by the sound of yet more raucous laughter, but I could have just been being paranoid. I detested Sarah Braithwaite to such an extent that I saw evil intent in every one of her actions, even standing in a stable yard, laughing with her friend, the evening sun glinting in the gold of their hair. I saw her mother leading Pepper and her own large bay horse, a gelding called Smartie, through the gate of the field, remove their head-collars and then stand and watch as the horses ambled away to graze. Pepper, who had become accustomed to my habits, immediately headed purposefully for my corner of the field, certain in the knowledge that I would inevitably have some treat for him in the pocket of my jeans. (I did. I had stolen a packet of Polo mints from Mrs Ayres' village shop just half an hour before). When he caught sight of me hiding in the dense grass, he whickered to me in that friendly way that horses do when they recognise old comrades.

'Get off,' I whispered, hurriedly stuffing a couple of mints under his tawny muzzle. 'You're going to give me away.' Indeed, even as I was hurriedly murmuring these injunctions to Pepper and pushing his nose away from my hiding place, I could see Sarah Braithwaite's mother watching the pony from the gate, her eyes narrowed with suspicion. She lingered for a couple of moments more; moments in which I hardly dared to breathe, before she moved away, the webbing of the head-collars dangling loosely between her fingers.

'Come on, Sarah,' I heard her call, her plummy upper-class tones ringing clearly across the stable yard. There followed more murmurings between Sarah Braithwaite and her friend, followed by a chorus of 'see you tomorrows!', etc, and then the girl clambered into her mother's small red car and they drove away. I breathed again. A little later, I watched as Jane Baker stashed the yard brush in the tack room and then she too left. Silence descended, beyond the stampings and snortings of the stabled horses and the odd bark from one of the many terriers that Denby kept to control the rat population of his yard. I emerged from the undergrowth and began to pet Pepper. I fussed over him for a little while, feeding him the mints and smoothing his mane before I hoisted myself up over his back. We took a few turns around the field, at a walk and then a trot. Finally, I permitted myself the ultimate luxury of a canter, sitting deep into Pepper's back, moving with the rhythm of his fluid and steady strides, my fingers curling in the black silk of his mane. By the time I saw the red car draw up in the stable yard, it was already too late. I watched as the car drove directly past the perimeter of the field. As it passed by, I caught a glimpse of Sarah Braithwaite's horrified features framed by the window of the car. Her features were exactly mirrored, I suppose, by the horror frozen upon my own. In that moment, two things happened. The first was that I lost my seat completely and slipped off Pepper's back to land in an undignified heap in the grass. The second was that the driver's door of the car was flung open and suddenly Sarah Braithwaite's mother was looming large and terrifyingly over me, closely followed by the smaller (but no less terrifying) figure of her daughter. Pepper, meanwhile, halted and ambled back to snuff curiously at me where I lay crumpled on the ground.

'What the...?' Mrs Braithwaite began. 'I knew there was something going on this evening...'

'You've been riding my pony! Mummy! She's been riding my pony!' I heard Sarah Braithwaite whine from somewhere behind her mother's large bottom.

'How dare you! This really is too much!' (Even through my terror, I couldn't help but notice that Mrs Braithwaite pronounced "really" as "rahly" and "much" as "mach"). 'You do realise that we would be perfectly within our rights to notify the police of this matter? Your behaviour is rahly quite crimina-r-l!

Now, hold on! Don't I know you? Sarah, isn't this one of your little friends?'

'No, it is not, Mummy!' I could hear Sarah Braithwaite respond through clenched teeth at the mere suggestion that I might be one of her friends. 'It's that horrid Emily Devlin who was so nasty to me at Brownies.' (Unfortunately for me at the mere mention of the Brownies debacle, I gave a tiny, involuntary smirk. It wasn't that the memory gave me any pleasure, you understand. Well not much anyway. It was merely at the irony of the thought that it might have been *I* who was nasty to Sarah Braithwaite when it had so manifestly been the other way around. It was *always* the other way around.) However, unfortunately for me, Mrs Braithwaite detected my look of amusement and misread it.

'I'm glad you find it funny!'

In fact, I wasn't finding these events funny at all; or even "fanny" for that matter, as she pronounced it. I was busy trying to think how I could extricate myself from this unfortunate situation, and more critically, how I could extricate myself from it without my grandmother ever finding out about it.

'I'm truly sorry, Mrs Braithwaite.' I smoothed my features and tried to mimic her clipped English tones in the hope that she would go easy on me if she thought that I was as well-bred as she was; if, in short, she thought that I was "one of them" rather than the trash I actually was in her eyes. Unfortunately for me, she just thought I was ridiculing her.

'You do think it's fanny! Well, I shall make certain that you are never welcome at this yard again. And think yourself lucky (lacky) that I'm not (nat) going to involve the police. But I'm going directly to speak to your moth... Er... Grandmother regarding this matter, young (yang) lady!' (Did I mention that everybody in the village knew about my mother?)

'But, Mrs Braithwaite, I really didn't mean any harm! I just thought what a beautiful little pony and so longed to ride like Sarah does.'

I did my best to appease the woman, even, resorting to flattering the detested Sarah Braithwaite. In fact, if Sarah Braithwaite had not been present, I might have stood some chance of persuading Mrs Braithwaite to let the matter drop with just a solemn promise from myself never to repeat the offence. Unfortunately for me, (and unfortunately for Sarah Braithwaite too, as it, once again, turned out) she *was* present; and so saturated with spiteful indignation at the atrocity I had found the gall to commit was she, that she, for once, dropped the façade of beautiful and perfectly-behaved little girl and aimed a savage punch at my nose. Her bony knuckles connected with a sickening crunch of ruptured membranes and I tasted the sharp metallic tang of blood at the back of my throat. For a moment, I almost saw stars. Dimly I heard her mother remonstrate; 'Sarah!', but something in that bloody woman's voice told me that when she related this story to somebody else, one of her cronies from the W.I. for instance, there would be an irrefutable element of pride in the woman's lah-di-dah tones. I could almost imagine her saying 'And then my little Sarah punched the cheeky little upstart on the nose!' and they would all laugh in an offhand way. I knew then it would be futile to plead my case any further. I had stepped way out of line. I had violated that most sacred of conventions and presumed myself to be on a level plane with them. I was not. In their eyes, I never would be. I would always be the grubby kid with the crazy mother who was not important enough even to be noticed. How dared I force them to acknowledge my existence? In that moment, my face a mess of blood and snot, tears prickling at the back of my eyes, still slumped in a heap in a field littered with horse shit, I knew all this. I didn't like the sinking feeling this sudden knowledge engendered in the pit of my stomach. My self-esteem was going down faster than the Titanic. And then, Pepper, who had stood next to me all the time as if listening intently to the opposing sides of the argument; brave, noble, generous-hearted Pepper who had never known a moment's kindness at the hands of his rightful owner, rushed to my aid.

42

He made a sudden dash at Sarah Braithwaite. Now I have seen horses charge at people many times. Generally, it is done in jest. A young horse might lower his head and gallop straight at you to tease you; as if to say, 'I *could* run you down. Have a care.' However, a horse will nearly always stop before he actually runs into you. All you need do is stand your ground and he will generally either alter his path or stop well short of you. And if he does run into you, ninety-nine per cent of the time it will have been an accident; the horse finding himself unable to stop at the critical moment, the ground being slippery or him missing his footing, or some such thing. A horse will *never* willingly step upon you. He will jump over you, shy around you, *anything* to avoid stepping onto something that is so unpleasantly squashy as a human being to rest his weight upon. In all the years I have known and been around horses, I have to say, this is the only occasion I have ever seen a horse deliberately set out to do this. However, on this one occasion, I watched in genuine amazement as Pepper, who had taken it into his head for some reason to defend me against the hateful Sarah Braithwaite, (his own appreciation of class barriers clearly not being as well-defined as Mrs Braithwaite's), deliberately charged at his owner, knocked her to the ground with his tawny head and purposefully planted his feet upon Sarah Braithwaite's prostrate body. He could easily have killed her. As it was, she just had a broken collarbone and a few bruised ribs. After that, confusion reigned. The still summer gloaming was distorted by the sirens and the blue lights of ambulances and police cars (Mrs Braithwaite had become somewhat hysterical at the sight of her daughter's broken body and immediately reneged upon her promise not to involve the police in the matter). Pepper was led away, shut into a dark green horsebox and driven away. I suspected the prognosis for him was bleaker than my own. Keith Denby arrived on the scene all bluster and charm. No, he had not had a clue what I'd been up to (liar). Certainly he would make sure that I never set foot on his property ever again (liar, liar). 'Don't you worry, Mrs Braithwaite, as one of my longest standing and most valued clients, I can assure you that this creature will never again be permitted entrance here.' (Liar, liar, pants on fire). In actual fact, it was only around a month later that Keith Denby gave me my first, and, incidentally, the only job I have ever held, at his stables. It was a position I held from around the time just after my eighth birthday up until my twenty-second, when, our relationship, shall we say, *soured*. Keith Denby had absolutely no problems defaulting upon any of the oaths he swore to Mrs Braithwaite on that evening, probably for two reasons: first and foremost, he was an unscrupulous shit, and, secondly, Mrs Braithwaite's teeth and bottom were far too large for him to ever be interested in taking her up into the hayloft and getting to know her better, as I had watched him do with so many of the other girls' mothers. If you work with horses all day long, it stands to reason that you don't want your latest squeeze to look like one.

I was escorted home by the local bobby, PC Anthony Bailey, who didn't seem to think that the crime I had committed, despite Mrs Braithwaite's hysterical witness testimony, was so very terrible. After all, I hadn't actually stolen the horse, had I? PC Bailey was jovially inclined, to put it all down to childish high spirits. Also, Anthony Bailey had walked the village beat for around twenty years. He knew my grandmother of old, and probably also knew that whatever punishment the long arm of the law could inflict upon me, it was never going to be anywhere near as bad as what my grandmother was going to mete out to me when she learned about this evening's work. For myself, I remained mutinously and defiantly silent. I knew I was in for it, and I no longer cared. I was aching all over from my fall from Pepper, my face was a mess of dried blood and I couldn't stop thinking about where that dark green horsebox that Pepper had been shut into was taking him to. I had a horrible feeling that I would never see him again. (I was right). As we arrived at the door to my grandmother's cottage, PC Bailey began to lecture me in earnest.

'Now, you'd better start showing some remorse, young lady, and think about what you've done. Things might go a bit easier for you if you can prove to your granny how sorry you are.'

44

I gave him a withering glance. Clearly, despite his twenty years' service in the village, he didn't know my grandmother that well. Nothing I could do at this point in time, *nothing* was going to make it any easier for me once my grandmother discovered what I'd been up to. PC Bailey rapped smartly at the door and then gave his most winning smile into the fiercely narrowed eyes of my grandmother as she swung the door open and took in the sorry sight of myself being brought home by a policeman. I suspected he was as afraid of her as I was.

'Brought one home for you,' he began, resuming his earlier bantering tone. Somehow, I was bundled into the confines of the cottage and shut away in the gloomy rear sitting room as PC Bailey informed my grandmother of the circumstances of my return home that evening, in the hallway. The door had been shut behind me, probably by my grandmother and I hovered behind the closed door, straining with all my senses to overhear exactly what PC Bailey was reporting to my grandmother. It sounded horribly like the truth, the whole truth and nothing but the truth. It could only be detrimental to myself. My heart sank further within my breast as I picked out random phrases from PC Bailey's narrative: '...Don't know how long it's been going on...' (This was bad. It meant that Mrs Braithwaite had correctly guessed that this evening hadn't been my first excursion upon her daughter's pony). '...Of course, the mother was very upset... Not really your granddaughter's fault but the mother seems to hold her responsible... badly injured by the pony... the mother feels Emily may have trained the pony to attack...' (Now how was I supposed to have done that? I could barely sit a trot, never mind start teaching Pepper new skills. Still, I doubted that my grandmother would believe that). '...All in all... best to keep a low profile... always out and about and up to mischief... running wild with that boy...' (Oh dear, oh dear, this just got better and better. I really was in for it, and it looked like Scotty, who, for once, was entirely innocent in the matter, would garner a share of the blame too). I held myself completely still, pressed as closely to the barrier of the door as I was able, desperately striving to hear my grandmother's response to the charges levied against me. However, my efforts were thwarted by a rustling, shifting sound behind me. Distracted and irritated, I half-turned towards the noise. In the semi-darkness of the room, I could just make out the shape of my mother, sitting in one of the old-fashioned winged armchairs at the far side of the sitting room. I was about to turn away again and renew my attempts at eavesdropping when my mother startled me yet further by actually speaking to me.

'Did I ever tell you, Emily, just how much you cried when you were a baby?' My mother's voice sounded cracked and hoarse. She had been through a particularly bad patch during that summer, even by her standards, and this was the first time I had heard her speak at all in a period of around five weeks. Still, unusual though it was for my mother to address anyone directly, much less me, I was unable to truly appreciate the magnitude of the moment, for two reasons. Firstly, I was terrified that at any moment, PC Bailey was going to conclude his interview with my grandmother and leave me to the mercy of her wrath; and secondly, my temperament as a baby had absolutely no bearing on the current situation, and was therefore, of utterly no interest to me whatsoever. In view of the above factors, I turned pointedly away from the shadowy form of my mother and attempted to renew my espionage of proceedings in the adjoining room.

'You were a difficult baby,' my mother continued, undeterred, in her strange, unnatural voice. 'But that doesn't mean I didn't love you. I loved you... I *love* you very, very much. It was just that you were... That *everything* was so demanding.' My mother's voice trailed away into silence. For a moment, it was as if she had gone away again into whatever land it was she went to when she blanked out like that. Wherever it was, it was one where I could not follow her. Certainly, her eyes suddenly had that flat, unseeing quality they held whenever she lost herself in her own head. Then, just as suddenly, she snapped back into our present again.

'I couldn't cope with it all. I can't cope with it all. I have let you down... Both of you... I am your mother... Your lives should be better than this... Oh, you think I don't know what goes on. You think I don't see, just because I lose myself sometimes... But I do. And I should be able to help you... To defend you against her... But I cannot... I have nothing left to give to you at all.' Her voice sounded more normal again, as if in the process of recalling her feelings she had also remembered how to speak. Her voice died away into silence. It was a silence which encompassed the whole cottage. With sudden shock, it came to me that PC Bailey had left. The realisation coincided almost exactly with my grandmother bursting through the door, throwing me back from it violently. With short, angry movements, she punched savagely at the light switch by the door so that the darkness outside sprang up around us, transforming from evening twilight to black as pitch in one sharp manoeuvre and throwing the details of the dismal sitting room into acute relief.

'After all the things I've done for you, young lady,' my grandmother began. 'And this is how you repay me. You do understand that you're the laughing stock of the whole village. *I'm* the laughing stock of the whole village.' (This was the part that really bothered her.) 'Pretending to be like that pretty little girl and thinking *you* could ride her horse. Well, you'll never be like her, *never*. Do you understand? She's worth two, three, *more* of you. And, once again, see what mischief you've caused with your stupidity. That little girl's collarbone is broken, you know. I should break yours right here and now for you and see how you like it.' She slammed her fist towards the bone in question and a red fog of pain swirled up around me.

In the background, just before I closed my eyes against the dizzying pain, I dimly observed my mother slip past us into the hallway, don her coat and slip her feet into her shoes. (She had pretty feet, my mother; something which I have inherited from her. They were narrow and delicately formed. Long after my mother's face was lost to me in my memory, I could still recall the shape and contours of her feet.) I saw her pick up her handbag and place it over her forearm. Then without a single glance behind her, and I am

47

quite certain upon this point, because I have replayed the moment over and over in my head many times; my mother did not once look back at me before she calmly left the cottage that night, leaving me behind with just my grandmother.

I think, perhaps with my description of events here, I am over-emphasising my mother's departure, as if at the very time of its occurrence, I realised the significance of the circumstance. Clearly, this is not the case. I was blissfully unaware of the fact that I would never see her alive again. The sad truth was that I was too busy dodging my grandmother's invectives and punches to even fully notice my mother's departure from the scene. I was too busy wondering if my collar-bone was actually broken, just like Sarah Braithwaite's, and trying not to vomit from the pain of a blow I had just taken square in the stomach. My mother was never much use to me on such occasions anyway, and she herself had just baldly informed me that I was to expect nothing from her, so she was hardly likely to be missed.

A little later, I was lying somewhat stiffly in my narrow bed, my bruises starting to swell and bloom purple and yellow beneath my skin when, once more, I detected a familiar rap at the door to my grandmother's cottage. Perhaps, this time, the knock was not quite so strident as formerly. There was a definite lack of the buoyant quality which characterised PC Bailey's usual cuffing at a door, probably in deference to both the lateness of the hour and the sobriety of the occasion. I knew it was PC Bailey again because I recognised the low rumble of his tones rising through the thin partition of my bedroom floor. I imagined my grandmother opening the door dressed in her quilted dressing gown, belted at her lumpy waist. I could picture her mouth pursing into lines of disapproval as PC Bailey removed his constable's helmet, tucked it into the crook of his arm and dipped his head as he stepped into the yellow pool of light that was the hallway to my grandmother's cottage. Of course, I couldn't hear the exact words. Perhaps I picked out the odd piece of salient information.

'..Bridge... River... Body...' Perhaps it is just that my imagination has filled in these words for me, after I learned the truth of the matter. However, I definitely heard the latter part of the conversation. I suspect the entire village heard the latter part of the conversation because it consisted of the normally convivial PC Bailey bellowing bad-temperedly at my grandmother at the top of his lungs.

'*Go and get those children out of their beds! They need to say goodbye to their mother. And you need to identify the body of your daughter-in-law. And, no, you cannot leave those children alone in the house while you do it. They are minors. They are too young to be left by themselves. And you need to remember this because you are all they have got now. Got that? You are responsible for them. You have to look after them now. You. Or do I need to call Social Services?*'

PC Bailey obviously wasn't so stupid as he was cabbage-looking. The merest mention of Social Services galvanised my grandmother into action; the picture of propriety - the caring, nurturing, matriarchal figure. The shame would have killed her if we had been taken into care because she had been deemed unfit to look after us. More to the point, the shame would have killed her if the village had discovered that we had been taken into care because she had been deemed unfit to look after us. Perhaps things would have gone better for us, my brother and I, if PC Bailey had called Social Services. But then, what reason, really, did he have to call them in? My grandmother (similarly not so stupid as she was cabbage-looking) made sure I dressed warmly for the occasion. That is to say, I was dressed to cover the bruises and PC Bailey, preoccupied as he must have been by the grim task ahead of him, and in the dimness of the night in which he saw me, probably noticed nothing beyond the pallor of my complexion. Something which he, quite naturally I suppose, attributed to the fact that my mother had just attempted to learn to fly from the bridge which

49

spanned the River Werriver and formed part of the bypass about a mile down the road.

As PC Bailey escorted us to the waiting police car, the flashing blue lights illuminating the dilapidated stable block eerily, I began to wonder about the river my mother had just thrown herself into. For instance, how had my mother managed to clamber over the high railings to pitch herself into the water below? Exactly how had she managed to drown herself in the gentle flow of the River Werriver? Why had she chosen this night out of all of the other nights of her desperate existence to end it all? And why had she taken her handbag with her? And I was wondering other things too; foolish, nonsensical things which flitted through my brain as I clutched onto the reassuring hand that PC Bailey offered to me, no longer the defiant child that he had encountered earlier that evening, but just a tired, stupid little girl who had lost her mother. For instance, as I walked, the blue lights of the panda car seemed to pick out a pattern in the concrete beneath my feet, a pattern of thousands of tiny blue stars which seemed to rush up to meet my eyes and dance before them. I wondered if my mother was in Heaven now, and if she was dancing too among the blue stars which seemed to swirl and sway in convoluted configurations before my sleepy eyes. Then I wondered if I too, like my mother, was losing my mind. I never did discover the answers to any of these questions. I don't know how my mother managed to clamber over those high railings. I don't know why she chose that night out of all the other ones she could have chosen to commit suicide. I certainly don't know why she took her handbag with her. However, I did manage to learn one thing, and that was this: in truth my mother had not drowned in the River Werriver at all. In reality, she had been killed almost instantaneously by hitting her head on the iron of the blue bridge as she fell. Of course, I didn't learn this fact until much later. Nobody; not the police, or the kind lady at the hospital chapel of rest, where my mother had been taken, or even my grandmother was prepared to tell a seven-year-old child and her brother the truth of the matter. Instead we were fed on platitudes: 'Your mummy's had an accident.' 'Mummy's gone to Heaven.' 'Your gran will look after you now.' All of these were probably lies – the last statement certainly was - and even though they were considered as a gentler, more child-friendly way of explaining matters, they certainly didn't make me feel any better.

By the time, however, we reached the police car waiting to drive us to the hospital, thankfully PC Bailey had run out of banalities to feed to us, and the drive to the Treeton Memorial Hospital was conducted largely in silence. I did not know the police officer who was driving the car. He nodded in our direction as PC Bailey handed us into the car, said 'Alright, Tone?' to PC Bailey and then drove off steadily down the lane.

It was warm in the dark car and I suppose I must have nodded a little in the car (after all, it was late and I had had a very busy day); anyway, it didn't seem to take very long to cover the thirty miles or so to the hospital. By the time we reached our destination, I was stiff and stumbling with exhaustion, and there seemed to be miles of too-bright corridors between the main entrance and the chapel of rest. Thankfully, in deference to the usage of the place, the chapel of rest was lit in a much more subdued fashion and the illumination ceased to hurt my eyes. When we arrived, PC Bailey muttered a few words to my grandmother who nodded stiffly in response before pointing at a bench, ordering us to sit, and not to move. She was then led into a small ante-chamber to the chapel, leaving my brother and I alone.

Within the chapel there was a small wooden table at the front covered with a large white cloth. On its surface there was a large cross. Hanging on the wall behind it there was a large picture of several pained looking men and women kneeling before a man who was clearly intended to be Jesus hanging from a crucifix. There was something odd about the picture, and when I stood to get a closer look, I noticed it had been minutely and painstakingly worked in intricate cross-stitch. There was a label on the side of the picture which read as follows: "This picture was worked in cross-stitch and presented to The Treeton Memorial Hospital Chapel of Rest by Mrs

Gwyneth Doyle." Jesus in the picture looked unnervingly like the lead singer from Iron Maiden. I would have liked to examine the picture further, but my brother called me back to the bench where our grandmother had placed us with a warning 'Em, she told us not to move.' There were several benches arranged in rows in the chapel, with an aisle parting the benches on the left and those on the right, just as you might expect in a real church. The walls were painted the same uniform white as in the rest of the hospital, but they had assumed a pinkish hue as the lights were shielded by red lampshades which cast a rosy glow over the interior. I wondered what God made of it all. Not the arrangement of the church, or the representation of His son as Bruce Dickinson in cross-stitch, but the actual use that was made of the place. The fact that relatives, friends would come here to look upon their loved ones for the final time and would then come to sit in here to berate Him over their loss. I wondered if he just wanted us to stop bothering Him, when it was clearly too late to do anything about those who had departed this life. If I was Him, that was how I would feel, I conjectured.

We heard the door to the anteroom swing open, and my grandmother appeared on the threshold. She looked smaller in the expanse of the chapel. Only God could dwarf her. She beckoned us wordlessly through and we, too, followed in the footsteps of all of those other bereaved relatives and friends, and went to look upon our mother for the final time.

Oddly, despite the fact that my mother's head had been bandaged, and in spite of her stillness, she didn't seem so very different in death as she had done in life. When we looked at her body, it was obvious that she, my mother, was not there. But then again, there had been so many occasions during her life when our mother had simply not been there, that there didn't seem to be so much difference between these two states of being; i.e. alive and not there, and dead and not there. The main dissimilarity, I suppose, was that when she was alive there was always the outside chance that she would pop back and be our mother again, at least for a little while, before the next blank spell took hold. This time her disappearance was complete.

Still, life goes on. Our lives had to go on; and I do not think I grieved so very much for my mother, despite the relentless sympathy of all of those I encountered in the weeks succeeding the event. She was always so much more of an absence in our lives than an actual presence. No, I do not think I missed my mother all that much. If I am truthful about the matter, I missed Pepper more. This sounds harsh, but it's just that if my mother was attempting to find her wings, well I had found mine. Pepper had given them to me. All those furtive visits to Sarah Braithwaite's pony, all those clandestine riding lessons; well, they hadn't just taught me how to ride, they'd taught me how my life could be. They'd taught me about the nature of freedom. I hadn't just been learning to ride, I'd been learning to fly. Now that he was gone, I felt the constriction of my existence more than ever. All of the incessant sympathy which was washing around us, my brother and I, didn't really help either. I just felt watched by the village, and the borders of my life became narrower than ever.

There was, however, it transpired, one advantage to this sudden outburst of empathy directed at my brother and myself, and it came, somewhat bizarrely I suppose, for me, in the form of Keith Denby. It was about a month after the death of my mother and I was (as ever when Scotty wasn't around) at a loose end. I was ambling down the lane swinging a large stick I had found against the hedgerow as I went, with a half-formed thought in my head that I would go and peep through the hedge at Keith Denby's place just on the off-chance that Pepper may have made a miraculous reappearance, when I heard the sound of a horse moving at speed in the field on the opposite side of the lane. Moments later the corpulent features of Keith Denby appeared astride his huge seventeen-hand-high Andalusian show jumper (Blackberry Wine, Winner BSJA South and West Yorkshire Regional Champion, 1978, successfully qualified for the Horse of the Year show during

53

the same year, but didn't manage to bring home any silverware). All this, however; these many accolades, are just incidental. The real crux of the matter I was considering as I caught sight of them, Keith and his horse on the opposite side of the hedge, was this: was I still in trouble with Keith and if so, how much? When I looked up into his face, however, he was smiling down at me as if he was pleased to see me. He pulled Blackberry Wine up behind the hedge adjacent to where I was and began to fall in beside me, the hedge still dividing us, but he could address me quite easily as we walked.

'You know, you didn't do too badly on Pepper; all things considered,' he began. 'I mean, it needs work, kid, it does, but you could be a decent little jockey given time.'

I was unable to speak. I could feel something suspiciously like happiness and pride swelling up inside of me; so much so, my tongue felt big in my mouth. I couldn't have spoken, even if I had been able to find the words. I nodded mutely. I was smiling though, I know that. I couldn't control it. I felt ridiculously, ecstatically, overjoyed that the great Keith Denby who had ridden at the Horse of the Year Show and competed against some of the greatest riders in the world had noticed me and thought my riding skills worthy of note too. I must have looked laughably eager to Keith Denby, but I expect it appealed to his monumental ego. I nodded fervently, anxious to see if any further crumbs of praise would be carelessly flung my way.

'You know, I'm a bit shorthanded at the yard. I could do with a new stable hand. Nothing fancy. Mucking out. Grooming. Can't pay you. Could give you a few lessons in return.'

I nodded again. I hardly dared to believe in what I was hearing. It was like the ending from a fairy tale, for me to hear those words, only better. Not *Cinderella you shall go to the ball*, but rather, *you shall muck out the stable*. I was beside myself with joyful anticipation, when a sudden occurrence shattered my illusions.

'But what about...?' My voice came out as a hesitant squeak. 'What about Mrs Braithwaite?' I hardly dared to even enunciate the woman's name after what had happened. It came out as a hoarse whisper. Keith Denby, however, had no scruples whatsoever about breaking any promises he had made to that woman.

'Forget her, kid. The Braithwaites are long gone.' He made it sound as if he had evicted them from his property on my behalf. The reality of the matter was that after what had occurred there, they were no longer prepared to be paying customers on Denby's yard, and as such, they were no longer of any interest to him.

'See you Saturday then.' Keith Denby dug his heels savagely into the Andalusian's side so that the large horse threw up his head and forefeet, snorting in surprise, before completing a swift transition from a stately walking pace to a rapid gallop away from me across the fields, leaving me grinning foolishly at their retreating figures. That was the thing about Keith Denby. If you saw him standing in a pub, or in a shop, he was just a short, fat, balding man, with coarse reddened features which spoke of a life of indulgence; too much good food and beer. You wouldn't look at him twice. When you saw him on a horse, however, wearing the leather chaps he used to wear over his jeans to ride in, or just saw him when he was around horses, the way he could assume command of those huge animals, animals which could have killed him as easily as I could have squashed a fly, he became a different man. He assumed a mantle of power which was irresistible. It was no wonder, really, that all of those pony-loving girls' mothers (and some of those pony-loving girls too) couldn't wait to scramble up the hay loft with him. There was definitely something about him. Even at eight years' old (it would be my birthday on the first Saturday I worked at Keith Denby's yard and was quite frankly, the best birthday present anyone could ever have bestowed upon me), I could see that. However, despite the riches he was offering to me, I found myself attracted and repulsed by him in equal measure. And, yes, if I am honest with myself, despite him acting as my fairy godfather at that time, and making all my childish dreams come true, I was more repulsed than attracted. There was something about the man which scared me. (I was right to be afraid). Still, there was no other way in which I was going to learn to ride, and even if he couldn't afford to pay me (I didn't appreciate until much, much later that, *of course* he could afford to pay me, but why should he when he could get away with not? He was a miserly shit); and even if I didn't get to ride much (hardly at all in the first few years) and even if it was all the rubbish jobs (they were the worst); at least I would be around the horses. Monica Dickens wrote that the love of horses and the longing to ride horses is like a disease. And I had caught it. Oh God, did I have it. And, of course, all Keith Denby did by inviting me into his yard was to fuel my obsession. It didn't really matter that he told me to sweep the yard in the snow, or clean up the pony's stable who had been out at grass too long and suffered with diarrhoea, or worse, wash that pony's tail. It didn't matter. I always just went back for more. Just to be around those horses, to feel the warmth of them, to smell the rich, horsey scent of leather and fresh hay was enough for me. It was healing balm poured onto my bruised and battered soul. So smitten was I by the horses and by the idea of Keith Denby as my fairy godfather that it was not until much, much later, that I came to appreciate just what sort of methods were being practised in that yard. For the time being, I asked no questions. I just wanted my wings back.

5. Childhood's End

(Written by Steve Harris. Appears on EMI Records: Fear of the Dark, 1992. Performed by Iron Maiden)

Grey, grey, grey. The colour of my life. My grandmother's house with its dismal, shabby furnishings. The silence all around us as my brother and I attempted to stay out of her way, broken only by the ticking of the clock on the mantle, marking the passage of the futile hours. The grey of the leaden Cheshire sky which loomed over all of our days. The dull monotony of the grey-green fields stretching into the distance as far as the eye could see, the gloomy waters of the sludgy rivers surrounding us, the dirty silver-white of the giant Lovell telescope at Jodrell Bank standing on a distant hill, looking at the stars which I would never see. The dreadful monochrome of my existence. It hurt my eyes to contemplate such nothingness. And then, out of the corner of my eye, on the periphery of my vision, the only gleam of hope: the golden gleam of hay in Keith Denby's stables, the gold of palominos, the silver of greys, the caramel of chestnuts and the dark chocolate of bays; colour at last. Stables filled with drowsy animal warmth; the solid companionship of his horses on whose warm withers I could lay my head and weep if the impulse moved me to it.

I was approaching my eleventh birthday and had been working for Keith Denby for three years. Birthdays ordinarily did not mean very much to me. After all, it was unlikely, if past history was anything to go by, that my grandmother would recognise the event. Scotty, if he did recall it (he had no memory for such niceties), had no money for gifts or cards. The best I could ever hope for was some small item filched from the village shop under the nose of Mrs Ayres, the owner. However, this year would be different. This year, just after I turned eleven, I would be starting at the secondary school.

In our area, there were two alternatives for secondary stage education. First and foremost, and skimming the cream from the primary schools and dominating in academic excellence was the old-fashioned Grammar school. This, obviously, was the preferred choice of most parents; the sole obstacle being that in order to gain entrance to this most revered of institutions, their precious offspring had to pass the Eleven Plus examination. For those who failed, and draining the dregs from the primary schools, the alternative was the shabby local comprehensive. The comp. was rough. I mean, it looked rough, due to years of neglect and failure to invest by the local authority. But it also was just rough. The pupils who attended that school were the misfits, the rejects, the just plain thick. They fought, they swore, they spat and smoked in the street. And if they didn't, they soon learned how to. They contributed wholeheartedly to the crumbling structure of their school by kicking, breaking and smashing their way through it every day. Scotty, who had failed his Eleven Plus examination in spectacular style just two years before had told me all about it. The kids who went to the local comp., well, they were just like me. Their fathers drank or gambled (or like mine had done, did both). Their mothers, also, like mine, were similarly absent; either off their faces with drink or drugs, or they'd just plain buggered off. Either way, we had a lot in common, those kids and me. We were all nothings. To my mind, there was never any doubt. I belonged there. At last, I had found a place I would fit; no longer the square peg in the round hole. There I would make friends, and even if I didn't, at least I'd be with Scotty. Yes, when the time came, I too would fail the examination in monumental style and go to the local comp. with Scotty.

It was the popularly accepted opinion that any child of moderate intelligence should be able to pass and have a fair chance of attending the Grammar school. In short, the general consensus amongst all of those upper-class parents who liked to think they belonged to the "Cheshire Set" was that if your child failed, he or she was a total imbecile. I held a different view. I would have to be a total imbecile to even consider attempting to pass that examination. There was no way I was going to get those questions correct and spend the next five years of my life being a target for Sarah Braithwaite and her ilk. (Somehow I just knew that Grammar school was going to be full of Sarah Braithwaites just waiting for a nothing like me to come along and make their academic year.) No, this was my chance to be rid of her and all those like her forever. At the comp., I would no longer be the minority. So when that fateful Monday morning came around which heralded the start of exam week, I was ready. I was prepared. I was fully focused. I was going to go in there and fail, fail, fail.

My strategy was quite clear in my mind. I had decided against merely defacing the paper. In order for it to be a credible failure, I felt I should strive to get a certain proportion of the questions correct and thus appear as if I had at least made some effort to pass; and I felt my approach to the examination was a sound one. I was confident, in other words, in the success of my failure.

At our primary school, the Eleven Plus examinations were completed over two days, with the pupils sitting the first two papers during one day and the final two papers over the second day. On the morning of the first examination, we were all of us lined up outside the large assembly hall by our teacher at her most officious. Some of my classmates, I noticed idly, looked, quite frankly, terrified. It was as if they were waiting to be herded into the gas chambers at Auschwitz. I, however, felt oddly dispassionate and detached from it all, since it was, obviously, going to be much easier to fail than to pass. Eventually, at a nod from the teacher, who seemed, if anything to be enjoying the spectacle of the terror of her charges, we were permitted to file into the hall and seat ourselves in the desks that had been lined up in rows, all facing towards the front of the assembly hall. Once we were all settled, and the fidgeting and shuffling had ceased, a further nod from the teacher, who was by this stage clearly exhibiting a species of sadistic glee at the extravaganza laid on before her, indicated we could turn over our papers and commence the examination.

59

All around me a sudden and concentrated hush descended over the room. All I could hear was the scratchings of pens as my classmates began to write their names on the front sheets of their papers. Pamela Casey, the girl who never washed her hair and belonged, with myself, firmly within the ranks of the school losers was seated to my left. I could see the greasy locks of her hair obscuring her plain face as she eagerly applied herself to her answer sheet. She was muttering the solutions to herself audibly in her desperation to succeed, completely oblivious to anybody else around her. She was utterly immersed in her own efforts to, presumably, pass. I, too, was concentrating; focussing all of my endeavours upon submitting a convincing fail. Some of the questions I consciously completed correctly. For every one I got right, however, I was careful to get a further two questions wrong.

After all of the papers had been completed, we were required, as a final swan song to the torture which had just been inflicted upon us, to compose a short essay upon a selected subject. This served the dual purpose of acting as a tiebreaker if there were more pupils achieving passes than places available. Also it was aimed at encouraging fairness, and assisting those pupils who, like Pamela Casey - who had spent the latter part of each of the examination papers sobbing quietly into her answer sheets - had gone to pieces during the exam.

That year the topic was as follows:

"Compose a short essay on what attending the Grammar school would mean to you."

I was particularly proud of my resulting composition. It read as follows:

"In the grand scheme of things, attending the Grammar school does not mean very much to me at all. If I was a typical ten year old child, attending the Grammar school would probably mean everything to me. I would be like Pamela Casey who is currently weeping next to me because she believes she has failed this exam. However, Pamela Casey is lucky because both of her parents are alive and probably love her, even though they won't buy her proper shampoo but make her wash her hair with washing-up liquid, which is why her hair is always greasy. My parents, however, are both dead. If they were alive, I do not think it would matter very much to them if I was awarded a place at the Grammar school, or not. My father, if he was still alive and had not thrown himself in front of the 11.32 a.m. to St. Pancras, would probably be too busy worrying about his gambling debts. My mother, when she was alive, and before she jumped off the blue bridge into the River Werriver never seemed to notice very much at all, so I do not think she would have minded whether I got a place at the Grammar school or not. I do not know if she notices things now that she is up in Heaven. Sometimes I look up at the sky, on those days when the clouds lower close to the ground and Heaven seems that little bit nearer than is usual, and I wonder if she notices me now at all and if she is watching what I am up to. Sometimes, when I am watching Mr Denby jumping his grey horse, Silver Destination, over the really high fences, I wonder whether, if I was riding that horse, if when he reached the pinnacle of his leap I put my hand into the air, I would be able to drag my fingers through the clouds and touch my mother again. Even if I could, and even if she was watching everything I am doing now, I *still* don't think she would care if I was awarded a place at the Grammar school or not. I think, perhaps, she would just want me to achieve what she could not, and be happy."

I felt my composition provided all of the pertinent points which I wished to convey to the Grammar school Entrance Committee; i.e. that I was a motherless (and fatherless, for that matter) brat who didn't particularly care whether she was awarded one of their coveted places or not. I certainly didn't deserve one. Unfortunately for me, the Examination Board disagreed with me; or maybe they just felt sorry for me; maybe you really did have to be a total imbecile to fail the exam. Maybe getting one question right for every two that you got wrong was sufficient. Maybe I wasn't as clever as I thought I was and when I had thought I was putting the wrong answer, I had inadvertently been getting them right. Whatever it was, I passed the bloody exam.

That first morning I attended the Grammar school was strangely reminiscent of my first day at the infant school all those years ago. Except this time there was no Scotty to hold my hand and reassure me. Scotty, no doubt, would have left already to slope nonchalantly across the fields to the comprehensive school. I, however, had to catch a bus to the Grammar school. It was a bus I would catch every morning for the next five years. It was a purple and white rickety double-decker. I loathed the sight of it. The stop was at the end of the lane. As I walked that first morning, I felt the familiar fear claw once more at my insides. Sarah Braithwaite would be on that bus. Her closest friends and comrades in harassing me, Jane Baker and Rachel Williams would be on that bus. I didn't even dare to speculate who else would be on that bus, which other pretty blonde girls who were all destined for sporting and academic excellence in equal measure; those who would all too readily be recruited into Sarah Braithwaite's clique and be utterly willing and able to make their own contributions towards her campaign of persecution against me. I was an outsider even before I set foot on that bus. I knew it already. I was always the outsider; and that was the way it would always be. More than ever before, as I made that first walk to the bus stop, I felt my pariah status as my destiny. As I waited at the end of the lane, I repeated the following words to myself like a mantra against what I *knew* was going to happen anyway: 'I will not cry. I will not cry. The bus is going to come and I will not cry. Dear God, I will not cry.' Nothing was going to prevent that bus from arriving to collect me. Only I stood between myself and tears.

It was an effort of will, but that day, at least, I did not cry. The mantra was one which I learned to repeat every day during my journey to the Grammar school. Sometimes it even *did* prevent me from weeping at my fate. At others, it failed miserably. That first day, as I alighted the bus, and took my first hesitant steps into the world of the Grammar school, I noticed that this world was probably not so very different from that of the comprehensive after all, for all the elitism attached to a Grammar school place.

Certainly, the school bus run was a riotous and raucous affair. Hardly any of the pupils remained seated throughout the journey. During that initial journey, I, along with the driver, tried to cower in an inconspicuous corner, but I had already been spotted by Sarah Braithwaite and her crew, and I had seen her eyes light up with malicious pleasure at the delicious sight of me. I was a tasty morsel to be gobbled up.

From that first day, and over the ensuing days, I learned that the pupils of the Grammar school could be every bit as vicious and unruly as the pupils at the local comp. were reputed to be. I quickly realised that they too could fight, swear and spit. They, however, had additional weapons at their disposal; for the girls of the Grammar school exhibited a level of sophistry and subterfuge in their bullying which was, quite frankly, of a degree which would have made Machiavelli gasp in wonder. It was not just violence. In fact, it was hardly ever violence, although the threat of it, the possibility was always there. (In actual fact, violence would only ever be used "accidentally" and when there was no likely probability of detection by someone in authority; such as the time one of Sarah Braithwaite's cronies, Amanda something-or-other, expertly flicked a hockey ball into my face and smashed out my front teeth. The "accidental" nature of this didn't make it any less devastating, I hasten to add). No; it was the rhetoric that was used against you that became the hardest to bear. The scathing comments and the put-downs, the derogatory looks and the campaigns of whispered lies about you, the gossip mongered about you until you almost believed it yourself. The slights, the snubs, the crushing humiliations, the awful names that stuck.

It's funny, but when I look back upon those years, I wonder why I let it all affect me so very much. When I think about all the events that came later, about how I flew so blatantly in the face of public opinion and didn't really give a damn what they thought – well, not until afterwards anyway, and then I was only sorry because of what happened to The Blank – but I wasn't the slightest bit ashamed before, even though I *knew* in my heart that what I was doing was wrong, and that I was breaking the rules - but I was taking one last chance, cocking one last snook at them all – still, when I think about the person I grew up to be, it amazes me to reflect upon the little girl I was then. I suppose I was just desperate to be approved. Maybe I just wanted to be loved. Still, when I reflect upon that time in my life, it astounds me that the cutting comments and the spiteful glances wounded me so very much. But what can I say? I was weak and easily injured. My grandmother had already begun a thorough indoctrination of me in my own worthlessness throughout those early years. The years spent at the Grammar school just compounded the view I already held of myself. Whatever it was, I felt their victimisation keenly.

Still, I suppose as time went on, I became hardened to it. In fact, there is no suppose about it. I know I became hardened to it all. It was a gradual process, but I became hard, so hard. Hard so that I would never show my feelings to anyone anymore. Hard so I could never admit when things were wrong and I was hurting inside. And it cost me, as I would come to learn later on. Hardness like that, well, it does cost. It's expensive.

I never liked school. I never fitted; but I learned to cope with it. I became defiant, and aggressive when challenged. And I played truant. A lot. Initially, I was subtle about it. I faked illness or forged notes from my grandmother requesting I be excused from this class or the other because of a dentist/doctor/optician's appointment. Then I became more brazen. I simply walked away from classes which were unpalatable to me, or missed whole days when the fancy took me. In the end, I simply didn't care about any of it. By my third year I was missing great chunks of school time. If I am honest about the matter, I was barely there. Like my mother before me, I was always more of an absence than a presence in that school. It was little wonder, really, that I failed to attract any friends. Even those other losers; the ones from my old school (Leon Rimmer *et al.*) and the new ones too, avoided me. There was Mark Trebor who was undersized for his age and who the bigger boys threw about during class like a rugby ball, Karen Ramburn who had a withered arm and was collectively called "clock" by the rest of the school because she had one big hand and one small (only children could be so cruel). All of them were as friendless and blighted as I was. I suppose I could have made overtures of friendship towards them, and maybe, just maybe, been accepted; but, as I have said, there is a hierarchy even amongst losers and I couldn't take the possibility of yet more rejection, yet more proof of my own worthlessness. Besides, by that stage I was wary of everyone and as prickly as a thistle. I could do nothing for them. I wanted nothing from them in return.

Most of the time when I played truant from the Grammar school, I just hung out around Keith Denby's stables. He didn't seem to care that I should have been in school. He was always willing to exploit an extra pair of hands at his yard, and I was always eager to be with the horses. And if there weren't any chores to be done, well, I just hid in one of the stables and dreamed. I dreamed about the day when I didn't have to work for Keith Denby anymore. I dreamed about the day when I would be free. Free from the oppressive regimes of school and my grandmother's house. What I would do with this freedom when I grasped it, I did not know. But it was going to be great. *I* was going to be great. I was going to jump faster, cleaner rounds than either my father or Keith Denby could ever do. I was going to own better horses. The skivvying work... The drudgery of the endless menial tasks which I performed at his stables... Well, that was just a stepping stone, a phase I had to pass through on my path towards this inevitable greatness. As I dreamed on those days, I could almost feel the thud and hammer of my heart bleeding into the rhythm of the horse's canter as we ran our approach to the first fence; the chalky taste of the dust in the arena as it rose up beneath the pounding of the horse's hooves to clog at the back of my nostrils and throat. My immediate surroundings melted away into nothing as I felt that last hitch of his feet as he cleared the final fence and then came the roar of the crowd as it rose in deafening tumult around our ears. The image was so potent, it was almost tangible. It was as if my destiny was waiting for me, just around the next corner.

Sometimes I just hung out with Scotty. We might go to the woods and build a fire to sit around. Anything to be out of the house and away from my grandmother. Anywhere where I could be safe from her, and any other prying eyes who might realise that I should have been in school. Scotty had left school by that stage, after somewhat predictably failing to gain any qualifications. He was unemployed and had become so foul-mouthed in recent times that he was probably unemployable. As a consequence, he had time on his hands. Our friendship, despite our many differences, had endured.

'Scotty,' I began, one wintry afternoon when we had lit a fire and settled ourselves around it on an old blanket. 'Where do you think we'll be in five years' time?' I suppose I could have predicted the answer.

'I don't know, do I?'

'Well, what about ten? Or fifteen?' I persisted. I must have been around fourteen years' old at that time. Fifteen years was a lifetime away for me. It seemed impossible to think that I would not have achieved the highest accolades that show jumping had to offer by that stage. Time would always be on my side. Scotty, however, had a limited imagination.

'I've just said, *I don't fucking know, do I?* We'll probably still be here. Hiding out in these freezing woods with nowhere else to go and nothing else to do. All those years gone by. I can't get a job and neither will you unless you start showing up at school and pass some exams.' It was probably the only serious piece of advice Scotty had ever offered to me before. As a rule, Scotty avoided serious topics of conversation. I knew he was being serious because by the flickering firelight I could see his eyes were blazing and his nostrils were flaring just as they always did when something really mattered to him. 'I mean, *fucking hell*, Em. You're clever. You're not like me. You could *do something*.' He held my gaze for a moment, but I had already let his words slide over me like water.

66

There was no way this was forever for me, hanging around in these wintry woods with nowhere else to go, no money, nothing better to do. The vision of my future shimmered indisputably before my eyes. I *was* going to *do something*. School... Examination passes... They were all unimportant in comparison with the greatness which loomed inevitably before me.

'Well, I wish we could see the future,' I concluded. Now I just wish I could see.

The moment passed and Scotty reverted to his usual flippancy.

'Anyway, what do you reckon? Should I have a skinhead or do you think I look better with a bit of hair?'

'You've already got a skinhead.'

'No way this is a skinhead. This is about two weeks' worth of hair.'

'Well, it looks like a skinhead to me.'

'Well, do you think I look better with a bit of hair or not?'

'I can't remember what you look like with a bit of hair.'

'This *is* a bit of hair. Do you think I should shave it all off or not?'

'God, I don't know, do I? Do whatever you think's best.'

And so we went on, talking trivialities until the evening closed around us and we judged it as safe as it ever was to venture home again.

I almost forgot about that conversation until it was time for me to actually sit my GCSE examinations. Then, when I somewhat predictably failed to gain any GCSE passes whatsoever, it came flooding back to me. However, I still don't believe I analysed Scotty's earlier advice and wished I had heeded it. I was just glad to be done with school. There was that day close to the end of August when all those pretty blonde girls with their slanting blue eyes and vindictive hearts who had made life so difficult for me during my early years at school, all traipsed back up to the school and hugged each other theatrically, exclaiming over their collective "A" grades and their brilliant futures before the watchful eyes and the flashing cameras of the journalists from the local rag. But I, of course, did not go. I had no place there. There was no-one to fold me in a congratulatory embrace, and nothing to congratulate me for anyway, for that matter. Seven GCSEs, graded "U" were hardly a worthy cause for celebration. I began to work for Keith Denby full-time. With no qualifications, it was as Scotty had predicted; I wasn't exactly inundated with offers from elsewhere. There was nowhere else I would rather have been anyway.

6.   Good Riddance (Time of Your Life)

*(Written by Billie Joe Armstrong.   Appears on Reprise Records:
Nimrod, 1997.   Performed by Green Day)*

Keith paid me the pittance of £30 per week, justifying this by
classifying my position under the heading of an "apprenticeship" or
a type of "Youth Training Scheme".   Under this heading he was
supposed to be providing me with some species of training to
accompany the slave wages he was paying me, but in reality, there
wasn't much of that going on.   Anyway, as time had gone on, I had
become increasingly dubious about exactly what I could learn from
Keith Denby in the first place.   There were, for example, a few
things that went on in his yard which I didn't like.   Quite a few
things.   Some of his training methods, for example.   Keith Denby
could take the most attractive, highly strung animal in the world;
you know the type, a horse that lived on its nerves, a horse that
would fly over fences and react almost intuitively to its rider's every
whim, and he could destroy that animal.   I had worked at Keith
Denby's yard since I was eight years' old and I had seen it occur
time and time again.   There are all sorts of horses in the world.
Young ones, temperamental ones, kind ones, half-wild ones, brave
ones, ones with rolling eyes and an evil streak a mile wide.   At one
time or another, I had seen an example of all of these types pass
through Keith Denby's yard.   They arrived as individuals, but they
all left in the same condition; broken, brow-beaten, miserable.   And
then there were the other things which I wasn't quite comfortable
with.   Nothing tangible, nothing you could put your finger on, but
somehow Keith himself - his very presence - made me feel uneasy.
He stood too closely to me.   When he wasn't standing too closely to
me, he was watching me too closely.   He made excuses to touch me.
He made lewd jokes which I didn't understand, and which I didn't
know whether to laugh at or not.   And it wasn't just me.   He was
like it with all of the stable girls.   The difference was they seemed to
know how to handle it.   They either laughed it off or played up to it.

I didn't know what to do, or how best to react. I tried to stay out of his way.

So why, then, did I stay? Partly because I had nowhere else to go. But there was more to it than that. There were some good riders amongst those stable girls. They knew a lot about horses and I wanted to learn. In fact, I was desperate to learn from them. It was they who taught me that it wasn't money or the best horses which made the greatest show jumpers; although having those things helped, there was no doubt about it. Show jumping is expensive, as my father had found to his detriment. But the best show jumpers had two things in common: Firstly, they wanted to win more than *anything else* in the whole world; and secondly, and, more importantly, they *believed* in it. They believed that nothing would prevent their horse from clearing those fences. It was no good half-believing, and thinking, well, he might run out on it, or he might stop before the fence. That was no good, because horses *know*. If you believe he is going to jump that fence, then jump that fence he will, and clear it too. Your faith in him is all he needs. If you doubt him, well, he'll start to doubt himself and then... Well, it's all over. I learned other things from them too. Things like you don't have to over-exaggerate your signals with a good horse. If you look at a fence and keep your mind focussed upon your route to the next jump, playing it out in pictures in your mind, then the horse will intuitively follow the path you have visualised. Also, if you *know* your horse is going to jump the next fence, which of course you do, because you *always* believe he's going to jump the next fence, then you can shave valuable seconds off the time of your round by taking tighter turns into the fences and cutting bigger corners. This was a tip which didn't always pay off. You had to be able to read and understand the horse you were riding to see if you could get away with it; but if you could, then it could mean the difference between first place and second if it came down to a jump off.

I didn't like Keith that much, as I have said, but I think after all those years, he had a soft spot for me; because after a while, in addition to exercising his daughter's recalcitrant pony when she couldn't be bothered to (she could never be bothered to), or mucking out the horses with the really evil temperaments who were likely to lash out at you if they were in the stall at the time; he also let me begin to compete. It was nothing amazing. If he was competing in a show, he might let me go along too, to take part in the novice/intermediate level class which inevitably preceded his own advanced class. In an unprecedented occurrence of largesse, he even paid for me to become a lifelong jumping member of the British Show Jumping Association.

There used to be show jumping every Tuesday night in the winter, just across the fields in the indoor arena at Scarbold. If Keith Denby didn't have anything better to do, he would ride with me across the dark fields by the glow of our stirrup lights and we would enter our respective classes; he in the advanced class, usually held at the end of the evening; me in the class before. The prize money wasn't much. It cost £2 per class to enter and the top prize was only £5 per event. Keith surprised me by his interest in these small scale shows at all really. I would have thought he would have sneered at them, but as it was he came along with me most Tuesday evenings, "just for the ride." I guess he wasn't winning much in other competitions at the time and so he didn't have any higher things to concern himself with.

He rode whichever of his horses he was trying to bring on. I always rode Miss Primrose, his daughter's fat palomino pony. He told me that when I won the novice class, he would enter me into a better, more prestigious competition and pay my entry fee. He didn't specify which competition. He left me to speculate upon this matter; and in my imagination it was always going to be one of the big events. It was certainly something to strive for. But...

'I'd like to see you win, kid. That novice class is always won by the same grey pony. It doesn't matter who's riding it. It always wins.'

There was always a but.

He was right about that pony too. It was called "Smart Sprite" and although it didn't have any wings, it could fly. It didn't even need a run up to the fences; it could jump them from a standstill, and turn on a penny. It never refused. It never upset a fence. It never even touched a hoof to one. It jumped for the joy of it and got consistently clear rounds in times no other horse could even come close to. Whenever Smart Sprite was in the competition, I didn't stand a cat in hell's chance of winning; unless, of course, I could have borrowed Smart Sprite and ridden him. Miss Primrose, too, could turn on a penny. Unfortunately, she refused to use this talent for my benefit. Instead of being able to use this skill to tighten up our turns and get a faster, cleaner round, she tended to utilise her genius for mischief. The first time I entered the Scarbold competition, I was nervous as hell. After I'd walked the course, I ran through the order of the jumps obsessively in my mind. Just the worst thing I could imagine would be to make a total fool out of myself by losing my way around the course. Enter from the warm-up arena and approach fence one, a rustic cross pole – low and easy – proceed to the far end of the arena allowing Miss Primrose to drift across to her left to fall into line with fence two, an oxer built out of yellow and white painted poles. Turn right at the top of the arena and follow the line of the corner around to fence three – a low wall jump. Clear the wall, turn right to fence four – nondescript and built from standard issue red and white show jumping poles. Back around fence one and along the long wall of the arena over a double jump before completing the round by turning and jumping fence four again. If several of the competitors jumped clear rounds then there would be a jump off, in which the course would have to be jumped again, but this time against the clock. The rider who jumped the fastest round with the least number of faults would be the winner. If it did come to a jump off, I could see that it would become necessary to risk a very tight turn after that double jump in order to get over that last fence quickly and thus complete the round in the fastest time possible. All of this ran through my mind as I cantered Miss Primrose around the warm-up area; a complete

72

strategy for victory, before we had even cleared a single fence. And it was all completely irrelevant, for Miss Primrose and I, did not, on that occasion even achieve the initial clear round in order to qualify for the jump off in the first place. For that evening, as with every other evening I competed with Miss Primrose, she was bent on trouble; something which I discovered to my cost. She completed the first four fences beautifully. I was just beginning to relax and enjoy it as I rode her confidently towards the double. She soared over the first fence and I relaxed totally as she cantered the three short strides towards the second element of the double. All we had to do was complete the double and the clear round was as good as in the bag. I even glanced away from the second part of the double momentarily, just to check out that last fence, and see how tightly I dared to make that final turn when it came to the jump off. It was the moment Miss Primrose had been waiting for; the moment when I lost concentration. She executed a beautiful turn upon the spot, swinging out wide and away from the second jump in the double, leaving me paddling somewhere in mid-air for one astonished instant before I plummeted to the ground, demolishing the second part of the double as I did so. There was an agonising silence around the arena from the watching spectators as I extricated myself, bruised and winded from the clutter of poles. I'm afraid I flailed around on the floor for a little time before I actually managed to achieve this. I had slammed my ribs against one of those poles and the breath had been smacked right out of me. I couldn't even speak to call to Miss Primrose, whom, meanwhile, had stopped innocently just a few yards away from me, her palomino bottom facing me but with her head turned towards me, large enquiring eyes regarding me benignly, as if to say, 'Well, what on earth are you doing down there?' I scrambled up to catch her to remount and complete the round, but, again, Miss Primrose had other ideas. With a gleam of mocking amusement in her eyes she gambolled away from me. She was in her element now, scampering around that show jumping ring, stirrups and reins flying, whilst everyone - fellow competitors, judges, and spectators - shouted advice as to

73

how to catch her again. All of it was wasted and none of it made the slightest bit of difference anyway. We were, eventually, eliminated from the competition when Miss Primrose exited the arena via the warm-up area.

I was almost too ashamed to return to the following week's competition with Miss Primrose; but I wanted to win. I wanted it badly. I was going to win. We were going to win whatever Miss Primrose felt about the matter; not just here at a poxy local show, but at the bigger event, whatever it might be, that Keith had promised me. But sometimes just wanting something isn't enough. The following week we still didn't win. This time, however, despite the knowing stares and expectant smirks of the audience at our reappearance, it wasn't quite so humiliating. The watchword with Miss Primrose was *vigilance*. If you maintained leg and mouth contact with her and held her together at all times, she would grudgingly complete the round. If, for even one split second, you relaxed and thought you had it all wrapped up, she'd start running out at fences. We returned week after week after week. We began to jump consistently clear rounds but we never could quite manage to match the ultra fast times set by Smart Sprite in the jump off; and if I took risks and forced Miss Primrose to take what she clearly felt to be too sharp a turn in order to cut down our round times, she would become indignant about the matter and begin refusing fences. We had a string of blue rosettes for second place, but no red for first. It began to look as if we would never achieve that elusive win; until, one Tuesday evening, fortune smiled upon us. Smart Sprite and his rider didn't show up for the event and that tricky first place was ours. I would like to be able to tell you that we had beaten Smart Sprite fair and square; that at the end of the day, my commitment and talent triumphed over all. Sadly, however, it would simply not be true. The only reason we won at all was because Smart Sprite wasn't there to beat us on that particular day. Similarly, I would like to be able to tell you that the bigger event which Keith had promised me entry into was a really grand one. Sadly, this was not the case either. It was merely one of the smaller

BSJA-sponsored events. Still, it was, as Keith had promised, a more prestigious event than the Scarbold show and it seemed I was on a winning streak, because I lifted the trophy there too. However, the only reason I won at this event was because of the horse I rode; and the fact that my horse, or rather Keith Denby's horse, outclassed every other riders' mount by miles. It was hardly fair, but what can I say? I still won. For when I returned home, giddy with triumph on that Tuesday evening and duly flashed my red rosette in Keith's direction (he hadn't accompanied me that night to Scarbold for some reason) and told him to get the horsebox ready because Miss Primrose and I were jumping at whichever big event he had lined up for us, his reply was unequivocal.

'Stuff that,' he said. And then, when he saw my face fall as I thought he was about to renege on his part of our bargain, he went quickly on to add; 'You're not riding that pony when you're representing this yard. You're going to win, not get chucked off at the first fence. No. Miss Primrose is retiring from the sport. You can ride Silver Destination.'

My heart leapt with elation at the prospect. You may remember Silver Destination from my concluding essay in the Eleven Plus examination; and you may gather from the time that has elapsed since that stage in my life, i.e. seven years further on down the line from there since that offering to the Grammar school Examination Board, to this point in my life, that Silver Destination was knocking on a bit. And, indeed, it's true, he was around sixteen years' of age when I rode him in that competition and would assuredly be deemed an elderly gentleman in the equine world. Certainly, he was no good for Keith Denby to ride any longer. He had suffered too much at the hands of Keith and could indisputably be numbered among the ranks of the broken that were strewn across Keith's path. However, he could still jump and for some reason, instead of getting rid of him, as Keith normally did when he'd abused an animal too much (he never could bear to be confronted with the evidence of his crimes; perhaps that was why he fired so many stable girls after he'd dallied with them), in Silver's case, he'd kept him on. In his prime, Silver Destination had cleared a wall of nearly seven feet in a Puissance competition, and although he would never have made that height in his later years, he didn't have to. The fences we faced in that competition were undoubtedly higher than the ones at the Scarbold events, but to Silver Destination, who had successfully jumped the course at Hickstead, the course for the small-time competition which Keith had entered us into was nothing. A walk in the park. I can remember that evening so clearly. If I close my eyes, shut out the blur and cast myself back in time I can almost live it again; every leap over every fence. I suppose I can recall it so well for two reasons. The initial one, of course, being because it was my first major win. The second reason was for what came after.

Keith Denby had loaded Silver into the horsebox himself. Silver hadn't liked it, of course. He was often tense and anxious when Keith was around, as were many of the horses. It had taken Katy, one of the other stable girls, to calm him down enough to stop him kicking out at the walls of the horsebox. Katy had also come along with us. She was seated next to me in the cab of the box. Keith was driving, I was in the middle, and Katy was on my other side next to the window. I was glad of her company, but I couldn't help but think that maybe she'd put on weight recently. I could feel her hip pushing into mine and generally squashing me in Keith's direction, where, frankly, I didn't want to be. Her face was all puffy as well, as if she'd been crying; but I didn't dwell on it too much, I must confess. I was too busy trying to quell the storm of nerves and nausea that was threatening to overwhelm me. My stomach felt like one of those volatile African countries. It was liable to stage a coup and erupt in rebellion at any time. When I caught sight of my own features in the wing mirror of the truck, I was startled by what I saw. My features were so pallid and drawn that I almost didn't recognise myself.

The drive there was conducted in near silence. Katy was obviously sulking about something; I felt sick, and Keith seemed to be in a bad mood too. It was only as we were drawing into the car

76

park for the venue that he flashed a smile in my direction, patted my (for once, immaculate) jodhpured thigh and said, 'Cheer up. You'll be alright when you get out there.' He was right too. Once I'd completed the first fence of the round, I was no longer nervous at all. I was exhilarated, buzzing with adrenalin. We could have taken on the world, and won. It was just prior to the event that I really suffered; in those moments when I was running the jumping order of the fences obsessively through my mind in the warm-up arena. When I heard the announcer call out our names as the next horse-and-rider team to compete, I could easily have vomited all down Silver's gleaming shoulder. But once we got in there, everything but the jumps faded from my mind. There were no spectators, no other competitors, no judges scrutinising our every move; no Keith and no Katy watching either. It all just disappeared around us. The whole world became just us, Silver and me; and nine fences to jump. It was beautiful. It was perfect. Silver's canter was light and springy. He cleared the obstacles easily. We flowed together with a smooth fluidity. It was over too quickly. We had our first clear round. The jump-off, the round timed to see which of the competitors with clears could jump the fastest, cleanest round and decide the winner, was similarly simple for us. There were only four of us with clears. I suspect for all of us, it was our first major competition. The other three weren't prepared to take risks with it. I was; but then again, somehow I knew that Silver was enjoying himself as much as I was, and would not refuse the fences, no matter how little run up to them I provided, so I wasn't really taking risks at all, when I cut corners and asked Silver to perform incredibly tight twists and turns between the fences, was I? Our round was a good three seconds faster with zero faults. Of the other competitors, two had managed to accumulate points for knocking down fences. The final competitor had ridden so slowly and exercised such care in the attempt to avoid this that she had begun to accumulate time faults. We had won.

I will never forget the presentation of the cup, the first place rosette (so much more expensive looking than the first place rosette from the Scarbold show) and that final lap of honour. I was almost delirious with exhilaration. Upon a whim, at the conclusion to our lap of honour, I rode Silver directly at one of the upright fences and as he launched himself over it, I threw my hand up just to feel the rush of air through my fingers.

I encountered differing reactions to this capricious action. The commentator and the crowd thought that it was a gesture of triumph. I heard laughter and the commentator saying, 'Emily Devlin, celebrating in spectacular style there. Well, why not? She's definitely one to watch for in the future.' His tone was humorously indulgent. On the other hand, my fellow contestants shook their heads mutinously at what they thought of as such a self-conscious act of victory over them and viewed it as bad sportsmanship on my part. Keith Denby chided me a little, but not as badly as he might have done, for showing off. But I didn't do it for any of those reasons. Just as I had completed my lap of honour, I had suddenly remembered that final essay in my Eleven Plus examination, when I had written about Silver Destination. I suppose it was riding Silver which recalled the words to my mind. *'...I wonder if I was riding that horse, if when Silver was at the pinnacle of his leap, I put my hand up into the air, I would be able to drag my fingers through the clouds and touch my mother again...'* Of course, I couldn't touch my mother again. I would never be able to touch my mother again. It was silly to do it really. But I did wonder if she was watching me, and what she thought of it all; if she thought anything at all. This was something I would continue to do every time I won. It became a species of tradition. My trademark signature of victory every time I lifted the cup in an event. As I have said, people exhibited differing reactions to it, but I don't care what they thought. I was only ever trying to reach my mother and make her notice me again.

After that first victory, I was consumed by the energy we had created, Silver and I, to win that competition. I couldn't sit still. I was in overdrive; and Silver was the same, prancing around the confines of the horsebox, tossing his head and snorting like an

Arabian stallion, flicking flecks of foam from his steaming neck until they clung to the boards of the box.

'Silver, stop it,' I was chiding him, but laughing at the same time, because I knew how he felt, because I felt like dancing too, because we couldn't help it. Still, he was steaming up dreadfully and I didn't want him to overheat and then become suddenly chilled afterwards. I threw an anti-sweat rug over his withers and grabbing a wisp of hay from his net, began to rub the sweat from his streaked coat. I figured it was the least I could do after he had effectively won my first major competition for me.

'Leave that,' Keith's sudden appearance startled me. I turned to face him and realised that he was standing much closer to me than I had anticipated. I began to feel a little uneasy; as did Silver. He had laid his grey ears flat against the side of his head and was rolling his eyes at Keith. He wasn't dancing like a yearling anymore either. It was hardly possible, but he almost seemed to have shrunk as he cringed against the wall furthest away from Keith Denby. It was a shame to see it. My heart hardened inside me. I could feel my lips tightening with disapproval. For a moment, before I got a hold of myself again, I must have resembled my grandmother. But then I pulled it back together. I couldn't afford to be angry with Keith Denby. I needed his sponsorship. I needed his horses. There were all the other events I was going to enter and win. I consciously smoothed the lines from my face so that it became impassively neutral. I think I even tried to smile at him, but it came out all wrong; a mirthless, crooked grimace. His features appeared too big in my line of sight. I could see all the open pores and thready veins on his nose. I wondered, self-consciously, if mine looked the same, and felt an irrational urge to cover it with my hand. I didn't know where to look. I turned away. It was easier not to look at him when he was standing so closely to me.

'It's alright,' I said with a too-bright cheeriness that came out all wrong. It sounded false, even to my own ears. I moderated my tone. 'I want to do it.'

No, leave it.' His voice was even closer behind me now. I could have sworn his hand was touching my bottom. 'Katy'll do it.' It was his voice that sounded all wrong now. Thick and husky. As if he was about to cry. It was all very disturbing. I was about to turn again and make some joke about it, but something stopped me. I couldn't be sure if he really had touched me; it had been the merest feather-light brushes of contact. I didn't want to accuse him of something he hadn't done and look a total fool. I began to rub at Silver Destination's sweating coat with the wisp with new purpose.

'Really, I'll do it,' I assured him. 'Katy's in a foul mood already.'

'Oh, forget about her. Stupid tart.' This last observation was made *sotto voce*, as if it was intended for himself, rather than for me to hear. However, I could tell by how clearly I heard this aside, just how closely Keith was still standing next to me. I didn't like the way things were going. Even if she was in a foul mood and she was a stupid tart (and she could be, sometimes), I wished Katy was there with us then. I felt a brush of air as if he was raising his arm to reach out and touch me. Silver Destination shrank even further away to press himself against the wall of the horsebox. I heard the boards of the box creak ominously under the pressure of his weight. He knew what Keith Denby's raised fist meant. I didn't; and I didn't want to find out. I moved with Silver. Not fast enough. I felt his fingers brush across the surface of my hair. I wished he wouldn't. My hair was all sweaty from being crushed beneath my riding hat. My back was prickling with an uncomfortable awareness of his presence; too much awareness. I didn't want it.

'You have beautiful hair,' he continued in the same undertone as previously.

'Huh.' I tried to snort derisively; make light of his compliment. Move back onto ground on which I felt safe once more. I tried to respond with a glib 'yeah, well, since when has mousy hair been beautiful?', but the words turned to ashes in my throat.

'It's fine. Like cotton. It looks almost golden when the light shines through it.'

There was no doubt he was touching me now. His fingers were almost tangling in my hair. I didn't know what to do. Panic was mounting too quickly inside of me. I recognised the feeling. It was the same as when I knew I was in for it with my grandmother. I was afraid.

'Em!' From the bottom of the ramp to the horsebox, just outside the pool of illumination from the dusty cobwebbed interior lights, I heard Scotty's voice. Oh, thank God. His voice sounded panicky too. I had absolutely no idea why Scotty should be there, but oh thank God that he was.

'Scotty!' The relief in my tone was almost palpable. I sprang away from Keith Denby's imprisoning bulk with lightening quickness. (I'm sorry, Silver, but you're on your own).

'Scotty! I didn't know you were coming to watch. I wish I'd known that you were here. Did you see? We won. We won first prize.' I gestured towards the sumptuous red rosette which was hanging from the wall of the horsebox, but Scotty didn't seem to see it. He was staring past me towards Keith, eyes narrowed with suspicion and lips tightened. As he moved further up the ramp to the horsebox and into the light, I noticed his features were blotchy and white, just like they were when he was really mad about something. His figure was tensed, all the muscles on his upper body standing out, like he was about to start throwing punches.

'I didn't see.' His tone was mean and angry. He didn't glance in my direction at all. He continued to look at Keith Denby.

'Oh.'

Then, just as suddenly as he'd appeared, Scotty shook himself loose and he was back to his normal self again.

'Come on, Em.' His tone was weary now and I noticed there were dark circles underneath his eyes. 'Something's happened. You've got to come home.' Scotty was already striding away. I turned to shrug at Keith Denby and then followed his figure retreating into the darkness.

'So if you didn't come to watch, why are you here?' I demanded as soon as I had caught up with him. The competition we had won had been a small scale event, but it had been held at one of the larger venues, some seventy miles away from where we lived. Scotty must have driven himself there in his ancient Talbot Avenger which he'd bought off one of his mates for fifty quid; but if he hadn't come to see me jump, then why had he bothered at all?

'I told you. Something's happened. I had to bring you home.'

'Well, what? What's happened?' We reached the rusting vehicle and Scotty clambered into the driver's seat, leaned across and pulled up the lock on the passenger door so I could clamber in beside him. I eased myself in carefully. There was a hole in the passenger seat which the unwary could fall through, ripping clothes and flesh on the decaying coils of springs within the seat. There was also a knot of wires hanging down into the footwell. The car itself could no longer be started with an ignition key. At some point in its career, and God knows why, but some thief had attempted to steal it and knocked the ignition point out. Therefore, it now started via a button attached to a tangle of wires hanging out of the space where the key would ordinarily have been slotted in to start the car. Scotty now jabbed at this fruitlessly a few times, before the engine sputtered into reluctant life.

'She's dead, Em.' Scotty was still fiddling with the car, but I knew he was watching me now, to see how I would react to this not-quite-revelation. He never was very good at handling the serious stuff.

It took me a moment to catch up; to read the look on his face, to realise he was not talking about his car. Comprehend who he must mean.

'Oh.'

I looked out of the window at the distant arena lights. Events were still going on over there. The competition I had just won was a relatively minor one, held early on in the event schedule. Over there, they would be working up to the grand finale, the main event.

Other people would be winning, just like I had done with Silver Destination.

'Oh.'

If I looked carefully I might still be able to make out the glow from Keith Denby's horsebox where Katy, probably still in a foul mood, would now be rugging up Silver Destination for the journey home.

'Oh.'

I'd left my rosette over there too. I began to laugh; softly at first, and then louder, until I was emitting great shrieks of laughter, borderline hysterical. Scotty turned to look at me fully then, dropping any pretence of fixing the wires to the car. There was a look of alarm on his face. Perhaps he thought I was going mad, like my mother. Perhaps I was. I only know that it was all too much to handle in one day. The elation of winning, the sudden panic I had felt in the horsebox, and now, *this*. I suppose I should have felt sorry. I should have been grieved at the news. That's what you did when someone died, I told myself. You grieved. All I could feel was an irrefutable sense of relief. It was over. The day was over. And now my grandmother was over too. Thank goodness. Terrible, I know. Almost bordering on the blasphemous, but I couldn't help the way I felt. She would never hurt me again. Why wouldn't I... *Why wouldn't anyone...* be thankful for that?

'Stop, Emily! Stop!' Scotty sounded really frightened now. And I knew he was serious, because he never called me Emily. It was always "Em", or "Emmy", or "our Em", and once, even "my Em". Never Emily. I hated that name. He hated that name. Nobody called me that. Nobody except my grandmother. And she never would again. I choked back another hysterical sob at the thought.

'For G-G-God's sake, Scotty, how do you expect me to react? She was alright this morning. What the hell happened?'

Scotty grinned broadly, as if he couldn't help himself, but then hurriedly struggled to hide his smile, as if he suddenly thought it somehow inappropriate. I grinned too, to show that I agreed with him. To show that I too, like him, was glad that she was dead. Scotty grinned again, and then laughed out loud.

'Christ-on-a-bike, Em, you wouldn't believe what happened. I only found Mrs Ayres wandering around in the yard outside the cottage.' Mrs Ayres was the woman who ran the local shop from where Scotty and I had liberated so much stock over the years. She lived in one of the other houses on our lane. I suppose she was one of our nearest neighbours, but we scarcely ever saw her beyond the dusty counter of her little shop. She was hardly likely to pop around to my grandmother's house for a chat. Nobody ever called in at my grandmother's house just for a chat. There must be more to it. There was. Scotty could hardly hold back his laughter as he recounted the tale.

'She was in a right mess. You should have seen the state of her. She came running up when she saw me and she started pulling at my shirt like this.' Scotty made his broad hands into the hands of a nervous old lady and began to pluck at the front of the ripped and sleeveless tartan shirt he was wearing. 'I knew it must be bad because she hasn't even acknowledged I existed since she caught me on the rob in her shop that day and barred me from going in. I mean...' Scotty rolled his eyes in exasperation at the unreasonableness of women. 'She never even looks at me, never mind starts groping me.' He pulled at his shirt again just to illustrate his point. 'Anyway, there's me, thinking I've pulled or something, when she only goes and starts crying all over me. '"Oh Scott, Scott,"' she says...' At this point, Scotty did a passable imitation of Mrs Ayre's thin reedy whine. I was laughing so hard it was hurting me.

'Stop it, Scotty. Just tell me what happened.'

'I *am* telling you, aren't I? Well, she starts going on with this great long tale all about how she went round for a chat, see?'

' I don't believe that for a minute.'

'No, neither did I. But I think she was trying to put it in a better light than it actually was. But then she breaks down and spills the beans anyway.'

I waited for Scotty to do the same.

'Chat my arse. She'd gone round to complain about that pissy little dog.'

'Ah.' I was beginning to understand. My grandmother kept (*had kept*. Past tense. Must remember that. My grandmother now firmly belonged in the past) a savage unprepossessing highland terrier named, rather appropriately as it turned out, since it spent so much of its life relieving itself on other people's property, Mr Tinkle. The conversation between Mrs Ayres and my grandmother, it seemed went something like this:

'Mrs Devlin, I've come to have a quick word with you about your dog.' I could picture the scene as Scotty sketched it before my eyes. I could imagine the tone of voice Mrs Ayres would employ, simultaneously appeasing but still managing to be slightly querulous. I could also envisage my grandmother's face as she peered suspiciously round the door to the cottage. I could visualise the narrowing of her eyes and her lipsticked mouth creasing into coral cracks and wrinkles as she pursed it in disapproval.

'I suppose you'll be wanting to come inside.' My grandmother would have (grudgingly) said. She didn't ever actually *invite* anyone into the house. She didn't know how to be welcoming.

'Well, yes. It might be better if I did...' Mrs Ayres probably wouldn't have wanted to enter anymore than my grandmother would have wanted her to be there, but she probably deemed it best to conduct this conversation behind closed doors rather than it denigrate into a slanging match in the middle of the lane. And, once inside, she probably hazarded a tiny glance around the little sitting room. After all, not many people got to see the inside of my grandmother's cottage, and I expect her curiosity got the better of her there. Not that there was much to see. A few ornaments still kept on their high shelves, even though my brother was now much beyond the age of stuffing delicate objects up his nose. Still, the lower shelves of my grandmother's cabinets were kept bare just in case the temptation should overwhelm him again. Once upon a time, those bare shelves would have been scrupulously dust-free, but recently my grandmother hadn't bothered so much, and there would have been a thin layer of dust on those shelves which Mrs Ayres' would probably have noted and tucked away with some satisfaction for future reference; some prospective material for a good bit of juicy gossip to proffer over the shop counter, to go with the paper or the quarter-pound of jelly babies which someone had bought. A couple of shabby armchairs, one of which, no doubt, would have been occupied by the malevolent presence of the little white terrier in question. Mrs Ayres would have caught sight of the dog and her features would have hardened, becoming set with new resolve at the sight of it. She was sick of it; sick of the bloody thing doing *its* business all over her dahlias and her path. And then when she tried to chase it off before it left another little "package" for her to step into on her way out to the shop, it turned on her. Nasty yappy little thing, jumping up with its filthy paws and snapping at her ankles. She couldn't bear it. She was sick of the damn thing laddering her nylons. Somebody had to take responsibility for the wretched creature. Still... She might have hesitated for an instant when she raised her eyes from the yellowy fur of the irascible terrier to meet the steely gaze of my grandmother. If only the girl was here, she might have wished, regretfully. She would have found me so much easier to chastise to her satisfaction over the matter. So much easier to bully. But of course, I wasn't there. I was never there, unless I absolutely had to be. I was always with my horses; and there was nowhere else I'd rather be. But Mrs Ayres wouldn't have understood that. No doubt she thought there was something going on between me and Keith. She wouldn't be the first to have thought that. She might even have had to suppress a smirk of satisfaction at the thought of me "getting into trouble" with Keith Denby. No doubt she'd have been pleased to see me come to no good. But I digress.

'Well, as I say, it's about your dog.' She would have begun innocuously enough, her caution of my grandmother and her famous/infamous temper keeping a check on the words she chose.

But Mrs Ayres had a temper too; and as I have surmised, she was heartily sick of that dog. What was more, my grandmother wasn't the type of woman to pour oil on troubled waters.

'I was just going to *tactfully* request that she keep a better watch on what that dog of hers was up to,' she had reported to Scotty, her voice high and hysterical still, but with a note of self-justification creeping in, just in case, anyone should think... Well, as she was so keen to point out, it wasn't her fault, after all... 'But she set about me, she did.' Scotty could only nod in agreement. What else could he do? He knew my grandmother. He knew what she was like.

'Well, spit it out then,' my grandmother would have rounded on Mrs Ayres. 'No doubt you've come to complain, you and all the other beggars around here who haven't got anything better to do than poke their noses into other people's business!'

'Excuse me, Mrs Devlin!' Mrs Ayres' tone would have become suddenly affronted at the very suggestion that she was merely "poking" her "nose in". 'I think it does become our business when that *damned* dog is coming onto other people's property and doing *its* business everywhere. My dahlias are practically dead this year, and I've entered best-kept garden again. I'd have won it too, if my dahlias were up to scratch, but thanks to your dog, Mrs Bury's bound to take the prize. And I'm sick of stepping in...' Delicacy would have forbidden Mrs Ayres from putting a name to the offending article which she had placed her foot in one time too many.

'Your dahlias!' My grandmother apparently snorted in response. "*Mrs Bury's bound to take the prize*, is she?" she mimicked in Mrs Ayres' carping tone. 'And, really, Mrs Ayres, there is no need to damn poor Mr Tinkle.' Mrs Ayres would have flushed with angry mortification at this. She prided herself on her clean-living and regular church attendance. Didn't she do the flowers before every Sunday service? And the coffees after? In short, she thought she was better than us and our dysfunctional family. She probably was, but still my grandmother had caught her out there.

'Well, really, Mrs Devlin, I don't know how you expect me to react. That animal of yours has driven me to it! Besmirching my paths. And not just mine! It's been out doing its business on other paths too. There was a bride stepped in something which no doubt that animal left on the churchyard path. So that animal of yours ruined what was supposed to be the best day of her life. But then that would please you, wouldn't it? Vindictive, vicious crone that you are!' (The gloves were well and truly off now).

'Vindictive! Vicious! Well, *you'd* know all about that!' They would have been shouting at each other by this point. They hated each other. They had always hated each other. To be fair, my grandmother hated most people. She had a great capacity for hate, something which I must admit is one of my own less desirable character traits, but then I must have inherited it from somewhere. Still, I doubt whether most people in the village hated my grandmother as much as she hated them. Mrs Ayres was the exception, however, to this general rule; and that hate had been waiting for just the right opportunity to burst its banks and spill over.

'I don't know how you have the nerve. You come around here *appointing* yourself the representative for the whole village. *If* the vicar wants to complain to me about a mess on the church path then *let him come himself.* But he won't, will he? Because the vicar's a *reasonable* man. He knows that it could be *any* of the dogs in the village who left that mess, not just Mr Tinkle! He's not the only dog in the village, you know!' (It was more likely that the vicar was afraid of her and did not dare come to complain. Having God in your corner can only get you so far).

'No! But it's the only dog that's left to run around unsupervised. It tried to bite poor Mrs Charlesworth's toddler, you know. You're lucky she didn't call the police, or the RSPCA! Looking at the state of the thing, it looks like it could do with the RSPCA!'

It has to be said that Mr Tinkle *was* getting on somewhat in years and had definitely seen better days. I have to agree with Mrs Ayres there. He was a bit of a wretched looking thing. His fur was rather matted and he was a bit smelly. I would have done something about it myself, but the dog was far too vicious to handle even by my grandmother, so it merely remained in the same sorry state.

'The RSPCA!' my grandmother continued, her voice rising even higher than before. 'Oh, so that's your little game, is it? Take an old lady's beloved companion from her, would you? You evil...'

'Well, look at the poor thing...' Mrs Ayres would have risked stepping closer to Mr Tinkle, now firmly ensconced in her new role as defender of a weak, helpless animal. She probably stretched out her arm to comfort the poor creature. I expect she was almost glowing with the knowledge of her own saintliness, but then Mr Tinkle would have bared his teeth in a warning grin at her and she would have quickly thought better of it and hastily retracted her hand.

'*Somebody's* got to take responsibility for the animal, and since you clearly aren't prepared to do it, perhaps I *should* intervene...' It was at this point that Mrs Ayres turned again to face my grandmother and was, as she put it to Scotty, quite simply horrified by what she saw. According to her description, my grandmother had 'blanched as white as a sheet, totally ashen. She wasn't saying anything at all, but her mouth was moving about as if she was trying to speak. But nothing was coming out. It was just sort of... Flapping. And then she fell down. Well, sort of slumped really... Onto the floor. And her eyes went all funny... Unfocussed, like she couldn't see me anymore.'

Mrs Ayres began to cry then and to pluck at Scotty's shirt even more than before.

'Well, what happened then?' I demanded in the darkness of the car.

'Well, I didn't know what to do, did I? I said to her 'Well, where is she now?' And she just points into the house, like she was still in there. So I said to her, 'Haven't you called a fucking ambulance or nothing?''

'Oh Scotty, you didn't say that to her?'

'Well, what do you expect me to say? She'd just left herself lying on the floor.'

'I didn't mean that. I meant you didn't have to swear at her, did you?'

'Oh, for God's sake. I wasn't even thinking straight or nothing by then. What would you have done?'

'Probably the same, but I wouldn't have sworn at her. You know what she's like.'

For a moment I visualised the small, slightly pointed features of her face, the auburn tinted bob of her wiry hair, the watery blue of her eyes, the broken thready capillaries that wove their way just beneath the surface of her pale skin. She considered herself refined.

'Oh... I don't give a rat's ass about that,' Scotty easily disregarded my misgivings on this point. 'I tell you, I hardly dared go into that cottage. The door was just hanging open and creaking in the wind; you know how it does...'

I nodded. It was an old cottage.

'It was spooky, I can tell you. But I had to go in and check and all the time that woman was coming in behind me, so close that she was clinging to me, you know. And I was just sweating... All down my back, where she was hanging on to me. I was hot as hell. Anyway, I got in there and she was just *there*. Just lying on the floor and, oh my God, it was horrible... There were great gobs of spit all hanging round her mouth, but I could hear her breathing, so I thought she must be okay. Well, I say breathing, it was more like snoring. Like she was asleep. In fact, I even asked Mrs Ayres if she hadn't just fallen asleep. She just got mad at that. Called me stupid. Asked me if I couldn't see there was something wrong with her.' Scotty shrugged in the darkness. 'It wasn't me who just left her lying there, was it? Anyway, I called an ambulance and then we just sat there... Waiting... I felt like I should move her. I mean... It didn't seem right just leaving her lying on the floor like that. I mean... She was always so fussy about that front room of hers. I wasn't even supposed to be there. She hated me in there. But Mrs Ayres wouldn't let me touch her. Not that I wanted to, mind. But it just didn't seem *right*. And that ambulance took ages to come as well. Or, it seemed like it, anyway. We were just waiting and waiting. And then she... *Her*... On the floor... She went all quiet and the snoring stopped and I just didn't know what to do because I knew... I'm telling you, *I knew* she was dead. And I think Mrs Ayres knew it too, because she said 'Oh! Oh! Scott! Scott!' and flapped her hands about a bit, but then she went quiet too, like she didn't want to think about it either. I don't blame her. I didn't want to think on it. Anyway, the ambulance came. At last. They'd come all the way from Chester and they'd only gone and got lost on the lanes. Anyway, they took one look at her and shook their heads and messed about a bit before they said she were dead and loaded her up in the ambulance and took her off. I didn't bother going with her. She hated me anyway and I hated her. Well, you know...'

I nodded again. I knew.

'I think they took her to the Treeton again.'

The Treeton again. The Treeton Memorial Hospital Chapel of Rest where they had taken the body of my mother all those years ago. I had a fleeting recollection of that dreadful sampler worked in cross-stitch starring Bruce Dickinson as Jesus Christ being crucified. I wondered if it was still there.

I never did get to find out. I didn't lift a finger to organise any kind of funeral. Instead, Mrs Ayres, took charge of it all. Perhaps she felt that it was somehow her fault; that my grandmother had suddenly dropped dead in the middle of an argument about a dog she didn't even care about. She would only have been arguing with Mrs Ayres for the sake of it, belligerent cow that she was. Perhaps it was as well that Mrs Ayres took charge. If it had been left to me, I would have done it on the cheap; one of those cardboard coffins made from recycled materials, no cars, no flowers or church service, just to spite her and her overdeveloped sense of propriety. I might even have just left it to the Council to sort it all out. Even after she was dead, I couldn't forgive her. I hated her still. Instead Mrs Ayres organised for a car to transport the body. She chose the coffin and probably paid for it too. She even bought flowers.

However, for all the care on Mrs Ayres' part, there were few enough of us "mourners" at her funeral. Mrs Ayres was there, of course. Beyond her, there was only Scotty and I. Even the professional mourners, those ancient old crones who never missed a good funeral and were ever-present at the funeral teas of the deceased, whether of their acquaintance or not, to partake in the bandying of embellished memories whilst simultaneously consuming as many curly sandwiches and cups of stewed tea as they could decently imbibe, had absented themselves from the affair. Like all of us, they had been afraid of my grandmother and that fear lingered on, even after death.

I wore my jodhpurs to the funeral. It was a sign of my lack of respect; but it was mainly because I wanted to get straight back to work after it was all over. I had been forced to take time away from the stables to attend and this I had only done grudgingly. I resented even the short space of the morning away from the horses. I saw the vicar looking at me strangely, but I didn't care. Neither did Scotty. He wore a pink T-shirt and when the vicar ran through the "ashes to ashes, dust to dust" section of the ceremony and crumbled a handful of earth into the open grave so that it fell against the lid of my grandmother's coffin, Scotty kicked a stone savagely in too which landed with an unseemly thud and chipped the veneer of the coffin. As we turned to leave, he said, loudly enough for us all to hear; the vicar, Mrs Ayres, me, my grandmother too if she was listening, 'Well. Good fucking riddance. No one's going to miss her.'

Nobody even bothered to pretend to be appalled. It was true.

As I swung down the lane away from the church, heading back towards Keith Denby's stables, Scotty ran up behind me, panting slightly as if he had been hurrying to catch me.

'Em, where are you going? Aren't you going to the Red Lion for a drink?' (Mrs Ayres had organised something in the upstairs room of the pub.)

'No. What for? I don't exactly have many happy memories I want to share of her. I just want to forget she ever existed.'

'I know. I *know*, don't I?' Scotty blinked hard as if he was trying to marshal his thoughts and then shook his head as if his efforts frustrated him. There was something he wasn't telling me. 'You don't have to go straight back to work though, do you? We might as well go and have a pint on her. You don't have to just run straight back to *him*. *He* doesn't even pay you that much. Take the afternoon off. You owe him fuck all,' he concluded bitterly.

I suppose I was a bit taken aback by Scotty's words. He caught me by surprise. I hadn't even realised he disliked Keith, but I could hear it now. There was a vehemence in his tone; as if all that hate, and yes, maybe even fear, he had felt for my grandmother had shifted onto a new target now that she was dead. I shrugged neutrally even though I was intrigued as to why he should suddenly hate Keith so very much, and turned to walk with him back to the pub.

The vicar was already there when we arrived, along with Mrs Ayres. They were chatting quite happily and making substantial inroads into the buffet as if they were both relieved the entire affair was over. They started almost guiltily as we entered. Perhaps they felt they shouldn't be enjoying themselves quite so much at my grandmother's funeral, but what did it matter to us? We weren't exactly grieving over her and somebody might as well be eating that food. We nodded to them in acknowledgement of their presence but then moved away to a table in the corner, away from their intrusive presence. A silence fell over the room which I supposed they felt was awkward, because shortly afterwards they withdrew, leaving us to ourselves. We sat in silence. The room was cold and smelt musty as if it wasn't used very much. Scotty kept taking long slugs at his pint and staring moodily into the distance as if he had forgotten I was even there. In the silence all there was to do was watch more dust drifting down onto the surface of the tables. I couldn't bear it. It was like being in the grave with my grandmother. I stood to leave. I had seen Scotty in this frame of mind before. He would drink until he fell over and nothing I could say or do was going to stop him. But as I reached the door to the function room, he suddenly called me back.

'Em, don't go. Don't go back there to *him*. I don't trust him.'

'Don't talk rubbish, Scotty. I've got to go back. I work for him.'

'You don't need him. Look, you're good at what you do. Much better than him. You can make it on your own. Look you won that competition on your own. You can do it without him.'

I shook my head.

'I didn't win it on my own, Scotty. Silver Destination won it for me. You see what I'm saying? *Keith Denby's* horse won it for me. Without his horses; without him, I wouldn't have won anything. I do need him, Scotty. I've got to keep on the right side of him, if I'm going to get anywhere with this.'

Scotty sneered derisively.

'So just how far are you prepared to go to do that?'

I was shocked.

'What do you mean, Scotty? What do you mean by that?'

Scotty shook his head suddenly as if ridding himself of unwanted thoughts

'Forget it. Just forget it. Just be careful around that bastard, alright?'

I had a sharp recollection of that night; the night I had won with Silver Destination, the night my grandmother had died. Amongst all that had happened, I had almost lost the memory of the sudden panic I had felt when I had been alone with Keith Denby in the horsebox. He had tried to touch me and I hadn't wanted him to. With the recollection came again that prickling feeling of too much awareness all over my body. It was my turn to shake the undesirable thoughts from my mind.

'Don't worry about Keith Denby,' I laughed half-heartedly. 'I can handle him.'

In that private room at the top of the pub, in the safety of Scotty's presence, I could almost believe it to be true.

7.   The Bleeding

(Written by Z. Bathory and I Moody.   Appears on Spinefarm Records UK: The Way of the Fist, 2007.   Performed by Five Finger Death Punch)

Time passed.   It passed by very much as before.   My grandmother was dead, but life went on, just as it had always done; and I never thought to break from the prison of the routine which I had constructed for myself.   I worked.   The hours were long and the work was hard, physical drudgery.   When I got home - and it was truly our home now, for the first time ever, since my grandmother had finally had the decency to die and leave it to us, my brother and I - I would fall straight into bed and into a deep, dreamless sleep. The next morning, I would rise early and begin all over again.   And so it was on the following day; and on the one that followed that. Thus, each successive day was filled, and the time passed.

Not so, Scotty.   He had ambled along since leaving school and although he had held, at one time or another, some species of dead end job or other, generally speaking, for the main part, he did nothing.   He drifted, purposeless, time passing him by and him seemingly unknowing, or uncaring, of the fact.   Sometimes, I envied him.   He didn't need a purpose.   He was just happy to be.   Me, I had to go on.   I was driven.   More so than ever before since that first success with Silver Destination.   More than ever I was determined I was going to make it; bigger than my father had ever done in the prehistoric times when he had jumped.   Definitely bigger than Keith Denby, although I didn't tell him that.   It was my secret and I kept it close.   Keith Denby was just a stepping stone; a temporary measure. Still, there were some changes when I returned to the stables on the day following my grandmother's funeral.   In the first place, Katy, who had always firmly occupied Keith's affections as his favourite stable girl, had gone.   At the time, I thought little enough of it.   If I thought of it at all, I suppose I thought that she'd just got sick of the job and decided to leave; she'd certainly seemed sick of it the last time I'd seen her, on the night I'd won that competition.   She'd been in such a foul mood. But as I have said, I didn't think very much about it at all. We weren't exactly friends. But, then again, barring Scotty, I wasn't exactly friends with anyone. Later, I heard that she was going to have a baby, which explained why she'd looked so puffy and ill on that last evening on which I saw her. The baby explained a lot of things, but I didn't think very much about that either. I certainly didn't think about that baby's father and who he might be. I didn't think *enough* about it all.

The other big change was, I suppose, as a direct consequence of Katy's departure; because suddenly, now that Katy was no more, I was Keith's favourite.

I call this change "big" and "sudden", but it wasn't just one "big", or "sudden" change at all really. In fact it was lots of little changes which happened gradually and subtly, but which, when I took them out and examined them in my mind, all added up to one "big", and "sudden" change in my status at the yard. Lots of little things which occurred almost imperceptibly and accumulated over time. I didn't have to muck out the stables Keith used for the livery horses anymore. Suddenly there was a more junior stable girl to do it for me. I wasn't to clean the tack anymore either, I was to concentrate on schooling Keith's show jumpers.

'Let someone else take care of it, kid. You've got more important things to concentrate on now.' He would always say these things expansively, with a definite consciousness of his own magnanimity. And each time, I could never be certain, but I would feel again those feather-light brushes of his hands upon me. I would never quite catch him at it; but I knew I couldn't be imagining it all the time. He would touch my lower back, my hips, but mainly my bottom. He took to standing very closely to me too; uncomfortably so. I didn't like it; any of it, but I learned to shrug and disregard these new developments. I learned to live with Keith's foibles in this area. I told myself they meant nothing. It was worth it to lose some of the drudgery from the work and to ride those show jumpers. Perhaps Scotty was right. Perhaps you did have to be prepared to give something in return for the things you wanted out of life. Perhaps there was always a price to pay. I wasn't comfortable with it, but it was easier to ignore it, pretend it wasn't happening rather than to confront it. The trouble was, the longer I ignored it, the worse it got. Perhaps Keith thought I liked it.

Still, small changes. Then one day, when I didn't have to muck out at all any longer, or clean tack, or pull the ragwort out of the field, or bag the manure up to sell to gardeners, or put the gag on or hold the horses when the equine dentist called to rasp their teeth, or indeed do any of the really unpleasant or laborious tasks that used to punctuate my days upon a regular basis; one day, after all of these little alterations had occurred without me really noticing them, one day there did come a really big change. I was in the indoor arena fooling around with a jumping course which Keith had constructed the night before. Just tinkering with it really; lowering the heights of some of the fences, altering the angles on others. Keith always set his fences much too high for young horses, the turns much too tight. He had a way of making a jump look uninviting; of suspending a single pole too high in mid-air with nothing beneath it; no filler. In some instances, it would look as if the horse would practically be able to run underneath it more easily than he could jump over it. But then Keith had a way of driving young horses at these fences relentlessly, with no mercy whatsoever for any misgivings they might be entertaining about the matter. And if they refused, or ducked out of the fence, he could be equally merciless in his punishment of them. He said it prepared them for the difficult obstacles they would face in an international arena. In reality, it just spooked them. If I did it cleverly, I knew Keith wouldn't notice the subtle changes I had made. He never really looked at the courses he had set up once he had put them out. He just jumped his horses over them until he was bored with them, and then would clear them all away (i.e. get someone else to clear them all away), before starting all over again. I would ordinarily have been able to alter those fences quite safely without any danger of Keith catching me red-handed. He was not an early riser. Why should he get out of bed when he had all those lackeys to run around and complete the early morning chores for him? However, on this occasion, the man himself breezed into the arena. He was looking impossibly pleased with himself and didn't seem to notice me start guiltily over the fences I had been fiddling with.

'Leave that,' he ordered glibly, rubbing his hands together with satisfaction and (thankfully) not really looking at what it was that he was ordering me to leave. 'I've got a surprise for you.'

'For me?' I felt slightly intimidated by the prospect. In my experience, surprises were not generally good things. In my experience, they ran along the lines of "your mother's just jumped off a bridge" and "you've passed your eleven-plus" and so forth. I hung back a little from him. I didn't want to follow him out of the doors of the indoor school to the yard where he was gesturing for me to follow him. But, of course, I had to.

Standing outside, in the September sunshine was Heidi, one of Keith's newest stable girls, a tall no-nonsense looking girl with masses of pale blonde curly hair. I think she was a German exchange student. She was holding a smart looking dark bay gelding, about 15.2 hands high, with neat little hooves, a white star on his forehead and a white snip curling over his muzzle. He had black intelligent eyes and at the very sight of him, something akin to a feeling of tenderness licked up inside of me. Before Keith had even said a word to me, I knew he was mine. I couldn't bear him to be anything but mine. I couldn't bear that bright glitter of understanding to be stamped out of him by Keith Denby and his methods of schooling him. He had to be mine; and as soon as I took one look at Keith and saw the impossibly smug look upon his face, and again that glow of conscious magnanimity, I knew it was so.

'What...? He's...?' I hardly dared give my hopes a voice, but I didn't have to.

'He's yours, kid... Yours to bring on.'

I couldn't help myself. Despite the fact that I habitually endeavoured to keep as much physical distance between Keith and myself as I possibly could, I felt I owed him *something* in return. I threw my arms around him. He responded to my embrace a little too enthusiastically for my liking. I had difficulty extricating myself from his arms and even when I did eventually manage to achieve this, he still retained a hand clamped firmly upon my left buttock.

'Thank you, Keith. Thank you. He's really mine?'

'He's yours to jump, kid. I expect big things, now. I want to see you win with him. He's a young horse. Don't let me down, now.'

'I won't, I won't. I promise, I won't.' I tried to move away to take a closer look at the horse, but his hand was on me too firmly. From the corner of my eye, I could see Heidi's no-nonsense mouth turned down into a grim line of disapproval. Perhaps, like Scotty, she thought I'd given more for that horse than just a grateful hug.

The horse was called Herbert Sherbet. That was his show name, you understand. The name that was set down on competition entry forms. I just called him "Herbert", or "Herb" or "Herbie".

'*Yours to jump, kid. Yours to bring on...*' Those were the words Keith had used. I should have analysed those words and considered them more carefully. I should have known that he wasn't actually giving Herb to me. I should have known better. You don't ever get something for nothing in this life, particularly from the likes of Keith Denby. But he *was* my horse. *Mine*. At least in my eyes, Keith had given him to me and he couldn't take him back again. He was mine and I coveted him. I guarded him more jealously than a first lover. I wouldn't let the other girls touch him. I mucked him out. I changed his water buckets. I gave him his feed and stood holding the bucket and stroking his head whilst he ate it. I groomed him and picked the mud out of his hooves. When he developed a stable cough from the dust in his hay, it was me who immersed his hay-net in a freezing vat of water to soak the poisonous particles out of it, and hauled it out again on the bitter winter mornings, using all of the strength in my body to take its weight, icy water pouring down my arms and soaking into my clothes as I did so. And when there was nothing else to do, but I still needed an excuse to be near to him, I would clean his tack sitting on his bedding which I had built up into high banks at the sides of his stable to prevent him knocking his legs against the walls of his stall. I would have slept in that stall if I could. Sometimes I did. I think perhaps everyone else at the yard laughed behind their hands at me when they saw how I went on with him. I think that they could perhaps appreciate the true state of affairs; that Herbert belonged to Keith really. They could probably see that Keith had lent this horse to me on a whim and that he could strip him from me just as easily. This was something which I failed to see. I averted my eyes from that uncomfortable reality, although I suppose I knew it really. Still, I coveted him. I was too jealous of him really. Herb became used to my cosseting of him and would not accept individual attention from any other. He would not compromise on this. If one of the other stable girls attempted to ride him; that is if Keith ordered that they should ride him and I had - grudgingly - handed over his reins, he would roll his eyes and toss his head and refuse to budge. If pressed on the matter, he would start to walk backwards shaking his head as he went as if to say "No! No! No!" In short, anyone except me, and he would sulk. I, who could not bear for him to be grieved or upset in the slightest manner, would quickly rush back to him to restore his equilibrium. Keith said that I was spoiling him; perhaps I was, but the results we got together were undeniable. It took us six months to reach the stage where we were ready to enter our first competition. It was six months of dedicated schooling and finding hills (few and far between in the predominantly flat Cheshire countryside) to ride up to increase our fitness levels. At the end of that six months, Herb, who was, as Keith had pointed out, a young horse, and who had been a mere stripling when he had been handed over to me, had begun to bulk up. After six short months, he possessed honed leg muscles, and the definition of hard muscle showed clearly beneath his gleaming dark bay rump. And from that first competition, we won. We were unstoppable. We entered the Cheshire Show and won the Foxhunters first round. We qualified for the Horse of the Year show, where we won again. We were the fastest; we were the best.

Nobody could even come close. By the time I was twenty, we were consistently qualifying for classes in the Horse of the Year Show and the BSJA Festival of Show Jumping. We had won both the Edy Goldman Trophy for the British rider gaining the most points under 21 years of age and the Martin Whiteley Trophy for the British rider gaining the most points on one horse (Herbert Sherbet, of course) who had never been entitled to wear any Union Jack badge and who had never won that trophy before. I suppose I could have got pretty pleased with myself about it all. But the fact remained that I always felt myself to be nothing. I was not popular at the stables. But then again, I had never been popular anywhere, except with Scotty. And even with Scotty in those days, we weren't quite as thick together as we had been in previous times. When I did see him, which wasn't often, we didn't have much to say to each other anymore. I was just too wrapped up in the life which was unfolding before me. It was a life which, I couldn't help but think that somehow Scotty didn't approve of. But I wasn't worried. He was still just drifting, and I, I walked alone; I always had done. Still, with Herbert Sherbet, I wasn't quite so alone anymore. Perhaps not so alone as I had been once; and we were winning, and I was Keith's golden girl, and when we were in the arena, we just couldn't put a foot wrong. We just won and won and won. By the time I was twenty-two I had accrued enough points to enter a competition which would bring me up against international riders. I had never competed at such a level before, and this one was important to me. This one would be the first time when I had come up into direct competition with Keith, and I wanted to win. I wanted to prove to him that I was worthy of his gift to me of Herbert Sherbet; that I had not let him down, as I had promised I would not.

Despite the fact that Herb and I were on such a winning streak, I was always afflicted by nerves prior to any event, and before this event, I was particularly sick and anxious. Not so Keith. He was as brash and confident as ever as we drove to the event together; he driving his flashy-looking silver horsebox with "Keith Denby – International Show Jumper" emblazoned across the side in the red, white and blue of the Union flag, just to illustrate that he truly was an international show jumper, representing Great Britain. In actuality, it was probably a bit optimistic of Keith to portray himself in this light. Keith, in reality, had never represented Great Britain for the sport, although he had certainly competed at an international level upon numerous occasions. Still, I suppose the sad truth was that he was a relatively mediocre rider with a lot of money to throw at good horses. Scotty was right about him really. But at this point in my life, after his gift of Herbert Sherbet to me, Keith was my hero. Okay, I knew that some of his methods were bad. I knew he shouldn't bully the horses quite so much. I definitely knew he shouldn't be using rapping - where two people would hold the pole and as the horse was jumping over it, lift the pole and rap the horse with it, just to scare the horse and make him jump higher over the fences, ensuring he learned to jump higher than he needed to - as a method of training; it was, after all, illegal. It never worked for Keith anyway. But I purposely blinded myself to his faults. Without him I was less than the nothing I knew myself to be; and anyway, who was I to tell him that he was in the wrong? It wouldn't be my place to. He was too far above me, I felt, in the stratosphere of the show jumping world. As I have said, at this stage in my life, he was as a God to me. He would continue to occupy this position for the space of a few more hours yet from the journey to that competition at which point my sight would clear and I would be able to see him for the scumbag he really was. Still, in those few hours, leading up to the event which immediately followed the competition, he was still my hero; and I was hanging on to his every word as he "prepared" me for the competition ahead of us.

'Just do your best, kid. Try not to let the nerves get the better of you and stuff it all up for Herb and yourself. There's a good chance you could get placed and win yourself a fourth or even a third place rosette here.' He shook his head as if slightly awed by the thought of that green or yellow rosette hanging next to his own red one in the horsebox; the first place rosette which existed at that moment in time only in his imagination and my own. 'You take third or fourth and you'll be in the prize money too. You could win yourself a couple of hundred quid here tonight,' he added, almost generously, as if he was giving me the money himself. (Still, what he said was true. If I was placed third or fourth in the event, I would still win some cash. The top prize of five thousand pounds, I supposed, Keith intended to keep for himself.) He rambled on in this vein for the hour and a half or so it took for us to drive to the venue. In his own mind he had already beaten me. In mine, as I have said, despite my habitual stage fright, part of me was more determined than ever to beat him, just to prove to him that I really had deserved the great gift of Herbert which he had bestowed upon me. (Upon reflection, I suppose, I should have thought this strategy out a little more carefully. Perhaps I only have myself to blame for the events that followed. Maybe I should have just let him win. From the way he was going on about it, I should have realised how much he wanted to... *Needed* to win that event. Perhaps, with the benefit of hindsight, setting out to beat him that night really wasn't the best method of proving my gratitude to him).

That night we were together right up to the start of the event. We unloaded our horses from the horsebox together and led them to adjacent stalls provided for the competitors. The walls were low so Keith was able to continue his preparatory lecture as we worked at getting our horses ready for the big event. Unusually for Keith, he had not brought a lackey along with him that evening to groom his own horse, Treacle Toffee, but was working industriously away at brushing a shine into Treacle's dark bay coat himself. I thought about this later, and wondered if this lack of a third party in the van with us was a deliberate omission on Keith's part. I wondered if he had realised all along that there was, in actual fact, a very good chance that Herb and I might beat him in that competition and that he had duly planned his retribution in advance... Just in case this should be the way that events panned out. But I could never bring myself to really believe that this was so. Yes, Keith Denby was a total shit, but he didn't have an ounce of cunning or, I didn't believe, even the capability for calculated thought within him. He was a just creature of instinct, and when it came to it, that's what he acted upon. His revenge upon me was entirely instinctive; he just did the things that he knew would hurt me the most. As for me, as I have already explained, nobody touched Herbert Sherbet but me; so I had no need for the services of a stable girl, not that I would have been cheeky enough to request them anyway. In my own eyes, if not in the eyes of the quietly watching show jumping world, I was still just a stable girl myself. Certainly, Keith had given me no indication that my status had subtly changed; that somewhere out there, other people were watching my performance with Herbert Sherbet, and that in private moments, conversations had taken place about me, and my future at his yard. I only realised much later just how close I had come to achieving my dreams of show jumping greatness; dreams I had cherished since my days of playing truant from school and hiding out with Scotty in the woods. In fact, it was much, much later that I realised just how nearly I had come to achieving these dreams; but by that stage, of course, they had been snatched away from me and reduced to ashes before my unseeing eyes.

Keith continued just has he had always done; imparting words of wisdom, interspersing these with various lewd comments about the snugness of my jodhpurs, the fit of my jacket over my breasts. If there had been no partition dividing us, his hand would have been clamped firmly upon my bum. I listened to his advice, as I had always done, but I was starting to feel sick now with the nerves, so I was listening in silence, clamping my teeth together to prevent myself from vomiting. Every time I bent down to brush Herbert Sherbet's lower legs or check his hooves, I could feel the bile rising up at the back of my throat. I had what Scotty would crudely call the "vurps"; burping because I had been too nervous to eat and had an empty stomach, and bringing up a little bit of vomit every time I did so. The queasiness lasted all the way from the competitors' stalls to, as usual, the moment when I placed my left foot into the stirrup iron, gave a couple of little hops to work up some momentum before swinging myself up into the saddle, and took a few turns around the practise arena and over the warm-up fence. Keith had come with me to the practise arena, bringing Treacle Toffee with him. He swung himself up into the saddle as I did and shadowed my movements around the practise area, despite the fact that he was not scheduled to jump until much later in the competition. He was watching me almost warily as I circled Herbert Sherbet into the approach to the practise fence again, but the banter continued as normal. There was no discernible difference in the manner he was behaving towards me, and I will be honest, I was too wrapped up in Herbert Sherbet and the competition; and I never was any good at reading people and their hidden motivations anyway. In short, I just didn't look hard enough. It was only afterwards that I thought about that cautious watchfulness and analysed it... Read it and understood it for the fear it really was. But all of this aside, these were the best moments of the night. My nausea had passed. Herbert's paces were at his smoothest. Each successive leap over the practice fence was lighter and more fluid than the last. We were at our best; we had never jumped better. By the time it was our turn to enter the arena, I was brimming with happiness. Nothing, nobody was going to get the better of us tonight. There just wasn't a horse that lived and breathed on the earth at that moment in space and time which could have brought us down.

For all that optimism, however, it was a difficult course. Twelve fences, one to be jumped twice from either direction, making (unlucky for some) thirteen jumps in total. They were tightly packed together too; a triple bar or staircase fence, with the rails at graduated heights, a fan fence with three separate poles fanning out from a central post to form a wide spread jump, a hog's back fence with the central pole set seemingly impossibly high, a wall jump with garish pictures upon it which I knew Herbert would find spooky if I didn't ride him towards it with conviction, a triple combination of jumps with a bounce in the first part of it and, a further wide spread jump. I'd walked the course before I'd gone to warm-up with Herbert Sherbet and taken it all in then. Keith, of course, had accompanied me, proffering advice to me for each of the fences as he did so. I say he was proffering advice to me; I suppose on the surface of it that's how it must have seemed to the other competitors who were also walking the course in clumps of twos or threes and working it out together. But half of what he was saying was muttered as if to himself. As he pointed out the various aspects of each fence to me/himself, I noticed his stubby fingers were shaking a little. His veiny nose was redder than usual, and his breath smelt as if he had been drinking. I put it down to nerves, although it was not like Keith to be nervous before any competition. Still, as we left the arena to take our mounts to the warm-up area, he did concede that it was a particularly tough course and that we'd be lucky if we, or indeed anyone, got clears. He was right about that too. I had been drawn to jump fifteenth and of the fourteen preceding me, not one horse-rider team had managed a clear. The closest had been Miranda Camberwell riding Winter Sunrise with just one fault for exceeding the time permitted for the round by a second. It was, as Keith had said, a tough course. It was going to be hard. Still, I felt elated as we cantered our entrance. Using an old trick learned from Keith Denby (and there could be no doubt that I *had* learned some things from him, no matter what I have said or may go on to say in the future about the man) I cantered Herbert Sherbet as closely as I dared past the high wall jump which I thought would spook him, just to give him the opportunity to take a look at it. I saw his ears flick back and forth at it, but then he settled into the rhythm of his canter and I knew we'd be okay. We headed purposefully for the first, an upright fence with brushwood fillers. Herb's canter was steady but I could feel plenty of bounce in his pace. He cleared it easily and we headed for the second, a tall upright fence constructed from traditional red and white poles. It was difficult to judge the fence without a ground line or any sloping outline in the fence to follow, so we checked our pace a little and increased our impulsion. It worked; again, we were clear. We cantered to the end of the arena and turned right, around the corner and cleared the staircase or triple bar fence, then across the arena and back on ourselves over a further upright fence – this time constructed from a five-barred gate. Around to the end of the arena to the triple combination; jump in and straight out between the first two elements - no time for a stride between them - the horse had to "bounce" in and out between the fences; then a larger space and time to fit two strides in before the final part. It was going well, but I concentrated hard on that final fence of the triple. I had learned a hard lesson from my time riding Miss Primrose about what can happen if you do not maintain contact with your horse over such combination fences. Around the corner and towards the wall. I tried to be as reassuring as possible for Herbert's sake, but despite myself I felt a stab of anxiety as we made our approach. It was big. Oh God, but it was big. It was only as we approached it that I could fully appreciate just how big it was. I felt Herbert waver and held my legs more firmly against his side. We slowed, we were almost cantering on the spot and it seemed to take an age to reach the point of take-off. At the last moment, he threw up his head as if to say "come on then, are we doing this today or not?" and soared over it. I felt his back hoof brush the top of the wall and there was a gasp from the watching crowd. Maybe it wobbled; I didn't turn to look. We pressed onwards towards the hog's back fence. I was beginning to feel reckless. I just wanted it to be over. We turned the corner and back on ourselves to jump the fan fence, and then turned again approaching the wide spread jump almost at a gallop; just desperate to get across. We did it. Two to go. I checked Herbert sharply before the upright, jumping it slightly at an angle in order to make the approach to the final fence, the upright with brushwood fillers which had also been our first fence. This time we were jumping it from the other direction. Seconds later it was over. We cantered across to exit the arena, hazarding a glance at the wall jump as I did so. It was still standing without any blocks missing from it. Whether Herbert had knocked it or not, it remained standing, seemingly unharmed, and we had the first clear round of the evening. The cheering of the crowd told me that I was not mistaken in this. I patted Herbert extravagantly as we cantered from the arena. He was shaking his head from side to side in triumph as we exited through the gate. I was about as close to weeping for joy as it was possible to be without actually shedding a tear, even though I knew we'd probably have to do a jump off and we wouldn't manage to jump such a clean round again if we had to jump it at speed. The course was technically too difficult.

What normally happens on such occasions is that the first clear round of the evening will mark the start of a run of other riders jumping clear. This time, in this event, it just didn't happen. Rider after rider was caught out by the height of the wall, or the width of the spread jumps or misjudged one of the uprights and tapped the highest pole off the top. Matters continued in this vein until it was Keith's turn to jump the round. I had put Herbert Sherbet back into his stall by this stage and was leaning over the railings to the arena watching as each competitor accrued faults. I hardly dared to breathe as each successive rider entered the arena. I could barely bring myself to watch their rounds, and yet I was powerless to move away. I was convinced that next time, the next rider would be the one who got the clear round and therefore would be the one I was facing in the jump off. I could hardly believe my luck in the way matters were panning out before me. Still, when Keith's turn came to jump, I was hoping that he would get the clear, although he looked in pretty poor shape, if I was honest. He was sweating profusely under the too-bright arena lights, his legs twitching almost convulsively against Treacle Toffee's sides. Treacle Toffee looked confused and ill at ease. He was sweating too. It did not bode well. As they made their initial pass around the jumps I could see that Treacle's canter was jerky and disjointed. The contact between horse and rider, the symbiosis that exists between and flows through the reins, the seat and the position of the rider to the horse, was not good. Treacle Toffee was tossing his head and each time Keith was becoming unseated. Keith aimed a savage blow at Treacle's side with his crop and Treacle started forwards, partly rearing up, striving to escape the burden of his rider. But Treacle couldn't help himself; he was a docile animal. Watching him then, his head tucked in desperately trying to understand the conflicting instructions Keith was passing to him, he reminded me of myself in my first few years at school; desperately striving to please the bullies, little realising that nothing I could do would ever placate them. I was never going to measure up. The way things were going, neither was Treacle. He was beginning to lather up, foam dripping from his bit as he headed for the first fence. He botched it and the first pole was off. Round to the second upright fence. Again, the approach was all wrong. This time the top two poles were dislodged.

'Oh, *come on!*' Keith's exasperated outburst was audible around the arena. Again, he lashed savagely at Treacle with his crop. An evil looking line appeared crossing through the sweat upon Treacle's flank. The foam around the line took on a pinkish tinge as if blood had been drawn. A disapproving murmur arose from the watching crowd. Treacle was beginning to panic. His head was no longer bent obediently over the bit. His eyes were rolling in terror. He gave an experimental buck and when Keith pitched forward in his seat, he bucked again, twisting to the side as he did so. Keith landed with an undignified thump in the dust of the arena floor. He was on his feet in a moment. I could hardly bear to see what would happen next. I had seen this a million times before. Treacle Toffee was really for it now. Keith made a desperate lunge at the reins.

'You bloody bastard!'

Treacle Toffee shied away from his grasping hands and bolted for the gate to the arena. Seconds later he had completed his only clean jump of the evening and jumped, rider-less with stirrups flying, from the arena into the warm-up area. Keith was eliminated from the competition. Ostensibly this was due to the fact that his horse had left the arena before the end of the round. However, afterwards, I heard a murmur that he had been removed from the arena under both the "abuse of horses" rule and the "inappropriate and dangerous riding" rule, whereby "any rider who affects the safety of any horse, rider or third party will be considered as dangerous and will be penalised accordingly.". This is very ironic, as I would later come to learn. However, the official line was that Keith had been eliminated because his horse had left the arena before the completion of the event. It was left to the media to speculate over any other, underlying reasons for Keith's disqualification; and this they did, vociferously, over the ensuing few days before the public tired of it as old news and moved onto some other scandal which had grabbed their fickle attentions. Not that I cared very much about what was being said by anyone at all by that stage. I didn't care about anything very much in those days after that event, although I could have done Keith a lot more damage and spun that story out for just a little bit longer, if I had spoken out. I should have spoken out.

In the warm-up area, I caught Treacle Toffee quite easily and did my best to soothe him out of the state of terror into which he had worked himself up. He was trembling with adrenalin and fear. I knew how he felt. I dreaded the moment when Keith would inevitably come to collect Treacle from me. I genuinely didn't believe that at that moment in time, taking into account Keith's phenomenal and very public display of anger at his mount of just seconds before, that Treacle was going to be safe in his hands. But when I hazarded a glance towards the space which Keith had occupied in the centre of the arena just moments before, that spot was empty. Keith had left already.

I had no choice but to leave Treacle Toffee alone in his stall next to Herbert Sherbet. There was still the chance I would have to ride again in the jump off and I had to be ready. I left him hanging his head over the low wall dividing the two stalls looking miserable. Herbert Sherbet was busy nuzzling at Treacle's black ears, as if consoling him for his woes. It was a comfort to me, at least, to see them together like this. I felt I hadn't abandoned Treacle entirely. I returned to watch the remaining competitors. After Keith there had been four more riders left to jump. By the time I returned to see how matters stood there was only Angela Radistock left to complete

112

her round. Her horse was spooked by the wall and demolished it just as I arrived. Sebastian Carling-Brooks, one of the other competitors, sidled over.

'You've completed a good round. I think you've got the only clear round. I suppose you're the winner. *This time*, anyway.' He was smiling at me. He seemed quite congenial even though I had beaten him, but there was something in his manner which I did not like. His unctuous, upper class accent reminded me of Sarah Braithwaite's mother's. It turned me cold. I could see what he must be thinking; I was just some upstart, barely better than a stable girl. I had no business beating him. He was an established name on the show jumping circuit. He bowed to me very low. I couldn't work out whether he was mocking me or not.

'*This time, you win*. Next time... Who knows?' I didn't like the way he passed this last comment at all. Despite his outward appearance of affability, there was something of a threat inherent in the undertow of his words. But I soon forgot about him. I didn't know anything about him except that he was ranked pretty high in the BSJA Top Rider list. Possibly for that reason, he had never spoken to me, or even noticed I existed as far as I knew, before that moment. I was just too far beneath him.

There was a jump off to decide the second placing between the three riders tied with the least number of faults from the first round, then the winners were announced. This particular victory had been tinged with bitterness but nothing can really detract from the elation of winning an event; and this was a big win for me. The cash prize for first place was substantial. As I collected the prize and completed the necessary final lap of honour on Herbert Sherbet, I almost forgot about Keith and his performance in the event. As usual, before we exited the show ring, Herbert and I completed the last jump again, my hand flung in to the air as we reached the pinnacle of the leap to touch the sky above. Fifteen years on and I was still trying to reach my mother.

I took my time preparing Herbert and Treacle for the return journey. I fussed over tail and leg bandages and travelling rugs and then, when they were all ready, and there was no further excuse to linger, I lingered still, hesitating over those bandages just a little longer; undoing them and tying them all over again. Anything to delay the dreaded moment when I would have to face Keith alone in the cab of the horsebox. I suspected he would have heard already that I had won, but I shoved the trophy into one of the kit boxes anyway. Out of sight, out of mind, I reasoned. The rosette and cheque I stuffed unceremoniously into the pocket of my jacket. There was no point rubbing salt into an open wound. (And I had realised by this stage – a little too late, admittedly - that my victory over him would be doing just that).

I wondered if he was still angry with Treacle. I wondered if he would be angry with me. I had the same feeling of trepidation and doubt about facing him as I used to have when facing my grandmother when I knew I was in for it once again. I was about to redo Treacle's tail bandage just one further time because I'd convinced myself it wasn't quite right (it was), when Keith himself appeared by the stable door.

'Come on, Em. Stop pissing about. Let's get these horses loaded up and get out of here.' His tone was brusque, but he didn't seem particularly upset or angry. Maybe things were going to be alright. He'd been drinking; I already knew that. I also knew that he probably wasn't fit to drive. Still I led those horses into that box and fastened them up without a murmur. I always was a coward. I despised myself for it, but I didn't dare to raise the issue. Instead I bit my lip as he drove fast and recklessly, closed my eyes and pretended to have dozed off. I thought about Treacle Toffee and Herbert Sherbet being jolted around in the back of the box and hurriedly pushed the picture out of my mind. It was easy for me to feign sleep, to cross my fingers and hope everything would be okay. They didn't know what was happening to them back there. They wouldn't understand why they were being knocked against each other and the sides of the horsebox. As if to emphasise the point, I heard one of them give a whinny, (Treacle, I think), high and frightened, and despised myself even more for my weakness. If only I was braver, I would have acted to prevent Keith from driving like that; but even as the words of reprimand formed upon my lips, my heart quailed within me.

Despite my pretence at sleep, there was still an atmosphere within the cab; a certain tension. Maybe things were not going to be alright after all.

Driven steadily and safely, the journey had lasted around an hour and a half. Driven like a maniac, it was considerably shorter. We were back at the yard in just under an hour. As we pulled into the yard, I stirred a little as if just waking and then yawned and stretched somewhat unconvincingly. I never was much of an actress. Keith looked across at me sceptically for a moment. I don't think he believed for a second I had been sleeping for the entire duration of the journey home. The complete effect of somnolence was additionally laid to waste by the fact that immediately upon the truck drawing to a halt, I leaped out with a display of athleticism which was highly improbable from one who had only moments before been profoundly sleeping. Out of the corner of my eye, I saw Keith shake his head, presumably in disbelief at my antics, before he looked away. In that moment, he looked as if he hated me. Perhaps he did; but me, being me, and the phenomenal coward that I was, did not want to confront the situation. I shut it away in the bit of my mind where I put all my uncomfortable encounters with people. I didn't go there very often, so this latest uneasy experience shouldn't bother me so very much in the future (a mistake). I went to let down the tailgate of the horsebox, shouting to Keith as I did so.

'It's pretty late. I'll get these horses into their stables.' I hoped he would take the hint, bugger off to bed and just let me get the job done in peace.

I led Herb and Treacle Toffee into their stable block, flicking the light switch as I did so. From the other stables came the muffled sounds of sleeping horses. From a couple of the boxes, some of the horses pushed their noses curiously over the top of their stable doors to watch our progress, blinking sleepily in the light as they did so. I led Treacle Toffee into his stable and let the lead rein from Herb's head-collar dangle on the floor as I untied Treacle's leg and tail bandages and swapped his travel rug for his stable one. Herb didn't wander away from me as other horses might have done, but poked his nose companionably through Treacle's open stable door as I worked. He used to follow me around like a dog. I never did need to use a lead rein with him. Even when I was leading him into the horsebox and he was as suspicious as horses are of such means of conveyance, and didn't really want to go, I never had to force him. I just used to let the lead rein dangle loosely from my fingers and walked slowly up the ramp into the interior of the box to show him it really was okay. He never resisted. He would just follow me inside faithfully. He trusted me. I suppose that's what made what happened later that night so dreadful. I mean, it was dreadful anyway, but Herb's utter faith and belief in me to keep him safe just made it so much worse. He trusted me to protect him. I let him down.

I didn't linger over Treacle. I wanted to fuss over Herbert, and, besides, Treacle seemed okay by then. He seemed to have recovered from the trauma of the evening quite quickly really, especially considering the jolts he must have received during the ride home. I left him busy with his hay-net and led Herbert to his own stable.

As I worked at removing the paraphernalia of travelling, I checked Herbert over carefully to make sure that the roughness of his ride home had not injured him in any way. There was a hard lump on the back of his offside hock. The flesh on his leg shuddered as I ran my hand experimentally over it, as if he was shaking off a biting insect; and I hated Keith even more for driving the way he had done and taking such a risk with my horse. I hated myself as well, cursing my own cowardice. I should have said something. Still, I consoled myself, Herb hadn't looked as if he was lame when I had walked him in. I would have to check on it in the morning, I told myself, when there was light to see properly. I fussed over Herbert Sherbet for quite a long time, talking to him all the while. I suppose I was going on a little, as was my wont when I was with Herbert Sherbet.

'Look at your coat. You're all sweaty. You can't go to bed all sweaty now, can you? We can't have that.' [Pause to pick up a dandy brush and begin to rub the old dried sweat out of his coat. Then as I neared the bruise on his hock and he shuddered again...] 'Your poor leg. We'll have to have a proper look at that bump in the morning. We'll soon sort that one out. Oh, yes we will!' [I talked to Herbert Sherbet as if he was a particularly cherished child, as you may have gathered by now.] 'We can't have those legs getting knocked now. Not when you've done so well. Those beautiful legs jumped over all those fences and you didn't knock a single one. Do you know? You were the only horse there who got a clear round. All those other horses; all of them knocked at least one fence down. Even Winter Sunrise who never puts a foot wrong for snobby old Miranda Camberwell was too slow to get a clear round. You beat them all. You beat them all because you're the best.' [Pause for Herbert Sherbet to take another pull of hay from his net and grunt at me contentedly, as if in general agreement with this analysis of the situation.] 'How does it feel to be the best of all of them? How does that feel?'

'Yes, how does that feel...? To be the best?' It was my turn to shudder, and violently, with fear. Keith's tone was bitter with hatred and contempt. I tried to jump around to face him, but I was too slow; his hands were heavy on my shoulders pushing me down into the ground with what seemed like his entire weight resting upon me, whilst simultaneously pulling me against him. I had a fleeting vision of St Christopher, in glorious technicolour, as he had appeared in my grandmother's copy of the "Bible for Children", carrying the infant Jesus upon his shoulders over a stretch of azure water. I seemed to recall that in the bible story, as St Christopher carried the child across the river, Jesus suddenly became as heavy as the weight of the world upon St Christopher's shoulders. For some reason, the childish Jesus in my mental picture had the facial features of Bruce Dickinson. I didn't know where that picture had come from, but the weight of Keith upon my shoulders felt like the weight of the world at that moment in time.

'Because I wouldn't know, would I? What it's like to be the best. Because I'm not the bloody best, am I?' He was shouting by that stage and slurring his words a little. Herbert Sherbet skittered away from us to the other side of the stable from where he regarded us with alarm.

'Keith,' I managed to gasp out. 'Let go of me. You're drunk. You're not thinking straight.'

'Yes, I'm drunk. A little drunk. Just a l-ee-tle bit drunk. But I'm thinking straight alright. Never thought straighter.' His tone was flippant now, almost friendly once more. If he hadn't been holding onto me so firmly, bearing his weight down so heavily upon me, I would almost have said he was his normal self. Still, it was an encouraging sign. I shrugged my shoulders as much as I was able to and attempted to revert to the usual irreverence I habitually employed to manage Keith.

'Keith, get off. Stop messing about. I've got work to do.' And then when he made no move to release me. 'Come on Keith, I want to get to bed.'

'Bed... Now there's an idea...'

The fear I had been feeling intensified. It settled into a cold hand of dread clawing at my guts. I had too much awareness of my body, and, worse, of Keith's too. I had a horrible, nauseating realisation of just what he had in mind for me.

'You didn't answer my question. What *does* it feel like to be the best?' Keith's voice had turned snide again. 'Because I don't know about you but whenever I win, it's a real turn on.' He pushed himself against my back. I felt sicker still. I couldn't see Keith; my back was turned towards him. Still, in my mind's eye I could visualise his reddened corpulent face, the stubbly receding hair line of golden hair, the pink scurfy scalp visible beneath; his stubby tobacco-stained fingers touching me. Now I, more than anyone

118

else, particularly at this juncture in my life, can tell you, somewhat authoritatively I might add, that appearances are unimportant. Take me, for instance. I haven't seen myself for several years. I have absolutely no idea what I look like now. I don't care. It's unimportant. However, it wasn't just Keith's appearance that was putting me off losing my virginity in this way. It was everything about him. The horses couldn't bear him to be near to them. Neither, I now realised, could I.

'Keith. Stop. Get off me.'

'You can forget that, kid. I think you've had enough of a free ride. I've done everything for you. I even let you ride that bloody horse you beat me on tonight. *My* bloody horse. It's payback time kid.'

I felt his hands slide from my shoulders and release the weight impacting on my spine. A moment's merciful relief and then the sound of fabric ripping, buttons pinging away, the feel of his hands forcing themselves inside my show jacket and shirt, cold air hitting my shrinking flesh. When I was younger, I had read books... Romantic novels, I suppose. You know the type. They are the ones where the front covers are always purple or cerise in colour and feature a dewy-eyed heroine clasped in the firm but loving embrace of an aquiline-nosed, granite-jawed, ebony-haired hero. In such novels, a standard feature would be, usually around pages eighty-seven to ninety-three, a sex scene; or, as the publishing company probably preferred to term it, a scene where the hero and heroine consummate their love for each other. In such scenes, the virginal heroine abandons any scruples she may have entertained during the first four chapters or so upon the nature of such licentious conduct and surrendered herself (usually upon a wave of ecstasy) to the caresses of the hero's (predominately tanned and muscular) fingers. In such scenes, her lips would part invitingly, her breathing would become ragged and her breasts would swell to meet the contours of the hero's possessive hands. Unrealistic, I now comprehend, but such novels had formed the entire basis for my sex education; as they probably did for many girls of that time. (It certainly wasn't a

119

core subject on the curriculum at the Grammar school, although I suppose I could have been skiving off when they covered it). I suspected, well knew really, that my own lips were not parted invitingly and my breasts certainly were not swelling to meet the contours of Keith's grasping stubby fingers. Rather, my flesh was cringing away from him, and my lips were probably compressed tighter than my grandmother's ever were. I suppose the nearest I could come to the romantic fantasy was the ragged breathing element of it. My breathing was certainly irregular; however, this was due more to panic and fear setting in rather than being motivated by any other reason. I made a last ditch attempt at reasoning with the monster that Keith had become; that I always knew he had the potential to become. I should have listened to Scotty.

'Come on, Keith. I didn't have you down for a *rapist*. I knew you liked a bit of fun with some of the other girls, but I didn't think this was your game.' I tried to make my voice sound severe; as bitter and critical as his own had been, but it came out all wrong. I was breathless with terror. The words I managed to gasp out sounded small and pleading. They merely added fuel to the fire. His hands became rougher upon me.

'Like I said, it's payback time kid.'

I became very still, staring at Herbert Sherbet bleakly and without recognition. We were both like frightened rabbits caught in the glare of a car's oncoming headlights, powerless to move and prevent the fate which awaited me. I wondered if Herbert Sherbet understood what was happening to me. I hoped not. Keith mistook my stillness for complicity and relaxed his hands for a moment. It was all I needed. Whether Herbert Sherbet understood it or not, I was not going to let him be the witness to this act of violence. I was not going to let myself be the victim of this act of violence. I sprang away from Keith to the open door of the stable and grabbed the pitchfork I used to titivate Herbert's bed of wood shavings into neat order and brandished it in the direction of Keith; but my hands were shaking and clammy with my fear and I thrust a little too enthusiastically. Before I really knew what I was about, I had jabbed it into Keith's thigh. He gave a shriek of pain and rage and collapsed sideways into Herbert's bed. The blonde wood shavings beneath his injured thigh began to turn pink. I staggered back, staring in horror at him, at what I'd done to him; at what he'd almost done to me.

'You bloody bitch!' He made a grab for my ankle but the pitchfork, still embedded sickeningly in his injured leg, impeded his progress. I didn't wait for him to recover. I ran. I ran out of the stable, out of the yard, into the quiet country lane where my footsteps echoed eerily in the silence. I ran to the end of the lane where the moonlight turned the high hedgerows from green to black and silver and vomited into the roots of them.

Then... Then I began to think; began to wonder about what I'd done and ask myself if I'd done the right thing. I'd just left Keith... And I had injured him; perhaps badly. Perhaps I had better go back and call an ambulance... Perhaps he'd just been drunk and angry... Perhaps if I went back I'd get to keep my job... Perhaps we could sort it out. Perhaps he'd let me keep Herbert Sherbet. I couldn't bear to lose him. (That's what it came down to. That's what really made me turn in the lane, no longer terrified, just a little nauseated at what I was prepared to give to keep my horse. As Scotty had predicted, there was always a price.) As I rounded the corner to the lane and turned into the yard, I heard the sharp metallic ring of hooves upon the ancient pitted concrete of the yard. A familiar beat of hooves... Herbert Sherbet's hooves. I was seized by a sudden and ominous dread. I almost knew what I was going to see before I actually saw it. Keith... The pitchfork no longer in his leg, but he was limping, one of the horses' leg or tail bandages tied around his wound, a reddish-brown stain on the white of his show jodhpurs, his stubby hands holding the head-collar of a frantically straining Herbert Sherbet, eyes rolling with fear, sweat lathering up on his neck and shoulders. Keith with his shotgun in his hand. He knew I was there. He turned to look at me triumphantly in the moonlight as he held the gun up to Herbert's head.

'You bloody bitch. I knew you wouldn't leave your precious Herbert. Well, too fucking late bitch. I always knew you were no good. Oh you ride alright with a decent horse, but without one, you're nothing. Just like your Dad. A waste of fucking space. Well, let's see how you do without a horse or my help. You're fired.' Keith paused and gave a twisted demonical laugh, 'And so is he.' The report from the gun cracked the stillness of the surrounding countryside and echoed eerily in the darkness. I heard someone say 'No!' A hoarse ghost of a whispered protest and realised it must have been me.

I must have made the walk home somehow. Like a zombie, I suppose. I can't recall it. I know I fumbled the door key from my pocket and found the cheque and the rosette from the competition earlier in the evening as I did so. I threw them on the floor. What did I want with money? I couldn't buy back Herbert's life. My fingers were shaking. It took several attempts to try and get the key to fit into the door. I dropped it at one point and ran through every swear word Scotty had ever taught me as I hunted around for it again on the darkened step. And then I began to retch and vomit once more, although there was nothing left to bring up, except bile by that stage. But the thud of Herbert's body falling onto the concrete kept reverberating in my mind and I couldn't help it. And that was how Scotty found me. He had been sitting by the fire in my grandmother's front parlour (curious how it was still her front parlour despite the fact that she had been dead for a while by that time), drinking pints of bitter and waiting for me to return to tell him all about it. It was nearly two in the morning, but Scotty didn't mind. In order to fill the blankness which his days had become, Scotty had taken to staying up late drinking copious amounts of alcohol before staggering off to bed at some ungodly hour to sleep most of the day away. Scotty took one look at me, still heaving convulsively over the bush at the side of the step, my hair all pulled out of its fastenings, my shirt all torn and spattered with blood and vomit, buttons missing from my show jacket.

'That fucking bastard. I'll kill him. I'll rip his fucking head off.' Scotty was already half out of the door, powered by alcohol-fuelled indignation. I shook my head numbly and staggered to my feet.

'Scotty.' It was all I could manage, but it was enough. He became very solicitous, but despite his attempts to console me, I could still see the murder in his eyes. I kept hearing him muttering to himself; 'I'll have him. I'll fucking have him.' And every so often he would slam his right fist into his left hand as if to emphasise his point. After a while I stopped noticing him do it. All I could see was those blonde wood shavings turning pink before my eyes. And the whites of Herbert's rolling terrified eyes in the moonlight. I couldn't see anything else at all. I was chilled and numb. I suppose I went to bed that way.

After a while I began to remember (or perhaps imagine I was remembering) other details about that night. The horror-stricken comprehension in Herbert Sherbet's eyes; the way his legs had buckled from under him. The days passed. I couldn't shake off the chill inside of me. It was cold in this new phase of my life. I was cold.

8. Time

(Written by D. Gilmour, N. Mason, R. Waters, R. Wright. Appears on Harvest EMI UK: The Dark Side of the Moon, 1973. Performed by Pink Floyd)

Let me tell you something about the next five years or so. I can't remember them. They are blurry and indistinct in my memory. At first it was because of the horror of that night. I couldn't seem to bring it back together again. Sometimes I would make a conscious effort to pull myself together. On those days the realisation would suddenly come to me that my life was simply slipping by; but then I'd remember it all again, and that memory, in turn, would make me forget I had my life to carry on with somehow. Scotty did his best. He lectured me about how we didn't need Keith Denby or his horses; how we'd buy other horses... We'd pick them up cheap, bring them on and then go out and win with them. (He didn't say where we would find these bargain champions of the future from and I was too apathetic to care enough to pick holes in his argument.) He was just trying to rally me, I knew. He kept on telling me how I could still do it; still be the best one day. (There were a few more f-words expressed with these encouragements, but I was so used to Scotty's perpetual foul mouth that by this stage, I had simply ceased to notice these). He even went so far as to strip down my father's old horsebox completely and put in new(ish) parts he had scavenged from a scrapyard and, against all the odds, he got the thing going again. Then when I didn't show any sign of doing *anything*, never mind being the best at it, he too lapsed into lethargy. The pattern of our days settled into a dull routine of nothingness. I too took to sitting up late with Scotty, watching late night horror films, drinking cider as he drank bitter, matching him pint for pint (I didn't like bitter). Then we'd collapse into bed around three a.m. and sleep most of the ensuing day away. When I woke in the early afternoon each day, I would strive to deny my wakeful state, do anything to extend the blessed unconsciousness of sleep. Anything to waste a few more hours of a dull day. And so we went on, just drifting along in limbo. The horsebox went back to rotting in an abandoned corner of my grandmother's yard. Once, almost in desperation it seemed, Scotty took hold of me by the shoulders and shook me hard as if he could jolt me out of my apathy.

'Why did you look, Em? Why didn't you look away when he had that gun in one hand and your horse in the other? Why didn't you close your eyes?'

I closed my eyes then; but nothing could remove the memory of that night from my sight. It would always be there. And with that memory came another recollection; a dark green horsebox all closed up being driven away into the darkness with Pepperpot Mill in the back. I had never seen Pepper again after that night either. I began to wonder if I was cursed.

One day I woke up and I saw, as if for the first time, that five years had gone by and it came to me in a flash of realisation that I should have been doing *something*. As Scotty had said in the early days of my non-existence, I *could* have made it on my own. I could have tried to get in at another yard. Keith Denby wasn't the only show jumper in the world. He wasn't even a very good one. I could have used the money I had won on that last evening to buy another horse and struck out on my own. Instead I had thrown the cheque on the floor. Then, in that sudden moment of epiphany, I realised that I had left it too late. It was over. I was never going to jump again. I was probably never going to ride again. It was just too late. I rolled over in bed and went back to sleep.

One morning I woke up and my eyes felt funny. Grainy. My vision was blurred. I thought I was just tired. (An excess of ennui can be incredibly wearing). But as the days wore on the blur didn't clear away. I couldn't see properly. I imagined I had a migraine and did what had become habitual to me; i.e. nothing. After several weeks of "migraine", however the blur was still there and I forced myself to go to the doctor. I do not like doctors and hadn't seen mine in several years. I hate the way they always make you feel as if you are wasting their time; that they have something infinitely more pressing or urgent to deal with than you and your trivial ailments. As Dr Sheldon picked up my medical notes, a single piece of paper slipped out of the file and drifted gently to the floor.

'We don't see much of you,' he commented drily.

Dr Sheldon hmm'd a little and looked serious. But then again, he always looked serious. He referred me to an opthalmologist at the hospital. He told me he would mark the referral letter as "urgent", 'just to put your mind at rest'; but it still took six weeks for the appointment to come through. By the time the letter did arrive, I could no longer read it. The blur in the centre of my vision had become much larger, making everything I looked at directly dim and fuzzy. My eyes were playing tricks on me. Sometimes things appeared much smaller than they really were, sometimes the lines of things I knew to be straight, doorways or oblong objects, such as the television or the fridge appeared wavy or crooked; and suddenly I realised that I had been seeing this warped view of the world for quite a while. Certainly, it was a phenomenon which had definitely been in existence for some time before the initial blur appeared in my eyes, but I had ignored it. I had been looking away from the world for so long by then, hiding my face from a world I had come to despise since the night of Herbert Sherbet's death that I had forgotten what it was supposed to look like. It was as if, just as I had found the strength to look it full in the face again, I had found it irrevocably changed in my absence. Instead of the future I had promised myself, golden and gleaming with my anticipated success, all I had earned was my just desserts for five years' worth of harboured bitterness; a distorted world, deformed and malignant with my rancour at it. This, however, was not the diagnosis I received at the hospital. The official diagnosis was this:

"A genetic form of juvenile macular degeneration – also known as or related to inherited juvenile macular degeneration, retinal degeneration disorder, geographic atrophy of the macular, fundus flavimaculatus, or a species of Stargadt's disease."

127

I liked the last name for it best of all. It was kind of pretty, as if it related to the twinkle of stars reflected in eyes (not that I would ever see those again); but it didn't really matter how you termed it. As Scotty put it, 'that's bad.' And I knew it really was bad too, because, for once, he didn't swear. It must have been the shock.

Dr Sheldon was much gentler and much less brusque when next I saw him. I suppose it was his attempt at reassuring me. I knew he was only trying to help but it wasn't much consolation to me, really, to know that I wasn't wasting his time after all; that, in actual fact, I *was* the more pressing matter that Dr Sheldon was hurrying through all of his other appointments to get to. He gave me something called an Amsler grid to take home with me. It was a chart of wavy lines and dots and was supposed to help me determine whether my eyesight was deteriorating or not (it was). He joked about my medical uniqueness. Apparently, this condition has nearly always manifested itself by the time the patient had reached the age of twenty. I was a late starter. For once in my life, I was outstanding. Well, whoopy-do. Eventually I couldn't face even looking at the chart anymore (not that I could see the bloody thing very well anyway). I gave it to Scotty. He pinned it to the wall and used it for his darts practice (where two wiggly lines hit was the equivalent to double top; three darts in a dot for ONE HUNDRED AND EIGHTY!) I went for regular eye checks with Dr Sheldon. He prescribed me a cocktail of vitamins high in antioxidants with zinc to slow down the deterioration in my vision, but it didn't really help. He hadn't been very optimistic about this treatment, even when he'd prescribed it. He'd told me then that there had been no proven research to support the success of the treatment, but anecdotal evidence indicated it might be helpful. (It wasn't). Gradually all of my detailed sight faded away until I could perceive nothing which was fine whatsoever. It was all just a blur. I suppose I got used to it; but that doesn't mean I got to like it. It was the stupid things I missed really. I missed seeing the contrails left by an aeroplane on a summer's day. I missed seeing the patterns the leaves of a tree make against the sky when you look up through them. Or bare branches in the winter time. I missed the way the street lights would light up those branches at night and throw them into relief. They were silly, trivial things; not the real life-changing consequences of my condition which were impacting upon me. For example, I could no longer read, and there wasn't much point in watching television. I couldn't work. There wasn't much I could usefully do. I would never be able to drive. Unlike some sufferers of Stargadt's Disease who were able to continue to drive, my vision had deteriorated too much and too rapidly as to preclude this. One day I went back to the doctors for the tests which had become depressingly routine. After the test was complete (or, rather, I had failed to complete it), Dr Sheldon sat down heavily and sighed. For a moment he sat unmoving, as if deep in thought, before he sprang into life again.

'Is that it? Can't you make out anything else at all?' His tone was exasperated as if I was a recalcitrant child, deliberately not trying hard enough.

'No.' He seemed to expect something more. I couldn't help myself. The old instinct to please started to take over, even though I've always despised myself for it, and I immediately began to apologise. 'I'm sorry, but I just can't do any better than that. I just can't see it very well...'

Again, he was very still. I wondered whether more apologies were required. He sighed again. There was an air of defeat about him now.

'I think the time has come, Emily, when we need to think about registering you as blind.'

I nodded. I had always known that it was coming; had been told to expect it at the rate of deterioration I was experiencing, but it was still a shock. I swallowed and nodded again. I told Dr Sheldon that I needed time to think it over. I didn't keep the next appointment. In fact, I never went back again. Life went on as before, without being punctuated by the fortnightly sight tests. They had always been pointless anyway. From the very beginning I had known I had been going blind. It had only ever been a charting of the progression of the inevitable; like watching the sands run out of an hour glass. It was always going to happen; nothing was going to prevent it. In addition to which, the sight tests had just depressed me more anyway. Still, there were some advantages. Now I had a real and tangible reason why I couldn't get a job, rather than just my own lethargy, I was entitled to claim disability from the Government. I didn't feel so guilty about the non-events which were my days now that I was getting paid for them. Time went on as before. I stopped drinking. I stopped doing anything very much, except just being. Sometimes I would feel Scotty's eyes upon me... I couldn't see him anymore beyond his blurred outline; even when I looked slightly above him as I had been taught to do in order to utilise the peripheral part of my vision that remained, he was still just a fuzzy shape. Somewhere along the line I had forgotten what he looked like. The memory had just faded, just as his features had faded into an indistinguishable blur. I knew he was getting older. Sometimes when I ran my hand through the stubble of his hair affectionately, I could tell that it wasn't quite as thick as it used to be. His hairline was receding. And if I couldn't recall how Scotty looked anymore, I certainly couldn't accurately recollect how I looked myself either. I supposed I was getting older too. Still, even though time was passing me by, at least, I consoled myself, I wasn't ageing along with it. To my own mind, if not to everyone else's, I was exempted from the ageing process. Another five years passed me by; a whole decade since the demise of Herbert Sherbet. (He alone remained precisely and perfectly preserved in my memory. He was pretty much all that was left.)

Then, one day, I got a letter from the bank. Scotty read it to me in his painfully slow and laboured reading voice, as he read all of my correspondence (at least there wasn't much of it so it was never too much of an onerous duty for him – which was good; he hated reading). The bank was writing to confirm a balance of £12,453.72 in my current account. The bank expressed surprise at the level of activity upon my current account. Or rather, I should say, they were surprised at the level of inactivity operating within my current account; for besides the monthly income from my disability allowance and a couple of standing orders for household bills etc, there was no activity upon my account whatsoever. No withdrawals recorded within the past five years. No deposits beside one large cheque ten years ago (so that's what happened to that cheque: Scotty must have found it and paid it into my account.) The bank was writing as a courtesy to check that everything was in order with my account. Perhaps I would prefer to transfer some of my balance into a high interest savings account and make my money work a little harder for me?

I was amazed by how much the disability allowance had amounted to over the years; and knowing about it suddenly gave me an idea as to how to spend it. It was an idea which Scotty described as "fucking stupid" and led me to The Blank. But for the first time in my life, I had some money and I was sick of the nothingness of it all. At least The Blank lent some structure to my days again. At least in looking after him, I didn't have to think about myself so much anymore and the nothing I'd become. Because I was nothing, as my grandmother had always predicted. I was worthless and useless; nothing was the sum total of me, and as I surely knew, nothing ever comes from nothing.

I never intended to jump again. My show jumping career was over, as was The Blank's. He'd never jumped very well anyway, according to Denby. No. The Blank was always just going to be a pet. The one horse which I had managed to save from Keith Denby's clutches and for whom I, blind and useless as I was, could give a better life than the one which he had (unfortunately for him) been born into. I didn't have much confidence anymore. Somewhere along the line, between my grandmother and Keith Denby and my eyesight fading away into blurry nothing, what little I had ever had had fallen away from me. I didn't even really believe I could ride all that well anymore. It took all of my efforts to find the courage to merely hack along the lane on The Blank. The Blank, really, was remarkably forgiving and generous towards my ineptitude. I mean, here was a horse who had been as ill-treated as my brother and I had been. Any other horse might have laid back his ears and aimed vicious teeth and heels at any human being who came within five feet of him. Instead, he greeted my clumsy attempts at kindness with compassion and gentleness of his own. Eventually, I came to trust him and I was no longer so fearful about riding him. I began to look forward to riding out on him each day. He, in turn, was no longer so afraid either. He would even sometimes allow Scotty into his stable to pet him. He was learning, once more, to trust in the ability of humans not to hurt him. I was learning to trust in my own ability to ride again. Suddenly, my life was not so futile as it once had been. In it, I discover, to my immense surprise, that there are still some good things to be enjoyed. When I think about what has been given back to me by this white horse, I know that The Blank is undoubtedly the greatest horse who has ever lived. He looks after me. He never lets me fall.

Or so I believe.

And I am utterly unshakeable in this belief; until one day, when I'm riding The Blank out along the lane.

It's just another day, another ride. I always rode around dawn. I couldn't get out of the habit of riding out early; partly because I didn't want anyone who knows me, or more specifically, anyone who knows I'm practically blind to see me out riding a horse on the road alone. I shouldn't really have been doing it; Scotty was right. I am probably a danger to myself and to everyone else around me. It's probably also illegal. As it is, I can never escape the feeling that I'm getting away with something illicit every time I hack out with The Blank. It has become more and more of a guilty pleasure every time I do it. But, I tell myself, anyone who knows The Blank as I do would know perfectly well that what I'm doing is not really dangerous at all. The Blank always takes care of me. That's what I thought that day, as I was riding out along the lane.

We make the turn towards a high wall which forms a boundary between a house and the lane, and I'm getting ready to turn right into another lane. From there I'll be able to find the bridlepath we need. It's only really just starting to get light and all is silent around us; no cars on the road, no people out walking their dogs or cycling by. It's just the way I like it to be, when suddenly The Blank throws up his head and pricks his ears as if he's heard or sensed something. He begins to move with tense little steps. He's suddenly very alert. It feels wrong. His head is held too high. I can feel the tension running down through his neck to his withers, on through his legs to his hooves. His nostrils are flaring, snuffing at the cold early morning air. I think: *another horse. He's caught the scent of another horse.* In a moment, I think, he will give that great baying whinny that horses use to call out to each other. The other, wherever, he is, will respond and The Blank will be satisfied. It's only natural that they should want to greet each other. Horses are herd animals and need contact with their own kind, from time to time. People are the same, but I had got into the habit of loneliness, and of thinking that I liked it that way. That was another habit that required breaking; but I didn't think that then, of course. After The Blank and this unknown other have greeted each other, I think, we'll be on our way again. But the seconds pass and The Blank doesn't call. He dances a little restlessly on his feet, tosses his head and then surges suddenly forward. Too late, I realise that whilst tossing his head, he's taken the bit between his teeth. The oldest trick in the book and I fell for it because of my utter belief in The Blank. Too late I realise that I'm just a passenger. The Blank's in control. I don't really see the wall looming up in front of us. It's too similar in colour to the landscape around it for me to distinguish it properly and, perhaps I was panicking a little by this stage as well. Not total panic; when The Blank surged forward part of the raw power he had been concealing within himself all of this time rushed through me as well. Perhaps what I was feeling was a combination of exhilaration and fear. So the wall, that same boundary wall I had been following, even though I should have realised it was there, came as something of a surprise to me. It was a high wall and The Blank had to do an enormous jump to clear it. He gave a tiny hitch with his back feet as he reached the pinnacle of his leap in order to pass cleanly over it. I remember being impressed in addition to being so surprised that in the end I simply bounced out of the saddle to hit the floor below. Fleetingly, before I hit the ground, I saw a house, painted an unnaturally bright white making it seem as if it almost shone in the early morning gloom, so white even I could make it out quite clearly; something too vividly blue to ever naturally belong in the dull Cheshire countryside, and then the ground rushing up to meet me before everything went black.

9. Snuff

*(Written by Shawn Crahan, Corey Taylor. Appears on Roadrunner
Records: All Hope is Gone, 2009. Performed by Slipknot)*

Swimming. My head feels like it's full of fluid. It feels like
I'm swimming. Well, floating really. Just floating along. Idly, I
wonder if that vivid splash of blue that flashed before my eyes was
water. It had the lurid artificial look of a swimming pool. Perhaps
I've fallen in. Perhaps I've drowned. Perhaps, when I fell off The
Blank, I fell in and drowned. Perhaps I'm dead. I don't feel wet
though. At least, I don't think I do. (Would I even be able to tell, if
I was dead?) But I'm definitely moving; being propelled through
the air. That seems like fairly conclusive proof to me. I'm dead and
I'm floating away. I begin to relax into this new dead state. Oddly,
it feels strangely familiar. I feel sleepy and lethargic and slightly
numbed. My head aches. Would my head hurt this much if I was
dead? My head is pressed against something. It's something warm,
and it comes to me all in a flash why the sensations I am feeling are
so familiar to me. I have experienced this before. Years ago, when
Scotty took me out once to the Red Lion pub. There was a disco in
the function room upstairs – the same room where we had sat just
after my grandmother's funeral – only this had been before she had
died. The room had been transformed by flashing red and green
lighting and a whirling silver disco ball. Even if we had known that
eventually we would end up in that room celebrating - and I do
mean that literally - my grandmother's death, we wouldn't have
recognised it as the same place. It had been after I had left school. I
had just turned sixteen. I was too young to be in there and too
young to drink, but Scotty had plied me with alcohol anyway, in the
mistaken belief that I would enjoy myself. Lagers and blacks. They
had tasted disgusting and I couldn't take them. I had been drunk by
the end of my second half. By the time I'd reached the fifth, I had
been swaying on my feet. At some point during the sixth, I had
passed out. I'd come to moments later, covered in purple, foamy,
blackcurrant scented vomit, and in the process of being carried from

135

the room by one of the bouncers. The sensations were the same. I was being carried. *Someone* was carrying me. *Somewhere.* Shit. I tried to move but my limbs felt like lead. I do not think I even managed to produce a twitch. I am being carried along by I don't know who to I don't know where. He (?) – I presume it is a "he" – smells nice. This is something. His T-shirt feels soft against my face. Perhaps I am dead after all. Perhaps he is an angel. The last thought which flitters through my mind is the hope that I'm not covered in purple sick.

As I swim slowly back up into consciousness again, the first thing I notice is the whispering. It is a frantic, almost feverish litany of hoarse urgent whisperings, like the rustle of dried leaves. The movement has stopped. The soft material which was pressed against my face like a security blanket has gone, as has the warmth of the arm which held me. From this, I deduce that I am no longer being carried. Wherever I was being carried to, we have evidently arrived. I am lying on something cool. My head hurts. My arms and legs feel like lead. There is a sharp stabbing pain in my collarbone and I wonder if it's broken again. To take my mind off the pain which is beginning to swell and bloom in my brain, I attempt to focus upon the words which are being feverishly hissed somewhere close by. I can't be sure, but it sounds something like this:

Looks okay. Looks okay. Moved her. Shouldn't have moved... Mebbe... I don't know. I don't know. Shouldn't have brought her in here. S'posed to be Mom's room. I don't know. It's not as if she's coming back. Nowhere else. Where else? I don't know. I don't know...

There's something odd about the way the words are being spoken. It's not just the hoarseness in the man's (it is *definitely* a "he" after all) voice which makes him sound like my mother used to do when she spoke for the first time after one of her protracted periods of silence, or even the frenetic manner in which he is uttering his words. It takes me a moment to pinpoint it, but then I realise. It's his accent. He has an American accent. It sounds fantastically exotic and out of place here in the dull Cheshire countryside. What a strange place for him to choose to live, I think. But then again, what do I know about America or Americans? I acknowledge to myself. Cheshire might be where all Americans want to come and live, for all I know. Somehow, I doubt it though. I try to remember just how the countryside looked here, before I lost my sight. I don't recollect it was all that stunning. Flat. Boring. Dull. These are the adjectives which spring to mind when I recall the look of it in my memory. I hope he's not some kind of nutter. Some species of reclusive psychopath. He sounds like a nutter. All of those late night slasher movies Scotty and I used to sit and drink through before I lost my vision resurface with disturbing clarity in my memory. Perhaps the thing I'm lying on feels cold because it is a cold metal butcher's style table. Any minute now he'll set to work hacking me into pieces. That would be just my luck, I think wearily. The only time The Blank pitches me off his back and I land in the garden of some weirdo. Trust me, I think, to land in the middle of the Cheshire Chainsaw Massacre. These thoughts, disturbing as they might be perceived to be, drift almost idly through my mind. I am not taking myself seriously, despite the fact that undoubtedly the man who has brought me into this room sounds very strange. But I feel so tired, I just don't have the energy to even react to them as if they were serious threats. I just want to lie here and listen to the murmuring voice. Okay, it sounds a bit odd, but it's also peculiarly soothing. This bed – because it's not the cold of a metal butchering table, but the cool of clean sheets – is comfortable. I just want to stay here and not move. I find myself not really caring if he is a murderer anyway. What is there to live for? I can't be bothered to fight anymore.

From somewhere outside, faintly, as if from a long way away, I hear the high whinny of a frightened horse; and for the first time, I feel the cold hand of fear begin to claw at my guts. Not being concerned for my own safety is one thing, but The Blank... Well, that's different. I begin to struggle; to fight against my overwhelming lethargy. My hands twist convulsively in the surface of the bed covers I am lying upon. The murmuring voice dies away into silence. He has noticed me move. *(Is this good? Or is this bad? Has he been waiting for this point in time; the point where consciousness is restored to me, so he can start torturing me properly?)* I feel the warmth of a body leaning over me. I can feel his eyes scrutinising me. I feel another stab of fear. I don't know this man. He could be anyone. I could be anywhere; *and I can't see to find my way out.* I feel a gentle touch upon my shoulder. Fortunately for me it is the uninjured one. I become very still. His hand slides over my shoulder with a gentle tenderness which almost brings tears to my eyes. His hand is very hard; callused as if he works with them somehow. A builder? A labourer? An American builder/labourer/murderer? Would a murderer have calluses upon his hands? *Rope burn?* Oh God, I wish Scotty was here. His hand stops at the top of my breast and then suddenly he snatches it away as if I have burned him.

'Jesus Christ, man, what are you doing?' I hear him mutter to himself. 'She's unconscious for Chrissake.'

I feel the space in the air open up between us again as he evidently wanders away, berating himself unintelligibly as he goes. I'm going now, I think to myself. I'm going right now, while his back is turned. I sit up suddenly, ready to run. The pain which shoots up through my shoulder and into my head, however, takes my breath away. Instead of running, I merely hunch over and groan.

'Oh-h-h-h-h-h-h-h-h...... G-G-G-o-d-d-d-d-d-d-d. Oh God. God. That hurts.' (So much for my survival strategy). Pain dances redly before my eyes before it subsides back into the slow throb-throb-throb of before. I breathe again and struggle back up into a sitting position. I stare around the room. I realise I must be staring blankly. (Of course I'm staring blankly...) I can't make out much anyway. A room of neutral tones. A Thomas Hardy poem of a room. Typical. I cast around for something – anything – to focus upon. Anything of note. I am panicking. I tell myself to calm down and focus on moving the blind spot, on using my peripheral vision. I breathe deeply.

'What hurts?'

The question makes me jump.

'Who's that? Where are you?' Oh God. Oh shit. I've tried – and failed – to make my voice sound normal, even a little bit severe. Instead, my questions come out high and frightened. If this man – whoever he is – is anything like Keith Denby, he'll exploit my fear now. It'll be rape and murder all the way. And worse, I suppose, I've not just told him that I'm afraid. I've also just given away the fact that I'm blind. *Afraid and helpless.* Keith Denby would find the combination intoxicating. If this man is anything like Keith Denby, then I am doomed.

I can find no movement in the blur in front of me. I take a deep breath and try again.

'Where's The Blank?' My voice sounds more normal now. *Thank God.*

'The what?' He sounds confused. I suppose he would be. Suddenly, I can see him. I see him raise a hand and rake it through his hair. The movement helps me to focus upon a mop of black curly hair. Cautiously, I inch myself towards the edge of the bed. I am about to explain when The Blank answers the man's question for me. I hear a whinny, urgently calling to me, much closer now. Immediately I forget my caution, slide myself stiffly off the bed and head towards the sound. I am careful not to step too close to the man though. I put out my hand to reach for where I think the sound is coming from and it slaps against the glass of a window. I half-turn towards the mop of black hair.

'Where is he?'

'He's outside....' he answers. His tone is even more confused than ever. 'That's a window.' I see his hand gesture towards where my fingertips still rest against the glass. His tone tells me that he feels he's stating the blatantly obvious – which, of course, he is – but only to a fully-sighted person.

'I brought you in the house after you fell. I thought... I guess I didn't think I should leave you just lying on the floor outside. I thought you'd be more comfortable... I'm sorry. I didn't think it through properly. I shouldn't have...'

I shake my head in confusion. I don't understand what he's telling me. Or maybe I'm just not processing the information he's giving to me very well. The pain in my head intensifies.

'Sorry... Where is he? My horse? He sounds like he's just outside?' As if to emphasise the point, I hear The Blank butt at the window I am standing at with his head. I feel the reverberation of the impact judder through the glass. I can almost make out the white shape of him.

'He is,' the man responds slowly, as if he thinks I might be a little bit stupid. His tone is even more as if he feels he is stating the "bleeding obvious" as Scotty would probably term it. 'He's just outside.' He gestures again to the window. 'This is a ground floor bedroom,' he adds.

I shake my head again, impatient now; ignoring the pain.

'Open the window. Please.'

I feel him move towards me. I can feel that he is being very cautious in his movements, sparing almost as if he realises that I am afraid of him, and is purposely keeping his distance so as not to intensify my fear. I hear the window slide open and almost immediately The Blank pokes his nose through and nuzzles at my still outstretched hand, shoving the man roughly aside as he does so.

'Hey, pal, steady on,' I hear him remonstrate gently. My fear falls away from me; mainly because I can feel The Blank's caress against my hand; but also because I am starting to like the feel of this man.

'Yes, steady on,' I chide in return, stroking The Blank's velvety muzzle as I do so. The Blank nudges gently at my palm with his lips, as if requesting forgiveness. 'You might well feel sorry,' I continue to admonish him tenderly. 'I wasn't expecting you to jump that. No wonder I fell off. You could have given me some warning. And silly old Keith Denby said you couldn't jump too. Well, what does he know?'

140

This last thought suddenly fills me with light, despite the throbbing bruise on the side of my head. We have jumped again. Okay, I fell off, but we did it. And if we did it once... Maybe, next time, I wouldn't fall. Maybe next time... A tiny flickering candle of hope putters into life. *Maybe, we're not as finished as we thought we were.*

'You're blind.' The man at the side of me emits the words almost in a rush of relief, as if they are the result of some intensely complex mental calculation.

'Hey, there's no flies on you.' I resort to a flippant Scotty-ism in my disappointment that he has, at last, it seems, reached the (sadly) correct conclusion about me. It's not just that he's realised though; it's also reminded me of the reality of the matter and effectively snuffed out any furtive, unworthy ambitions I might have been nursing about getting back into the show jumping arena. *Of course, we're finished. I'm blind; and The Blank isn't going to be doing any show jumping without me, is he? We're finished with all that. We're both finished. QED.*

I paste a brave smile over my face – it's the same brave smile I've been using ever since I developed Stargadt's – I'm sick of it. I wheel around to face him, but then stagger a little as I do so, feeling suddenly dizzy and a little sick

'Hey, take it easy, sugar.'

I feel him put an arm around me, presumably to steady me. For one second, one tenth of a second even, I permit myself the luxury of leaning against the solid warmth of him. My head rests just below his shoulder. I don't know this man. I can't see him; but there is something so *nice* about him. Nobody has ever called me "sugar" before. Something else – not just some base meaningless ambition this time – licks up inside of me. I make a conscious effort to pull myself together and move away from him. I feel the warmth of him seep away from my body. As the cool air begins to circulate in the space between us again, I feel momentarily – stupidly, I suppose – bereft.

'I bet you've got a concussion,' he says, following me, moving a little closer again.

I wonder if he feels the same as I just did, but then dismiss this crazy notion quickly from my mind.

'You'd better rest here for a while,' he continues, almost cheerfully.

I hesitate. I don't know what to say or how to answer him. I gnaw at little at my lower lip – a bad habit I know – but one I always seem to take refuge in when I am uncertain of anything.

'I don't know,' I say eventually. 'I don't want.... I don't want to inconvenience you or anything. I mean... I don't even know who you are.'

He laughs a little. (He has a nice laugh, I note).

'Hey, I'm safe. I promise. Scout's honour.'

I laugh a little too, but then a wave of nausea claws its way up from my gut, threatening to overwhelm me. I sit suddenly back down upon the bed. If I don't I will faint again and then the next thing I know I will wake up covered in purple, foamy vomit and I'll never get to talk to this strange and wonderful person ever again. Okay, maybe not purple, foamy vomit – I have never been able to drink lager and black since that first awful time - but any kind of vomit is nasty, and something of a turn off, I suppose, if you are trying to impress a person. (And why would I be trying to impress him? The whole situation is just so... bizarre... I tell myself. I make a determined attempt to order my thoughts. A last crack at rational behaviour.)

'But what about The Blank?' I ask uncertainly. I can't stay here, I tell myself rationally. *I can't.*

'The what? Oh, the horse... Don't worry, there's some stables in the back. They're pretty decrepit, but he'll be okay in one of those, won't he?'

'Oh, yeah,' I nod. I can't ride home. *I can't. I won't make it.* I feel so tired, I cannot think. My eyelids are heavy. My head throbs. If I don't lie down and sleep, I'm going to die, I know it.

Before I can argue with myself anymore, I find myself agreeing with the man. 'They'll be fine. He's used to decrepit anyway.'

'You should sleep if you're tired,' he says. His tone is kind. I can't focus on anything other than that. 'You've definitely got a concussion,' he adds. 'Nothing makes you sleep like a bang on the head.'

I lie down. I cannot help myself.

'I do feel really tired,' I mumble, knowing I am being stupid; knowing that Scotty, when he finds out about this, is going to kill me. But I can't move. There's nothing else I can do, I think, before a warm comforting nothingness envelopes me.

10. Brain Damage

(Written by D. Gilmour, N. Mason, R. Waters, R. Wright. Appears on Harvest EMI UK: The Dark Side of the Moon, 1973. Performed by Pink Floyd)

I wake up slowly. It seems to take me ages to resurface properly. I can hear noises coming from somewhere in the house – rhythmic thumping sounds – and I lie and listen to them lethargically for a long time before I decide I can move. When, eventually, I do muster the energy to open my eyelids I notice that the light in the room is even more dim; no longer just a room of neutral tones now, but a dark room of neutral tones. I cannot make anything out at all in the gloom. I feel my way around for some time before I locate the door. I have, I realise, slept through the entire day, from dawn to dusk. This is terrible, I tell myself. Scotty is going to be so angry with me. He's probably really worried as well. I should go home straight away. But, then again, I tell myself, already making excuses, I can't just leave, can I? Not without saying thank you. Or goodbye. And I don't really know if I am up to facing the swearing at this present moment in time. My head is still throbbing dully. I decide to track down the source of the drumming sound which I can hear first.

It takes me a while, but eventually I find it. A large room at the front of the house which, as far as I can tell, (and I can't tell much because the light is so bad), contains nothing much excluding a large drum kit. At the drum kit, the man sits playing them. I don't know anything about music, but it sounds amazing. The entire room is permeated with the energy of the rhythms he is creating. I can't see hardly anything but I can feel the presence of him, can feel, rather than see, the whirling mop of black hair. I am just beginning to really enjoy the sound when suddenly, disappointingly, it stops.

'Any chance I could turn the light on in here?' I ask as the last reverberation dies away.

'I thought you were... well... blind?'

I shake my head quickly.

'Not totally blind as such. I just can't see very well. It's all a bit... blurry. Well, very blurry really. I can't see you at all in this light. I can't even see the drums you were playing. If the light were better, I might be able to see a bit.'

I hear a clatter as if the man has casually tossed the drumsticks onto the surface of one of the drums and angle my head towards the noise.

'What was that?'

'Huh? Oh that. It's one of my floor toms. I just threw my sticks on there.'

'Oh.' Needless to say, I don't really know what a floor tom is.

I feel a brush of air as he walks by me presumably to get to the light switch and I angle my head again, this time trying to get a decent look at him. For a moment, he stops and stands quite still, as if he realises this will be helpful to me, but I still can't see him. I shake my head in despair at myself. All I know of him at this point in time is that he is a small man of slight build with a mad mop of black curls on his head.

'Sometimes looking slightly above something moves the blind spot up and out of the way so I can look at things, but I can't see you at all in this light,' I say. Without thinking, I reach out my hand (*not* to touch his face, you understand – blind people only do this in films) but, shamefully, because I want to touch those black curls. Aghast at myself, I snatch my hand away at the last minute and force it down by my side. He is still standing utterly motionless next to me and I wonder if he has noticed my odd impulse; and if he has, how he feels about a strange blind woman standing in his house groping at him. The thought makes me want to laugh. Get a grip, I tell myself sternly. Strange blind groping woman is bad enough. Strange, crazy, blind groping woman insanely laughing at nothing is much, much worse.

'Oh yeah. The light,' he mutters softly, almost to himself, and reaches past me to flick the switch. Immediately, he springs into view. I can see him now. He *is* a small man, but he is taller than me. He is wearing black and I can't tell whether it is the darkness of his clothing, or just his natural colouring, but his complexion seems very pale, as if he doesn't get out much. His eyes are grey (I think). It is very hard to tell. The only thing I can really be certain of is the wild mop of black curly hair on his head. I long to touch it. I turn away from him to distract myself from this mad urge.

'Oh yes, that's much better. Thank you.' I turn towards where the drums stand again. 'Is that what you do then?' I nod towards the kit.

'Yeah. I just play drums.'

He sounds devastated about the fact.

'There's no need to sound so down about it. It sounded pretty good to me,' I say lightly. 'Better than being an unemployed show jumper,' I add, to myself, really.

'I thought you were blind,' he says.

'I bet I can see a few fences yet,' I am still speaking to myself. You see, even though I *know* we're finished, I still can't shake the fact out of my head that The Blank jumped that wall. I'm still dreaming, in other words, that we might have some kind of future after all. Stupid, I tell myself. Snap out of it. 'But, okay, yeah, point taken,' I say, 'A *blind*, unemployed show jumper.'

'So,' I continue, taking a few experimental steps towards the drum kit which dominates the room. 'Tell me about these drums.' My foot stubs against something which makes a hollow sound in return. 'Ouch. Sorry. What was that, for instance?'

'That's a bass drum. A 22 by 18 bass drum to be exact. Either side of it you got your floor toms and then just here,' the man grasps my hand and lifts it onto something smooth. The sensation takes my breath away. Not the feel of the drum, you understand – but the feel of his hand. I feel like I've been given an electric shock. I see the man snap his head up and wonder if he felt it too. He

147

carries on, however, as if nothing has passed between us. 'This is a rack tom. And this... This is my favourite.' He raises my hand again and places it onto a different drum, one that makes a slight rustling sound as I touch it. 'This is a 14 x 6.5 Ludwig Black Beauty Super Sensitive Snare drum.'

'Black Beauty, huh?'

'Yeah. Like the horse, y'know.'

I nod. Of course I know. The horse anyway. The drum I have utterly no idea about.

'And then you've got the cymbals... I got six on here in all. I use Zildjian.'

I nod again. This time blankly. This time, I really don't know. I suppose he notices, because he laughs a little at my confusion.

'There's a special Hi-hat here. I got a K Hi-hat on the top and a Z custom dyno beat on the bottom. Then I got this one.' He moves my hand again and I touch metal.

'This is a Dark Medium Thin Crash. This one's a Medium Thin Crash. Then this one... This is a Ping Ride. Then I got this one... This is a K 20 Crash/Ride and finally... This is an FX 20 Oriental Classic China.'

Each time he has moved my hand onto a different metal circle. Each time I get the electric shock.

'Bloody hell,' I say, and I'm not just talking about the facts I've been overloaded with. 'Well... It sounded great. It really did.' I nod quickly in affirmation and then wince a little at the pain in my head.

'Hey, how are you feeling now, sugar?' I feel the man lightly brush his fingertips against the bruise which must have swelled purple by now and long to lean into his caress. I force myself to pull away a little, but then find myself saying almost recklessly;

'Hmmm-mmmm, that's nice. I mean...' I backtrack quickly, 'no-one's ever called me "Sugar" before. It's nice. A nice thing to call someone. But I still feel a bit shaky. And I feel terrible... I mean, just sleeping it off in your bed like that. You don't know me and I don't know you. I don't even know your name. How bad is that? I just felt too tired to move though. But I'm really sorry. Really, really sorry. I'm so sorry about The Blank jumping over the wall and me falling off and passing out and everything, I really am. And I can't believe I slept all this time. It's terrible, it really is. I should go. I'll just get The Blank... My horse... And we'll go. We really must go now. We really must.' I say the words quickly. I'm afraid if I don't, I'm never going to muster the will to leave.

'No! Don't go. You can't go yet,' he says immediately. There is something nice about the way he says it. As if he really does want me to stay. As if he has been waiting for me to wake up. I can't help but smile at the shape of him. 'What I mean is,' he continues slowly, ' I mean, I don't think you should ride that horse home with a concussion. Anyway, I'm actually terrified of horses. Seriously. I mean really. I had to completely overcome my fear to get him in that stable in the first place. I think you should stay for a while and keep me company just to reward me for that. Also, I don't think you really can leave, because I think I broke the horse's bridle when I took it off.'

'Oh. Show me,' I say, and follow the black shape of him through the house, outside into the garden. I hear The Blank whinny to me and focus upon his outline almost immediately. He is secured in one of a pair of run-down looking stables, weaving restlessly around it. He's probably starving. He usually spends the whole day grazing.

'Hey, let him out, if you need to. He can eat my lawn,' the man says.

There seems to be plenty for him to go at. The grass on the man's lawn is overgrown as if he hasn't bothered cutting it for many months. It catches damply at my ankles as I make my way cautiously towards The Blank.

'If you're sure you don't mind,' I say politely, but I've already slipped the bolt on the stable door and I feel The Blank brush past me as I open it for him. He nuzzles my hand momentarily but then wanders away almost immediately and I hear him begin to tear and chew at the grass vigorously. I am amazed that he even let this man put him in the stable. After all he has suffered at the hands of Keith Denby, The Blank can be a little suspicious of strangers sometimes, and rightly so. The only reason I can attribute to it is that The Blank, like me, likes the feel of this man too. He must be alright, I tell myself, because The Blank would surely know if he was some kind of psychopath.

On the top of the stable door, I find The Blank's saddle and his bridle. All of the straps to the bridle have been undone and it is lying in many pieces. I know immediately what has happened here.

'You've unfastened all the buckles on the bridle, that's why it's fallen into pieces. It's not broken really, it just needs fastening back together. When you take a bridle off a horse, you only have to undo the throat lash and the noseband and then you can just slide it off.'

'The what and the what?'

'It doesn't matter,' I am laughing now. 'You did amazingly well to get him in there and get this stuff off him if you're as scared as horses as you say you are.'

The man nods his head solemnly.

'I am absolutely terrified of them. Seriously. I don't go anywhere near them. They had some police horses at one of our shows once. They were using them for crowd control. Jesus Christ, they looked like vicious bastards. Like they couldn't wait to trample you into the asphalt, like they were relishing the prospect. I stayed away from those things. I stay away from them whenever I can.'

I half-smile at the thought.

'I suppose some horses can be vicious. I don't know many that would purposely trample on you though.' I smile again. I am thinking about Pepperpot Mill all those years ago. 'Only one I can think of.'

'These ones would. I'm not lying to you. I could see it in their vindictive looking eyes.'

I laugh again and gather together the pieces of the bridle.

'I can fix this. I just need a little light.'

'Come inside and do it.'

I follow the shape of the man towards the block of light which is flooding from what must be his lounge and illuminating his garden. I am careful where I step and stop to stroke The Blank a little on the way there, just to reassure him; just to reassure myself really. He grunts at me companionably and once again I get the feeling that this man is okay. Just as I am about to step inside the house, I hear the man say,

'Hey, I wouldn't drink that buddy...'

I turn quickly and almost bump into the man who is following closely behind me. For a half-second, I think I see him reach out with his arms to steady me, but then, disappointingly, he drops them again.

'He's trying to drink my swimming pool. He spat it out pretty quick though. There's a pond over there. He can drink that.'

'He'll find it,' I say and turn back into the brilliantly lit room once more. I find a place to sit on a pale "L" shaped sofa and sit, my legs crossed, fastening the bridle back together. I am doing this by touch really, feeling at which point the leather in each individual strap is most creased and knowing that this must be the point where the strap was originally buckled. Occasionally, I hold the leather up to a height where I can get a half glance at it, just to check it looks okay. The man follows me and sits down on the other side of the sofa. I flash a quick, nervous smile in his direction. He is silent for a moment, but I can feel him watching me. It makes me even more nervous still.

'So,' he begins eventually. 'I guess I'd better keep on calling you "Sugar" since I don't know your name.'

This makes me laugh.

'You can keep on calling me that if you like. It's nice.' I fiddle with the bridle for a moment before offering, 'But my name's Em.'

'Short for... Emma?'

151

'Emily.   But no-one ever calls me Emily.   Except my grandmother did. But she's dead now.'

'So she doesn't call you that anymore, hey?' he replies lightly.

'No,' I say. 'Thank God.'

'Huh.'

There is another pause.

'So, you're the world's only blind show jumper, hey?'

This makes me laugh again; makes me forget about the shadow of my Grandmother.

'Actually, I'm the world's only *nearly* blind, *unemployed* show jumper. There is a subtle difference.'

'There certainly is.   So which happened first?   The blindness... Sorry, the *near* blindness, or the unemployment?'

'The unemployment. I lost my vision after. It didn't seem to matter that much at the time. I lost the horse I used to jump with and well... After that... Nothing seemed to matter very much. Not even losing my sight. Nothing meant very much to me at all for a very long time.' Something catches in my throat as I say the words, reveal these things about myself.

'God, I know that feeling,' the man says.

I nod quickly. Suddenly, I can feel his despair. Perhaps that's why The Blank jumped over the wall into his garden after all, I think to myself. Perhaps what The Blank had sensed beyond the wall was indeed a fellow creature. That is to say that perhaps what he sensed in that man's presence was something of the creature he himself had once been; standing up to his hocks in the mire, abandoned and desolate. I do not really know this, of course; but I do know all about despair of the type the man is feeling. I know it very well indeed. I cast my eyes up again towards the man and realise that he has slid a little closer to me whilst I have been involved in these cogitations. I do not know if he has done this purposely or not. I continue to scrutinise the bridle, even though it's almost fixed now.

'But you got yourself another horse?'

I nod, and let my eyes follow the shape of The Blank as he grazes his way around the man's garden.

'You can see him?' the man prompts.

'Yes. Well, sort of. I can see him because he's so white. He stands out. But I can't really see him, if you know what I mean. He's just a blurry white shape. Just like you're a blurry shape with loads of black curls... But I can see him enough anyway...'

'Should you even be riding him? I mean... If you can't see that well?'

'Oh God, don't you start.'

'Sorry? Say again?'

'Never mind.' There is a short lull, before I feel pressed into further explanation. 'He's really quite safe.' The silence which surrounds this statement resonates with the man's scepticism. 'I mean, he is. I know. I know. He jumped over your wall and I fell off and banged my head and everything. And nobody ever wants to fall... But he's never done anything like that before. And I've owned him for a while now. I can't explain it. He's quite trustworthy really.'

'Well,' he says, still dubious. 'I guess it's up to you. I mean... You know him best. I guess.'

I fidget a little bit. The bridle is back in one piece. I make a show of scrutinising it for a second before I glance up at the man again. I suddenly realise I still don't even know his name. I don't know anything about him, except that he lives in a big house with a big drum kit and a big enough garden for it to have stables, a big swimming pool and a big enough lawn for my horse to graze; and that he apparently lives here all by himself. Oh, and that he must play his drums in big enough shows to need police horses for crowd control. Or he says he does. Suddenly, I am racked by curiosity.

'You know, you haven't told me your name yet.'

'Oh no, I didn't, did I? It's Jimmy.'

'Jimmy. Nice to meet you Jimmy,' I say. The man smiles at me. At least I think he does. It's very hard to tell. He seems to have moved closer to me, but that also, is very hard to tell.

'Well, Jimmy, I suppose I'd better get The Blank home. I can't just leave him eating your garden all night.' I move to stand, but Jimmy stops me, arresting my progress with a hand on my arm. *That settles it, I think, he was never within touching distance before. He's definitely moving closer.*

'Yes, you can,' he says quickly. 'He can eat the whole Goddamn lot for all I care. Stay a bit. I haven't spoken to anyone... Oh God, for weeks now.'

And then Jimmy tells me a story. It is quite frankly, the strangest story I have ever heard and it means either one of two things. (1) Jimmy is telling the truth about himself which, I suppose, could be the case. The truth is, after all, stranger than fiction, they say. Or, more likely, (2) Jimmy is a complete and utter nutter after all, but a nice one, and one with a knack for telling a good story. Perhaps more delusional than psychopathic. I hope so anyway. The story goes something like this:

Jimmy's full name is Jimmy Bridges. He tells me he is the drummer in a punk rock band called *"Lights Out"*. (I have to say, the name sounds familiar, but whether Jimmy is their actual drummer or not, I would never be able to tell. This sort of thing would be really easy to lie about to a visually impaired person. I mean, it's not as if I can see him to recognise him – not that I would recognise him anyway – I only really think I *might* have heard of this band anyway. It's all very vague). He was born in a small town in New England and was brought up by his mother (or his "mom" as he calls her). His father died in a ski-ing accident just before he was born, but it didn't seem to matter to him, because he adored his mom and his mom adored him. So far so good. As he got older, he started to do something called "flunking out" of school. I am not sure about this, but I think it means that Jimmy's progression through his school years were comparable to my own, in that we both failed to meet expectations. The difference between us was that Jimmy, it seemed, was popular and, being as he seemed to have something of a reputation of being a "bad boy", nobody dared to pick on him. He certainly wasn't the underdog that I was. He also, it seems, had two friends who were like brothers to him. These were (and, I suppose, they still are) called Pete Darlow and Si Pelton. All three of them were doing that flunking out of school thing because they were just messing around and hanging out together all the time. (This, I have to say, certainly sounds much nicer than just skipping school on your own). Well, that's what the school (and his mom) had thought they were doing. What they were actually doing was forming their band and practising together. It was a serious business, or so Jimmy tells me. It should not be lumped under the heading "goofing around" (his words) at all. When they had all been 17, they had got their big break. They had been spotted by a record producer during one of their gigs in the diner where his mom had worked and he had commissioned them to record an album. The record producer is called Damien Deadly. He is a man who appears as cadaverous as his name implies. Their first album had gone platinum. (I don't know what this means, and I don't ask). He had been forced to drop out of high school because of the tour they'd needed to do to promote their album. He says he was "forced", but he'd been failing anyway. The only thing he was ever any good at, he tells me, is playing his drums; and, if truth be told, he admits, he was glad to be able to leave school. (Oh, I think, if only someone had given me a get out of jail free card like that – I would have been so happy too). That first tour, he tells me, was a complete and utter blast (his words, again). They had money for the first time in their lives and they spent it like it was going out of fashion. It slipped through their fists like water. Booze, drugs – anything to keep the party going. As time went on, it started to take increasing amounts of both to keep it going for any length of time, but that didn't matter – there was always plenty more. They had the money to spend on it and spend it they did; but by the time their first tour had ended and their record company was demanding they get some new material in the bag, they were burnt out. None of them were able to function without the booze or the drugs anymore. Somehow, they manage to throw something together for their second album, but it's not as good as their first. They know it. Damien Deadly knows it. Their fans know it too – but for some reason they keep coming to the shows. After a while, it becomes apparent that the fans are only coming for the trouble which they know will inevitably start at these shows. Pete and Si are out of control. Well – he somewhat reluctantly admits - he is himself. Damien Deadly encourages this insane behaviour in his prodigies. He tells them that the madder the behaviour, the more publicity they will get. The venues they are playing are crappy little shitholes filled predominantly with assholes; and the biggest assholes in them are themselves. The problem is they've started to believe in all of Damien Deadly's hype. They've fallen under his spell. It was hard not to, Jimmy tells me. Damien Deadly told them that they were Gods of Punk Rock; hence they *were* Gods of Punk Rock and they were damn well going to act like it too. People love it. Their shows start to sell out. They start to play bigger shows at bigger theatres. The money keeps coming. The booze and drugs keep on flowing. The second tour ends with all three of them being arrested on the UK leg of their tour. Jimmy is charged with resisting arrest, disorderly conduct and the possession of class A drugs. The charges were dropped, but enough is enough. They call it quits and head for home. Days later, Pete goes into rehab. Jimmy and Si are lost without him. Their whole existence – Jimmy's whole existence, he tells me – has become the band. He is nothing without them anymore. Eventually Pete comes out again. When Pete arrives home he shows them their third album. He wrote it whilst in the hospital and it is utterly amazing. Their third tour, he calls their "clean tour". No booze. No drugs. No nothing. It is during this tour that Jimmy falls in love with Italian born lingerie model Isabella Grazio (now I've definitely heard of her – Scotty has spent many a happy hour mooning over her pictures in magazines – whether Jimmy actually met and married this person is, however, another matter). Damien Deadly sees that Jimmy really wants her and what Jimmy wants, Jimmy gets. He fixes them up together. After a while, Isabella falls pregnant. She isn't too happy about it, but they agree to get married. Isabella, it transpires, is a bitch. Their marriage does not last. At the end of it, Jimmy has a daughter (Juno) who he never gets to see, and a new nickname "Mad Jimmy" (Jimmy does not tell me where this nickname came from – to be fair by this stage in this extraordinary narrative, I am beginning to think it is somewhat justified, whatever the reasoning behind it). The next few years, Jimmy tells me, all seem to fuse into one. Album – tour – album – tour – album – tour. He can't remember anything about any of the places he has visited (suspicious, and very convenient, I think) – everything, he tells me, just seems to merge into one big blur. A bit like my eyesight, he tells me. From the last tour, he tells me, he has only one clear memory. It is this: they are playing in Sheffield. With time to kill, they spend the afternoon visiting the Museum and Art Gallery. The place sits by the side of a small but immaculate park near to the University. There are signs everywhere telling people to "Keep off the grass" which seems crazy to him. Surely grass in a park is there for running and playing on? The museum itself is nothing special. The exhibits consist of a few mummies, a Natural History section boasting several stuffed animals including a very moth-eaten lion whose tail is half hanging off, the victim of numerous toddlers who have swung their weight upon it, despite the notices surrounding it pleading with their mothers not to let them do this, and then, at the back of the building, the Art Gallery. None of this is especially interesting to Jimmy; or Pete or Si for that matter. (To be fair it's not that interesting to me either, but then a partially sighted person isn't ever going to find an art gallery interesting, are they?) However, in the Art Gallery, at the back, there is a special exhibition of art produced out of the Bethlem Hospital in London; or "Bedlam" as it was popularly known. The works on display are the paintings and drawings produced by the depressed, the mentally ill, the deranged, the downright insane. The end products are beautiful, thought-provoking, haunting, he tells me. One of the pictures particularly stands out in his memory, even now. The artist who painted the picture was unknown. The painting depicted two horses, one white, one black; galloping along what looks like a beach. The white horse is marginally outstripping the black; but it is a close run thing. Both horses are running at the edge of their strength. Their tongues loll from their mouths as they gallop, much as one sees racehorses do as they finish a race. The blurb to the picture, he tells me, explains how the horses are a manifestation of the unknown artist's depression. The black horse (his despair) keeps pace with his healthy mental life (in the form of the white horse). Suddenly, that day, looking at this picture, Jimmy can see it. He can see his own despair, his own depression, keeping pace with him all the time. He is losing himself in the misery of his non-existence. All his life he has been the drummer in a band. He doesn't know how to be anything else. He has never been anything else. He manages to keep going, but like the horses in the picture, it is a close run thing. He becomes desperate. He buys a house in England – this house – just to have a project, to have something to focus upon. He commissions interior designers and landscape architects. It's going to be amazing. He nearly starts to enjoy himself again, but then, in the middle of it, this new project he has assigned himself to save his sanity, he is once again called back to tour with the band. He gets a flight out of Manchester to Newark. (This confuses me, but apparently the Newark he is talking about is near New York, and not the one near Nottingham). He is met at the airport by Pete and Si. Pete is wasted. He's been struggling creatively and he's back to drinking too much and relying on the drugs once more. He is frustrated and angry and looking to take it out on someone, *anyone*. He takes it out on Jimmy. Initially, however, it is Si who steps forward to meet him from the plane.

'Jimmy,' (Si says) 'I'm really sorry, man. Really sorry. I don't know how to tell you...'

'Oh stop fucking around Si. Just tell him,' Pete (apparently) interrupts. He is giggling beneath his words. Jimmy tells me there was a manic look in his eyes.

'Pete,' Si says warningly, but Pete isn't listening to anyone anymore.

'Your mom's dead, dude...'

Jimmy cannot believe it. She hadn't been that well, he had known that. She had been a lifelong smoker and during her later years, there had always been a sinister rattle in her breaths, but he cannot believe that she is really dead. He has just finished preparing a guest room in his new home for her (the room of neutral tones where I have just slept off my concussion). She can't be dead, can she? He gapes at Pete. Pete, however, is only just warming to his theme.

'She's dead. No more. Stepped off this fucking mortal coil. Deceased. Defunct. Departed. Perished. Gone to Heaven. She's fucking dead, Jim.' Pete, it seems, turns breaking the bad news to Jimmy into a particularly famous Monty Python sketch, only this time they're not talking about a parrot, it's Jimmy's mum. Jimmy is heart-broken. He feels numb. He can't get over it. Suddenly, he sees himself for the nothing he has become. His ex-wife won't speak to him, his daughter is apparently afraid of him and won't go anywhere near him, his mother is dead. Even the people who he thought were his best friends, Pete and Si, seem strange to him now. He begins to fall apart. He feels he is being torn apart. There is a solid lump of misery in his throat the whole time now. He can't concentrate anymore. People tell him to do things, and he doesn't do them – not because he doesn't want to – he simply hasn't heard them ask. Too much noise, too many people speaking at once, confuse him. He finds himself unable to follow the events of his daily life. He has no appetite. He is already full with something else; something black; something like despair. He struggles to eat a single mouthful and sheds more weight. He begins to have blank spells. Jimmy feels as if he has stepped outside of himself for a moment. For the first time, he begins to fully understand the true meaning of the epithets applied to the mentally ill; *he's not all there, he's not feeling himself, the lights are on but no-one's home.* All of these are true in his case. When he is inside of his own head, he doesn't feel like himself at all. He doesn't know who *he* is anymore. It's surely not the true Jimmy there. Sometimes all he can hear inside his head is screaming. He becomes forgetful. He

159

forgets how to play the songs. Si is sympathetic, but Pete just gets mad with him.

'Jesus Christ, Jimmy,' he says, 'Pull yourself together. You were fucking useless before. You're even worse now.' Jimmy says nothing in response to these jibes, but something inside of him is hitched up a notch. He takes a further step closer to the edge. And then, one night, he steps over that indefinable edge. One night, for some reason, in the middle of one of their songs, he just stops playing, throws down his sticks and walks out on the tour. He hasn't seen them, Pete or Si, since. He had run; and there had been nowhere else to run to except here, his "home". And so home he had come, even though it really was just an empty shell of a house where he had been even more miserable. Jimmy tells me that he knows that life goes on. He knows this, but that he just can't seem to go on with it. He is still, nine months after walking out on that tour, a complete and utter mess. (I have to say, he certainly seems to be a mess. By this point in time, he is crying. His words are choked. No doubt his face is soaked with tears).

'All I can think about,' he tells me, 'is the picture in that gallery. The white horse barely outstripping the black. 'Well,' he says, 'in my head the black horse is winning that race now... And so you see,' he concludes this astounding and utterly unbelievable story, 'you see why it was so amazing that a *white* horse should jump over my wall. It's gotta be a sign. *You* coming here like this. Well, it's just gotta be a sign that things are gonna get better. They've got to get better. They can't stay the same. They just can't. They've got to get better.'

This last is said so desperately that I ache for him. A silence falls between us. I don't know what to say. Even if it is all - and it's fantastical enough to be - a complete and utter pack of lies, there's no doubting that this last bit is real. The last part, the bit about the blank spells, I have to say, all sounds horribly familiar – he could be describing my mother – or myself, really - in those empty years after Herbert Sherbet; and only someone who has

160

experienced it would know). I understand. I want to tell him I do, but I don't know how. In the end, this is what I say:

'Pink Floyd. *Brain Damage*. Do you remember that song?'

'What?'

'It says something about how the members of the band are all playing different tunes. In their song. It sounds like you were all playing different tunes in your band. Like you'd fallen out of time somehow. Sorry. I'm not saying this very well.'

'Huh.'

I am failing to convey my comprehension of his misery to him. I'm just not very good with people. Only with horses, I realise. In the end, I act instinctively. I reach out with my hand and gently touch his face. It is, as I had surmised, soaked with tears. For a moment he rubs his pale, pale face against my hand, like a cat, drying the tears against my palm.

'I'm sorry,' I say. 'I'm sorry for you. I know how you feel. I really do. I lost my mum too you know. It wasn't like yours. It wasn't as bad really. My mum, I never really knew her. I can't even remember what she looked like. And when I used to look at the photographs we had of her – I mean, this was when I could see well enough to look at them – well, it was like looking at a stranger. I didn't recognise the woman in the pictures at all. She jumped off the blue bridge on the dual carriageway at the end of the road. I spent... I've *spent* years trying to find her again.' I shake my head, almost in disbelief at the sorry pair we present. 'Perhaps that's the problem. Perhaps we just need to let go and get on with our lives. Such as they are...' I gesture towards my eyes. 'Speaking of which,' I continue, 'I *really* must go.'

'Oh no. No, don't go now. It's nearly one in the morning. We've talked nearly the whole night through. And you must be starving. *I'm starving*. Do you want some supper? Stay a bit longer, please.'

I do not go. I am weak and easily persuaded. Besides, The Blank seems quite happy out in his garden. Every so often, he pokes his head in through the open patio doors, seemingly just to check on me. Once, I note, he even sets a hoof inside the house, just to see. He doesn't like the feel of the carpet though, I can tell. He drops his nose to snuff suspiciously at it and then backs out into the garden again. He isn't showing any inclination to jump back over that wall, and Jimmy doesn't seem to care about the flowers and lawn that The Blank is munching his way through, so I'm not too concerned about him. Eventually, I notice, the texture of the light in the blur begins to change. It is getting light. A grey April dawn is beginning to flourish around us. I have now been missing for a whole twenty-four hour period from home. Scotty, I think once more, is going to kill me. The thought makes me tired. I yawn.

'Tired, huh? Well, it looks like we talked the night away.'

'It's been nice,' I say. It has. 'Nice of you not to mind about him jumping over your wall and eating your garden and letting me sleep my headache off and... Well, everything really.'

'Looks like you could do with some more sleep now, hey?'

'I could,' I say. Suddenly, I am crushed by fatigue once more. 'I could just sleep.'

'Well, sleep,' Jimmy says. 'You can use that room again, if you want.' I hear, rather than see, Jimmy give a huge yawn himself.

'I might take you up on that,' I say. I am being stupid I know, but Scotty is going to be so mad with me now anyway, a few more hours of continued absence really isn't going to make much difference in the total amount of swearing-this-is-going-to-result-in stakes. 'I could really do with a sleep... ' I continue. 'And, after all, like you said, you're safe...'

'I'm not that safe, honey.'

He leans over and kisses me. For a moment I don't know how to react. The sensation feels strange, but not entirely unpleasant. I feel myself sagging against him. I am tired. I have never met anyone like Jimmy before. Would it hurt so desperately to let someone in? My lips part. His tongue flicks into my mouth. He tastes nice. I attempt an experimental flick of my own. He pulls me harder against him. I cling to the curls at the nape of his neck, stroking them as I have longed to do all night. The strips of leather of The Blank's bridle are still dangling through my fingers. They brush against Jimmy's shoulder and neck. Then, two things happen very quickly. First, The Blank is suddenly standing over us. He bumps Jimmy on the head with his nose and whinnies loudly. Our teeth crack against each other and Jimmy springs back. The noise of the 'ouch' he manages to emit is drowned out by the second thing that happens: the doorbell rings suddenly and this is followed by a rapid and urgent hammering against the door.

'What the hell...?' Jimmy says. 'Nobody's supposed to be able to get through the front gate.'

'Fucking open the fucking door you *fucking, fucking* bastard.'

'Oh,' I say, a sinking feeling beginning to engulf me. 'I think I know who that might be.'

I don't know if he hears me. He is already at the door. He flings it aside violently. I hear a crash as it hits the wall. I stand and follow him into the hallway.

'What the...?' Jimmy manages to say, and then I hear a slamming noise, and dimly make out the shape of him flying backwards through the air. He skids across the hard tiled entrance hallway and comes to rest against my ankles. Even I can see the angry red blood pumping from his nostrils.

'Oh, God, no! Scotty! Scotty, stop it! For God's sake, what are you doing?'

'You know this person?' Jimmy asks weakly from his prostrate position.

'This,' I say sadly, 'is my brother.'

Scotty's mad; even I can see that. Matters are going to be much worse than even I had anticipated they would be. He has the same air about him as he'd had that day he'd caught Keith Denby trying to mess with me in Silver Destination's horsebox. I can imagine he's currently got both hands bunched into fists; all of the muscles in his chest and the veins in his throat will be standing out with the tension.

'Oh,' Jimmy says.

'And I've been worrying about you all fucking night, you stupid bitch. What happened?' Scotty demands of me. 'And *you*,' just as easily, Scotty switches the target of his anger from me to Jimmy. '*You fucking fucker*. You'd better not have harmed a hair on her head.'

'Jesus Christ, man, take it easy,' I hear Jimmy say. He's on his feet again now. He has the feel of a man who is squaring himself up for the fight. I really hope they are not going to start throwing punches. 'I was taking care of her,' he says.

'Just stop, Scotty,' I push myself between them. 'It's true. The Blank jumped over the wall and I fell off and knocked myself out. Jimmy's been looking after me.'

'I told you didn't I?!' Scotty rounds on me again. 'I told you that stupid horse was a stupid fucking idea. Which wall? Hey, hang on a minute. Jimmy. You're Jimmy Bridges. I thought I knew you. Come on Em, let's go. This is that smackhead from that band. You know. Lights On or something like that. Some mad nutter who beat up his wife and kid and then went bonkers. Where's that stupid horse? We're going?'

'Oh for God's sake, Scotty,' I sigh, exasperated now – and, yes, okay, just the teensiest bit amazed that the incredible story I've been told tonight, is in fact, *true*, after all.

'Sorry,' I say to Jimmy. Then I hear the sharp clattering rhythm of The Blank's feet as he comes into the entrance hall. The ring of his hooves against the hard floor echoes around the house. He's evidently come to see for himself what's going on.

'Oh, for fuck's sake!' Scotty shouts. 'What are you doing letting the thing in the house for? You are a bloody idiot and all. Complete and utter nutter. I don't know why I'm even surprised. *Jesus Christ!* Right. Give me its bridle.' I feel Scotty snatch the strips of leather from where they are still dangling through my fingers. He shoves The Blank's nose roughly into the bridle and pulls it over his ears.

'Saddle?' Scotty demands

'It's out back,' Jimmy says. I see his head move as if he is gesturing with it to the stables at the rear of the house.

'Right.' I hear Scotty stride quickly away.

'You never mentioned the beating up your wife and kid thing,' I hazard worriedly.

'It's not true! None of it was true. You have to believe me. I would never... Oh God.' There is a pause. I see Jimmy rub his hand under his injured nose and examine his fingers for blood. 'You never mentioned that your brother was a foul-mouthed maniac.'

'No,' I concede. I shrug lightly. 'It didn't seem important.'

There's no time to say anything else. Scotty has returned. For the first time ever, I think, Oh God, I wish Scotty wasn't here. There's no time to even reach out and touch Jimmy's hand, which I find myself desperately wanting to do, but Scotty is still moving with sharp angry movements and there's no predicting what he'll do to me or Jimmy if any sign of affection is exchanged between us. Not that Jimmy's probably feeling that much affection at the moment. He's probably sorry he kissed me by now. Scotty flings the saddle over The Blank's back with just a little more force than is absolutely necessary. I see The Blank throw his head up in surprise.

'Careful, Scotty,' I breathe. 'Don't take it out on The Blank.'

'You do it then.'

I stoop and fasten The Blank's girth.

'Well, what can I say?' Jimmy says. 'It's been fun.' I see him gesture ironically to his busted nose and my heart sinks within me. I'm never going to see him again.

'Open those bastard gates,' is Scotty's only response.

'Sorry,' I say quickly. 'Sorry about your nose. And your garden. And everything.' I half-reach out towards him with my hand, shake my head in despair at myself, and turn quickly to follow Scotty and The Blank. Some high security gates (I guess Scotty must have climbed over those to get in) are buzzed open and we walk slowly home together.

'You should have seen the size of the wall he jumped, Scotty,' I venture eventually.

'You're lucky you didn't get jumped there.'

'What? The wall was huge. Six feet, maybe more. And he cleared it easily. He's got a beautiful jump, Scotty,' (I am warming to my theme now). 'He hitches his back feet right at the top of it to make sure he's clear. It reminded me of the way Herb used to jump. It made me think...'

'Oh no! No fucking way. You can stop right there before you get anymore stupid ideas into your thick head...'

We argue all the way home.

11. King for a Day

(Written by Billie Joe Armstrong/Green Day. Appears on Reprise Records: Nimrod, 1997. Performed by Green Day)

When I returned from my short sojourn at Jimmy's house, I had two thoughts on my mind. These were as follows: firstly, the way it had made me feel when Jimmy had called me "sugar". Even a couple of days later, the mere memory could produce a twisting, lurching sensation in the pit of my stomach. And when I thought about the fact that he had kissed me; and, I have to be frank, I did think about it, *a lot*, well, it did very strange things to me indeed. But, I told myself sternly, after the way Scotty had behaved, and taking into consideration the fact that someone like him wasn't going to be interested in someone like me, then the best thing I could do was to try and forget all about it. After all, I was hardly likely ever to meet up with him again. I'd optimistically described where I lived to him in the hope that he might call around, but I never was any good at giving directions and I had to face the truth, we hardly moved in the same social circles. No. All in all, I had to admit that it would be for the best if I just put him out of my head. Not easy; but I did have something else to keep me busy, which brings me to the second item preying on my mind, which was the phenomenal jump The Blank had done to get us over Jimmy's wall and into his garden in the first place. Now that I really couldn't stop thinking about. After all, it had been an extraordinary jump. Okay, okay, so I fell off; but then again I hadn't been expecting him to jump the wall in the first place. But jumped it he had. And that wall, well it was enormous. Not even Herbert Sherbet, who would have jumped through flames if I'd asked him to, would have cleared a wall like that. I couldn't help myself. Despite what Scotty had to say about the matter (and he had plenty), I couldn't stop myself from thinking, what else might he jump?

And it was with this in view that the moment that Scotty popped out for a pint or two with some of his pals, I got busy in the paddock constructing obstacles out of whatever I could find; straw bales, old tyres, any old poles I could find lying around. I tried to make them big and colourful; not to test The Blank you understand, but just so I could see them. Then I tacked up The Blank, explaining myself to him in a self-conscious, self-justifying monologue as I did so.

'You did such a big jump, and such a good one too, it seems a shame never to let you jump again, just because I can't see very well. Now, I put some fences up, but you don't have to jump them if you don't want to. You don't have to do anything you don't want to. But we could just try. Now I can't see them very well. I did my best to lay them out right but sometimes I don't judge things very well anymore... But I think we should just try. I'll try not to fall off this time, I promise.'

I continued in this vein at length and for some considerable time before we actually managed to get out into the paddock and begin the process of warming up. Round and round and up and down the paddock we went; walk, trot, canter. I felt so nervous, I felt ill. It was like that first major show with Silver Destination all over again; only this time there were no judges, no spectators, no commentators. No indoor floodlit arena and immaculate fences. Just the rutted and trampled open grass of the paddock and a few ramshackle straw bales and old tyres for fences. It wasn't great; but it was a start.

'Come on then, let's do it.'

I steered The Blank in the general direction of one of the fences. Moments later we were soaring through the air and the fence was behind us, still standing, cleared and easily so.

That afternoon, it was fantastic. I thought I'd forgotten how to jump. I hadn't. The memory was always there, the techniques and rhythms unforgotten, just concealed within myself. We jumped and jumped those fences, over and over again, for much longer than I would ever have schooled Herbert Sherbet, or indeed Silver Destination or even Miss Primrose over such fences. I couldn't help myself. Every time I told myself that we should stop now, that The Blank would be getting tired or bored, or both, I would press on to jump just one more fence. I think part of me was terrified that we'd never get to do it again, that I might never find the courage within myself again, or that it might be another ten years before I did. I wasn't taking any chances. I was making the most of it. I would probably have continued until darkness fell (or Scotty returned and started shouting at me again, whichever happened first), if it hadn't been for The Blank. For we had just completed another pass of the spread jump I had constructed and were about to make a sharp turn to jump the wall I'd thrown together out of straw bales when suddenly The Blank veered round and trotted over to the hedge which formed the boundary between our property and the lane. He didn't however, it seemed, intend to jump it. When he reached it, he merely poked his head over the top and whinnied as if calling to someone.

'So this is where you are,' I heard a familiar American accent calling up to me from the lane. I squinted over the hedge and could just make out Jimmy's mop of black curls, the pale of his upturned face in the lane below.

'You found us.' I tried hard to keep the pleasure at seeing him again out of my voice. I guessed it wouldn't do to be so obvious.

'Yeah. Eventually... I thought you said you turned left at the end of my drive to get here? You have to turn right to find the place. It took me ages to track you down.'

'Oh. I guess I meant the other left,' I shrugged apologetically. I'm torn between shame at my own ineptitude with directions and utter delight that he's obviously tried so hard to find me again. 'Sorry. I told you I was no good with directions.'

'It's a good job I'm not easily offended. A guy might think you didn't want to be found.'

'Oh no! No, no, no! Not at all. No.' I stop suddenly, realising (a little too late) how pathetically eager I sound. (Did I mention I was rubbish with people?) I fall into silence, cursing myself inwardly, but Jimmy seems, if anything, quite pleased by my fervour. By this time, I've moved The Blank to stand lengthways

169

along the hedge so that I can look at Jimmy using my peripheral vision. It's still not really any good but I distinctly mark his lips stretch into the broad curve of a smile. Encouraged, I add, 'Would you like to come in?'

'Sure. Let's see you ride this horse without falling off.'

'Oh, we're just finishing off here anyway.'

'But I'd like to see you ride him a little bit,' he protests. 'The question is, how do I get to be on the other side of the hedge with you there?'

I pretend to consider the question carefully. 'Well,' I begin slowly. 'If you had a horse, or really long legs, you could jump over.'

'And if a guy had neither of those things?'

'You could walk along the hedge to the corner and come down the drive.'

'Right. See you in a minute.'

I sit for a moment on The Blank's back, feeling ridiculously pleased that Jimmy has called around to see us. I have a foolish grin plastered all over my face and no matter how I try, I can't make it go away. I run my hand over the arching muscle in The Blank's neck and pat him lavishly.

'You see that? He came. He actually came to see us. Just for us. To see us again.' I felt so happy, I could have burst with it. Instead I aimed The Blank at a couple of the fences and at the pinnacle of The Blank's jump I put my hand in the air to drag my fingers through it; just as I used to do in the old days when I'd won a big competition. Then we trotted over to the gate of the paddock to go and meet Jimmy. Too late, I realise, he's already there.

'I don't know how you do that,' he says. 'It looks... *awesome*... And you can't even see. How do you do that when you're blind?'

'I'm not totally blind. I can see a bit. You know, red blur, blue blur, blur of straw bales...' I gesture at the fences I have constructed. 'But, you know, The Blank is an amazing horse. I trust him a lot, and he trusts me too, I suppose, and that helps. I

170

know I fell off him when he jumped into your garden, but he really is an exceptional horse. I mean... Let me show you...'

I urge The Blank into a steady trot around the perimeter of our small paddock. When he's going along quite nicely, I drop the reins and put my hands out to the side. 'You see, he's got such an even pace, I don't really have to do anything to ride him.' I urge him into a canter and kick my feet free of the stirrups. One by one I pick up the stirrup leathers and cross them over his withers. This achieved, I swing my legs up behind me and cross them. Finally I pull myself up into a kneeling position in the saddle and place my hands on my head. The Blank continues to canter around quite steadily, quite contented in his new role as performer of circus horse tricks.

'You see? He's so even in his paces and I trust him so much, I don't need arms or even legs to ride him. So you see, a little thing like being almost blind, when you ride a horse like The Blank, well, it's hardly a disability at all.'

I let my arms and legs fall back into position, turn The Blank back to the gate and dismount. 'Want to have a go? You don't even need to be able to ride. He'll look after you.'

'Noo-ooo. No way. I told you I was afraid of horses. Anyway, I can't do that. I don't wanna do that. And you say anyone can do it. I think you're doing yourself an injustice. You can do it because you're obviously a great rider, and, like you say, The Blank trusts you. You can do it because you're *you*. I couldn't even think about doing it. I'm not even gonna try.'

I open the gate and start to lead The Blank back to his stable. I'm overflowing with the praise Jimmy has bestowed upon me. For the first time in my life, I feel really good about myself. Everything about him, I tell myself; even the way he says my name, makes me like myself. It's as if his approval makes me see myself in a new and somehow better light. I am allowed to like myself, simply because he does.

'I over-exercised him a little. I got a bit carried away.' I untack The Blank and start to brush the sweat out of his coat with long sweeps of his dandy brush. The Blank takes regular pulls from his hay net, his back turned towards Jimmy. He is totally relaxed. It clearly hasn't bothered him at all that Jimmy has followed us into his stable. As for me, all I can feel are Jimmy's eyes upon me. I feel as if I'm burning up inside with nervous excitement. Totally relaxed is the one thing I'm not.

'You know when you were over at my house... Just before you're brother called around for you... Well, I could get carried away myself here with you.' He reaches out and runs his finger almost tentatively over my hair.

'I...' I know what he means. I can feel my lips parting invitingly. In other parts, surprising things are happening to me. Inner thighs are turning to water, breasts swelling in anticipation of his touch upon me. In short, I have reached page eighty-seven in my life at last. Or perhaps, more like page twenty-three or the end of chapter one where the heroine realises that she has feelings for the hero in those romantic novels I was telling you about earlier; because there's no way I'm undertaking any of the actions detailed in pages eighty-seven to ninety-three of such books in a stable. It reminds me too much of Keith Denby; and what he tried to do to me in a stable once upon a time, and what happened after. This, however, leaves me with a problem. I don't want to offend Jimmy, or deter him at all; but at the same time I'm not committing myself to anything here with The Blank watching us.

I attempt diversionary tactics. In this instance, I find the barrier of a horse especially when utilised against someone who obviously isn't that keen on horses, is a particularly useful asset. I move around to brush The Blank's other side.

'You know, today's the first time I've even attempted to jump any fence at all in a very long time; not counting accidental jumps, of course...'

Jimmy nods seriously. 'Don't fancy me, huh?'

'No! I mean, yes... I mean, no... Oh God. It's not that. I do, I mean... Oh God, I'm making a mess out of this. If I'm truthful, I've spent the last few days hoping you'd call around. I spent such a long time trying to describe to you where I lived in the hope that you would do,' I shrug apologetically. 'But I'm so stupid with directions I told you the wrong way anyway. And Scotty...' (I'm talking to... Well, haranguing myself now really). 'Scotty just keeps shouting at me and going on about you being "Mad Jimmy" and how you beat up on your wife and kid and what a f... Well, you saw what he's like. But somehow what he was saying about you just didn't add up... I mean it didn't sound like *you*... Not that I know you... But it didn't sound like the person who took care of us... The Blank and I; and so every time Scotty stepped out I'd flip Scuzz channel on just to see if I could hear what your band's like and what you were like in it. And, now, here you are, and I look like shit and smell of horses, and I've probably got hay in my hair.' I lay my head on The Blank's withers and feel his reassuring warmth. I feel exhausted. I also feel like crying. 'And now I bet you really think I'm a total idiot. I shouldn't have said any of those things, should I? Especially not to you.' (*Did I mention I was rubbish with people?*)

I jump suddenly, momentarily startled as I realise that Jimmy has conquered his apparent distrust of The Blank and followed me around to stand on the same side as me. He puts his hand up to my face and runs his fingers through my hair. I have to fight an impulse to rub my head against his caress, like a cat.

'I'm so glad you did, honey. And I don't think you look like shit at all. But there is some hay in your hair.'

I smile. 'There always is. I don't want to do this here.'

'Okay.'

And, simple as that, he backs away and retreats to the other side of the stable to lounge against the wall.

'So why don't you tell me about the last time you jumped a fence instead? I mean, not today, or when you jumped over my wall, but the last time you jumped, a very long time ago.'

And so I do. I tell him everything about the last time I jumped; and all about Herbert Sherbet and how promising it had all been and how it had all crumbled away like ashes. Then when I'd finished telling him all about that he came into my grandmother's fusty old house and had what I call "tea" and he called "supper"; and then Scotty came home slightly worse for wear after a long session in the pub with some of the wasters he hangs around with sometimes, and Jimmy had to go then, because Scotty was still mad about it all and inclined to take it out on Jimmy. It was hardly romantic, but by the time he'd left he'd exacted a promise from me to return to his house the following evening so that he could cook what he called "supper" and which I could only presume would be my tea in return.

I couldn't sleep for thinking about it. My mind, my whole body was alive with fantasies of what would happen when I arrived there. I couldn't settle to anything all through the following day. That *something* would happen, I was certain. My whole body ached for him. Transparent as I had proved myself to be in revealing my feelings about him, how could he fail to notice it? And after such a build up, how could I fail to be anything but disappointed? I don't even know what it was that I was tense with the expectation of when I arrived on his doorstep to ring the doorbell. I mean, it's not as if I imagined he'd pull open the door and ravage me right there and then on the threshold. I would have been horrified if he had attempted it. The problem was, I didn't know how one even approached the run up to such things. It was an obstacle I'd never tackled before. Did one approach slowly but with plenty of forward-going impulsion as when advancing towards the high fences, or as fast as possible with plenty of outgoing-expansion in your stride, as with the wide spread or the water jump? Either approaches seemed formidable and somehow not quite right either. But I didn't know anything about how one deals with people; I only knew about horses. Still, there I was, standing upon the doorstep, pushing the buzzer to the door with trembling fingers, half-elated, half-terrified by what it was that (I imagined) I was about to do.

'Hey, come in,' Jimmy opened the door immediately as if he had been standing behind it, waiting for me to arrive, which was, I had to admit, somewhat reassuring. But then he followed this up with: 'Hey, how come you got past the security gate?' In actual fact, I'd done what Scotty had done in order to gain access to the house. He'd climbed through the gate in the next field and then crawled through the woods at the edge of Jimmy's property which brought you right out in front of his house. Scotty had told me about it, although he sure as hell hadn't wanted me to come back here again; and I wasn't sure whether Jimmy would want to hear about the fact that his security could so easily be breached, particularly as that high electronic gate at the end of his drive looked like it might have been expensive.

'Never mind that now.' Jimmy puts his hand on my arm and pulls me inside the door, and I think, *oh God, this is it. This is what people do. This is how it will all begin*; and I suppose I look confused and frightened. Certainly I look towards where his hand is covering my wrist and I feel as if it is not the hand of a man at all, but the hand of a creature totally alien to me. I'm guessing it shows because he immediately drops his hand from my arm, leaving me, contrary creature that I so obviously am, feeling bereft. Still, he's all het up about something, I can feel that. Just as he can probably feel that I'm in a similar condition. He looks down at the hand he's just removed from my wrist and laughs a little, almost as if he's suddenly as nervous as I am. 'Never mind that now,' he repeats a little softer this time, as if he's not talking about the security gate at all, but something entirely different. 'I've had an idea.' He gestures for me to follow him. I follow the movements of his body through the dimness of my vision and feel, rather than actually see the reservation in his movements, as if he's holding something back; as if he's deliberately holding himself at a distance from me. He leads me into the room where I'd found him drumming just after I woke up after that really long, concussion-induced sleep. I can see the glint of the shiny metalwork around his drums and the duller brass shimmer of the cymbals even in the subdued evening light. In my imagination, I can see him as he was in those first moments. The blurry mass of frantically waving arms, the mop of curls whirling around his head. In those moments, for probably the first time in my life, I had felt I wasn't disadvantaged in my lack of vision. I didn't need to see. I could feel the energy emanating out of him. He flicks the light on behind me.

'This is my studio. You know, where I practice... And stuff...'

I nod.

'I remember the room. And you drumming. The sound was amazing. It led me right to you through this house; even though I didn't know where you were. And then when I got in here, even though I couldn't see you in the light, I could feel you and the energy of you through your music. It was... well... amazing.'

Jimmy nods. I can feel he's pleased and I realise all in a rush that this is what I like the most about him, that I can feel his emotions so clearly. He's as transparent as I have proved myself to be. But then his pleasure suddenly seems to subside.

'Hey, hang on... You could hear the noise outside the room?'

I nod enthusiastically, unaware that I'm giving the wrong answer. 'Yes, the sound led me right to you.'

'Those Goddamn piece of crap builders. They haven't done anything right. They were supposed to heat the pool, it's out there covered in ice. They were supposed to soundproof this room, and you say you could hear me from the guest room.'

I nod again, sheepishly this time.

'Was it loud?'

'Quite loud. Very loud. But I liked it. Sorry.'

'It's not your fault. Those bastards. I hope I never see them again. I'll bust their asses for them.'

'You sound like Scotty now.'

'Sorry. Anyway, that's not why I brought you in here. I had an idea. You could jump again. I mean, professionally, like you used to.'

'I was never a professional,' I shake my head, interrupting him. 'I never reached that status.'

He waves my protestations aside. 'Well, whatever. You could do it again. And win prizes, like you used to. But on The Blank.'

'That's exactly what I've been thinking about.' My enthusiasm for this, my favourite daydream, takes over. 'That's exactly why I had those fences up in the paddock and why I was putting The Blank at them. He's got the most breathtaking jump. He just jumps and jumps. He doesn't put a foot wrong. He does this little hitch with his back feet over the high fences so he doesn't catch the poles. He's as good at jumping as you are at drumming. And all this time I never knew. I reckon I could see a course enough to get around, if the jumps were big and bright enough...' (I'm off in a world of my own now, thinking through all the arguments I've played out in my head, by now a thousand times, in those few days since The Blank first jumped over Jimmy's wall). 'But I can't do any of the shows around here because everyone probably knows I should be registered blind and I'd just get eliminated before we even jumped the first fence. And I can't ask Scotty to drive us anywhere... Not yet, anyway. If we won a couple of things first, he might be more open to persuasion... But he thinks it's madness even owning The Blank, never mind competing with him.'

'Ah, well, like I said, I had an idea to throw the odds in your favour.' Jimmy opens his hand significantly before me. Of course, I can't see what he's trying to show me. I can't make out what it is even if I squint at it out of the periphery of my sight, where my vision is better. I give up.

'What is it?'

'It's an earpiece. You put it in your ear and then someone else... A third party, say, could speak into a walkie-talkie and convey instructions to you. That way if the course was difficult or the fences hard to see, someone... Me for instance, or Scotty, if he could be persuaded, could talk you around the course... Well... It would give you an edge. It's not really cheating. I mean, you are... I don't wanna offend you here, but you're the one who's handicapped. All those other riders can see.'

177

I'm silent for a moment, thinking it over. I could probably do it. I could probably see those fences and get around a course. But he's right. It would give me an edge in a competition, especially with those sneaky little rustic fences which look so simple but which are so easy to knock down and so hard to see if your vision is like mine. (You see, even after all this time, even after nearly a decade of despair, I still wanted to win.) More importantly, however, that tiny piece of additional equipment might convince Scotty to help me out with my plan. There was a show on at Abbey Hall over the following weekend. It was only a local thing but it was a qualifier for the summer county show; which, in turn, was a qualifier for a national show. Also, even if we didn't win, and I must admit I doubted we would after so long off the circuit, it would be the opportunity to start accumulating points if we got into the placings; and points meant rising up the ranks of the BSJA top-rated riders, and the higher up the ranks you were, the more eligible you were to jump in higher-class, more prestigious BSJA affiliated shows. This thing at Abbey Hall might only be a minor event, but it was worth the journey just for the couple of points we might pick up if we were lucky. We could do it, The Blank and I, I knew it. We could be great. We could wipe the floor with Keith Denby and his ilk. My heart filled with a species of vindictive triumph at the thought. (I know, I know. It's hardly an attractive sentiment to admit to, but after all we had suffered at the hands of Keith Denby, The Blank and I, and after all the times I'd been made to feel second-rate by the Sebastian Carling-Brooks's, the Miranda Camberwell's, the bloody Braithwaites, can you blame me for such vengeful reasoning? Yes, it was low. Yes, it was nasty and malicious; but justifiable surely? Anyway, I told you I had a great capacity for hate. It hadn't just gone away with my eyesight, you know.)

'It goes in your ear?' I am already reaching out my hand to take it from his; but it's too small for me to see accurately. Jimmy grasps my groping hand.

'Here. Let me.' I feel his breath on my face as he leans closer towards me to fit the earpiece into place. His hands pull back my hair. I'd forgotten about it in the midst of all my spiteful scheming, but I'm suddenly very aware of my body again; and the warmth emanating from his too. The earpiece fits neatly into my ear. It tickles as he fixes it into place. This new awareness makes me question if he has seen the passage of my thoughts across my face. I feel suddenly ashamed and pull back a little from him. I don't want him to see that aspect of me.

'What is it?' he asks. 'Is it against the rules?'

'I don't know. Probably. But then so is not being able to see the course. In for a penny, in for a pound, hey?'

'Huh? Oh, yeah, I guess.'

'Do *you* think it's cheating? What would you do? Would you use it?'

'Hell, yes. Hey, honey, I'm the one telling you to use it and not to feel bad about it. I don't think it's cheating at all.'

I accept his approbation eagerly and file it away in my brain underneath the heading of "Justifications for breaking British Show Jumping Association/British Eventing rules."

'So, how does it work?' I ask.

'Right. Well, you stay here and I'll go into the other room and talk to you. You should be able to hear me through the earpiece quite clearly.'

'And I can talk back to you?'

Jimmy shakes his head. 'No. It's a receiver only. You're not supposed to talk back. It's only really used for issuing stage directions, etc. We used them when we made some of our videos to go with our songs.'

'Oh. Can you see it?' I turn my head to the side.

'Only if you knew it was there to look for it. It's pretty small. Plus, it'll be hidden by your hair and your hat, or whatever it is that you wear.'

I nod.

'Just stay right here, honey. I'll go and say something from the other room, just to see if it works or not. Give me a minute.'

Whilst I am waiting for Jimmy's voice to magically materialise in my inner ear, I wander around the large predominately empty room. It is empty, apart from the drum kit, of course, which I squint at narrowly as best I can. I can't really see it any better and I bump my leg against the corner of some unidentifiable piece of equipment as I am travelling around the room, so I stop moving about and just stand in the centre of the room, the drum kit directly in front of me, before I injure myself against anything else I can't see.

'Hey, can you hear me?' Jimmy's beautiful voice floods into my ear. It's unnerving. It's like he's standing next to me addressing me, but, of course, he's not there. There is only the slightest crackle of the walkie-talkie he's using which reveals the fact that he's speaking to me remotely. This is how it would be if ever I lost my sight completely; hearing people but not being able to see them. I should, I supposed, be grateful I could at least see the blurred outline of Jimmy, if nothing more.

'Okay,' he continues to speak to my inner ear. 'I'm going to say these things whilst I can't see you because you just look so afraid of me every time I try and touch you.'

'I'm afraid of everyone,' I say to the empty room, forgetting that although I can hear him, he, of course, cannot hear me. My voice echoes eerily around Jimmy's vacant studio.

'And because I can't bear to see your face if you don't want me as much as I want you. Because I do want you. From the first moment I saw you. And believe me, sugar, I haven't felt like this in a very, very, very long time.'

When he calls me "sugar" again, something curls up inside of me and makes my whole body ache with need for him. It is focussing my entire attention upon this, I suppose, which distracts me from the fact that suddenly I'm hearing Jimmy's voice in stereo.

'I've never felt like this before, ever,' I tell the drum kit. 'But, God, I know how you feel. I'm dying with longing for you.

180

But,' I continue to confide to the kit, 'I don't know anything about this sort of stuff. I don't even know where in your house you are.'

'I'm right here, sugar.' Suddenly he is standing over me and I don't know who reaches for who first but we are kissing and it's deliciously familiar and somehow *right*, and then he has scooped me into his arms and he's carrying me back to his guest bedroom again, much as he must have done that first night when The Blank jumped over his wall and I fell and knocked myself out. I feel him kick the door open and then he is laying me down upon the bed, laying down beside me and all the time kissing and kissing me; on my mouth, on my neck, on my breasts and peeling layers of clothes from me as he does so, and I suppose I'm doing the same because somehow we're both naked. It is like the first time I saw him as a blurry shape beating at his drum kit. He is just a mass of energy. I can't really see him at all when he is so close to the blind spots in my vision. It continually surprises me where he touches me. When he covers my nipple with his mouth and draws it slowly inside, scraping it against his teeth as he does so, I arch against him in delighted surprise. When he drags his hand over the notches of my ribcage, over my hips and pushes his fingers inside of me, I feel a sensation as of a thousand cords being dragged up through my gut. I could die with pleasure. But then, he tries to force himself inside of me and I just know, it's never going to work. I'm hot and tight and dry; too small, and the burning pain makes me begin to panic. Suddenly he could be anyone. He could be Keith Denby trying to inflict himself upon me in a stable. The weight of him is crushing me. I would push him away but I am powerless to move. The panic rises like a silent scream inside of me.

'Are you alright, Em? I'm not hurting you, am I?' The sound of his voice brings me back to myself. The panic begins to subside. His hands stroke the fear away from my body and reassures me, just as I might soothe The Blank, by running my hands over him. 'I'm sorry, honey, I'm sorry,' he continues to mumble into my hair. I feel myself yielding, warm and fluid, my body melds and adapts to the shape of his own. He pushes himself deeper inside of me, and I don't mind. I let myself float, ride the wave of it. If I think about it too much, I'll drown.

Jimmy makes a sound as if it's me who is hurting him now and collapses against me.

'Oh God. I'm sorry. I wanted it to be longer than that, I really did. Oh God; it felt so nice and it's been so long. But I wanted it to be nice for you too, especially as it was your first time...'

'Oh...' I don't know what to say. 'I had no idea it would... be so... obvious...'

'You've bled, Em... There's blood on the...' Jimmy gestures towards the cover of the bed. There's a reddish brown stain streaked across the coverlet that even I can see. It stares out at me from the snowy surface of the bed like an accusation against my own inadequacies as a woman. I was always too busy with the horses, chasing hopelessly after a dream that I would never achieve to do what other women my age were doing. I have failed in so many ways, not just failing to achieve my dream, or failing to pin my mother down and relate to her in any meaningful way, or even failing my GCSEs, or failing to fail my Eleven Plus examination, or failing to be a Brownie; I have failed at my entire life.

'I thought all those years of horse-riding...' I mutter, ashamed. 'Sorry. I didn't mean to mislead you.'

'Hey, you didn't mislead me at all, baby...' Jimmy mumbles into the skin of my neck. 'I could see you were afraid. It didn't take a genius to work out why.'

'Oh.'

Jimmy curls around me and hooks a hand possessively over my left breast. 'You don't have to be afraid anymore, honey,' he continues sleepily into my hair.

'Oh.'

He doesn't specify what it is that I don't have to be afraid of. Clearly if it's just the physical act of intercourse, then it's a little late for that. It doesn't really matter. It sounds reassuring anyway, whatever it is that he's referring to. He nuzzles against my ear, which suddenly reminds me that the earpiece he fitted earlier is still in situ. I put my hand up to my ear and Jimmy sucks my finger into his mouth. Those warm, aching, wanting, sensations begin to draw up in my stomach again.

'I've still got the thing in my ear,' I say.

'Hmm?'

'The earpiece... It's still in my ear.'

'Uh-huh, really?' He releases my finger and puts his hand up to my ear to remove it.

'It just shows really, doesn't it?' I say. 'If it stays in place all through... Well... *That*... It'll be okay while I'm jumping. It won't fall out or anything like that in the middle of a round.'

'No, it won't fall out. It's supposed to be pretty secure. Pete... Y'know... Our singer, used to wear one when we were filming some of the videos which went with our songs and he jumped around all over the place in them. They always stayed put.'

'Oh, that's good,' I say. I think he sounds a little sad when he mentions his friend and I wonder if perhaps he misses what he used to do in the same way I missed jumping in those dead empty years when I was doing nothing except drink and stay in bed. But then he hasn't been away from it for a whole decade like I was, has he? And he's already told me that his friends from his band have said that he can go back whenever he's ready and whenever he wants. At the back of this thought, I wonder what will happen to the "us" that we seem to have become if he does return to his own world. I don't like the thought. It leaves me feeling cold. I put it out of my mind. Jimmy runs his hand over my rib cage.

'I'm gonna feed you up. You feel way too thin.'

'It takes a lot of energy keeping and riding horses. It's a lot of work. No matter how much I eat I never seem to keep it on. I've been six-and-a-half stone ever since I was fifteen years' old.' I don't tell him about all of those missed meals whilst I was a child. All those punishments which my grandmother inflicted upon Scotty and I for wrongs either real or imaginary; the meals we were not permitted to eat and the ones we were which were barely edible.

The out of date mould-covered filth that she told us was all we deserved. It was no wonder we grew up so stunted and undernourished, the both of us. Scotty was as thin as a snake, as well as I, and he'd never ridden a horse in his life. We spent the better part of our childhoods starving, desperate for nutritious food. No amount of food I consumed in my adulthood ever seemed to be able to compensate for this.

'Six-and-a-half stone? Hmm... That's about ninety pounds. You're pretty light. But I knew that anyway. I bet I can feed you up a little. Hey, I didn't make your supper yet.'

'It's okay.' His hand's still idling over my breast and, to be honest, food is the last thing I'm thinking about.

'Maybe we'll eat in a little while...' and he pulls me towards him once again.

The next day, I show Scotty the earpiece and explain its use. Then I quite calmly tell him of my intention to enter the Abbey Hall show.

'Well you can fucking drive yourself there because I'm not being any part of this insane scheme,' is his (somewhat predictable) response.

'It's okay,' I tell him serenely. 'Jimmy says he'll drive us.' Now, this, for the record, is a lie. Jimmy never even mentioned the possibility of his driving us. I didn't even know if he had a UK driving licence or if he could even drive. He certainly hadn't volunteered his services. However, it was a lie whose purpose was twofold: firstly, I knew Scotty would never let Jimmy anywhere near his beloved horse box. He'd stripped it down and rebuilt it and reincarnated it so many times, it was practically his baby. Secondly, if Scotty knew Jimmy was coming too, then I knew he'd want to come along. It hadn't been as bad as I'd expected when I'd first told Scotty that I was visiting Jimmy at his house again, but Scotty still didn't trust him. The lie worked beautifully.

'Fuck that,' was Scotty's response. 'I'm not letting any damn Yank drive my truck, least of all him. He doesn't look as if he knows his arse from his elbow.'

'Since when has it been your truck? It was Dad's truck. It's *our* truck.'

'Well you can't drive it, can you? And it certainly wasn't you who fixed it. No,' Scotty nods as if it's all his own idea. '*I'll* do the driving.'

And thus it was that we arrived at the end of Jimmy's drive and Scotty leaned on the antiquated horn of the horsebox to let Jimmy know we were there.

'God, Scotty, shouldn't we go ring the gate buzzer or something? That horn sounds terrible. It's like something out of a 1950s film. And it's barely half-past-eight. You'll wake the whole village up.'

Scotty's only response was to lean on the horn even harder.

'Who cares? And I'm not getting out and ringing any buzzer. You can if you want. Anyway, if he wants to come with us so fucking much, he'll have to get up early.'

Scotty probably would have continued in this tirade for a considerable amount of time longer if Jimmy hadn't at that moment arrived and hauled open the passenger side door to the horsebox. I shunted up a little, he squeezed in beside me and we set off for Abbey Hall.

Our show jumping careers, The Blank's and mine, had begun again.

Abbey Hall was probably about forty miles away; far enough I hoped for me not to be recognised by anyone who might happen to know that I was, for all intents and purposes, blind. It took us two hours to drive there taking into account the slow speed of our ancient transport and a short detour when we lost our way in the maze of lanes surrounding Abbey Hall. Even so, I enjoyed the journey. Jimmy's hip pressed pleasantly into mine and for the latter part of the journey, he held my hand; a fact which Scotty noted with a disgusted: 'Oh, for God's sake.' Still, Jimmy's presence and his touch upon me helped to calm my nerves, if only a little bit. For, I had started to feel that awful sickness of fear creeping over me as we got closer and closer to the showground, and matters were only going to get worse; I knew that.

Even allowing for our lengthy travelling time, we had arrived too early by far. By the time we'd parked up in the competitors' area and I'd unloaded The Blank and tethered him to the side of the horsebox, it was still only half-past-eleven; and I wasn't due to ride until twenty-past-four. I couldn't eat lunch; the thought of it made me want to heave. We wandered around the showground watching snatches of the events in the various rings: the leading rein gymkhana with the toddlers seated on fat recalcitrant ponies being hauled around by bossy-looking mothers, the ridden Arab class with the chestnut and grey ponies cantering around their arena with nostrils flaring and tails held high in the air as if newly arrived from the desert and looking exotically out of place in this lush and leafy English country village. We checked out the jumping arena. Our class, the advanced adult show jumping class was the final one of the day. When we checked in for a brief look at the layout, they were still doing the novice show jumping class there, and it was impossible to tell how difficult the advanced course would be. Still the fences looked bold and bright, and I could see them in a blur of colours which I took to be an encouraging sign. Time passed. Scotty went to sleep in the horsebox and I was no company at all. I supposed Jimmy must have been bored. By this stage, I was a wreck of nerves, chewing at my fingernails, gnawing at my bottom lip. Jimmy was too kind to show it though. Every so often he would squeeze my hand encouragingly and say, 'you'll be fine, honey,' and then he would laugh and say, 'you remind me of Si just before a show.' At three p.m. we went inside the horsebox and fitted the earpiece. Scotty had identified a spot by a large oak tree where he could stand and watch the event and surreptitiously guide me around the course through the walkie-talkie, should I seem to need his guidance. We had agreed he would let me get on with it unless I seemed to be floundering. Somehow it seemed less like cheating that way. Then it was time to tack up The Blank, put on my show jacket and fix my competitor number, given to me earlier by the show secretary, to the back of my jacket. I was number 463. Scotty stayed with The Blank whilst I walked the course with Jimmy guiding me just in case I should walk into a fence or fall into a ditch or do anything else stupid which might give the true nature of the state of my eyesight away. As we walked away from Scotty towards the ring, I heard Scotty's voice flooding through the earpiece, evidently addressing The Blank:

'You'd better look after her out there. I don't know why I went along with this crazy plan, but you put a foot wrong and you're *glue*, you understand me?'

I heard The Blank grunt in response. He was as comfortable with Scotty as he was with me by now and so probably knew Scotty didn't mean his words, but I guess it meant that Scotty was worried about me; which was nice, I suppose. Jimmy kept pace with me as we entered the roped off section of field which was being used as the show jumping arena. I was feeling truly ill by this stage and matters were not helped by the fact that I completely missed the first fence, a small brown rustic jump.

'Em, there's one here,' Jimmy grabbed my arm as I was about to walk straight past it. 'Can you see it?' he muttered into my ear, taking care that the other competitors who were milling around us should not hear. 'It's a little brown fence. Can you see it?'

I shook my head, a sense of panic threatening to overwhelm me. What had I been thinking? This was going to be a disaster. I couldn't even see the first fence.

'Well, look, let's go back to the start,' Jimmy said, taking hold of my arm and leading us to retrace our steps. 'And it's one... two... three... four... five... six... of my strides in. It's not quite by the rope. It's out a little, more into the middle of the arena.'

'Between X and E then?'

'What?'

'Imaginary points in an arena used for riding. There are letters around the arena to be used as points of reference. "All King

187

Edward's Horses Carried Many Big Fools"; A, K, E, H, C, M and F.' I point out the location of where each of the letters would be in the arena as I recite them. 'And X in the middle. Never mind, it's not really important. Thank you. I think I can get where it is now.'

The second fence, an upright built out of bright red and white traditional show jumping poles I can see. I can also see it's a hard one too. From the number one fence we're going to have to swing around, first veering left to give ourselves enough run up and then sharp right at the perimeter of the ring to get a clear approach to the jump. Following this was a triple combination along the length of the far side of the arena. Again it was bold and bright and I could see all three elements of it; but when it came to jumping it, I'd have to decide whether to take a risk, opt for speed and cut the corner in the approach to it, or go deep into the corner of the ring and give The Blank a proper run up to it. I decided to go for the latter approach in the first instance and only adopt the former if it came to a jump off (if I even made it that far). The first part of the triple combination was of average height, the second after two or three strides was larger and the final element after three strides more was enormous. I ran my hand over the topmost pole and felt my breath catch in my throat. After the combination, the course followed the natural corner of the ring to a small wall. Again, being as this had been built out of blocks of grey, it was difficult for me to see. This, coupled with the fact that I knew from experience how flimsy these walls were intended to be, how easy to demolish, it made me feel very nervous of it indeed. After the wall, again the natural line of the arena was followed to a parallel bar jump. Both high and wide, we'd need plenty of speed to clear it. This was followed rapidly by a tall upright fence in blue and yellow poles. I could see it easily enough but I knew I'd have to get right into the corner of the arena before we made the turn towards the fence in order to achieve the right angle of approach. Finally, fence number nine was a high ascending oxer about two strides after the upright fence. After that, all that would remain for us to do would be to hot foot it out of the ring and hoped we'd jumped the course within the permitted time without incurring any time penalties, and, more critically, anyone realising I was blind. I did my best not to grope at the jumps or do anything else which would reveal my impairment to the judges or other competitors, but I simply had to feel some of the fences: the ascending oxer for instance, just to check the angle of it, and the parallel bars to get an idea of its width. Jimmy continued to talk me around them too. Just his being there was reassuring to me, although his presence was undoubtedly drawing attention to us, which was the last thing we wanted. As Scotty pointed out later, however, a diminutive punk rocker with tattoos running up and down his arms is always going to attract attention at an equestrian country show. Still, as he said, at least if folk were looking at him, they weren't looking at me, and I couldn't bring myself to feel sorry that Jimmy was there, no matter how much he drew their stares. After I had gleaned all I could from the walk of the course, I returned to mount The Blank and headed for the warm-up area and practice fence.

In previous years, as soon as I had mounted my horse and entered the warm-up arena and had completed a couple of passes over the practice fence, my nerves would have subsided entirely and I would have been ready for anything. Not so this time. I circled that warm-up arena at a walk, a trot and a canter but I didn't dare approach the practice fence.

'Oh God,' I was muttering to myself.

'OhGodOhGodOhGodwhathaveIdonewhathaveIdone?   I can't do this. I've lost my nerve.' My thoughts ran together almost incoherently with panic. I cantered around the perimeter of the practice arena again and did not dare approach the fence. One of the other competitors swam up to me out of the blur and called to me, 'Aren't you going to try the jump?' before they were gone again. I think the question was meant kindly, but it just threw me into even more of a panic. Now the other competitors had noticed that I was acting strangely and would be watching me to see what I would do. *OhGodOhGod.*

'Competitor 463!' A female voice trilled over the tannoy and I realised with even more of a sinking feeling that it was too late. With a lurch of my stomach I understood that the first fence we were actually going to be jumping that day would be in our round proper, over a fence I couldn't even see. *OHGOD*. I felt sick. Scotty's voice swam up to me out of my impending hysteria.

'Okay. Pass behind the jump and follow the line of the rope to the entrance to the arena.' This, I have to be honest, was not a great deal of help. I couldn't even see the rope, but I completed another half-circuit of the warm-up area until Scotty's voice appeared again, 'You're at the entrance now. Okay, do a circle. Just a little one... Jesus Christ, Em, pull back a bit, you nearly ran straight into the rustic.'

Now I really am panicking. I can't see the first rustic fence at all. I'm going to be eliminated before I've even put The Blank at anything, or worse, I'm going to injure him through my own gross stupidity in entering this event in the first place. Why did I even think I could do this? I could weep with shame. I have no confidence and The Blank's feeling it. His pace falters. He's practically stumbling along. We have no impulsion whatsoever.

'Okay, keep going straight, Em, now. You're nearly there.'

My heart sinks. Half-heartedly, I put my leg to The Blank's side. He lurches into a faltering canter. He's not going to jump. He won't jump. I know it. Right at the last minute, The Blank half-halts before the first fence before doing an enormous cat leap over it. I am pitched forward in the saddle and scrape my chin against the coarse hair of his mane. Suddenly, we are flying. My nerves are gone. I was born to do this.

'Veer left, Em, LEFT!!! Other fucking left, you stupid bitch. Now! Turn! TURN! Right! Now!' I'm ignoring Scotty now. I can see the next fence. I ride The Blank deep into the corner and swing around. He clears it beautifully. Around to the triple combination. I misjudge the strides and he only puts in one when it should have been two between the first two elements of it. It doesn't matter. We clear them anyway. The wall which I couldn't really see so well looms up at me. I ask The Blank to jump it just a little too late. He struggles, but clears it somehow. I let him have his head and he gallops towards the parallel bars. We clear it easily, but then struggle to slow enough to make the turn for the next upright.

'Too fucking fast, Em. Slow down,' Scotty states the obvious in my ear. In the nick of time, we slow just enough to clear the upright. We are at the ascending oxer and I let The Blank do it his own way. We're home clear. We gallop out of the arena, no time faults incurred. I hear the woman over the tannoy trill, 'Competitor 463! Clear round!' and head back towards the warm-up arena. One of the other competitors, probably the woman who had asked me if I was going to try the practice fence, slows her horse to a trot and falls into step with us as we enter.

'Bit of an odd round, but I suppose it's going clear which counts.' Her tone's not so friendly now, and it's apparent from it that she doesn't approve of my style of riding at all. I guess she's realised that I'm a contender now. The Blank and I might actually beat her, despite the poor first impression we've given.

'Em,' I hear Scotty's voice call to me from the perimeter fence and draw The Blank up to a halt next to it. The other rider halts her horse too, as if interested to hear what Scotty will have to say about the matter.

'Fuck off,' is all he has to say to her about the matter. I hear her shocked intake of breath and 'Well, ra-h-ly,' in those horrible lah-di-dah Cheshire tones I loathe so much. I'm glad Scotty has offended her. When she has gone, I turn to Scotty and Jimmy.

'It wasn't a great round. Was it as bad as it felt? Oh my God, The Blank...' I suddenly notice a splash of colour on his snowy mane. 'Oh God, he's bleeding.'

'It's your blood, Em. Your chin's bleeding where you bumped it on his mane,' Jimmy says.

'Oh.' I put my fingers up to my chin and touch the sore spot.

'It looked fucking awful. I don't know how you even fucking got a fucking clear round in the fucking first place,' Scotty cuts in. I know he's nervous because he's swearing even more than ever. 'You'd better look lively too. The jump off will start any minute. Fuck knows what a disaster that's going to be. I can hardly bear to watch.'

'Well, it's not much use to me if you don't, is it?' I hiss at him, before the woman's voice rings over the tannoy once more.

'Competitors 427, 431, 452, 463, 470. You are required for the jump-off. Please attend in the warm-up arena and await the call of your number! Competitor 429, with the least number of faults after the clear rounds, you qualify for the sixth place rosette. All other competitors please clear the area.' Then, after a short pause, 'Competitor 427 for the jump off please! Competitor 427!'

The woman whom Scotty has just insulted departs the arena, and shortly after I hear the gratifying clatter of broken poles as her horse demolishes one of the fences.

'Four faults, competitor 427!'

'Scotty, quick, have a look. Have they changed the course at all?'

'No. Just the same. The wall's higher. It's the same, Em. You'll need some speed this time. You're going to have to fly around the course to get first.'

I begin to circle The Blank around the warm-up area again. I even complete the practice jump. I'm not afraid anymore. I know the course. When they call my number, I ride purposefully; my destiny... Our destiny is awaiting us.

This time, I count the strides in to the rustic and when we are upon it, I'm ready for it. We jump clean and clear.

'Okay,' Scotty's voice is in my ear again. 'Just cut the corners. Run straight and veer right straight away.' I do as he says and we're upon the upright immediately. The Blank clears it easily. I don't bother with the next corner either. I've realised that The Blank won't refuse whatever I put him at. He doesn't even need a run up. We complete the triple combination easily. I don't cut the

192

next corner because I can't see the wall too well and Scotty said it was higher. I stick to the line of the arena. The strategy pays off; we clear it without touching it. Again I let The Blank have his head and gallop at the parallel bars before swinging violently right towards the upright. It's a mistake. We don't have enough impulsion and The Blank touches the topmost pole. It rocks in its cradle for a moment and then clatters to the floor. Four faults. Shit. We clear the ascending oxer and gallop out of the arena.

'Competitor 463, four faults. Fastest time so far. Competitor 470 please!'

Scotty is waiting for me.

'Shouldn't have cut that last corner so much.'

'Well I know that now, don't I?' I'm annoyed with myself.

'Hey, everyone else knocked that fence down too, so if you got the fastest time, doesn't that mean you're winning?' Jimmy asks.

Scotty and I look at each other. I hardly dare to breathe.

'Competitor 470, four faults! Second fastest time!'

We both break out into enormous grins.

'You did it! You fucking did it!' Scotty ducks under the rope of the practice arena and throws his arms up around The Blank's neck; who throws his head up in surprise at Scotty's uncharacteristic gesture of affection. '*Fucking hell*! Who would have believed it?'

'Steady on, Scotty, everyone's looking at us. They'll guess something's up.' I hiss at him. I give what I hope is a winning smile in the general direction of the other competitors and the spectators leaning against the rope barrier of the ring and walk The Blank back into the jumping arena.

'Results of the advanced adult show jumping are as follows' the woman speaking through the tannoy announces officiously 'From the jump off, no clear rounds. Competitor with the least number of faults in the fastest time, and taking first place, competitor 463! In second place with the least number of faults and the second fastest time, competitor 470...' And so on, and so on. I ride The Blank down the centre line of the arena and join the line up of other competitors waiting for their prizes.

'Interesting-looking horse you've got there, my dear,' the elderly judge comments as he hands me the rosette and the twenty quid prize money. 'Poor confirmation. I would never have said it would have jumped so well.'

'His sire's Tar Barrel, his Dam's Cotton Queen. His pedigree is excellent,' I respond in my best upper class Cheshire accent.

'Ah. Ah really? Tar Barrel, hey?' The man's voice tells me he's never heard of either sire or dam. He's just another blustering fake. He's got no more right to stand here and judge The Blank than the woman serving tea in the refreshments tent would have. I hate him.

'Well. We'll see how he gets on in the county show. You knew this was a qualifier, didn't you? The course will be a lot tougher there.'

I have to bite my tongue. I wish I was Scotty. I long with every fibre of my being to tell him to fuck off. The man moves along the line dolling out praise and criticism to each of the other placed winners. I wonder if any of the others feel moved by a similar impulse to insult him. Somehow I doubt it. There's definitely something wrong with me, I am forced to acknowledge to myself; that I hate these people so very much. Then the tannoy crackles into life again.

'Round of applause please for our winners in this class today. Lap of honour, competitors, please!'

I've taken first prize. It's my role to lead the lap of honour. I'd much rather, I have to say, not have to do this. It would be much easier to let The Blank follow another horse than lead the way when I really can't see it. Just as the tannoy has crackled into life, so the piece in my ear does too.

'Fucking Hell, Em, try and avoid the fences. Careful. Move over!'

Too late, I realise I have ridden The Blank directly at the wall jump and before I know it, he's jumped over. His jump stirs an old memory into life and just as we reach the pinnacle of The Blank's leap, I put my hand into the air and feel the rush of air once again through my fingers. The organisers of the show are not impressed.

'Competitor 463, restrain yourself!'

I giggle with delight and canter The Blank out of the arena.

Scotty catches hold of the reins as I pull him up to a halt.

'Fucking hell, Em, you don't want to be doing things like that. People will start recognising you from before. There. Take a look at her. That posh bird who was talking to you before. She's looking at you all suspicious-like now.'

'It was an accident, alright? I couldn't see the wall. I forgot it was there.'

'Well, putting your hand in the air wasn't an accident, was it? I'm telling you, people'll start remembering you as the Emily Devlin of ten years ago and start asking questions about where you've been all this time.'

'Ten years is a long time. They won't remember who Emily Devlin was, and they won't care who she is now. It'll be alright. They'll think I was just showing off.'

'Well let's just go. I don't like the way that bitch is looking at you now.'

We get The Blank back inside the box in record time and get moving before anybody starts asking difficult questions. Once inside the cab of the horsebox again, I start to stuff the rosette into the pocket of my jacket casually.

'Hey, lemme look at that,' Jimmy says, taking it from my hand.

'This all you get? This ribbon? For winning?'

'I got twenty quid as well.' I hand the note to Scotty who shoves it carelessly into the front pocket of his jeans. 'Oh and I got some competition points too. They're worth the most really. Points make you eligible to enter bigger and better competitions which are worth more prize money if you win there too.'

'But you qualified for the county show. You can relax now. You don't have to do anymore.'

'Fuck that,' Scotty interrupts. 'We need the prize money if we're gonna keep running that hay burner.' He gestures impatiently with his head towards the back of the horsebox where The Blank is now safely ensconced. 'You need to win more shows.'

It becomes something of a routine on Saturday mornings. We'd load The Blank up into the horsebox and drive over to Jimmy's house, where Scotty would lean on the horn of the truck with scant regard for the shattered peace of the sleepy early morning village until Jimmy appeared to clamber up into the cab of the horsebox beside me. Wherever there was a show and wherever there was prize money to be had and points to be accumulated, we went. And we won. We won, and won, and won again. The Blank was the king of any show jumping arena he set foot in. As the summer wore on and the show season progressed, he just got better and better. For my own part, I found I could control the ever-present nerves a little more effectively, although I was always seized by a feeling of absolute terror just before we completed the first jump. And Scotty became more proficient at guiding me around the courses through Jimmy's earpiece with each successive competition. We took to recording his commentary on a dictaphone and analysing the progress of the round after the event. By listening to himself, he became more adept at describing the courses to me. I think he even swore less. We gained more competition points, The Blank and I, and slowly but surely, began to climb up through the ranks of the BSJA top rider list in the UK. By the time of the county show, I was ranked joint fifty-ninth. By the time of the national show, which of course, The Blank breezed through, I was forty-second.

Despite the fact that we were trying to be careful, and despite the fact that we were travelling further and further afield to avoid to being recognised, I began to notice some of the old familiar names from the circuit of ten years ago. Miranda Camberwell was still competing. We beat her a couple of times. And Sebastian Carling-Brooks; Scotty recognised him swaggering around one of the larger events we attended. We did our best to stay out of their way and hoped they hadn't noticed me sneaking up on them in the ranks of the BSJA top rider list.

But it was not just all about The Blank. Suddenly, and for the first time ever, my life was about more than horses. Suddenly, there was Jimmy; and the time I spent with him. Not so much the time spent at shows, or travelling between them together, although he always came along too, and it was nice that he was interested. But I couldn't concentrate on him then. I was always too petrified (before), or too elated (afterwards), to pay him the attention he deserved. Plus Scotty's presence and his perpetual foul-mouth hardly provided a romantic backdrop for any burgeoning relationship. No; it was the time we spent alone which counted. The long summer evenings spent on his sun terrace sharing confidences about our lives past and the nights spent twined together in his bed.

When I was with him, I felt safe. The merest brush of his callused fingers could soothe any fear away from me. I adored his energy; not just when he was playing his drums, but in everything else he did. When he walked, when he talked, he simmered with a pent up vital force. Even when he was just sitting beside me, it was impossible for him to just be still. His fingers were perpetually tapping out rhythms upon my wrist or the skin of my inner arm. He exuded life; and somehow just being near to him brought me back to it too. I was no longer the faded, shadowy creature subsisting on the margins of an existence I did not want. Not when I was with Jimmy. He made me feel good about myself. He made me feel it was okay to like myself, simply because he so clearly did.

When I was with him.

197

But when we were apart, it was a different story. Without his presence to reassure me, I would begin to doubt myself; and my own interpretation of the Jimmy I thought I knew. I could not, for instance, tally the Jimmy who would fidget restlessly beside me, playing with my hair, tickling me, making me laugh, with the Jimmy he himself had told me about, the one who could be utterly consumed by a despair which annihilated every crumb of life within him; the one who was only capable of staring blankly into space, lost in his own depression. This Jimmy sounded alarmingly like my mother and it made me wonder... Would, one day, when I least expected it, Jimmy too take a walk down the lane and take a flying leap from the blue bridge which spanned the river there? I couldn't bear it. I couldn't bear another such loss. But just knowing about this other Jimmy who I had not seen since that first meeting, when he had told me that story, tears soaking his face as he spoke, made me question, what else did I not know about Jimmy? Not so much about where he came from – I realised I would never fully understand his past. His upbringing, the life he had led... It was all just too far removed from my own experiences. From what he had told me of his former life, much of it seemed to have been spent living on a tour bus, driving from city to city, country to country, across entire continents even. He had told me there was no respite in this way of living. No peace to be gained from it – at least not for him. He had been perpetually pestered by newspapers, magazines, fans; hounded by a fame which once he had courted but later he had come to loathe. How he couldn't even bury his mother without it turning into a media circus. Well, what did I know about such things? Nothing. Oh, I listened to his stories. Some of them made me laugh out loud. Some of them made me ache for him. But they could have been any stories about anyone. If he was exaggerating, or not telling the truth, I would not have known it.

But there were things about his past which did worry me; things which I did long to clarify in my mind and understand. For instance, why did his ex-wife hate him so very much? To my mind, there was nothing whatsoever to dislike about Jimmy. So why did she loathe him? Why was she so hateful of him that she would not even let him see his own daughter? In other words, what did she know that I did not? He himself had admitted that his daughter was afraid of him. Now, why would that be? Scotty had once called him "some mad nutter who beat up his wife and kid"; but it couldn't be true... Could it?

Once, when we were lying in bed together, Jimmy had been stroking my hair, when suddenly he had tangled his hands roughly in it, pulling me fiercely towards him. It had hurt. I think I even cried out a little. He was immediately remorseful. He hadn't meant to hurt me, he had promised.

'But I was just thinking,' he had said, ' about the man you used to work for.'

'Keith Denby?'

Jimmy's hands had tightened in my hair again. I suppose I must have winced a little because he immediately relaxed his fingers.

'Don't even say his name in my house! God! When I think about him being the first to touch you. To try what he did... It just makes me so goddamn mad...'

Something about Jimmy's choice of words disturbed me a little. Was he angry because of what Keith had tried to do to me in that stable? Or because he'd come before Jimmy? Did Jimmy believe he owned me so completely that he could even erase my past?

To be fair, part of me wished that he could. But there was another portion of me which worried about this possessiveness; about the way in which it had been expressed. Was it possible, I sometimes asked myself, in those doubting moments when I was alone, that all of this good energy Jimmy carried within him would one day turn bad? That was another prospect I could not bear to face. There had been too much violence in my life already. Scotty and I had faced the promise of it every day of our childhoods. I just couldn't face living through all that again now.

Sometimes, when we were alone together, when Jimmy was not around, Scotty would see me doubting myself and worrying, and I knew that he was worried too. I knew that whatever he had read in the papers about "Mad Jimmy" Bridges would rear up in his thoughts again. But these uncertainties – they only ever occurred to me when Jimmy was not with me. I don't know about Scotty - if Jimmy's presence reassured him at all – but when Jimmy and I were together my worries would dissipate, as transient and intangible as dreams. Jimmy, my Jimmy, was happy and loving and careful of me; respectful of old wounds. Full of promise of much joy to come for us, despite the fact that the one thing we didn't talk about was his future. For my own part, I was almost afraid to broach the subject. I suppose I knew that one day he would go back to his former way of life. As time progressed, I would find Jimmy playing his drums more and more whenever I called around. I suppose I knew that he missed his old life. But I didn't want to think about it; about the prospect of him leaving, getting on those tour buses once again, driving across those continents. I didn't want to think about anything that was going to take Jimmy away from me.

However, I was deluding myself if I thought that my ignoring my fear of him going away would be the same as actually preventing it from happening. I was a fool.

My folly caught up with me late one summer evening, when the chill of autumn was just beginning to creep into the air. I had called around at Jimmy's house, as usual, but this time, unusually, as I rang the doorbell, I could hear the sounds of raucous laughter spreading through the house. Jimmy didn't open the door within seconds of my ring as he normally always did. I wait on the step, dithering. I don't know whether Jimmy's just busy and I should go away again (to be frank the thought of such stridently jolly company frightens me a little; but then the thought of just going away again without seeing Jimmy doesn't seem very appealing either), or if he just hasn't heard the ring of the door. As if to emphasise the possibility of this point, I hear the beating of drums emanating from Jimmy's "sound-proofed" studio room, plus the noise of electric guitars mingling in with them as well. It sounds good. It sounds good enough for me to overcome my fear. Curiously I wander around to the other side of the house. The music stops and I hear Jimmy call to me, 'Hey, Em!' His voice sounds unnaturally loud and over-bright. 'Hey, c'mon in. Meet the guys.'

"The guys" are "Pete" and "Si", the other members of his band. The former; Pete is tall, much taller than me with dull blonde hair. I can't see him too well at all. He's too tall for me to look above him to move my blind spot out of the way. He's so tall I can't get the angle of my head right to manage this, and I don't know if it's down to the fact that I can't see him too well, or just the feeling in my own gut, but there's something about him that makes me feel uneasy. He seems familiar to me somehow. He reminds me of someone and the thought fills me with unaccountable dread for some reason. Si is shorter with a strip of long bright pink hair growing out of the middle of his head. The sides of his head are shaven. At least I can see him.

'Hey guys,' Jimmy shouts as he pulls me through the French windows into the house. 'This is my lady I was telling you about. Isn't she somethin' else?'

I feel very uneasy as the guys inspect me. I feel equally uneasy about the way Jimmy has introduced me. It sounds sarcastic. Or is he just trying to be cool in front of his mates? I begin to wish I'd run whilst I had the chance.

'Is this the blind bitch he's screwing?' Pete asks someone; presumably not me. Probably Si.

'Blind. Not deaf. Nice to meet you too,' I respond to him anyway.

'Hey, take it easy. Jeez, Jimmy, she's touchy,' Pete responds.

I begin to feel a little ashamed, like I should make more of an effort with these people. They are, after all, Jimmy's lifelong friends. They knew him first. They have more claim upon him than I do. They know him better than I do.

'Sorry,' I begin to apologise, hating myself for it all the same. 'Just not used to...' My words trail away into nothing. Not used to what? Being called a blind bitch? Well, why should I be? I lapse into confused silence. I can't say anything right here. I look to Jimmy for help.

'Hey, hold on there,' Jimmy says happily to me, as if blissfully unaware that anything is wrong at all. 'You all get to know each other a little better while I fix us all a drink.'

'Oh no,' I hurriedly protest. 'I should leave you to it... You haven't seen each other for ages...'

'Yeah, Jimmy, we haven't seen each other for ages,' Pete repeats, his voice dripping with derision. I see by his movements that he has thrown his arm around Jimmy's shoulders. 'We got loads to catch up on, don't we?'

'Huh?' Jimmy says distractedly. 'Oh, yeah. Plenty of time for all that. Stay, Em, and meet the guys. I don't want you to go.' He ducks out of Pete's embrace and reaches out to touch my hand. I feel momentarily reassured.

'Okay.'

'I'll go fix those drinks.'

Oh God, don't leave me with these people, I think, the transitory sense of comfort which I have derived from his touch crumbling away from me. Too late. He has gone. I attempt a winning smile in Si's direction.

'So, if he's Pete, you must be Si.' I walk towards the blurry neon pink shape, tripping over something as I do so. I just manage to prevent myself from falling.

'Pete...' I hear Si say warningly.

'What?' Pete's voice oozes innocence. 'She should watch where she's fucking going. Hey, you kicked my foot.'

'Sorry...' I begin again. A hard knot of misery solidifies at the base of my stomach. I know who he reminds me of now. Sarah Braithwaite.

The evening progresses from bad to worse. Pete seems to derive exquisite pleasure from pushing obstacles into my path. Whenever Jimmy is not there, I'm almost afraid to move for fear of the boxes, chairs, feet, I'll trip over or bruise myself against. But Jimmy won't let me leave. Halfway through the night, Pete drops the bombshell that Jimmy's agreed to tour with the band again.

'It's all down to you, honey,' Jimmy whispers happily against my ear. 'I felt like nothin' at all until I met you. You've made me all better.'

'Yeah,' Pete chimes in. 'You made him all better so he can leave you.'

I look up sharply in Pete's direction. *If Scotty was here*, I think, *he'd smash your face in*.

I see Pete start back as if he can feel my white hot hatred of him and hear Si mutter, 'You deserved that look, man. Leave her alone.'

'Yeah, well, if looks could kill. And I thought she couldn't even see,' Pete responds *sotto voce*.

The night drags on. They're all drinking, even Jimmy. I can't keep pace with them. I don't even try. By the time we fall into Jimmy's bed, Jimmy's blind drunk. He pulls me roughly towards him and holds onto me so tightly it hurts.

'Now, don't be shad about me leavin' for a little while...' he says. He's so drunk he's slurring his words. 'I'm comin' right back to you,' he says.

'Jimmy, let go, you're hurting me,' I whisper, but he's already asleep. I lie awake for a long time, uncomfortable and worrying. I think about his ex-wife again. Was this how it was for her? I can't conquer my uneasiness, and, for once, Jimmy's actions are only exacerbating my fears. I can't move. I can't extricate myself from his grasp. His hold is like iron. Like a vice. Like Keith Denby's once, in a stable. Eventually, I fall into an uneasy, fitful sleep.

The next morning over breakfast there is less raucous laughter. The atmosphere is more subdued and serious. The talk is of the proposed tour and the conversation runs as if I'm not even there. From their words, I glean the fact that Jimmy will be away from just before Christmas until June the following year. The stone of misery at the pit of my stomach settles deeper. I toy with my food. I can't bear to listen to the conversation. I long to leave.

'I love you,' Jimmy says suddenly. I'm lost in a miserable world of my own. I barely hear him. The guys, Pete and Si, fall into silence. It is this sudden silence, rather than Jimmy's words which recall me to the present.

'Well, say somethin',' Jimmy says, reaching out his hand to touch me. I stroke his finger. The touch of his hand feels nostalgic.

'Sorry. I didn't realise you were talking to me.'

'Well, who did you think I was talking to?'

'Could have been Pete for all I know. I'd better go. Got to feed The Blank.'

I leave as fast as I can. I've realised much, much too late that I can't afford to fall in love with Jimmy Bridges.

The next few days are miserable. Jimmy doesn't come around and I daren't go over to his place. I don't want to be anywhere near Pete ever again. For the first time, we don't call around to collect him before Saturday's show. Instead, we go alone; Scotty, The Blank and I. It's only then, in his absence, that I realise just how much his presence at these events means to me. Without him and wretchedly miserable as I am, I am rubbish. The Blank feels it too. For the first time ever we leave with a yellow third place rosette, in place of our customary red first. Scotty harangues me about it during the entire return journey.

'What the fuck were you playing at out there? You were shit, I mean you really were. You knocked two fences down. You didn't even make it to the jump off.'

'I got third, Scotty.'

'Third's no fucking good,' he comments disgustedly, and then continues in his tirade. I let his words wash over me like the water that flows over the pebbles at the bottom of a stream. I am too wrapped up in my own suffering to consider his feelings as well. As Scotty makes the turn into our drive, however, I do catch his final words.

'I knew this would happen. I knew Jimmy fucking Bridges would spell trouble.'

The next day, however, Jimmy calls around. I've given The Blank the day off and I've turned him out into the field to take some grass. I'm sitting in the corner of the field watching the blur of his white shape as he ambles around. It reminds me of the days when I used to hide out in Keith Denby's fields watching Pepperpot Mill and the other horses, and waiting for everyone to leave so that I could ride; except this time The Blank is my horse and there's no-one to say whether I can ride him or not. I lie down in the grass and bask in the warmth of the late summer sun. I'm feeling pleasantly drowsy when Jimmy collapses beside me and kisses me full on the mouth by way of greeting.

'Scotty told me you were here,' he says when he, at last, releases me.

'I'm amazed he told you. He was swearing his head off about you yesterday.'

'About me? What have I done?'

'I only got the third place yesterday in the Area Sixteen regional competition. He blamed you. He said I was pining for you because you weren't there.'

'And were you?'

'Yes.'

Jimmy kisses me again and lets his hand wander over my breast. 'Don't let's fight, Em. I don't want us to fight. Particularly not about me going away on the tour. It's not worth fighting over. It's the fighting about it that wrecks relationships, not the being away on the tour itself. I learned that with Isabella. Time passes real quick, honey. I'll be back before you know it, and you know I'll be thinking about you every single moment.'

'It's not the tour,' I shake my head. 'It's not that. I always knew that you'd have to go back to what you do one day. I didn't want to think about it; and I'll miss you too, but I knew you'd have to go. It was more...'

'Pete?'

I half-nod. I'm reluctant to insult his friends, but I'm not going to lie to him either. Jimmy rolls away from me onto his back and looks up at the flawlessly blue sky, his arms folded behind his head. It's probably the last proper hot day of summer we'll have this year. Even I can see the sky is blue, blue and more blue; not a cloud in it. I want to freeze it in my memory forever. 'It's funny,' he says, at last. 'Isabella and Pete always got on together. Maybe he was so down on you because you're not like Isabella. I mean you're nothing at all like her. She and Pete, they had a lot in common, y'know? They were kinda one and the same person, in a way, they were so alike. Isabella... Jeez, she could be mean, y'know? Just nasty for the sake of it. And Pete... Well, don't get me wrong, we've been friends for a long time. In some ways he's like a brother to me; but I know he can be that way too. Vindictive... Hurting people in petty ways jus' so's he can show them that he's the great Pete Darlow. That he can do it to them.'

Jimmy laughs a little.

'I remember once,' he continues, 'when we were kids. We... Pete, Si and me... We were all playing this game with a rope we'd found in my mom's back yard. Pete wanted me to go up into this scrawny old tree my mom had growing there and tie the rope up so we could make a swing out of it, y'know?'

I nod, but Jimmy ignores me. He is lost now, in this memory from his childhood.

'I didn't wanna go. I didn't wanna be the one to have to climb up into that tree on account of how I was scared, you see? I never did like heights. Pete got mad at me. He knew how I felt but he just kept on pushing it. And I just kept on refusing. I wouldn't be the one to go up there, but he wouldn't have it. In the end, he said he was gonna teach me a lesson. Y'know what he did? Y'know what he persuaded Si to do? They used that rope to tie me to the base of that tree and then they just left me out there in my mom's yard. Mom was working a double-shift that day. By the time she found me it was dark. I'd fallen asleep a little, I guess and when I woke I could see the lights of Pete's house in the distance were on. Those squares of light in his house just seemed to make it darker in my yard somehow.' Jimmy shakes his head at the memory.

'Mom was mad when she found me out there. Mad as hell. Mad at Pete. And at Si, too, for going along with it. And I was really mad too. For a long time, I couldn't forget it. How it had felt to be tied up for so long. How they'd just gone off and left me there not knowing when my mom would be home to cut me loose. How I couldn't walk properly after she did because they'd tied the knots so tight. How my hands had swelled up like two big balloons. Y'know, you think you forget these things. We were only kids. But Pete can be a bully... Can be real nasty. And I sometimes wonder if I didn't hold it in all those years. That last night... When we were out on tour... That last time I played a show with the guys... Well... God, I felt awful. Just like nothing at all. I didn't even know if I'd remember how to play the songs. I was kinda alright as long as I didn't think about things too deeply. If I just went onto automatic pilot... But that last time, well we were playin' somethin' slow and some of the audience were holding lit cigarette lighters in the air. Suddenly all I could see were yellow squares of light in the distance. I didn't know what it was, but suddenly I just had to be away from Pete... From Si... From everyone really. Everyone on that bus who was anything to do with that tour. I ran. I threw down my sticks, got up off that stage and ran. I couldn't stay. I didn't know why, but I just had to be away from them all. But maybe... Just maybe, seeing those yellow squares of light brought it all back to me. Of how Pete can be sometimes. All I know was I hated them in that moment. I wanted nothing more to do with them; *not ever.*'

Jimmy shakes his head again, as if dismissing the recollection from his mind.

207

'But Pete... Well, you saw how he was. He can be charming and funny and a great guy to be with too.'

I bite my lip hesitantly. My truthful answer would be: 'No I don't see how he was. He seemed like a cretin to me,' but I bite back my words.

'Also, Pete... Well, he's seriously fucked up. Sometimes he can be so full of anger and bitterness. I mean he's been through *a lot*. Rehab, twice. Getting clean ain't easy y'know, after an addiction like Pete's. Sometimes, I don't think he even knows how to like people or be happy for the happiness of others anymore, even that of his closest friends. Ignore him, hon. Cut him some slack. He's nothing to do with us.'

Of course I can't appreciate it then, as Jimmy rolls back towards me and kisses me again, first gently, and then more insistently; of course I can't even begin to know just how wrong Jimmy is about that.

The glorious summer begins to fade away. The days begin to have a sad autumnal aspect about them. The shows move from outdoors to in, but still we're winning. By the time mid-November arrives, we've accumulated enough points to be ranked fifteenth in the top UK rider list. People, as Scotty had predicted, have started to take notice of us. We have to be extra cautious at the shows. One of the leading equine magazines somehow gets hold of our telephone number and an incredibly posh woman phones up asking for an interview about, in her words, 'The phenomenal season The Blank and I have enjoyed so far.' She wants comments for the magazine about where I've been during my long absence from the show jumping circuit and our plans for the future. Scotty responds with: 'fuck off, how's that for a comment?' Offended, the woman exacts her revenge by running an article about The Blank's poor confirmation. He is described as a "circus horse", with myself as a mere "trick rider". My future prospects and riding ability are not rated very highly at all. Other riders also pass comment about my performance in the article, including words from Sebastian Carling-Brooks.

'Listen to this,' Scotty reads aloud to me. '"I'm not worried about Miss Devlin elbowing her way up through the ranks. Yes, I agree, she's had a good season on that rather peculiar horse of hers, but other riders have had good seasons and ascended the ranks in this way in previous years. What you find is they can't do it consistently and you often discover they plummet through the ranked rider list as quickly as they've climbed. It's staying at the top that counts. Anyway, Miss Devlin would have to be in the top *twelve* not the top *fifteen* to qualify for an invitation for entry to a *really* prestigious event, such as the British Open, so she won't be coming up against any of the really top riders such as myself any time soon..." What a fucking wanker. That man really is stuffed up his own arse. I'll tell you what that is. He's scared. He's only ranked twelfth. You could easily whup his peasy ass out of the top twelve.'

I'm sick of listening to it.

'God, Scotty,' I respond shortly. 'You've taken all the advantages out of being blind. I don't usually have to take any notice of this crap. Chuck it on the fire.'

I had to admit it though, Scotty was probably right. Sebastian Carling-Brooks did sound a little fearful in that article, particularly of losing his right to qualify for entry into that most coveted of show jumping competitions, the British Open. The main reason the winning of the British Open Show Jumping Championship is so coveted within the show jumping world is because only the best as defined by the BSJA are able to participate in the competition. In short, only the top twelve ranked British riders as at 1st January each year qualified for entry. Leading riders from abroad were also invited to compete to make up a total of thirty riders who are able to enter the competition in all. The rewards were great; the prize money was immense and the kudos associated with the winning of such a prestigious event was unbound. No wonder he was afraid. I was getting much too close to that number twelve spot which he currently occupied and the Blank and I, well, we were still winning. His own form was, at best, indifferent, this season, and the horses he owned couldn't hold a candle to The Blank.

At the end of November, Scotty and I drive over to Jimmy's house and sound the antiquated horn at his gate for the final time in what feels like is going to be a very, very long time to come. We're not driving to a show this time. We've left The Blank at home and the back of the horsebox is empty. This time, we're running Jimmy to the airport so he can fly out to join his band for their tour. It's not as bad as it could have been. We've worked out that his schedule means he'll be performing in London the night after I'm due to jump in a major competition at one of the large arenas. He's even due to perform at the same arena the next night. He's planned to arrive early, watch me compete and then we can grab a night together before he moves onto the European leg of his tour. It's not much, but it's something to hang onto.

As he kisses me goodbye, he whispers into my ear, 'Don't miss me. Just keep winning, honey. For me.'

But I do miss him. I cannot help myself. The three weeks until our arranged rendezvous in London takes an age to pass. I feel his absence from me like a physical ache inside of my body. I remember that first evening I spent in his arms, how just before he kissed me I had stood in what I believed to be his empty studio and said the words, "I'm dying of longing for you." Now I really know the meaning of these words. In my weaker moments, I lay my head against The Blank's withers and take comfort from the warmth and solidity of him, the pleasing smell of warm hay and apples that always lingers about a horse. It reminds me of when I was a child and I used to lay my head against the withers of Keith Denby's horses and weep when it all became too much for me. I had considered myself hardened and above such emotions. It just shows how wrong a person can be; even about their own self. I don't know myself at all.

Still, as Jimmy had promised, time passes; and so it does, even if it does not pass, as Jimmy had also promised "real quick".

Scotty drives the horsebox with The Blank and I down to London and we prepare to compete in our event. It's a big one for us; an opportunity to win some substantial prize money as well as qualify for yet more valuable points. As usual, we do our best to stay out of the way of the other competitors, but Scotty tells me there's a lot of pointing and whispering wherever The Blank and I are out together these days. We're not popular. We haven't endeared ourselves to anyone with our uncooperative, even positively hostile attitudes towards the other competitors. We've added insult to injury by perpetually beating the very people who consider themselves so much better than us in so many ways at these competitions. But we can't afford to make friends. We can't afford the risk of these people knowing anything about us. They don't expect me to converse with them and I certainly don't expect them to do anything other than pretend we don't exist. So, it's a surprise when Sebastian Carling-Brooks saunters over to where Scotty and I are standing with The Blank, just as I'm preparing to mount up and enter the warm-up arena.

'Hello again,' he says, affably enough. 'Long time, no see. It's been a while since we competed against each other. Last time was in, let me think, 1998 was it? Or 1999? I forget. You beat me. On that pony of yours. What was it? Liquorice something.'

'Herbert Sherbet,' I respond automatically.

'Oh, I knew it was something sweety-ish like that. Listen, my dear, I hope you're not thinking of doing anything silly like beating me tonight. At the moment, my qualification for the British Open's in the bag. If you win here and I don't... Well... I wouldn't like to be you. Or that horse, for that matter.'

I suddenly recollect that meeting of a decade ago. His words then had been affable enough too, but there had been a veiled threat undeniably present. I wondered just how far he'd go if he didn't get what he wanted from me. Would he, like Keith Denby, be capable of terrible atrocities against myself or The Blank? My mouth flaps open helplessly. I don't know what to say. I'm not risking The Blank as I so foolishly risked Herbert Sherbet ten years ago.

Unfortunately for Sebastian Carling-Brooks, however, Scotty has heard every word he'd said.

'You fucking bastard,' Scotty swings a meaty fist at him. I hear an unmistakeable crunching of bones.

'Agh! God. Fuck. You've broken my nose, you lout. I'll have you arrested.'

'Oh, you will, will you? Well they're gonna be very interested in the fact that you've just threatened my sister; as will the BSJA. If I was you I'd keep that,' Scotty presses his fist into Sebastian Carling-Brooks' curling upper lip, 'schtum.'

'They won't listen to a lower-class yob like you,' he retorts, but there's a quiver in his speech. He's afraid.

'Oh, yes, they will,' Scotty brandishes the dictaphone we use to analyse Scotty's commentaries of our rounds after each event out of his pocket. 'I don't trust you people. Never have. Never will. I don't trust those equine journos either. I always carry this and turn it on every time any one of you comes anywhere near us. I always knew that when we started beating you, you'd get desperate and start playing dirty. You're as bad as the Arsenal football club for that. Well now I've got the proof, haven't I?'

Sebastian Carling-Brooks has gone very pale. He stumbles away from us, and moments later we hear the tannoy announcement that he has withdrawn from the competition due to a facial injury.

'Oh, Scotty, that was so clever. Recording him like that,' I breathe. I am in awe at the genius of my brother.

'T'weren't turned on. I never got a word of what he said. Still,' Scotty shrugs. 'He doesn't know that.'

And here's something we didn't know, Scotty and I, in those moments either. In the short space of time it had taken for Scotty to break Sebastian Carling-Brook's nose, Miranda Camberwell (ranked number thirteen in the UK top rider list) discovered she was pregnant and decided to take a break from the sport for the period of her gestation, and Frederick De Lacey (ranked number fourteen in the UK top rider list) was arrested on the suspicion of possession of Class A drugs and removed from the rankings by BSJA officials in disgrace. All of these events added up and became equal to one result and one result alone: I was now ranked number twelve in the top rider list and, being as this was the final competition before Christmas and the New Year, I had qualified for an invitation to compete in the British Open, and all before we'd even jumped the practice fence. We didn't even need to win our class; but we did anyway, just to show them that we could do it and so I could give the rosette to Jimmy and prove that I was still winning for him, and also because The Blank was the king of the day and couldn't be beaten and we had to let them know what they were up against come next April, when the British Open Show Jumping Championship was scheduled to take place.

Back at the horsebox, we find Jimmy waiting for us to arrive. Now that he's emerged from his self-imposed exile back into the public glare, the paparazzi have been following him again.

'I couldn't stay until the end, honey,' he tells me. 'I wish I could have done just to see you ride, but they were all over me and I had to sneak out back. I didn't want them following me back here to you.'

I'm just so glad to see him, I don't care whether he saw me ride or not.

'It doesn't matter,' I tell him. 'You must have seen me ride The Blank a thousand times by now. You must be sick of seeing me ride.' I hand him the red rosette.

'Never,' he responds, stroking the satin of the ribbon through his fingers as he does so. 'I really wanted to stay and watch you win. But I knew you would win, so I guess that's all that matters. Hey, we've got our tour buses parked out back in one of the secure car parks next to the arena. We won't get bothered by anyone there. Wanna see how we live when we're on tour? Wanna see one of our buses?'

I nod. 'I wouldn't mind seeing the blurred outline of one, but I've got to sort The Blank out first.'

'Leave it,' Scotty interrupts. 'Just this once. And I *mean* just this once being as you two haven't seen each other in three weeks. I'll sort him out.'

'Thanks, Scotty.' I hand over the reins and turn to leave with Jimmy, which just shows how utterly desperate I am to be somewhere where we wouldn't be bothered at all with him, because ordinarily I wouldn't leave The Blank with anyone, not even Scotty.

There are three buses with trailers attached to them parked in a small private car park adjacent to the arena, along with a couple of big lorries. They all, Jimmy tells me, contain people and paraphernalia relating to their show at this same arena tomorrow evening. There are noises; shouts and laughter coming from one of the buses, but mercifully, Jimmy leads me into the second of the three which is blissfully dark and silent. The moment we step through the doors, he begins to kiss me and fumble at my clothes. I am racked with desire. I collapse against his body and let him tear my clothes from me, pulling me deeper into the interior of the bus as he does so.

'God, honey, I've missed you so much,' he mumbles. His voice sounds thick and hoarse with need. 'This is my bunk,' he pushes me into a small, curtained space that contains a bed which fills the entire space and kisses me again, my face, my neck, my breasts. His lips travel over my stomach and he peels off my underwear with his teeth, muttering feverishly against my skin as he does so.

'God, I wanted this to be special. I wanted to savour you, take you slowly. I can't do it. I need you so Goddamn much.'

He plunges inside of me and ejaculates almost immediately, arching against me; before collapsing shaking on top of me.

'God, I'm sorry, I'm sorry. I can't tell you how much I've wanted you... Missed you...'

In all my life, I have never felt such power, that this man should be reduced to this by his desire for my body. I arch against him, rubbing myself against the length of his body, like a cat. I nuzzle against his face, nibbling at the lobe of his ear.

'I've missed you too,' I say, continuing to arch against him.

'Hey, I've got a surprise for you when we get back,' he says.

'Oh.' This revelation stops me short.

'What's wrong? Don't you like surprises?'

'Err... No, not much really.' I think about all those other surprises in my life "Your mum's just jumped off the bridge", and so on, and so forth. 'In my experience,' I add neutrally, 'surprises are not generally good things.'

'You'll like this one.'

'Will I? You promise?' I'm too occupied with my rediscovery of the wonder of Jimmy's body to even pose the question seriously. I begin to rub myself against him again. 'God, I'm going to miss you after tonight. It's going to be even worse then. You're going to be gone for six whole months before I'll see you again. You'd better give me something to remember you by. You'll have to do better than this, you know... C'mon Jimmy, I want more.'

'So, I've been away for only three weeks and you've become a minx, have you? Well, I'll give you something to remember me by...'

His fingers stroke me until I'm gasping, almost sobbing with my desperate need of him.

I wake later to see the light in the room has altered. There is a grey watery glint filtering through the flimsy material of the curtains which tells me its morning. Jimmy is sleeping peacefully beside me. Outside of the compartment which forms Jimmy's "bunk" all is still and silent. I'm desperate again; this time with the need to urinate.

'Jimmy,' I prod at him, but he barely stirs. He seems so peaceful. I can't bear to wake him. I fumble around in the tiny space and rediscover the clothes that Jimmy tore from my body the previous evening. Then I venture outside to find the bathroom. I locate it to my relief towards the rear of the bus and start to make my way back towards Jimmy's bunk.

'Hey there,' Pete's voice startles me. I hadn't even seen him. He must have been sitting very still, unfortunately right in the centre of my blind spot.

'Oh... Hello again. Jimmy's still sleeping,' I offer by way of explanation and turn, once again, to get back to Jimmy.

'Hey, don't run away. It's been a while, hasn't it... Emma?'

'Em,' I correct him automatically.

'Yeah, whatever. It's so hard to keep track, don't you think? What with all the girls who are in and out of the bus all the time. Everyone's so pleased to have Jimmy back. You saw what a great time we all have when we get together. You saw how it was over at his house that time. You know, us all drinkin' and partyin' and carryin' on. The groupies love him. And, boy, does he love them back. Did he tell you that? No? It's a different one every night with him. Well, with all of us really. The thing is,' Pete's tone drops to become suddenly hard and serious, 'we can't afford to get distracted, any of us, or hung up on just one girl. We've got our careers and our music to think about. It's more important to us than anything. Jimmy particularly. He's had so many problems focussing that he really can't afford to get hung up on some *nothing* who just happened to breeze in at precisely the moment that Jimmy was looking for something more broken than himself to fix. Now I know for a fact that he's just looking for an excuse to lose you from his life. Let's face it, you're not very rock n' roll are you? Some blind nothing of a hanger on. Jimmy can do so much better than you, don't you think? I think it's time you left, don't you? And make sure you leave Jimmy alone from now on.'

I left pretty quick after that. Not because of what Pete had told me about all those other girl groupies and how Jimmy had slept with them. I didn't know if that was true or not, although it left a nasty taste in my mouth to think it might be, I also knew that Pete was just nasty and had probably made it up to hurt me. No; it wasn't that. I left because of the other stuff Pete had said; the stuff about me being nothing and just a hanger on and how Jimmy could do so much better without me. All that stuff, it was all true. After all, it was only ever Jimmy who made me feel like it was okay to like myself anyway. When Jimmy was away from me, I went back to how I was before. How I had always been. Pete was right. Without Jimmy's approval, I really was just nothing. And, perhaps the surprise Jimmy had for me was the fact that he wanted to, what was it Pete had said? "Lose me from his life". In my experience, surprises never were anything any good. Yes, I told myself as I headed back across the grey car park to our ancient horsebox, I was no good for Jimmy, or at least not good enough. Pete was probably right.

12. When Two are One

(Written by Atreyu. Appears on Roadrunner Records: Lead Sails, Paper Anchor, 2007. Performed by Atreyu)

The weeks pass. I feel numb. There is a weight of emptiness lodged within my gut which feels like a permanent stomach ache. I can't think about Jimmy, or his band, or his tour. If I picture him in my imagination, if anything reminds me of him and what I have lost, misery threatens to overwhelm me. I am close to tears at all times. The emptiness metamorphoses into a physical pain which rises up through my belly, progresses through my chest and sticks in my throat. I can't speak at such times. I am more like my mother than ever. Only now can I fully understand the loneliness and the wretchedness of those final years of her life; the ones she was forced to spend without my father. Even The Blank is no comfort to me, although he is the nearest I can come to finding empathy anywhere. Scotty just swears at me. He is mad as hell at everything about the situation. He doesn't know the full story. I do not tell him about Pete and what he has said to me. I can't face telling him. But he's mad at me for getting involved with Jimmy in the first place when he warned me not to. He's mad at Jimmy for apparently dumping me. Most unjustly of all, I suppose, he is mad at himself for letting me get hurt. He's spent his entire life looking out for me. Getting in my grandmother's way whenever it looked like I was in for it again. Taking my beatings for me. He can't bear to see me like this. His anger at himself is the hardest to bear. It just makes me feel guilty, but I haven't got it in me to hide the pain.

I spend longer and longer with The Blank. He, at least, neither judges nor swears at me; but I am even letting him down. Selling him short. The British Open is looming. The official letter has arrived from the BSJA informing us of our place in the competition. It's the biggest thing that's ever happened to me. It is the culmination of a lifetime's dreaming, but we haven't done nearly enough to prepare. I can't face it. I can't face anything. I can't even face riding anymore. At night I sit in The Blank's stable and watch the outline of him as he moves around. During the day, I sit in the roots of one of the trees in his field. I feel tired and sick. I feel heavy. My breasts hurt. I've missed a period. I know I should be doing something, some kind of decision making, but I don't feel like doing anything. I can't tell Scotty; not yet. I don't know if I'll ever feel up to it. I know it is terrible. I know it is wrong, but I just stare into space, like my mother did before me.

One day, I walk into the cottage and find Scotty hunched over the computer. He has a furtive, secretive air about him. He tries to hide what he has on the screen as I walk in.

'Scotty,' I say wearily. 'You do realise how pointless that is, don't you? Look I don't care what horrible pornography it is that you're looking at. I can't see it.'

There is a momentary silence before Scotty turns towards me slowly.

'It's not porn. Look, Em, it's about Jimmy. He's got a Twitter page and a Facebook page too. He's got a blog... Look, www.jimmybridges.blogspot.com' Scotty reads the web address out in his painfully slow and stilted reading voice. 'You could contact him,' he suggests tentatively.

I laugh almost hysterically.

'Oh yeah, great idea, Scotty. Fantastic. I could join his Facebook fan group and be a "friend" along with his 531,878 other special "friends". I could post a message on his wall: "Jimmy, am pregnant. Please come home."' I stop in horror at what I have just revealed and then flop down helplessly into the chair. Scotty turns slowly away from the computer monitor to face me.

'What?'

I am silent. I put my hand over my mouth. I can only nod in affirmation of what I have just let slip. I didn't mean it to be like this, but at least now, it's out in the open.

'God, Em, what are you going to do?'

Tears spill down my face. What am I going to do? I hate the way that I have to make this decision alone.

'I don't know Scotty. I just don't know. I feel so alone.'

220

'Well, you're not alone. *You're fucking not, alright?*' He pulls me fiercely towards him, presses his forehead against mine. I suppose he is staring into my eyes, except I can't see him. 'You will never be alone as long as I'm around, alright. We don't need some fucking mad punk rocker. I don't know what I was thinking... It's just that you've been so sad... But I told you he was an headcase! Just fucking off and leaving you like this... If ever I see him again, I tell you... Well, never mind. You're not alone. You've got me. You've got The Blank. You've got the baby now too. Come to think of it, this place has never been so fucking crowded. How can you say you're alone?'

I laugh a little through my tears.

'I think we'd better leave the Open though, don't you...? You shouldn't really jump, you know. Not in your condition...' Scotty continues almost hesitantly.

I shake my head emphatically.

'No, Scotty. No. I'm going to jump. We... The Blank... Me... The baby too... We're all jumping. I'm never going to get this chance again. Not ever. I've spent my whole life dreaming about this moment and suddenly, impossibly, it's here. I never thought it was going to happen. It shouldn't ever have happened really. I mean, I'm blind for God's sake. I've got to do it now. There won't be any other time. Please, Scotty. Don't leave me now. One last time. And it will be the last, I promise. No more after this. But just once more, even if we get knocked out in the first round.'

But we don't get knocked out in the first round. Nor the second. Nor even the third. Incredibly, and despite the fact that I feel as sick as a dog (and it's not just nerves this time either) we make it through to the final.

The final is televised. There is a blonde, horsey looking woman leading the commentating with Will Somebody-or-other, some ex-show jumper with her. She tries to collar me as I go into the warm up arena with The Blank just before the final, but Scotty swears so excessively at her that the BBC reporting team stay away from us after that. They're afraid of infuriating old ladies with bad language before the watershed. For the first time ever in my life, I am grateful for women in the world like Mrs Ayres, who would find the time and energy to write to the BBC and complain about such things.

The final of the British Open is probably about the toughest course we have ever faced. The fact that The Blank is doing it with a hidden extra passenger certainly doesn't help. I feel so nauseous because of the baby that I actually vomit down The Blank's shoulder just after I mount up. The BBC exact their revenge on me and my refusal to co-operate with them by gleefully reporting this fact, although they just put it down to nerves. Scotty tells me they show a full screen shot of The Blank's shoulder streaked in my gastric fluids. I viciously hope someone writes and complains about that. Thankfully, they don't know anything about the fact that I'm carrying "Mad Jimmy" Bridge's baby. They would have a field day with that one, if they found out, I know. The female reporter argues that The Blank and I are the ones to watch in this championship. Will Somebody-or-other expresses his doubts about this. He doesn't think we can pull it off. He's of the opinion that I'm a trick rider and The Blank doesn't have the necessary pedigree. He thinks that because The Blank is an albino and has wall eyes he won't be able to see the fences very well. He thinks this will lead The Blank to make a mistake. Oh, the irony there.

Scotty and I walk the course together. There are fifteen fences in all. Fence number one is a high upright. Next is a yellow gate. I am grateful for the fact that it's yellow and that I can see it. I am less grateful for the fact that it has been deliberately built to be flimsy and easily knocked down. Fence three is a parallel bars jump which is both high and wide. After that, we will need to swing around in an "S" shape (never an easy thing for me to do and be completely sure I won't run The Blank into something) to reach jump four, which is an ascending oxer. After the oxer, there's a tight turn to the right to reach fence five which is just an upright with a brushwood filler. Fence six follows straight after. It's a wide spread jump and I realise there isn't going to be much room for The Blank and I to get the necessary speed up to clear the width of it. Also, and more worryingly still, the approach to this sixth fence is hampered by fence number ten, a fan fence which sits slightly in the path of the sixth. We are going to need to swing out a little and then move back on ourselves to get the line to the jump right. Fence seven is the highest wall jump we will have ever encountered. After the wall, The Blank and I need to turn the corner to fence eight, a staircase triple bar fence. Again, it has been built so that it would be incredibly easy to chip a pole off the top of it. It's a similar story with fence nine, an upright around six strides after the triple bar. After the ninth, we're going to need to swing around fences three, four and five to gain a clear approach to the tenth, that tricky fan jump. After this, if we even make it this far without crashing into anything, it's straight up to the top of the arena to jump the triple combination. Once more, these have been laid out in such a way as to test horse and rider to the maximum. The first element of the combination, fence eleven is very high and there's no room for a stride in between fence eleven and fence twelve. I'm going to have to ask The Blank to bounce in and out between the jumps; never a simple matter for a horse to achieve, particularly when the jumps are high. There is room for one small stride between fence twelve and thirteen, but only if I get the timing right; and let's face it, what are the chances of that, I think bleakly to myself. The final two fences are not so bad, I think, in comparison with the rest of the course. I suppose, really, the issue there is that it's unlikely that any horse and rider team is going to complete the course in the allotted time. By the time they reach those final two innocent looking fences horse and rider are going to be both tired and rushing; and this will inevitably lead to mistakes being made.

The whole course is a nightmare. It's a nightmare to an experienced, competent, fully-sighted horse and rider team. To a relatively inexperienced horse and rider team, one of whom is pregnant and can't stop vomiting, and both of whom cannot see well, it's a complete and utter disaster. I don't even know why I am there at all at this point in time. We trot around the warm-up arena, The Blank and I, and I listen to Scotty swearing reassuringly through the ear-piece which sits hidden in my ear. I am going to need Scotty to give me some very good directions indeed tonight, I think to myself, if we are going to make anything out of this. He's going to have to come up with something better than just F-words this time.

The first horse and rider team to jump is the German Siegfried Humbert and his horse Goethe. The Blank and I swish around the warm up area as Scotty, hidden in a quiet spot, watches and talks me through his round.

'He's doing alright. Not bad. I think it's too slow. He's asking Goethe to speed up' (Scotty pronounces this "goat". I smile to myself as we make circuits of the arena but then notice one of the other competitors regarding me narrowly. *Careful, Em*, I tell myself). 'He's going to get time penalties. He's panicking now. You should see his fucking face.' I hear "Goat" clip the final fence myself. 'That's done it,' Scotty says triumphantly in my ear. 'He's knocked that last fence – the white gate - down. Be careful on that one, Em. The horse barely touched it but the whole bloody lot came down.'

Indeed, there are no clear rounds from the next few competitors. Then, the Frenchman, Jean-Paul Patrice jumps clear with his flashy grey horse, Printemps. This is bad, I know. He's been close behind me throughout the competition. If he beats us tonight and takes the 240 points which are on offer for first place, then he will win the title. A flicker of that old desire to win starts to build up inside of me. We take a turn over the practice fence, and wait for further reports from Scotty. Jonno Hamilton, a man I seem to remember as being what Scotty once described as "some

224

impossibly smug middle-class twat" is the first English contender to jump clear. Helena Goldsmith, who I do not know at all, also jumps clear. Gerald Jacobs, who I seem to recall was one of Denby's old pals, also gets a clear with Minstrel. In between, there are many more crashes and casualties, than riders jumping clear. Then, suddenly, sickeningly, it is our turn to jump.

The ear-piece which Jimmy gave to me for just such occasions crackles into life once more. *(Jimmy, oh Jimmy, where are you now?)*

'Okay, Em, this is it,' Scotty says. *I know,* I think. *God, he's going to have to do better than that.* I am panicking. I know I am. I force myself to breathe and urge The Blank to canter down the arena towards the first fence.

'Careful, Em. Slow and steady. You're doing good. You're on course...'

The Blank leaps almost silently over the first.

'Straight on to the yellow gate... Beautiful,' Scotty breathes in my ear as The Blank executes another faultless leap.

'Now, turn left. Do a tight one, Em. Keep the time down.'

We follow the corner of the arena and clear the parallel bars.

'Okay, swing out to the right... Not too far... That's it... Back in. You've done it. You're on course.'

We clear the ascending oxer and then execute a further tight turn to clear the upright with the brushwood filler.

'Okay, Em. This is the one where the fan fence sits in the way. Push The Blank out and away to your right. Right. *Right! Other fucking right....* God you're going to hit it... *Oh Jesus Christ, don't do that to me!'* At the last minute we swing around the fan fence and clear the sixth.

'Wall jump,' Scotty says, slightly unnecessarily. It's so high that even I can see it. I almost wish I couldn't. I feel a sharp stab of fear and resist the impulse to close my eyes as The Blank and I canter a slow approach to the fence. Slow, slow, slow, putting as much impulsion into our pace as we can, it seems to take an age to reach the point of take off. Eventually, however, we are there. There is a rush of air as The Blank jumps. Is this wall as high as the one into Jimmy's garden? Or higher? I cannot decide. For a second, I wish we were jumping into Jimmy's garden once more. I feel The Blank give a tiny hitch with his back feet, just as he did that night when we jumped over that other wall, and we are clear. I am beginning to feel exhilarated. Fences eight and nine seem easy to us. We almost gallop our approach to the fan fence which I nearly collided with just moments before. We clear it easily. We are unstoppable. Moments later we have done it; we have cleared that final white gate fence and with no time faults either. We've got it. We've got our clear. We canter out of the arena and back into the warm up area. Scotty is waiting for us.

'For God's sake, Em, what the fuck are you playing at?' He demands savagely as we draw level with him.

'What? We got the clear. What are you complaining about now, for God's sake?'

'You nearly ran into that fan fence. Jesus Christ. When are you gonna learn left from right?'

'Oh Scotty,' I sigh. 'We got away with it, alright. We're doing alright.' I pat The Blank's neck lavishly; lean forward and tickle his ears.

'Oh God, they're changing the course now for the jump-off.' Scotty sounds terrified. I suddenly realise that I'm not the only one who suffers from nerves at these events. As if to confirm this, Scotty turns angrily towards me.

'I tell you what, I'm fucking glad this is the last time. I can't be doing this much longer. It's put years on me, I'm telling you. Or knocking years off my life expectancy. One or the other. Either way, if I die young, looking old, *it's your fault.*'

I laugh a little and lean down and squeeze his fingers.

'Once more, with feeling,' I say, and go off to warm up The Blank for the final jump off of our careers.

As we swish our way around the warm up area, Scotty whispers the alterations to the course to me through the earpiece.

'Alright, Em, they've put the wall up. It's massive now. I don't think even The Blank will clear it. The only consolation there is that that smug middle-class twat and his smug middle-class horse won't clear it either.' I smile to myself. Scotty has undoubtedly got a point. Jonno "smug middle-class twat" Hamilton's horse, Hello Dolly, has got an undeniably smug air about it. I guess it's an extension of the myth that dogs grow to look like their owners, perhaps horses get like their owners too. I think about The Blank and his poor-seeing pale blue eyes and suppress a further ironic smile.

'They've taken out fences four and five. Got that? No ascending oxer and no upright with brushwood fillers. Don't go looking around for them. They're not there. So after three, the parallel bars, it's straight round to six, which is the spread jump. Then the wall, fences eight and nine... You were okay with them last time... Then that fan fence, the triple combination... Fence fourteen's gone, so just the white gate and then out. You're going to have to be quick, Em. Cut the fucking corners. No-one's gonna get clears here with this. It's time that counts now.'

First up, it's Jean-Paul Patrice. There is a tense silence from the audience and amongst the riders in the warm-up area. He is clear over the first three, but then he evidently takes a big risk and cuts a corner in the approach to the wall. His horse, Printemps, demolishes it. Next, it's Jonno Hamilton. Amazingly, they jump clear. I dread to think just how smug he looks now. Still, there's no denying, his time is not fast. I think, maybe, just maybe, we might be able to beat it. Helena Goldsmith, like Jean-Paul Patrice, takes risks, cuts corners and knocks the wall down with her horse White Sails. Nerves have clearly affected Gerald Jacobs quite badly. Reassuringly, I hear Scotty sniggering in my ear.

'You should see the state of this fella. He's sweating like mad.'

Jacobs goes on to demolish nearly every fence in the round.

'Oh well, at least he did it quickly,' Scotty says. 'You're up, Em.'

I canter down the side of the arena and enter. I feel light and confident for the first time since I stepped off Jimmy's tour bus all those weeks ago. This is the one moment The Blank and I are going to have. Everything is in our favour. We are going to wipe the smile off Jonno Hamilton's smug middle-class features. Even the crowd is with us. The English, with their love of the underdog, is chanting "The Blank! The Blank!" as we make our entrance. The Blank flicks his ears back and forth, before evidently deciding to ignore it. We clear the first easily and he puts in a couple of massive strides before clearing the second, the yellow gate. We cut around the ninth fence and clear the third, the parallel bars. Scotty is talking to me all the time, but I am not really listening to him anymore. I can see the fences. They're so big, it would be hard to miss them really. I can see them; and I'm visualising them in my mind at the same time (the images are much more detailed in my mind's eye. It's nice to know that I haven't got Stargadt's of the imagination). I'm playing our round out in pictures; envisaging each perfect jump before we have even completed them. There is no way we can lose here tonight. We are the greatest show jumping horse and rider team that ever lived. We veer around to jump what had been the sixth fence in the previous round, but is now the fourth. I seem to remember this is a wide spread jump. Plenty of outgoing impulsion required, I tell myself, and ask The Blank to speed up. There is a hush in the audience, but all I can really hear is the rush of the blood in my ears. Suddenly I hear something else.

'*Fucking look out!!!!*'

Scotty's voice almost screams in my ear, but it is too late for me to recall the fan fence – that tricky number ten fence which sat slightly in the way of the approach to the number six fence – I have forgotten all about it and in galloping The Blank straight at what I

228

believe to be the spread jump, we are heading directly into where the wing of this jump sits.

It is too late to alter our course. A sense of horror at the inevitability of it all engulfs me. A tenth of a second later, I feel The Blank stagger beneath me as he catches his shoulder on the wing to that number ten fence. His head drops momentarily and I think I am going to fall, but then he flings his head up again, and I fall against his neck. He recovers himself and puts in an amazing stride to clear the spread. I am mortified. I can feel the alteration in The Blank's pace. He is undoubtedly injured; but we have to carry on.

'*Is it still up, is it still up?*' I whisper to Scotty, forgetting of course, that though he can talk to me, I cannot talk to him through the earpiece which Jimmy gave to us. I wonder if the fan fence is still standing, or if we have just demolished it. I do not have to wait long for the answer as I hear Scotty hiss angrily in my ear.

'*Stupid fucking bitch. You're lucky you didn't take out both fences there. I don't know how you got away with it, but they're both still up. But you're getting some funny looks now I can tell you. If this doesn't give the game away, I don't know what will.*'

I think Scotty is probably right. I wonder if this will lead to us being discovered. The audience is no longer chanting for us. They evidently think that I have tried to shave too much corner off the approach to the fence and have injured my horse in the process. In a nation of animal lovers, that's never going to endear me to anyone. We canter slowly towards the wall. It is, as Scotty has said, even higher, but The Blank is determined now. I can feel him take the bit between his teeth, much as he did that first night he jumped over the wall into Jimmy's garden, and decide to let him do it his own way. His pace does not feel as fluid as it normally does. I know he has hurt his shoulder. *I have injured his shoulder.* The least I can do now is to let him finish this the way he wants to. He jumps clear. I steer him towards the next fences, and once again let him do it his own way. Next up, the triple combination. I let him have his head again. I am just a passenger. I think about Miss

Primrose all those years ago and how, now, if she were The Blank, she would run out at the last moment and then probably go and bite one of the judges or something, just out of spite. All of those years since Miss Primrose, I tell myself bleakly. All of those years filled with stupid, unworthy, unthinking, blind ambition to get to this precise moment and all I have achieved is a past littered with dead horses, and one injured one. Pepperpot Mill, Herbert Sherbet; and now The Blank. I have been instrumental in destroying them all. I am jinxed. I am a Jonah. The baby within me is as cursed as I have ever been. His daddy's gone too. Oh God, where will it all end? On the blue bridge at the end of the lane, taking the final jump of my life? Tears are pouring down my face and I don't even realise it. The Blank, however, is finishing this for us. He completes the three elements of the combination faultlessly and then charges down the arena to the final jump. Moments later it is over. We limp out of the arena into the warm up area. Scotty rushes over to me, as do a whole crowd of other people I do not know. I can hear him pushing and shoving his way through the crowd, swearing profusely as he does so. He pulls me into his arms, forcibly removing me from The Blank's back really.

'He's okay, Em, he's okay,' he whispers to me. 'It was just a knock. It wasn't as bad as it looked. He'll be okay. We'll poultice it.'

And from this, I know it is bad really. I put my hand up to The Blank's shoulder and see it judder convulsively before I can touch it. It's hurting him.

'Oh God, Scotty,' I say. 'Get us out of here. I don't want any part of this anymore. Let's just go home.'

We don't even wait for the results of the competition to be announced. We just get The Blank back into the horsebox and head for home.

13. I'm Not Okay (I Promise)

(Written by My Chemical Romance. Appears on Reprise Records: Three Cheers for Sweet Revenge, 2004. Performed by My Chemical Romance)

When we get back to the cottage, there is a crowd of people already waiting for us, congregating in the yard. We have not stopped to collect the trophy, the cheque or take any part in the prize-giving ceremony, although I suppose, as our time was faster than Jonno "not-so-smug-now middle-class twat" Hamilton's, we have won. As soon as we emerge from the cab of the horsebox, the flash of photographers starts.

'How do you feel?' I hear somebody yell at me. 'Are you and the horse okay?' I try to shove my way through.

I can hear Scotty swearing as well, from somewhere around the other side of the horsebox.

'I bet you're not!' I hear a jeering voice. I recognise the voice immediately. It is Keith Denby's. 'I bet you feel like shit. I bet that's just how it feels to win and then be disqualified from the British Open!'

Suddenly, Scotty is standing next to me. I don't catch all he says, but what I do hear sounds something like this;

'I suppose it feels better than being a fucking horse-murdering rapist. You get the fuck off my property. Go on. All of you. Any one of you on here by the time I count to ten and I'm calling the rozzers. Get out. All of you. Before I start getting really mad.'

He already sounds really mad to me. About as mad as Scotty gets. Somehow I am bundled into the gloom of the cottage and Scotty slams the door behind us.

'We can't leave him out there,' I whisper into the darkness. The Blank is still in the horsebox. As if to emphasise the point, I hear him whinny, calling to me from inside the shut up box.

'Oh for fuck's sake!' Scotty barges his way out again. Minutes later he returns, leading The Blank. The three of us wait in my grandmother's lounge. If she had been alive, she would have gone crazy at the sight of a horse standing on her best carpet. If she had been alive, the shock would probably have killed her. I am unsure, however, which she would have preferred: to die in an argument over a dog, or one over a horse. There couldn't be much in it really. Still, whatever she would have said, she wasn't there and we can't leave The Blank out there alone. He's been through enough today because of me.

I huddle into one of the armchairs. I cannot get warm.

'Do you think it's true?' I whisper after a bit. Scotty has been around and shut all the curtains to the cottage, but we can still hear them out there. I hope they can't hear me. 'Do you think we've been disqualified?'

'How the fuck should I know? What does it matter now anyway? I just wish they'd piss off.'

We sit in silence. The Blank stands with his head nodding over my lap. He, alone, seems utterly unfazed by this turn of events. I boil the kettle and make a poultice for his injured shoulder. I feed him all the carrots and all the apples we have in the house. The hours pass. Night becomes day, and then night again.

At some point during the following day an official from the BSJA telephones. It has come to their attention that I may have been riding with a visual impairment. Keith Denby, it seems, has grassed me up. I tell them the truth. There doesn't seem much point in lying to them now. I tell them that I should be registered blind, but that I do have some vision. I tell them that I was wearing an earpiece and that I was being guided around the course. I think this will make matters better. In actual fact, it makes them worse. Now, it seems, I have broken two of the fundamental rules of British Eventing. I am disqualified from the British Open under rule number fifty: "Inappropriate and Dangerous Riding, Part One (b)" whereby "any rider who affects the safety of any horse, rider or third party will be considered as dangerous and will be penalised accordingly". Riding whilst blind, it seems, is considered dangerous. When I think about The Blank, still standing next to me whilst this telephone conversation is taking place with his injured shoulder, I find I cannot argue with this reasoning. Due to my confession about Jimmy's earpiece, I am also disqualified under British Eventing rule fifty-three (a) concerning electronic devices, which states, the man tells me, "No receiving, recording, transmitting or monitoring device may be used by a competitor during any phase of a competition." The man, despite talking like a glossary of equine policy documents, is kind. His kindness reduces me to tears. Perhaps it is the sound of me snivelling down the phone which determines the leniency of my punishment. I will not, I am told, be prohibited from further membership with the British Show Jumping Association. Indeed, the BSJA, Rules-and-Regs-man tells me, is an organisation which embraces equal opportunities for all. They would certainly encourage my continued participation in the sport, but only in the *appropriate* competition. He then goes on to tell me that I may be approached to represent Great Britain in the paralympic games. The man's stress of the word *"appropriate"* just depresses me more, I have to say. All my life, I've been held back by the people in charge just because I'm not the right quality of person. I don't want to play their games by their rules anymore. I don't want to only enter the competitions that they say it's okay for me to enter. The prize which I have been stripped of, I am told, will now go to Jonno (smug-once-more-and-with-good-reason) Hamilton and Hello Dolly. In fact, if anything they'll both be even more impossibly smug now.

I suppose this information is leaked out. The clamour outside the cottage by the waiting journalists, if anything, increases. In the middle of all of the noise, I suddenly hear a rustling, tapping sound at the back window. The Blank throws his head up and whickers in a friendly way, as if in greeting to someone.

'Oh for God's sake!' Scotty says fiercely. 'They've started coming round the back now.'

From outside we hear a whispered voice.

'Em! Em! It's me! Jimmy. Lemme in.'

I look frantically at Scotty.

233

'I don't know, Scotty. I don't think I can face...'

I can feel the heat of the withering glance Scotty gives to me in response. The tap comes again and Scotty marches over to the window, with sudden decisiveness. He pulls the curtains and flings the window open with more force than is strictly necessary. I hear him struggling to pull Jimmy in through the window.

'You've got timing haven't you?' I hear him berating Jimmy. 'Where d'you think you've been, hey? When we actually needed you, you're nowhere to be found.'

I hear Jimmy land in a heap on the floor. Scotty rapidly pulls the window closed and draws the curtains once again. I have my back turned towards Jimmy, my chair facing away from him, and to be quite honest, I don't want to even think about turning around. I don't want to see the blur of those black curls again, unless they're staying for good this time, which seems unlikely after what Pete told me. I shiver at the memory and hunch down even further in the chair. The misery is like a physical ache inside of me. The Blank regards Jimmy sleepily, his ears hanging slackly to the sides. After everything we've been through, he is a horse for whom nothing holds any surprises anymore, not even a punk rocker falling through the window to land at his feet.

'What's The Blank doing in here?' Jimmy asks.

'You might well fucking ask,' Scotty spits out in his most disgusted tone of voice.

'We couldn't leave him out there,' I say pleadingly to Scotty. 'They would have been all over him. Flashing their cameras at him. He's been through enough. He would have been frightened. He had to come inside with us.'

'Oh,' Jimmy says.

'More to the point,' Scotty says, 'what the fuck are you doing here?'

'I had to come,' Jimmy says. From my peripheral vision, I notice that he has moved around to stand near to me. Scotty moves to bar his way. Jimmy continues to address me over Scotty's shoulder.

'Pete... Pete came clean and told me it was him who told you to leave. I thought you'd just left that day. I thought that I hadn't... Well, that you'd had enough of me. That's what Pete said after I woke up and found you gone. He said that you didn't want to be involved anymore and that you'd just left. I was so... I was just so... Sad. When you left. I thought... But then Pete told me what he'd done... What he'd said to you... And I had to come back and see if you still... If we could still... Be together, y'know? After all. Because I can't live without you, Em. I've left the band. I've told Pete where to shove it. He had no right... He Goddamn near broke my heart. When I thought you'd gone. Jeez.' Jimmy shakes his head in apparent disbelief. 'They'll never bother us again. I promise.'

I am silent. My misery seems to have been part of me for so long now, I'm not sure if I can just let it go so easily. I mean, I think to myself, here is Jimmy telling me what I've been longing to hear for weeks now, but what if it's all some kind of sick joke? More lies. I don't know what to believe. What I don't want to do is believe him and then get hurt all over again. I just couldn't bear it. That way, I know, lies the path to the blue bridge over the River Werriver, leaving a motherless child behind to stare at a dreadful cross-stitch picture starring Bruce Dickinson as Jesus Christ. I can't bear the thought of that; but I can see now, after all the hurt I've been through, just how my mother came to be the way she was. All those years of reaching out for her, and finally I've found her. I wish I hadn't.

'He said you were sleeping with other women,' I say. My voice is barely audible. '"Groupies", he called them. He said I was just some nothing you wanted to lose from your life. He said that the only reason you were with me was because you'd been looking for someone more broken than yourself to fix, and that I was it.'

'Oh! That was harsh. But it's not true. None of it. I never slept with anyone else. Not after I met you. We used to... With groupies... Sometimes... Before... Oh God.' Jimmy stops suddenly as if he realises that he's just making the whole situation worse. 'But not after I met you,' he adds hurriedly. 'Not ever.'

'What were they like though? These groupies?' Scotty enquires eagerly. He sounds impressed.

'I didn't know what to think...' I say. 'I *don't* know what to think. Except that I knew that Pete was probably right. At least, I felt like he was at the time. I am just some nothing... And you... Well, you're *you*. But I've been hurt enough.'

'Oh, for God's sake!' Scotty rounds on me suddenly, leaning over me in the armchair as he does so. 'You're so stupid sometimes! Tell me Em, tell me this one thing. The last time you had sex with this knob...' he jerks his head in Jimmy's direction, 'what was it like?'

'Scotty!'

'No. Tell me. Seriously, I *seriously* want to know. Did he take his time over it or did he come right quick? Tell me. I wanna know. It's important, see?'

'Well. It *was* quite quick. I suppose,' I mutter reluctantly.

'Well, there you go then,' Scotty says as if that proved everything. What everything was though, I still wasn't sure. I awaited clarification. 'Look,' Scotty bends even further over me. 'He's not going to come real quick if he's been shagging every other bird from Blackpool to Boston, is he? He's only gonna come quick if he's not got his rocks off for ages. That proves it. That Pete's a lying wanker, and him,' Scotty jerks his head in Jimmy's direction once more, '*he's* been waiting for you all-fucking-faithful like'

I can just make out Jimmy's eager nod of acquiescence on the periphery of my vision.

'And I don't know why you look so happy,' Scotty snaps at him disgustedly. 'I wouldn't be that pleased to be holding my hands up to premature ejaculation.'

Scotty turns towards me again. This time his tone is gentler.

'And as for being hurt enough, can't you see that you're never going to stop hurting as long as you're not with him. You've been a mess. Heartbroken. Give him another chance. Please. I can't stand how miserable you've been without him.'

'Please, Em,' I hear Jimmy plead too. 'I've been miserable too. I need you.'

'I can't believe it,' I say slowly. I turn fully to face Jimmy for the first time. 'He must be serious because that's the most I've heard him say without swearing in about twenty years. I suppose I'll have to give it another go, just on that basis alone.'

Scotty nods, evidently satisfied.

Jimmy edges a little closer towards me, but he's still wary of The Blank. He's not coming too close. He seems to hesitate and then stops just a little way away from me.

'I saw you win the British Open,' he says eventually. 'You were... You *both* were awesome. Oh, I know... I know you were disqualified...'

'Jonno...'

'*That* smug bastard,' Scotty interrupts sotto voce.

'... Hamilton has won it now. Keith...'

'Horse-murdering rapist,' Scotty interrupts softly again.

'Denby told them about my eyesight.' I gesture futilely at my eyes. 'So I got disqualified under some dangerous riding rule.'

'Oh...' Jimmy says.

'Oh, God,' I say. The penny has only just dropped. 'Oh, the irony there. British Eventing Rule Fifty: "Inappropriate and Dangerous Riding, whereby any rider who affects the safety of any horse, rider or third party will be considered as dangerous and will be penalised accordingly." Do you remember, Scotty, there was a rumour that Keith Denby had been disqualified under that rule that night with Treacle Toffee... How perfect is this? He must be laughing his head off.'

'Oh stuff him,' Scotty says. 'I'll give him something to laugh about if he ever sets foot on our yard again.' He swings a meaty fist into his other hand meaningfully.

'I guess not being able to see the course is against the rules, after all,' I say.

'Well I think you should have been able to keep the prize. You still won. You were a hundred times better than all of those other riders. I think you still won,' Jimmy says.

'Well... Thanks,' I reply uncertainly. 'The Blank's been lame ever since I ran him into that fence though. I've been poulticing his shoulder. It was my fault. They were right. I shouldn't have been out there. It was dangerous. For The Blank most of all.'

'He looks alright,' Jimmy says. As he speaks, The Blank straddles his back legs and urinates luxuriously all over the floor.

'Oh, for fuck's sake,' Scotty mutters, shaking droplets from his hands as he does so. There's evidently been some splash-back.

'I bet he'd do it all over again for you, if you gave him the chance,' Jimmy says evenly. 'We watched it from the green room of the stadium we were playing. Even Pete and Si watched. Hey, they were so impressed. They thought you were somethin' else out there. But, boy, did you look nervous before. I never saw you look so fraught.'

I shake my head.

'That last round, I wasn't nervous at all. I felt utterly and completely exhilarated. I was so sure that I had got what I had wanted all these years; that, at last, I had made it. That I was going to waltz off with the prize, the greatest show jumper that the world has ever seen. All I've ever wanted,' I repeat sadly. 'None of it was worth it. I shouldn't have done it. I shouldn't have risked The Blank.'

'Oh, C'mon!' Jimmy says. '"Not nervous at all"! You were sick. In the warm-up arena. All down The Blank's shoulder. They said so. They said it was nerves. On the television.' Jimmy shakes his head wonderingly. 'I never saw you so nervous that you were actually sick before.

'That wasn't nerves,' I repeat stubbornly. 'I wasn't sick with nerves. I was sick because I'm pregnant.'

'Oh...'

'And before you put your foot in it again, yes, it's yours...' Scotty interjects fiercely. 'And thank fuck you're back or I'd be the one who was stuck with it.'

I focus all of my efforts onto moving my blind spot out of the way. I wish I could see Jimmy's face more clearly, and I can't be utterly sure, but it looks like he's grinning to me.

'We need to get out of here,' he mutters at last.

'That's the most sensible thing I've ever heard you say, but how?' Scotty demands.

'We'll go back to my place. Bring The Blank too. We'll wait until it goes properly dark and then just muscle our way through. We'll take them by surprise.'

Scotty shakes his head.

'I don't rate our chances very much. There's hundreds of them out there now.' Scotty moves to take a cautious peep around the edge of the curtains. Outside a clamour begins to rise as the movement at the window is spotted. Scotty hurriedly lets the curtain fall.

'No. I'll go out there,' he says with finality. 'I'll tell them that you're gonna go out and make a statement or somethin' and ask them to move out into the lane. While they're moving out, you sneak out the back and cut through the hedge, over the field and up to Jimmy's house. Then I'll pretend to come back in here and get you, Em, and I'll just do one myself. I'll meet you there.'

'I don't know,' I begin to protest. It all sounds a bit mad to me. 'What about his poor shoulder. I don't know if he can walk.' I reach out to run my hand over The Blank's shoulder and feel his flesh judder convulsively again, before I barely even touch it, as if in anticipation of the pain.

'We'll take him slowly,' Jimmy says. 'He'll be better off at my house than in here, believe me.'

I suppose he is right. There is an acrid stench of warm ammonia beginning to permeate the air of the cottage, rising from the carpet beneath where The Blank is standing.

'Too right,' Scotty agrees, rubbing his nose. 'C'mon Em, get his head-collar on. Let's get out of here.'

Seconds later, Scotty emerges from the cottage to an uproar of journalists' questions and flashing cameras and, whilst they are busy, Jimmy, The Blank and I are busy too; hotfooting it across the fields to the lane where Jimmy's house stands. As we walk, he grasps my fingers.

'Hey, I've got a surprise for you when we get back to my place.'

'I don't like surprises,' I reply quickly. 'In my experience they're never anything any good. You told me you had a surprise for me that last night before Pete... Well after what Pete said I guessed that it was that you wanted me out of your life. It's not been nice living with that.'

'Well, Pete, as Scotty so eloquently put it, is a lying wanker. And my surprise was *never* gonna be that, d'you hear me?'

I give a snort of laughter.

'I'll tell you what the surprise is and then you can decide for yourself whether it's anything any good or not before we get there.'

I nod silently in acquiescence to this idea.

'I had the stables fitted out for The Blank. They're gonna be the best stables ever. Anything a horse could ever want, apparently. I had the swimming pool filled in and the whole garden turned into one big paddock for him. It's gonna be awesome. Although I haven't seen it myself, yet, I have to admit. I left some guys doing it while I was out on tour.'

'You did? Why?'

'Because I was kinda hoping that The Blank would move in with me... But you'd have to come too, because he needs taking care of, and I'm afraid of horses.'

This time I laugh out loud. I stop in the centre of the field and reach up with my hands to stroke at those wild black curls which frame the pale of his face.

'God, I've missed you. I've really, really missed you.'
Jimmy pulls me towards him and kisses me ferociously.

'Don't leave me.   Don't ever leave me... Not ever, ever again,' he mutters hungrily against my lips.   'C'mon.   Let's go home.'

When we arrive at Jimmy's house, Jimmy seals the security gate behind us and leads us around the back to the stables.   I lead The Blank inside the first one and let him snuff at the deep bed of wood shavings which has been prepared for him, banked high against the sides of the walls so that he won't bump his legs. Whoever Jimmy got to do the job, did a good one, I think.   The stables are perfect.   I locate the empty water buckets and take two outside to fill them at the tap there.

'Any car tyres?' I ask.

'Any what?'   Jimmy sounds confused.

'We could do with a couple of car tyres to stand these buckets in.   Just so The Blank doesn't knock them over in the night and ruin his bed.'

'Oh,' Jimmy says.   He sounds disappointed.   'It seems such a shame to put old car tyres in here.   It's such a fine-looking stable.'

'I know,' I sympathise.   'It is.   But he'll only knock them over and ruin this bed if we don't get some.'

'I'll get some,' Jimmy promises reluctantly.   'From somewhere.'

'Don't worry,' I say.   'Scotty will get them.   We've got some in the yard.   We'll get them later.   When they've all gone again.'

The Blank takes a pull of hay from the hay-net which has been hung in preparation for his arrival.

'I wonder how long that's been there?' I worry, pointing to the hay.   'I bet it's dusty.'

'I don't know.'

'Oh well,' I attempt to dismiss the anxiety from my mind. 'He's eating it.   It must be okay.   Your poor shoulder...'   I stroke The Blank's neck.   'You poor thing.'   The Blank grunts and flicks his ears back and forth at my words.   I stroke the long arching

241

muscle of his neck. 'At least you're safe here. They won't bother you here.'

I back away and move to join Jimmy at the threshold of the stable. As I walk towards him, something brushes against my face. I stop and grope at it, whatever it is.

'What's that?' I ask eventually, when I have failed to locate the mysterious object again. 'It felt like thread. Don't tell me you've got spiders in your new stable already?' I find the thread again and travel the length of it. Something cool and metallic hangs from the end of it. 'What *is* that?' I ask again.

I feel Jimmy move towards me. He takes my hand.

'I didn't want you just to move in here with me. I wanted you to... Well... Stay with me forever. I can't live without you, Em. I've already proven that to myself. Marry me, Em. Will you? Please?'

I pull at the thread and it snaps in my hand. Between my fingers I hold the ring which Jimmy has left for me to find. I hold it up to my eyes and squint at it as best as I can.

'Pretty,' I say eventually.

'I was going to get you the biggest diamond cluster I could find, but then, somehow, after I'd got it, it didn't seem quite right. Y'know, *for you*. I just couldn't imagine its brash extravagance on your fairy fingers. I took it back and got you this fire opal instead. My mom would never have approved. She always said opals were unlucky and refused to wear them. And then when you'd gone that day, off the bus, I thought she must have been right all along. I mean, there was me, leaving you an opal engagement ring to find when we came back here, and suddenly it seemed like you wouldn't be coming back. God, Em, I've been to hell and back without you. I'll never forgive Pete for what he nearly did to us.'

He pulls me towards him and kisses me once more. I am crushed against him. I can feel his desire and am suddenly afraid.

'Come inside,' he mutters thickly into my hair. 'Come inside *now*.'

I pull away from him a fraction.

'Do you think... Do you think it's alright?' I cover my stomach with my hand in a subconscious movement to protect the child within.

'I know it's alright,' he promises. 'You forget. I've done all this before, honey. With Isabella. Well, sort of. Anyway, I'll be real gentle with you... With both of you.'

I lean against him, pushing myself against him, wanting him savagely now.

'Don't be too gentle. I've missed you Jimmy. God, you don't know how much.'

When we wake, Scotty is lounging in one of the recliners on the sun terrace. As we appear, he leaps impatiently to his feet.

'At fucking last. Talk about reunions. I thought you said he was quick?' he snaps.

I can feel myself blushing to the roots of my hair.

'Hey, that was only one time,' Jimmy chides.

'Whatever,' Scotty dismisses him. 'I had a right job shaking them off. I don't know when we'll ever be able to go home. This place is okay though. I don't mind hanging out here a bit. You should see it, Em. You should see the stuff he's got. This pad's flasher than a rat with a gold tooth.' Scotty gestures around us to all of these amazing things which I cannot see and don't care about anyway. He shrugs when he notices my disinterest. 'I had to laugh though,' he continues. 'I hid out in Mrs Ayre's village shop when I was trying to shake them off and just happened to pick up a copy of *Rock Review*.' Scotty throws a copy of a magazine onto the table before him. 'Check out the review of your concert on page sixteen.'

Jimmy slowly picks up the magazine and reads:

'"Live Shows:
Lights Out, Plus: *Pandora's Box*
Olympiahalle, Munich.

Nobody here tonight has come to see Pandora's Box, a ramshackle, if enthusiastic pop punk quartet, and despite playing, (and in the case of lead singer, Andrea Boccelli screaming) their little hearts out (Ahh, bless) the crowd never progresses beyond luke-warm in their reception of them. It's equally true that nobody here tonight has come to watch the British Open Show Jumping Championship on a large screen at the back of the stage. In fact, if anything, it has to be said that this is the *last thing* any of this audience here tonight would have thought they would be doing; but that's exactly what's happening, and it's all because, as the management apologetically explain, *LO*'s stickmeister, Jimmy Bridges is refusing to come on stage until he's watched the event through to the end, AND, they go on to explain, none of the band will play at all unless Emily Devlin takes first prize on The Blank. What follows is a surreal and extremely tense hour when several thousand German punk rockers cheer when their own man knocks down a fence on his horse and go into raptures of relief when Miss Devlin and her, quite frankly, ugly-looking horse take the prize. Yes, *Lights Out* are still as mad as geese but would you want it any other way? The answer has to be a resounding "No!" for their performance this evening, despite the unscheduled and slightly bizarre equine interlude is easily the best I've ever seen. Throughout their set of some twenty-five songs, with selections from every album and spanning their entire twenty year career, they maintain an intensity level which threatens to blow the equipment, set the joint on fire and peel the skin from your face simultaneously. Frontman Pete Darlow is awesome; Si Pelton wields his bass like a weapon and, if the sound he manages to wring out of it is anything to go by, it's one of mass destruction too, and Mad Jimmy, despite clearly being off his rocker, is still the king of the sticks. Rumour has it that tonight's performance may have been unique for other reasons too; for there's been some gossip coming through the grapevine that it may have been Bridges' last with the band. The gossip says that Bridges flew out of the *LO* camp after the show last night and he's not scheduled to return any time soon. Rumour has it that he's going home to his show jumper girlfriend. No prizes for guessing who that is.'"

Jimmy throws the magazine down and Scotty grins at him.

'They got that right, didn't they? You are off your rocker an' all making all those people watch the fucking show jumping.'
'Scotty, did you steal that?' I put in accusingly.
Scotty shrugs.
'I had to have something to do while I was waiting for all those journos to piss off.'

Night settles over Jimmy's house. The peace of the Cheshire countryside is as it always is. No one would guess that just half a field away a storm is raging outside of our house. We could even begin to forget about it all and relax into the tranquillity of this new situation we have found ourselves in, until Scotty turns Jimmy's television on and the storm bursts around our ears once more.

'Good evening and welcome to Look North,' a woman with too much bronze make-up on her face says to the camera. 'And tonight on Look North... The local man who's spent a month on a desert island for charity... The pensioner robbed at knife point in her sheltered accommodation unit... Bus drivers threaten strike action again... And Emily Devlin, the local woman who's rocked the world of show jumping by winning the British Open Show Jumping Championships, only for her to be stripped of her title less than twenty-four hours later when it emerged via local show jumping legend Keith Denby that Miss Devlin is actually blind...'

'Legend in his own lunchtime,' Scotty murmurs disparagingly.

'...We gauge your reactions to the controversy,' the woman continues.

I cannot stand it. I go outside to poultice The Blank's shoulder again, even though it's starting to seem less swollen now. In the background, as the first article starts, I hear Jimmy ask Scotty conversationally, 'Hey, what would be the one thing that you'd take with you to a desert island?'

'Ray Mears,' Scotty snaps in response.

I grin, but then try and purposefully shut out the sound of the television. I don't want to hear the public's reactions to the controversy I have caused. When the article rolls around though, I cannot help but hear what people have got to say.

'Well it were just bloody stupid,' I hear the voice of an elderly man state. 'She could'a killed herself and the horse. It were cruel.'

I wince.

'She won. She should have been able to keep her prize. The fact that she did it and she was blind all along just makes it all the more impressive,' I hear a woman's voice saying.

'Oh, it was awful,' another voice swims out of the television towards where I am hiding at The Blank's stable. This voice is plummy and well-to-do. It sounds like Sarah Braithwaite's mother. I hope to God it's not. 'The way that poor animal bumped its shoulder against that fence when she rode him straight at it. She should have been expelled from the BSJA, never mind just the competition.'

I make my way back towards the lounge where Jimmy and Scotty are watching in slightly uncomfortable silence.

'Turn it off, Scotty,' I say. 'I can't stand it.'

Scotty flicks the remote of the television over to one of the music channels, just in time to hear the dying bars of "We Won't Stop the Party," the anthem by which *Lights Out* became known by during their 1994 "Into Darkness" tour.

'*Lights Out* there with "We Won't Stop the Party",' a nubile young presenter (wearing only slightly less bronze make-up) announces. 'But it looks like they have and will, being as this is the second tour drummer Jimmy Bridges has walked out of and this time, nobody's that optimistic he'll return. Looks like the party's well and truly over for *Lights Out!*' the woman bears her perfect white teeth at the camera in a predatory fashion.

'And I can't stand this. Turn it off, Scotty,' Jimmy says.

Scotty switches the television onto standby and a blissful silence permeates Jimmy's lounge room. It is me who breaks it.

'Do you think I was cruel?' I ask.

'No way!' Scotty leaps immediately to my defence. 'You were just better than everyone else out there and when they found out they'd been beaten by a blind woman, they didn't like it, did they? They had to disqualify you, else it makes them look crap. Let's face it, they didn't like you beating them before they found out you were blind. They were just looking for an excuse to disqualify you anyway. You being blind, well it's given them one. They still look crap though. They are crap compared to you. No way were you cruel to that horse.'

Another silence permeates the room. This time it is Scotty who breaks it. 'What about you?' he nods to Jimmy. 'Is the party over or what? Are you going back to them?'

'No,' Jimmy says. 'Never. I'd rather teach drums in High School or whatever else it is that you guys have over here. Or else be a session drummer for other bands. Or produce the music of other bands, I could do that. I don't really care. I'd rather wait tables in a diner and be happy here with you, Em, than go back to that life.'

'There aren't many diners around here,' I observe matter-of-factly.

'There's a McDonalds,' Scotty suggests, helpfully. 'I don't think any school would have you. The parents round here wouldn't trust you with their snotty-nosed stuck-up kids.'

'One thing's for certain,' Jimmy continues. 'We are... *Both* of us, going to have to answer for what we've done. We are going to *have* to talk to the press, Em. If we don't and they don't get some answers from us, they'll never leave us alone. If we don't

247

give them something, they'll just start making stuff up. Trust me, this is *one thing* I *really* do know about.'

I shrink back from him. The thought is utterly, terrifyingly, devastatingly, horrible to me.

'I can't...' I eventually manage to breathe. 'I can't go out there and talk to... All those people...'

'Listen to me. Listen to me,' Jimmy places his hands on my upper arms. I can feel the urgency of what he wants to convey to me by the pressure of his fingers upon my flesh.

'I'll tell you a story. Once upon a time I thought I was in love with this girl. I'd have done anything to have her. I wanted her to belong to me. Jeez, when she walked into a room, I couldn't concentrate anymore... God, but I had it bad.'

'Oh, for fuck's sake,' I hear Scotty interrupt.

'Scotty!' I chide distractedly.

'Okay, I'll take an interest in this *pointless* story. Did this bint have big tits?'

'Scotty!'

Jimmy makes a move with his head in Scotty's direction, but continues addressing his words solely to me.

'It's not pointless, but as it happens, she did. She was Isabella Grazio. She had enormous breasts. Magnificent breasts. She made a fortune out of them. Until she started hanging out with me. I got her pregnant, see? She didn't want the baby. She lost her modelling contract because of our baby. And because of that, she started to hate me. Well... Maybe because of other things too, but I think it was mainly down to that. But... God... I wanted her. I loved her. I adored her. I just wanted us to be a family together.'

I don't want to hear this. I don't want to hear about this woman who Jimmy... *My Jimmy*... Loved and wanted so much. I don't want to hear about this woman who didn't want to carry Jimmy's baby, when I'm standing here, carrying Jimmy's baby. I attempt to twist away from him, but his hands on my arms won't let me.

'No, wait! I don't want her now. I was wrong. I'll only ever want you. You and our baby. Our family. Surely you must know that, right? But there is something you must know about Isabella and me. She hated me so much that after the baby was born, she started to sleep around. She slept with my manager. She slept with Pete.'

'What about the other one?' Scotty interrupts. He's interested now, in Jimmy's story; now that it contains models and sex and large mammaries. 'Si?'

'I don't think so. I don't know though. She slept with a lot of people. Maybe. I couldn't hold it against Si if she did. She was beautiful. And persuasive.'

Scotty might be enjoying this story, but I'm not. I feel slightly sick. I don't want to hear about this beautiful, persuasive being, who isn't me. Perhaps Jimmy notices my rising pallour.

'But, God, she was a bitch. I wanted to get back at her. Just to get even. I started sleeping around too. I don't know why I thought she'd care, but I did it anyway. Anyone would do. Groupies. Whoever happened to be around. Then, one day, it must have been on one of the rare occasions when we actually slept together, she caught somethin' off me... Or I caught somethin' off her, and it all came out. Jeez, we had the biggest row. I just lost it. I really did. I punched out at the wall behind her. I was just so mad. I can't lie to you. I wanted to kill her. I wanted to squeeze the life out of her lying throat. But then... Suddenly, I realised what I was doing. At some point during our argument, she'd picked Juno... the baby... she'd picked her up. Juno's screaming and screaming at me. She never liked me all that much that kid. In fact, let's be honest, she hated me. But suddenly she's afraid of me as well. And when I look at Isabella, I see there's fear in her eyes too. I back off. I felt... Just... Well, *mortified* by how I'd been behaving. I say I'm sorry. I apologise over and over again, but I can't deny that I only just stopped myself from hitting her... Hitting the woman who's holding *my* child in her arms. I can't deny that just moments before my hands had been fists. Just moments before I was bending over her, breathing too hard, with my heart full of murder.'

I'm breathing way too hard myself now. I don't want to hear any of this. I ask myself why I ever wanted to know or understand any of this stuff about Jimmy's past in the first place. Scotty makes a move towards me, the old instinct to protect me evidently reasserting itself, but Jimmy raises his hand to stop him.

'Wait. This is the important bit. I know it hurts to hear it, honey, I do, but this last bit you really need to know. I left. Fast as I could. Got back on the Goddamn bus and went on another Goddamn tour. But Isabella... Well, she got even. I'd given her the ammunition she needed against me, see? She went to the press. She told them I beat her. They believed her. They said it was because I was a drummer. I had to have something... *Anything* to hit. They started to call me "Mad Jimmy", the little man who made himself bigger by beating up his wife and child. I never spoke up for myself then. And the name "Mad Jimmy"? Well, it stuck. If I'd just spoken out for myself. If I'd just had a go at clearing my name, who knows? Maybe I could have proven her a liar. Made a case for myself. Instead, I let it go. I let her have that one. After all, I'd come pretty close to beating her, that much was true. Or maybe I was just afraid to speak up for myself. I never could stand up to the bullies either, y'know? Bullies like Pete can be and your Sarah Braithwaite. Whatever. *That name.* "Mad Jimmy" Bridges. I've been stuck with it forever. Even you. I've even seen you believe the lies. I've seen fear in your eyes too sometimes. As if I'd harm a hair on your head.'

Jimmy turns away from me now. He is disappointed in me. I can feel it.

'No... No, I...'

Jimmy faces me again.

'Ask yourself. Why did you just walk off that bus that day? How could you just leave me behind so easily if a part of you didn't believe I was the person you should know me to be. Face it, honey, part of you believed I was "Mad Jimmy" too. Those lies. Isabella's stories. They've even tainted us.'

I shake my head emphatically.

'No! It's not true. It's just that...' My words trail away uncertainly.

'Of course it's fucking true,' Scotty interrupts. 'You wondered about those stories and so did I. We both believed that there might be a grain of truth somewhere in those stories. Where there's smoke there's fire and all that.'

And then, when I say nothing, Scotty presses on.

'Well, I know I did. And... Fuck it... I know you did too. I used to see you worrying sometimes. And I couldn't weigh him up half the time...' Scotty jerks his head in Jimmy's direction. 'And that used to bother me, you know? I was convinced that one day you'd start coming home with bruises... But then it never did start. And you seemed so happy most of the time. Still... I always had my doubts.'

Jimmy places his hands on my upper arms again. This time his touch upon me is gentle but insistent.

'I don't blame you, honey, for believing that those stories might be true. Those papers... They can be real persuasive too. But just imagine if you get stuck with some name now, like I did... Some label of animal cruelty or somethin' like that just because you don't speak up for yourself.'

Jimmy places his hands over my tummy. '*He's* gonna be the one who's got to grow up not knowing whether to believe those lies about you or not. You gotta clear your name, while you still can...'

'He's right, Em,' Scotty interjects. 'You've got to get out there and explain it all. Imagine what they're gonna say about us if they start digging around. I mean, Christ! All these years, we've been living off your disability benefits. It's only really because of those that we could buy The Blank in the first place. Benefits have financed your entire show jumping career. Can you imagine what the *Daily Mail* would make of that? And that's just the tip of the iceberg. The stuff they could put about mum. About dad. The stuff Keith Denby could make up about us. You can't let them do it to your baby. Think about mum. How she never helped us. And I *know*. I *fucking know* she couldn't fucking help herself. But she should have been able to. It was her job. As our mum. And this is your job. As his mum. To get out there and clear his name before he gets launched into this shit.'

I swallow convulsively. They are right. Both of them. I have to speak out. I have to set the record straight, and fast, before any more damage is done. Before those papers turn into Grammar school bullies and start spreading lies about me until I almost believe them myself. It was always the rhetoric that was used against you that became the hardest to bear. The scathing comments and the put-downs, the campaigns of whispered lies about you, the gossip mongered about you. I can't let them do it to me again. But then I think about all those people; about that faceless, blurry crowd baying for my blood.

'I know I've got to. You're right. You're both right. I know it. But I don't know if I can just walk out into that lane and explain it all. Oh God. What a mess.'

'You don't have to,' Jimmy squeezes my hand reassuringly. 'We'll do it on our own terms. There's a man... My manager... He owes me a favour... Lots of favours really.

'Is he the one who slept with your ex-missus? I should say he owes you a favour,' Scotty grins.

'Yeah, well,' Jimmy shrugs this jibe aside. 'He'll get us set up on a prime time television show. You know, one of those talk shows. One of the good ones that everybody watches and we'll explain it all then. You can tell them why you weren't being... would never be cruel to The Blank. I'll tell them I'm finished with *Lights Out* and that'll be the end of it. We can get on with the rest of our lives.'

I nod slowly. I know I don't have any choice in the matter really. This will be going on forever, unless I face the music now.

'The only thing is...' Jimmy continues somewhat reluctantly. 'Well, Pete and Si will have to be there too.'

The feeling of horror seizes hold of me once more.

'Both of them?' I ask in a voice that comes out as a hoarse whisper. 'Pete too?'

'Yes, Pete too. Especially Pete. He's the frontman. They're gonna want to hear it from him.'

Thursday finds us in a television studio for the recording of "*Last Night with Graham*". It is worse than even I anticipated it would be. I am, putting it quite simply, petrified. My terror blinds me even further. I am unable to calm myself down sufficiently to be able to concentrate; focus upon moving my blind spot aside when I need to. As a result, everything is just some indefinable shape dancing in the blur. Scotty has not been permitted to accompany me inside the building. They spout some crap about "authorised personnel" and "security risks". I can't really blame them. I suppose Scotty looks like a security risk to people who don't know him, with his skinhead and his ripped clothing. Instead they provide their own "assistant" for me. She is of no assistance to me whatsoever. She watches me fall up stairs and clip myself on door frames. Every time I commit one of these acts of clumsiness, she will tut a little and say "careful, Dear". After an hour in her company, I am longing to be away from her. When she tries to take my arm in a manner in which she has clearly seen blind people being led about in films, I shove her away from me with more force than is necessary.

'Tut! Careful, Dear,' I say, as she stumbles backwards, and try not to laugh.

It is only a minor victory. It doesn't really make me feel any better about the situation; but it is something, and at least, after that, she leaves me alone a little.

Jimmy, I know, is somewhere inside the building. He was with me, at first, but then they took him away too, leading me off in

253

the opposite direction. It seems to take an age to be taken back to him. They fuss over me endlessly. Eventually I am led into a room crowded with other people. The "assistant" clearly as sick of me as I am of her now, abandons me, leaving me floundering and panic-stricken in the midst of all of these strangers, none of whom I can focus upon properly. I freeze momentarily. I think I'm going to be sick.

'Hey, Em,' Jimmy touches my arm and relief floods through me. 'They put make-up on you,' he observes. 'You look... Different.'

'God knows what they've done to me. They've just been fussing over me for what feels like days. I'm sick of them.' I hesitate for a second. 'Do I look ridiculous?' I ask quietly, suddenly, and possibly for the first time in my recent history, concerned as to how I look.

'No! You look... Pretty.'

'Oh... Thanks.'

A blurry figure approaches Jimmy. I recognise the strip of shocking pink hair.

'What up, man?' Si says to Jimmy. He stoops to kiss my cheek somewhat awkwardly. 'Nice to see you again.'

I take an almost involuntary step backwards. There is a tall, equally blurry shape behind him who I am guessing is Pete. The knowledge causes a stab of anxiety in my gut.

'I wish I could say the same,' I say coldly. I direct my eyes behind him to Pete's tall figure. I'm glad I can't see him properly.

'Hey! I thought she couldn't see,' I hear Pete remark flippantly.

'Just the blurred outline is bad enough,' I say shortly.

'Hey, hey, take it easy,' Pete says. He lifts his hands in what is probably a mocking gesture of surrender. 'I'm sorry, okay. I told Jimmy so. But, Jeez, I thought you were hard. There's me supposedly breaking your heart and telling you to stay away from the guy who I'm thinking is the love of your life, allegedly the only guy you've ever screwed, and you walked off that bus like you didn't have a care in the world. When I saw that, I thought I'd done right. Our Jimmy's a sensitive soul. He doesn't need another hard as nails woman fucking him up some more.' Pete reaches past Si to cup Jimmy's chin. Jimmy jerks his head away violently.

Pete's words trouble me. Suddenly, I'm seeing myself as other people must see me. It's not as pretty as Jimmy says I look. Prickly. Hostile. Hard. It's how Pete views me. It's probably how all those people out there in the studio audience view me too. A cold, callous, show jumper who deliberately rode her horse into an obstacle, injuring it in the process, just to cut seconds off my jump-off time and win, even though I had no right riding in that competition in the first place. A wave of misery engulfs me. I feel Jimmy's hand close around my fingers, and for the first time ever, his touch does not make me feel any better. I feel tears pool in my eyes. Jimmy squeezes my fingers again. I feel the pressure of the calluses on his hands, calluses formed over all the years he has clutched drumsticks in his hands. I suppose I remain unresponsive, because after a moment he stoops down and whispers in my ear;

'Look, I'm sorry, okay? I didn't mean to let slip about you being a virgin. It just kinda came out in the middle of the conversation Pete and I had just after you'd walked off the bus... Y'know? When I thought you'd walked out on me? I'm sorry. I was upset. I wasn't thinking straight...'

'Oh that,' I say disparagingly. Who cares what Pete knows or doesn't know, I think. But then I realise that it's not just Pete, is it? This room is full of people; strangers to me, all of whom also, by default, know this most intimate fact about me now. I can suddenly feel myself blushing right up to the roots of my hair.

The assistant returns and we are directed into seats. As she does so, she introduces each person in the room. Mad punk rockers *Lights Out* and the blind woman who fooled the British Show Jumping Association are not the only guests on Graham Last's show. There's an actress too. Her name is Senga Winters. I seem to think her name might be familiar to me somehow. Jimmy whispers to me that she's a Hollywood A-lister and that she's

Graham Last's guest of honour here tonight. As such she will be interviewed last this evening.

'Ah, last by Last,' I say and feel a bubble of hysterical laughter build up inside me.

There is also a painfully shy young man who takes a seat on my left. He wears his self-consciousness like a mantle. I feel nearly as sorry for him as I do for myself.

'I thought you were marvellous,' the Hollywood A-lister, says to me suddenly. She has an horrible clipped English upper-class accent which reminds me of Sarah Braithwaite and Sebastian Carling-Brookes too much for comfort. I wince involuntarily and keep my gaze directed down at my hands in my lap.

It transpires that the room we are in is called a "green room". We will be filmed, we are told, as we wait in this room, and as Graham Last introduces us, our images will be projected onto a large screen in the television studio for the benefit of the studio audience. Then he will call us out, one by one, to be interviewed. I am so focused upon my own fear, however, that I barely listen to the instructions being conveyed to us. I continue to stare (unseeingly, of course) at my hands in my lap. I ignore the rustle of activity around me: clothes being smoothed, hair being fiddled with, smiles being pasted across faces. I don't care how I look. This is only ever going to look bad, no matter how nice my hair looks or however much I smile. The weight of the misery inside of me intensifies.

'Heads up, everybody, you're on,' another assistant calls into the room. This one stands by the door, as if she is fearful we will try and make a break for it. As Graham Last makes his entrance in the studio outside and we hear what he has to say about us, it becomes clear why.

'And what a show we've got lined up for you tonight, Ladies and Gentlemen. We've got Meuthen Matthews, the baby-faced winner of *I Can Be a Star!* Look at him, Ladies and Gentlemen! Just have a look at those boyish good looks. He's right

256

there in my green room! No, you're right... He doesn't look all that stellar, does he?'

Oh God, I think. I feel the man next to me sag against his seat, apparently crushed by what Graham Last has said about him.

'Ha! Ha!' Graham Last continues, apparently oblivious to the agony he has caused to the boy next to me. 'But we have got some *real* rock stars here tonight, too. Yes, Ladies and Gentlemen, it's *Lights Out!*'

On the other side of me, I feel Jimmy stiffen and guess that the camera is now trained upon him.

'Try not to smash anything up, guys!' Graham Last calls gaily out to them.

'Jeez, who the fuck is this guy?' I hear Pete mutter.

'We've also got something of an exclusive for you here this evening. She's refused to talk to anyone else, but she's agreed to come here tonight to talk to me about what's become the biggest scandal in the show jumping world since Ivan Howley tried to marry his horse... Yes! It's a woman who's definitely got some explaining to do. It's Emily Devlin everybody!'

A further wave of nausea engulfs me.

'No, don't adjust your sets, viewers at home. She really is that shade of green at the moment.'

I feel Jimmy start forward angrily, as if he's about to go out there and start throwing punches. I lay my hand on his arm.

'S'allright,' I mutter in a barely audible whisper.

'And no need to adjust your sets here either. Yes, she really is that beautiful! We've got Senga Winters here to tell us all about her new film *Black Wood*. It's going to be another box office smash... But, first, Ladies and Gentlemen, Meuthen Matthews! Here he is.'

I feel the young man square his shoulders before he shuffles out to face Graham Last almost reluctantly. I know I should be concentrating on this interview, listening in on what sort of questions Graham Last is asking to see if I can glean from these just how bad it's going to be for me out there, but I can't seem to focus upon it. I hear Graham Last make a few jibing comments about Meuthen Matthews' sexuality and can imagine how utterly crushed that shy young man is going to be by the audience's mocking laughter at these comments. In the background I can hear Pete begin to complain about Graham Last.

'Who the fuck is this guy? He'd better not be some asshole or I *will* start smashing stuff up.'

'He's the biggest asshole there is, Sweetie,' Senga Winters interjects. 'But he's also got the biggest ratings. He might be pure poison, but this is the place to be seen if you've got something to sell...'

Oh God, I think again. What will he do to me? Me, who has nothing to sell and nothing to offer except explanations and excuses. And not very good ones at that. Distantly, at the back of this thought, comes the realisation that an expectant applause is filtering through into the green room.

'Well, he'd better not fuck with us,' I hear Pete say. He is standing up now. Jimmy gives my hand a final squeeze.

'See you out there,' he whispers to me.

I make a concerted effort to focus on just what is going on out there.

It all begins amicably enough. (What I don't realise and what Senga Winters could probably easily have told me, is that with Graham Last, it *always* begins amicably enough.) They talk about their twenty year history as a band together, focussing upon their successes, of which there have been many. There's a lot to talk about. I can feel by the way that the conversation is progressing that Jimmy is beginning to relax. I suppose they all are. It doesn't sound so bad. They almost sound as if they are starting to enjoy themselves. Maybe, this isn't going to be so terrible after all. Still, I can sense something. I'm not sure what, but something... Something which fills me with unaccountable dread. Seconds later, as Graham Last's tone alters perceptibly, my premonition proves correct.

'So, here we are guys, twenty years on, yet another tour and *yet again* your drummer walks out of it. What is it this time, Jimmy? *Lights On* and no-one's home again, or is it just *lights out* for *Lights Out*?'

The audience roars its approval.

Evidently encouraged, Graham Last continues, 'Lost the plot *again*, have you?'

'Hey... You make it sound like I'm always walking out on tours... I've walked off of one... Once... In twenty years... And I was ill...' I hear Jimmy say.

'Yeah, yeah... *Mentally* ill. And I thought all drummers could count to *at least* four. Well, I guess you can't, can you, because I make it *two* you've walked out of now...'

'Well, there was the last one too, I guess...' Jimmy must know that he's playing directly into Graham Last's hands with this helpless casting around to excuse himself. Graham Last doesn't let him finish anyway.

'And this time, before you walk out on the tour, you firstly force all of your German fans to sit through the final of the British Open Show Jumping at your Munich concert, and then, and I really do think this is insult to injury, Jimmy, *then* you announce you're throwing in the towel. I mean, couldn't you have done that before the concert... Save them all sitting through what has to be the most pointless sport ever invented in the first place. You could have at least let them watch the football. It sounds like you were losing your marbles to me.'

I wonder if Jimmy is getting angry. Or Pete. I don't think that he will take this lying down, and for the first time ever (oh, it's a night of firsts alright: first time on a TV talk show, first time Jimmy's touch has not comforted me, first time I've been outed as a virgin in a room full of strangers) I am glad for the person that Pete is.

'Yeah, man, you got us,' Pete interrupts suddenly. 'It's *lights out* for *Lights Out*. Ha ha. You're so funny. Ha fucking ha. But we ain't through yet. Alright, Jimmy's got his own plans, but

I'm gonna do a solo album. I got songs comin' out of my ears, man. The best is yet to come for me. And Si's formed a new band too.'

'Yeah, man, *"April Showers"*. We've got ideas comin' out of our ears too, and they're all *killer*.'

'So, a *shower* to watch out for in the future, then?'

'Too right!' Si responds, totally oblivious to the ironic emphasis Graham Last has employed with Si's new band's name. The audience laughs wholeheartedly, joining in with the joke at Si's expense. I don't think Si will get it though. He's probably just feeling confused right about now.

'Well, let's hope it's not a *washout*.' Graham Last says conspiratorially, addressing the audience, who, once more, titter along with the joke dutifully.

'And what are your plans, Jimmy? Next stop the funny farm is it? Or going to form the world's first show jumping to music show?'

'Nah, I don't think so. Reckon I'll just kick back and relax a little. I might even become a house husband.' Jimmy sounds unperturbed again now. He sounds like he doesn't care anymore.

'House husband, hey?' Graham actually winks at the audience this time. 'You really have lost it big time, haven't you? I mean, correct me if I'm wrong, but didn't your wife *leave* you and take the kid with her. Isn't it a bit late for all that now?'

'You don't bother doing your research very well, do you?' I hear Jimmy chide lightly. 'You really should make an effort, y'know. Earn that obscenely huge pay cheque you get. I mean, even *Rock Review* knew that Em Devlin and I are an item.'

The audience laughs a little uncertainly and I am gratified to note that Graham Last sounds less assured now as he wraps the interview up.

'Ha ha ha, Jimmy Bridges and *Lights Out* everybody. Still crazy after all these years. But now let's meet the woman who made her accidental debut into the punk rock world when these guys insisted her performance at the British Open be broadcast live, as we have heard, at their Munich show. This just hours before she was disqualified from the competition when the event organisers discover that she's actually *blind*! Astonishingly brave or foolhardily cruel? You decide... Let's hear what she has to say for herself... It's Emily Devlin, Ladies and Gentlemen!'

Somehow I force myself to stand up and walk through the doors. My actions feel clumsy. I feel as if I am moving like a robot. I vaguely recognise that Jimmy has stood up to meet me. Pete, Si and Meuthen shunt themselves further down the long couch to make room for me to sit. I take a cautious seat in the space nearest to Graham Last. I think I'm going to be sick. Jimmy sits down beside me. All I can focus on for the first few seconds is the thump-thump-thump of my heart and the noise of the rushing of blood in my ears.

'Find us alright?' Graham Last quips. I feel myself flush to the roots of my hair. I hate this man already. I wish I was quick-witted like Scotty. I wish I could think up funny responses. Instead, I don't know what to say to this moron; how to respond. He doesn't give me chance anyway.

'Just my little joke. Welcome! Welcome to the show, Emily Devlin. Just before we begin let's take a look at your performance in the final of the British Open Show Jumping Championship.'

The large screen which must have been previously used to introduce us as we waited in the green room, flickers into life and shows a montage of clips of me riding The Blank. The Blank clearing the enormous wall jump. The Blank turning on a penny to clear one of the other upright fences. Finally, The Blank bumping his shoulder against that fatal tenth fence.

'Well, it was some performance, I've got to say,' Graham Last begins flippantly. 'I'd have to be blind before I'd even consider tackling those fences. I mean, they were enormous! Were they as bad as they look there, or couldn't you see? Was it all just your brother guiding you around the course through the earpiece - and not very well, either, when we look at those pictures there?'

'No, it wasn't,' I hear myself saying. 'I could see the fences. I'm not totally blind. Of course, I could never have gone out there and done it if I was totally blind. I have something called "Stargadt's Disease". In my case, it's very progressive and it's created a blind spot in my vision. I wouldn't be safe to drive, and I can't read, or anything like that. My sight's just too poor. But I genuinely believed that I was safe to compete with The Blank. I could see the fences, even if they were a bit blurred. I thought I could see them well enough with my brother helping me. That last was just a terrible accident...'

'Well, those fences are certainly big enough for even a blind person to see,' Graham Last remarks affably enough. 'I mean, Ladies and Gentlemen, just take another look at that wall.' The screen again flickers into life to show The Blank clearing the wall jump at the final of the British Open.

'Even I had my eyes closed over that one,' I murmur.. 'Although my condition can make things look smaller than they really are, which, in this case, might have been an advantage.'

'It certainly might. But seriously,' Graham Last's tone alters perceptibly. Alarm bells begin to ring in my mind once more. 'The very fact of that terrible accident only goes to prove the mindless cruelty of your actions towards that horse.' Graham pauses to let the import of his words settle over the audience. 'I mean, was the horse injured at all?'

I nod slowly. I'm not going to pretend anymore. I swallow convulsively before I begin to speak; to attempt to explain.

'Yes, he was.' The studio audience gives a shocked gasp. I jerk my head up. I know, or at least I think I know, that sometimes audiences are given directions in television studios as to how to react; i.e. "Applause now" and so on. I seriously doubt, however, that there is a sign saying "Give shocked gasp now". I have a horrible feeling that their response is genuine. This is going to be harder than even I had thought it would be.

'Yes, he was,' I repeat. Suddenly, shockingly, I feel my face crumple. Tears are clawing at the back of my throat. My

262

words become thick. 'He was lamed. He's alright now. But you're right. I did that. I thought I was being so clever, getting one over on them all. I thought I could still do it, even though I'd lost my sight, lost everything really since I last stood any real chance of making it in show jumping... and I know you think it's the most pointless sport ever, but to me... to me... it's *everything*. At least, it *was* everything. You have to understand, it's all I ever wanted to do, *ever*.' I am appealing to the studio audience now, ignoring the noxious presence of Graham Last at my side. 'It was everything to me, and suddenly, bang! Overnight it was gone. But I didn't deliberately set out to be cruel. You have to believe me. I've been accused of being hard. And I have been hard... I was always afraid of letting my emotions show... Of seeming weak...' I turn my head momentarily in Pete's direction. 'There are always those who are willing to exploit weakness... People like Sarah Braithwaite who bullied me when I was at school... People like *you*, Graham. You two would get on well together, although I'm told she looks more like a horse than her mother ever did these days... But, I'm wandering away from the point. You're right about one thing. I didn't act in the best interests of The Blank, but the last thing I ever wanted to do was for him to get hurt. When I found The Blank he was standing up to his hocks in a muddy field. His next stop was the *Whiskas* factory. At least I saved him from that. Surely that's worth something...' Tears are coursing unchecked down my cheeks now. For the second time in the same night, I worry how I look. I look dreadful when I cry; all blotched cheeks and red swollen nose. At least I used to; and I doubt that the Stargadt's has changed that; transformed me from a noisy, messy crier to a graceful one - one for whom an audience would feel sympathy. A single pearl-like tear drifting gently down a cheek is always going to be so much more palatable than great gulping sobs and streams of snot. I cannot even begin to imagine how I would look if they projected my image onto the enormous screen behind me; and I bet that's just what they are doing. As if to confirm this, I note Jimmy shift a little uncomfortably and glance behind him at the screen. They shouldn't have put so much make up on me. I bet there is mascara running in rivers down my face now. I bet I look like a giant weeping panda. Graham Last, to his credit, almost appears genuinely shocked by the reaction he's provoked (further, and also to his credit I suppose, I bet only a *very* small part of him is rejoicing at what this display of naked emotion is going to do to his ratings. I bet he'd rather not have to deal with the tears.)

'Well... Er... Yes... I'm sure the Ladies and Gentlemen of the audience all agree that *that* is definitely worth *something...*' Graham, from the corner of his flashy-looking desk, produces a tissue from the box he's probably kept on it for all these years in the hope that just this eventuality would occur at some point during his show, that one of his guests would actually feel *some* real emotion; and proffers it to me with a flourish. I start to hate Graham Last with a vengeance now. Similarly, I can feel the heat of Jimmy's hatred of the man. I don't think I would try very hard to prevent it if Jimmy decided to start throwing punches now, I reflect.

'Are you okay now?' Graham Last oozes unctuously.

'No, Graham,' I say shortly. I am suddenly very, very angry. 'I'm not O-fucking-kay. And before you ask me anymore stupid questions, I won't be riding The Blank again professionally. I'm certainly not riding in the paralympic games. The Blank's retiring from the sport, as am I. We're finished. Through. So I guess that that's us through too, unless you want to take the piss out of my visual impairment some more. I mean, you've had a good laugh at my blindness and at the fact that Jimmy's had a mental illness now. Perhaps there's someone else you'd like to take a pop at. Gays? Oh, sorry, you already did that with Meuthen, didn't you? What about a nice spot of Jew-bashing instead? That's how you people work, isn't it? You and the fucking Sarah Braithwaites of the world? Jeering at anyone who's different from you. Poking fun at the freaks. Well, I've got news for you, it's the freaks of the world who get things done. It's the freaks who win the British Open when they can't even see properly. It's the freaks who've got a

264

string of platinum-selling albums beneath their belts and who have changed the face of punk rock forever. It's the freaks who think differently enough to change the world. What have you done, apart from leech yourself onto people like us and make yourself a fortune, you fucking parasite?' I stop suddenly, horrified. I've gone much, much too far. Graham Last's mouth has flopped open almost helplessly, even I can see that. He closes it again, but then lets it fall open once more. (Later on the director of the programme will congratulate me on my interview. He will tell me that at this point in time he was utterly engulfed by a feeling – and one that he was not entirely displeased with – that Graham Last would never speak again. In the entire eight year history of the show, the director tells me, he has never known Graham Last to be utterly dumbfounded by one of his guests. He is genuinely lost for words. "Graham Lost" the headlines will read in tomorrow's newspapers; when suddenly the tabloids are on my side again when fickle popular opinion swings back towards me being the underdog who should have won the British Open after all.)

'Oh...' Graham eventually manages to emit. 'I see. Well. Any plans for the future then?' he concludes somewhat lamely.

'I thought I'd get married and have some children,' I reach across and take hold of Jimmy's hand.

'Oh. I see! Well, well, well! Who'd have seen that coming?' Graham addresses his studio audience, winking at them again, trying to get them back onside once more.

'Don't ask me. It's not as if I could see anything coming, as you've been at such pains to point out, you winker.'

From the end of the couch, I hear Pete give a high-pitched giggle.

'You know, I'm starting to like her,' he says.

14. Breaking the Habit

(Written by Mike Shinonda. Appears on Warner Bros, Meteora, 2003. Performed by Linkin Park)

So here's something: a baby, just a few months' old nestled in my arms, suckling gently at my breast, his eyes closed. And here's something else, I'm not hard anymore. I'm soft, yielding; everything a mother should be. What Pete said was right. I did act like I didn't care when inside my heart was breaking. It was an old habit and they die hard, but by doing it, in the end, the only one I hurt was myself. Now, if my heart aches over something, I cry. I show my emotions. It's no longer possible not to; not when this little person is relying on me to teach him about being a human being. I will not fold myself up and hide myself away inside and become a blank of a person, like my mother before me. He is relying on me to tell him about how it hurts sometimes, how it's not always good, but that's okay. We'll deal with it in our own ways and the good bits, well they are there too. There will be joy as well as sorrow. I'd rather have both, than nothing at all. Laughter as well as tears.

Pete's proven that too, in a way. For it was as he said, for him, the best was yet to come. His solo album was at number one in the album charts for months and Jimmy says that he seems to have found a kind of peace, a sort of happiness in his achievement. It's been a long time coming for him, Jimmy says, so I suppose I should be happy for him too, even though I will never like the man (oh, yes, I can still hate). Si did well too, not that we move in those circles anymore. Even Scotty, at last, has managed to achieve *something*; a steady job in a call centre taking telephone calls from people who want their gas boilers or central heating serviced. After every single call, he says 'F-ing bitch!' or 'F-ing bastard!' or 'F-ing people f-ing asking me about their f-ing central heating!'; but at least he manages not to swear during the calls and he's taken to going out and about with some blonde bombshell with very long legs who fields calls alongside him. I think he's happy.

As for me, I'm happy too. Perhaps I am the person to whom wonderful things happen, after all. All that remains for me is to get quietly on to my next adventures and be content with them.

He's going to sleep now. The Blank's nuzzling at my arm, his snowy head reaching in through the half-stable door in our kitchen. He's begging for attention too. Absentmindedly I push one of the apples from the bowl under his muzzle. In a little while, I'll lay our son down in his cot for his nap and when Jimmy returns from the studio where he produces the music of up and coming bands, I'll leave him with his daddy, tack up The Blank and go for a ride. Then I'll just be an ordinary woman out riding a plain-looking horse through the flat, nondescript, Cheshire countryside.

Acknowledgements

I wish to acknowledge the use of a number of sources within the text of this book:

Enid Bagnold, *National Velvet* (London: Mammoth, 1992)
Monica Dickens, *Talking of Horses* (London: Pan Books Limited, 1977)

The titles of the chapters are all the titles of songs from various musicians and bands, the music of whom, coupled with the dedication and creative efforts of these, much inspired and facilitated my own creative effort in this work. The song titles and where they can be found are detailed in the chapter headings.

I am indebted to Tré Cool, drummer of Green Day/Foxboro Hot Tubs, whose drum kit from the *American Idiot* tour I borrowed on the basis that it's not possible to plagiarise a drum kit (I hope).

I also owe a great debt of gratitude to a number of people/organisations without whom this book would never have come into being. These are: my husband, Martin, to whom this book is dedicated and who was forced to read it twice. My first reader and comrade in misfortune at the call centre, Tracey Allen (again read it twice – thank you so much), and my lovely friend Emma Dearing-Coupland. Thank you for your honest opinions and the time you spent on it for me. My Mum and Dad for reading the book and encouraging me to keep the faith. Pompey and Steve also for all of the encouragement you offered and advice on a most practical level. I would also like to thank all the other numerous people who have provided advice and have helped make this the book it is today. Thank you also to the Inky Newsletter/Signposts Writing Development Project for the "free read" with The Literary Consultancy and to the TLC for their honest opinions and encouragement. I am indescribably grateful to The Bethlem Royal Hospital and Archives for kindly granting permission for the picture "Two Horses" by anonymous male, aged 33, to be used as the front cover to this book. The exhibition to which Jimmy refers when he describes the painting of the two horses was a real event – an exhibition held at the Weston Park Museum/Mappin Art Gallery in Sheffield some time during 1995/96. In the book, Em advises that galloping on a horse should be the one thing everyone should experience before they die. To add to that, I would advise that you include looking at the immense and amazing collection of art works held by The Bethlem Royal Hospital and Archives onto your list of "things to do before you die." Last, but not least, I would like to say a big "thank you" to The Music Rooms in Chesterfield for permitting me to experience the feel of the sticks for myself. Okay, I was crap, but at least I could describe it accurately. Thanks for your patience with me, guys.